INK

The first time Lizzie dies is a learning experience. Then again, anyone new to an ancient Egyptian reincarnation cult would have no idea what to expect once they've made it past the Hall of Judgment.

Now that she's been sent back to find out why her husband from her past life is missing, the last thing Lizzie expects is to wake up in the wrong body, stuck with the mess its previous tenant left behind. In fact, she's in agreement that whoever ran Ashton Kennedy over with a big shiny SUV did the world a massive favour.

Some secrets, she soon discovers, are better left buried, especially in a world where enemies are eternal, and death does not offer a final solution.

Inkarna
Copyright © 2012 Nerine Dorman
ISBN 9798648239098

First published June 15th 2012 by Dark Continents Publishing

Second edition published by Ba en Ast Books 2020.

All rights reserved. No part of this book may be reproduced in any form by any electronic or mechanical means including photocopying, recording, or information storage and retrieval without permission in writing from the author.
This book is a work of fiction. Any resemblance to actual events, real persons living or dead, is entirely coincidental.

Cover Illustration by Jodie Muir
Cover Design by Tallulah Lucy
Interior Design by Nerine Dorman

This first paperback edition was printed by Amazon.

An e-book edition of this title is also available.

www.nerinedorman.blogspot.com

INKARNA

NERINE DORMAN

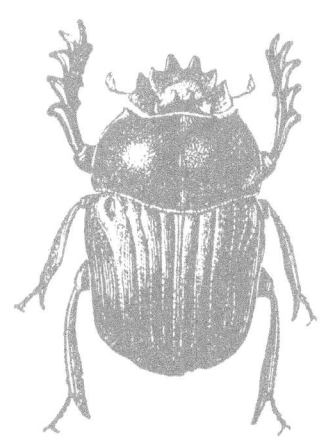

DEDICATION

This goes out to Peter, Shaen, James, and others we've lost too soon. Wherever you travel, my friends, know that you are loved – you are star stuff.

CONTENTS

Acknowledgements	6
Foreword	7
Chapter One	9
Chapter Two	16
Chapter Three	32
Chapter Four	65
Chapter Five	86
Chapter Six	104
Chapter Seven	124
Chapter Eight	141
Chapter Nine	159
Chapter Ten	187
Chapter Eleven	226
Chapter Twelve	265
Chapter Thirteen	275
Epilogue	341
About the Author	345
Other Books by Nerine Dorman	346

ACKNOWLEDGEMENTS

I am forever indebted to my fellow Skollies at Skolion. Without your help this revised edition of Inkarna *would have been mouldering on my hard drive for the next twenty years.*

FOREWORD

Inkarna came into being thanks to grief, and that existential sense of loss that creeps in when you hit a particular age. For me it was my early thirties, with the growing sense of the ephemeral nature of our fragile existence, that the icons who are the hallmarks of our particular generation are frail, that they too will pass.

And then there was the dream, where I clearly remember walking down a street, but in the wrong body—the body of a man—and how alien that entire experience was. This was how Ashton Kennedy came to be, and the rest of the story grew from there.

I am grateful to my friends and fellow authors who've walked this path with me to bring the revised edition of this adventure to life. It's always somewhat strange revisiting older writing. I was a very different person back then, and I don't think I'll ever write a novel with quite the same energy as this one.

Thank you for joining me on this journey.

"The United Kingdom has Tanith Lee, the United States has Caitlin Kiernan, and South Africa has Nerine Dorman. An interesting Dark triangle."
– Don Webb

"Nerine Dorman is a master of building a dark and secretive world beneath the one you think you understand. Her writing is lush and seductive, and her characters are flawed and all too human, walking that indeterminate grey line between good and evil."
– Cat Hellisen

"Nerine Dorman's bright clear prose is at the forefront of modern fantasy."
– Storm Constantine

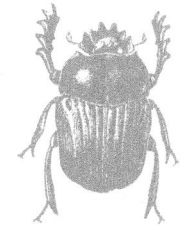

CHAPTER ONE
*Maitland Cemetery,
Cape Town, 1966*

TOMORROW WILL be the first time I die. It seems appropriate that I visit Richard's final resting place among the mausoleums and monuments of Maitland cemetery. The wind's bite chews through my new Turkish leather coat. The cold goads the deep-rooted pain lodged in my bones, all the way through to my marrow, and each step I take offers a fresh blaze of agony shooting through my joints to make my heart shudder and my breath catch.

Leonora is at my side, as always. At thirty-four she still retains her youthful bloom, the chill having brought a blush to her cheeks, the wind whipping her dark bangs in her face. So young, so serious. We haven't discussed any of this, but I think she already knows. Although I don't want to, I lean heavily on her. Almost nine decades of knocking around on this earthly plane makes one grateful for support when it is freely given, and I honestly don't know what I'd do without this brave woman who's served me so loyally for the past fifteen years. The gods know she's given up a lot for House Adamastor.

She bites her lip, grey eyes scanning the uneven gravel pathways as we pick our way between ornately carved marble slabs. Lichen-encrusted crosses are stark against an aquamarine sky. Winter howls between the statues, the truncated columns, draped urns and weeping angels. Weeds spill over granite kerbs where wrought iron fences act as borders between the real estate of the dead and the byways of the quick.

I can feel my death approach. He has waited many years, biding his time. That is the blessing of our kind, of those who are Inkarna of House Adamastor. We know when we have to keep our appointment with the Keeper of the Black Gate. It is a subtle knowledge that speaks on a cellular level, whispering in our dreams: *Come to me, come to me. You will feel no more pain. It is time. Close your eyes and go to sleep.* Death will come for me in the early hours of the morning, when the veil between the realms is at its thinnest, when those who must be born into this life often make their squalling entry and those who are ready to depart lose their tenuous hold on this existence, leaving with a whimper, a sigh.

Will it hurt?

I keep telling myself I have nothing to fear. It seems strange that the next time I consciously look up toward Table Mountain, it may be a few decades hence, after I've spent time in Per Ankh, our House of Life. Many millions of lives don't have the surety of the Inkarna. They don't know the truth. Death is not the end if one has access to such arts to preserve the sanctity of one's souls after the physical body's passing.

The thing is, I don't know whether the past sixty-odd years of study and practice have been for a pile of horse droppings. I'm an old woman. I've had a good innings, so

I can indulge in some of these fears. If I am to pass into eternal slumber, of not-being, so be it. If I am to return, that is as it should be. Either way, it's been a good ride.

I can look back on my life without regrets. I have not caused great pain. I have not killed. I have not consciously set out to do evil. I have not withheld from the poor. I have not slandered my neighbours. When I stand before the scales of Djehuty I can say with honesty that I have followed the way of Ma'at. My heart will not be cast to Ammit, the Devourer. Anpu Upuaut will open the way for me. I will travel in the Sun Barque of Ra into the Splendour of Splendours. Set will slay Apep and the unknowing, and I will pass through into the Tuat, to complete my journey to Per Ankh, the House of Life, where my brethren will welcome me until it is time to return.

The silver scarab pectoral is heavy and warm on my chest. The fingers I raise to trail its much-scarred surface are clawed and bent with age. How will it be to shuck this flesh, to be freed of the physical aches and the heaviness of matter?

Do not be afraid, the texts tell me, but those are the words of those who have gone before. Words can be fabricated. It is only Leonora and I who remain of our House, and neither of us can claim to know the words for fraud. Richard went many years before, almost a lifetime ago. He assured me of the truth held in the texts, yet I never held his hand in those last moments, so I have only his journals and the records of others left behind as assurances that death isn't final, and that he will be waiting for me when...

Richard. My chest feels tight as I tug at my memories of him, even after all these years. Leonora has brought me to his memorial. He has a beautiful grave and, compared to the others surrounding it on this plot, it is well tended. His headstone is the palest marble, carved in

the style of the pylons of the Temple of Amun in Karnak. A scarab, sculpted in relief, flares its wings at the top. Set and Har-wer stand on either end, each raising a hand in benediction. A cartouche bearing Richard's *Ren*, or true name, inscribed in Middle Egyptian is the only writing on the marble slab, apart from his death date, that is?
June 21, 1902.

Siptah, a name worthy of a pharaoh, the date, strangely apt. He passed as the sun began its return for those of us in the southern hemisphere.

Trust Richard to have hung on until the longest night.

There is space here on this monument for my own cartouche, and Leonora's, and all those of House Adamastor who choose to leave their *Kha* of this life here once the breath of life is extinguished.

Will I see Richard soon? There is no surety in this business. Without the old photographs to remind me, it is difficult to recall his features—merry brown eyes, hair to match, and a round face framed with bushy sideburns. He always looked so dashing in his top and tails. The men nowadays dress so slovenly, especially with some of the dreadful fashions and the long hair…

Leonora glances at me. "Mrs Perry? Are you all right? You haven't said anything these past ten minutes."

"Just lost in thought, my dear." I pat her arm. Have I really been standing here for so long? My body has gone numb from the cold and the dull buzz of weariness crawls through my flesh.

Now's as good a time as any to do what I must. I turn and, with care, seat myself on Richard's grave, although I daresay superstitious passers-by would cast us filthy looks. Richard won't mind me taking my ease on his most recent *Kha*'s final resting place. Leonora supports me so my creaky knees don't give in at the last moment. Her eyes are large. She knows, oh, she knows. I don't have to tell her that today is the last. She sits next to me, pressing her body against mine, seated to shield me from as much of the wind as possible and lending me what warmth she can.

I know her fear. I was in exactly the same situation all those years ago when Richard knew he was breathing his last. It still burns me that he sent me away.

"I don't want you to see me like this," he'd said. By then the malaria he'd contracted in Zambia had taken its toll. So young, snatched away at the age of thirty-six.

"Continue the good work, study, meditate and *become*," he'd said, before reaching beneath his nightshirt for the very same pectoral I'm about to give Leonora. Yet I wasn't there at his death. It feels as if he rejected me.

My fingers are so numb I struggle to unfasten the chain. "I can't... Help."

Wordlessly Leonora obeys. Whether her shaking is from the cold or her sorrow, I don't know, and it doesn't matter, but her fingers fumble at the catch and she pauses, dropping her hands in her lap.

This act of passing power from one to the other is necessary. House Adamastor is not a big House. Not like the others, who squabble and machinate, and consider us beneath their notice. Richard said even at House Adamastor's height there was normally only ever one master and one or two initiates. I have placed my confidence in him. Leonora is to become Mistress of the House at my passing. I have left behind a great legacy at our chapter house, an exquisite library comprising many tomes and even some ancient papyri. I must trust that Leonora will take up the staff of office and rule in my stead until another of the Inkarna return.

"We watch from afar," Richard told me the day before he died. "We are just on the other side of the veil, and sometimes we can cross over to the land of the dreaming to speak with you, to impart knowledge. We learn from the Blessed Dead before they return to the Sea of Nun. Know that you are loved. We will see each other, and the intervening time will seem as a heartbeat."

I never did dream of Richard, or any of the other mysterious Inkarna he spoke of with so much love and respect. Ah, it matters not. I am here, now. Tomorrow I shall have no need of this flesh, which shall go the way of all mortal matter, to dust and ashes. What waits for me on the other side of the Black Gate I shall discover in a few scant hours. I should be joyous. My heart beats painfully, and it's difficult to draw breath.

Leonora is a pretty lass and I'm sure she'll find love, and perhaps start a family. My passing will cause her grief. A partner will likely assuage some of that. Even if she chooses to live with the sorrow, perhaps in the next life, she will have more luck. We have all the time in the world. For all we know, the one who will complement her is yet to be born, or might already exist in Per Ankh. When one has more than one opportunity to grasp life, it teaches one to be patient. *No haste, my dear.*

She gazes at me, her eyes wet with unshed tears.

"Oh, Leo, don't cry. It will be all right, you'll see." I caress her face and try to project my sense of love.

The girl buries her face in my lapels, terrible sobs wracking her slender frame. She is the daughter I never had and I stroke her shoulders, rocking her slightly while I smooth her hair. "Now-now, Leo, we both knew this day would come. We shall be parted but a short while, you'll see. It shall be like a heartbeat and we'll stand together in Per Ankh, and we will know no pain. The Tuat's skies will shine with stars, and we will be strong and unfettered by mortality. You'll know me by my *Ren*, Nefretkheperi, and by then you'll have spoken yours, and nothing will keep us apart, not geographic distance or death. Death, where is thy sting?"

She pulls back and smiles at me, the edges of her lips quivering. "What if..."

"Hush now, my daughter." *Don't voice my fears. They are mine alone.*

"Come, you must help me take off this chain." I gesture at the back of my neck.

Leo twists behind me. This time she has more resolution in her movements.

The pendant slips into my hands and I turn it over a few times, tracing its edge, taking one last, longing look at the list of *Ren*s engraved on the reverse. I was responsible for adding *Siptah*. Before that there was *Sethotep*, *Thothmose*, *Siptah*... Richard has worn this exact piece more than once.

I slip the item into Leonora's hand. Her fingers won't quite close over the scarab and I cup my hand over hers, bending her digits so that she accepts the gift.

"Choose your *Ren*, daughter. This is our way, the way of the Inkarna."

Above us, rattling about in the windswept umbrella pines, the pied crows rasp at each other as they hop from bough to bough. A gust brings the traffic noises to us in brief bursts. It's time to go.

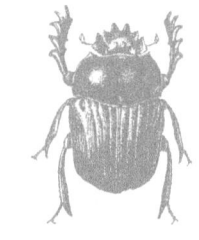

CHAPTER TWO
Disorientation Games

SOMETHING'S WRONG. It's a gradual realisation, a slow sinking into flesh. Like a dream, everything that has taken place before becomes hazy; smiling faces, a sense of being loved, of farewell. I want to go back but that door has been shut. The light of Per Ankh is extinguished, for now. I have unfinished business here.

Now.

Which is *where*, exactly?

I'm supposed to do something but the heaviness drags me down into discomfort. Dim memories assail me, vague knowledge, which slips through fingers like drops of mercury.

Something's wrong. This isn't how it should have been.

Lub-dub, lub-dub. A pulse. I have a pulse? That much I know, and the air rasps into my lungs

painfully, as though fighting a great resistance.
Live, breathe!
We love you; we are watching.
Who is watching?
A roiling dense fog tugs at my limbs, holding me back from wakefulness. The Sea of Nun. Forgetfulness.

A measured, bleating tone becomes a continuous electronic whine.

A sensation, as of falling, of snapping into solidity. Someone cries out, a man. Something's wrong.

A continuous *bleep* gives way to a measured *bleep-bleep-bleep-bleep*.

Open your eyes, damn you. Open your damn bloody eyes.

The flesh obeys the spirit, albeit with great reluctance. The light blinds me, and another strangled cry escapes my lips.

Bleep-bleep-bleep-bleep.

"Ash?" a woman says. Her voice is heavy with grief, and warm fingers enfold mine, squeezing.

Another time, another place, someone holds the hands of a much-older woman. Grey eyes fill with tears. The recollection slips into dull opacity.

This time I dare to open my eyes again, slowly, filtering the glare through my lashes until I can focus on where I am and what the hell is going on. The woman who holds my hand is silhouetted against a window covered by vertical fabric blinds that were once white. An antiseptic stench clings to this place, a hospital ward some fragment of my memories informs me.

My companion is in her late teens or early twenties; it's difficult to tell for sure. Auburn hair spills in ringlets down her shoulder, escaped from a knot pinned loose and skew on one side. Wide brown eyes study me intently, reminding me of...

Siptah.

Who or what is Siptah? No memory responds. It's as if neural pathways that should have been there are excised. I need time...time to figure out what the hell is going on here.

"Ash?" Tears run freely down her cheeks and she gives my hand another squeeze. She is a pretty girl with a round face, a small spattering of freckles across her slightly upturned nose.

The hand she has trapped within her grasp is larger than I'm used to. *What?*

This is wrong!

The fingers are long, the bones bigger than... Dark hairs on the wrists, but I gag when I see the ink on the skin that starts just above the wrist, travelling up the arm—skulls, demonic faces, writhing snakes, flaming pentagrams—the stuff of fanciful imaginings of amateur occultists.

This is a man's arm. This should not be.

Pinching shut my eyes won't help.

The first memory smacks me from the side, of Meritiset flowing ahead of me, tugging at me. "It is time, Neffie, we must hurry. They cannot wait any longer, you must punch through. There has been a change in plan."

Where time should be is a nebulous grey haze.

I gasp, shifting, but the body doesn't respond properly. The *Ba* must yet take root and the flesh is weak. A great ill has befallen this *Kha*. This knowledge to move slowly, to grow into the situation, is clear, but impatience causes me to twitch, my hand to slip from the woman's to claw at the bedding.

"Ash!"

"That's not my *Ren*!" I want to shout, but my voice comes out a croak, like dry leaves, my tongue cleaved to my palate.

"What are you talking about?" She entraps my hand again, shifting closer so her scent washes over me—mint and roses.

"Who are you? Where am I? *When* am I?" The *when* seems more important than the preceding questions.

"Don't you know me? The doctor said?" The woman turns her face away from me, probably because she doesn't want me to see how upset she is. Her grip on my hand is fierce.

"Answer me, please?" I breathe out, stare up at the ceiling. My stolen *Kha* belongs to that of a man, not the... *It was supposed to be a girl*, my treacherous memories inform me, locking into place. *Her name was Catherine van Vuuren, and she was three years old. She fell into a coma after drowning in a swimming pool. You were supposed to have her* Kha *when her* Ka *and* Ba *fled for judgment.*

"There's been a mistake," I tell the woman at my bedside. "I'm not the right..." Stupid fool, I can't tell her. I clamp my lips shut and keep my gaze firmly on the strip-lighting on the ceiling. How does one explain the existence of the Inkarna—Those Who Return?

We are the few who remember, who refuse the lure of the Sea of Nun and its promised cycle of eternal forgetfulness.

"There is no mistake! How can you say that? You don't remember anything?" Hysteria tinges her voice.

I close my eyes then inhale. Exhale. "No, I don't remember a bloody thing." What else can I do but play dumb until I figure out what the hell is going on?

Per Ankh, so distant, remains a blur.

Richard wasn't there. No Siptah. We don't know what happened to his blessed Akh after his last Kha perished.

That recollection brings a hot stab of pain and this time I sit up, despite the physical body's weakness. He wasn't there. He never returned to the Tuat and never entered through the pylons of Per Ankh. Some misfortune befell him as he passed through the Black Gate. And now this.

"Gods." I try to swing my legs around but my limbs won't respond, my arms straining to keep me in a seated position.

The young woman lets go of my hand and staggers back against the wall, her features pale and her eyes white-rimmed. "I'm going to get the nurse." She dashes out the room, leaving me to my own devices, which is a good thing, for now.

With the assumption I'm not going anywhere in a hurry, I slide back down onto the bed and peer about the ward in search of clues. Two of the other three beds are occupied. A thin Indian man with a clear plastic pipe crawling out of his nose is attached to a variety of machines I can only imagine are there to keep him alive. The soft hiss of oxygen accompanies the steady rise and fall of his chest.

The old man in the bed opposite mine watches me with bright, beady eyes. "She's been sitting at your bedside for four months now," he says.

"Four months?"

He nods, offering me a toothless grin. "They took you off life-support yesterday. Pumped you full of morphine. Even had some minister here to offer last rites and all a big fuss. But you didn't die. She's been sitting here the whole time, praying and pleading, though for what reason I'm not sure."

"Who're you to pass judgment?" A small twinge of annoyance makes me snap out the words. *I have not killed, I have not coveted my neighbour's possessions.*

He shrugs. "Been listening to the arguments between the gal and your poor parents. They've gone through hell with you, it would seem." What's with this man's smug tone?

The idea that he knows more about my *Kha*'s past than I do rankles. "How so?"

"The way I see it, you'd be doing them a favour if you'd just gone and died."

I don't have an answer to his words and resume staring at the ceiling. What went wrong? Why am I here? Now. "What year is it?" I ask him.

"It's two thousand and twelve. What, you remember nothing?" His laughter is dry and raspy, as though he's gargled thumb tacks. I almost smile when his laugh turns into a hacking cough.

"Oh." It was supposed to be 2007. Play stupid—memory loss, the best card until I have all my scattered marbles. The nothingness obscures the turning of five years.

Damn, a man's body. What went wrong? I'm too scared to touch my face. I don't want to know.

The girl arrives with an overweight matron in tow. It's easy to lie back, allow my muscles to go slack while the fat woman pokes at me, takes my pulse and gauges my temperature.

"Glad to have you with us, Mr Kennedy. You've had your girlfriend and folks worried."

Girlfriend? I study the auburn-haired girl, and a wave of sickness washes over me. This man—black scribbled lettering on a whiteboard above my bed catches my attention—Ashton, he must have *slept* with her. If he has tattoos like a ruffian then he must have... Oh. My. God.

"I'm glad to be back." I try to muster cheer I don't feel. My smile is pasted on, the body's facial muscles slack from disuse.

My...*girlfriend*...grimaces. This is going to be difficult. She is a stranger to me and I think she's beginning to realise that, likewise, I'm not the person she knew.

Sister Elton—for that is what the matron's nametag proclaims—pushes the hair back from her face. "Your vitals are...stronger than expected. It's still early days but I think you'll make a full recovery. It is most remarkable." Are those tears in her eyes? Well, I'll be damned.

"W-what happened?" I ask. "I'm afraid I don't remember...much." That part isn't a lie.

"You were brought in four months ago. Severe head trauma after an em-vee-ay. You've been lying in a coma ever since then."

"Where is here?"

"Groote Schuur hospital."

I want to ask what an MVA is but I don't want to let on exactly how ignorant I am. For now I'm content to know my name, my new name, that is. I don't really want to know too much about this body. Not yet, at least. It was 1966 when I died. This means Leonora would be an old woman of eighty. That's if she's even still alive. A horrible strangling sensation closes my throat, and hot tears prick at the corners of my eyes. House Adamastor hadn't had the gathered daimonic strength to punch an Inkarna through sooner. Our inability has been a great source of worry. And now this.

This time I turn my face away, preferring to look toward the comatose Indian man. "Leave me," I tell the two women.

The memories flood me and I remember *everything*, and it burns with a cold fire, of loss and the distinct realisation that a lot more has gone south. If I'm not in the right body, *who* is? I pray the chapter house is still standing. House Adamastor was never supposed to have more than one full Inkarna in the material plane. That was drummed into me upon my arrival in Per Ankh. Who inhabits the *Kha* of Catherine van Vuuren? Or did that *Kha* pass and this is why I'm here now? Is this why it has taken me almost five years to return?

On the day I am discharged, I wake screaming from the same recurring nightmare that has plagued me for the five days I have been stuck in this *Kha*. The grey, the nothingness of oblivion, is a vast pool through which I flounder. Each time the waters of the Sea of Nun close over my head, I cannot draw breath, and begin the slow descent into darkness. I jerk upright, a terrified cry escaping my lips.

This *Kha* is still too weak to walk unaided, its muscles atrophied from months of being supine. It is embarrassing the first few times the nurses help me to the bathroom now that the catheter is removed—all this flesh and appendages that are in the wrong places. The first few times I urinate I want to shrivel into myself from the mortification of inhabiting a man's body. This is so wrong.

Yet it is also utterly fascinating, this heaviness of flesh, of gravity tugging at my limbs as I stretch, watching skin slide over muscle. This is my *Kha* now. Being able to move fingers, watching flesh twitch at the simplest command of a thought. This is a wonder in itself.

Ashton Kennedy would have been a comely man if it were not for the tattoos covering both arms. Oh, and the hair. A vain creature, he was, his hair long and black, all the way down to his buttocks. Marlise—the girlfriend—takes great pride in the fact that she didn't allow *his*... No, I must now consider them *my*... parents let the nurses shave my head. She seems to think long hair is important to me and bemoans the small section they had to shave when I was first admitted. Long hair on a woman, perhaps, but on a man? I look like a savage, not to mention the tunnels in the soft flesh. Tribespeople in the Amazon would stretch their lobes with discs. The few times that I face the mirror, for really, I cannot accept this face yet, I creep a pinkie finger through the shrivelled skin where Marlise tells me the disk went. It seems unnatural for my digit to fill the space and to tug. A shiver crawls down my spine.

Nine millimetre tunnels, she'd told me proudly, and all I can think of is what sort of surgery must I undergo to close those holes again. She brings me plugs before I'm discharged. Rubber things that stretch the skin back to about six millimetres, and I spend most of the evening tugging at the alien objects. It's easier to play along with others' whims until such time as I can figure out the way forward.

I don't want to argue. I am like some sort of doll and allow her to fuss over me, brush the hair while I stare at the television screen, at the tiny figures in the illuminated box. It doesn't matter what they do, just so long as there is movement to distract me from this entire situation. But I have to admit there is something strange and wildly beautiful about this man, his patrician nose, the high cheekbones, the cleft in the chin, the narrow face and those cold grey eyes that cut into the very depth of my heart when I stare into the mirror. My eyes.

Who are *you?*

I ask myself that question over and over again, fascinated by the musculature, tracing the hard lines of sinew in the wrists. Beautiful and arrogant, Ashton Kennedy, and you knew it, didn't you? And you used it to your advantage, you sod.

Of my old powers, there is not a trace. Maybe it's too soon. That doesn't mean I don't try. I wait until late on the last night, when the nurses dim the lights to cast everything in a dull amber glow and it's only the hiss of the machine keeping the patient next to me alive.

The man in the bed across from me snores softly, and I'm fairly certain no one is awake. My eyes closed, I pull at my surroundings, questing with my thoughts at the electrical energy, the residual motion of the world, but it's like bumping into a wall. Nothing budges, and a terrible dull throbbing starts at my temples. In a last-ditch attempt, I glare at the chair next to my bed, willing it to shift even half a metre to the left. Nothing.

I choke back the strangled cry that forces itself to my lips, instead biting the soft skin on the inside of my hand. Encased in strange flesh I am stripped of my powers and prestige. Lost. What came easily to the aged Lizzie Perry proves impossible for Ashton Kennedy, and suggests another reason why Inkarna would never seek out a mature body for a return. It's too early to get upset by this. I need time.

Mr and Mrs Kennedy visit every day—a thoroughly unremarkable pair. They have worn themselves grey looking after this son. The only similarity I can see is Mrs Kennedy's eyes. They are the same storm-blighted shade as mine. There all resemblance ends. The father is stooped and says little, preferring to stare out the window while the mother natters on about someone else's past and how glad she is I'm awake. I play the amnesia thing to the hilt, offering minimal words and gazing into space with a blank expression whenever they are near. The doctors say there is always a chance for some sort of impairment after a prolonged coma. I can use this to my advantage while I gather my strength and figure out the dynamics of this new life. The doctors are just surprised I have so much control over my motor functions. Most who awaken are lucky if they can move their hands or speak without some sort of impediment. Although doddery, I can walk unaided. I speak without slurring my words. If only I didn't have these nightmares. My fellow patients complain bitterly, and the sleeping pills the matron prescribes help not one whit.

I should be happy I'm alive.

Instead I spend hours recalling Per Ankh, my friends I have now left behind, drawing on the memories of the Blessed Dead I encountered. So many lives. So many stories. My first triumph is tapping into my first Blessed memory, a fleeting thing, a child's fears of this very hospital, of visiting a sick relative. There is hope my other powers might return.

"I'm sorry we had to sell the house, Ashton," Mrs Kennedy says. "We didn't really have a choice, but we've kept some of your things from where you stayed in Observatory. You may want to look through them."

Oh gods. At these words I fix my gaze on the ceiling, not wanting to maintain eye contact. I am an interloper, a cuckoo's offspring. Why don't I feel love? I should be grateful.

Instead Ashton's mother grasps my shoulder and squeezes, as though she gives me comfort and all I want to do is rip myself away from any physical contact. I want to tell her, *You are not my mother*, but those words blessedly, remain a mere thought.

What prospects do these two people have now? Their only child is a miserable failure by anyone's standards. Marlise tells me I'm a barman and a musician.

And they've given everything up to keep *this* alive?

I'd box the young man's ears if he were still around. To the people who tend me I'm pleasantly vague without committing myself. The clothing they bring doesn't fit me properly, the jeans baggy about the waist, the T-shirt and fleecy top gaping at the neck. I allow them to push me out to the parking lot in a wheelchair.

While I'd been awaiting discharge, I had pointedly not gone to the window. Besides, the vertical blinds had been drawn most of the time. One trauma at a time, I'd reasoned.

The world outside the hospital is the first shock to my system. The few memories I can draw upon, of my time in Per Ankh, I'd been aware, to some degree, and informed, about how society and the environment has changed during the intervening years. But even these remain, unfortunately, in fits and starts. Yet, in our designations as Inkarna, we've often waylaid the Blessed Dead to learn of the world we've left behind, before they forget, their knowledge lost for eternity. It's the only way we can initiate a return without wasting precious time.

Nothing has prepared me for how much my city had grown.

First the roads, so much bigger, the cars sleeker and faster than I could ever conceive. It is one thing delving into a person's memories, it is quite another faced with the stark reality. Gleaming monsters roar past at astonishing speeds on a highway near the hospital grounds. I try not to gape, conscious that Mr and Mrs Kennedy, and my ever-present shadow, Marlise, watch me intently as they wheel me through the parking lot.

And it is so cold, the sky low and heavy with cloud, the wind biting through my jacket and reminding me of my death day. It was winter when I first shuffled off this mortal coil. My gaze follows the contours of the cars, registers the wheels of my chair turning in the chromed hubcaps and metallic paintwork of vehicles almost alien compared to the ones I recall from so long ago.

Lizzie never learned to drive. What must it be like to be behind the wheel of these monsters? Could Ashton drive? I assume so, but there is no way for me to access those memories with the spirit fled.

It is Marlise's car in which we go home, a battered hatchback with more patches to its paintwork than its original white. Mr Kennedy sits ramrod straight in the front, a scarecrow of a man, while Marlise drives and Mrs Kennedy is seated in the back with me. Ashton's mother keeps touching me, as though to remind herself I'm real, that I'm breathing and functional.

"I'm fine, Mother, really," I say for the umpteenth

time then content myself to stare out the window. What I really want to say is *if you ask me one more time whether I'm all right, I won't be.*

This new world is Cape Town but it's not. Old houses lining the highway have been renovated. Some demolished. Some buildings are new, their lines stark and alien. Marlise pulls up in front of a residence in one of the older parts of Newlands, blessedly familiar. Progress hasn't touched the stately homes here built during the early nineteen-hundreds. Only the trees are different: some missing, others larger. I can only handle so much strangeness in one day. Thank goodness for some permanence, even though these people have essentially imprisoned themselves. Many of the properties have six-feet-high walls topped with spikes.

Marlise takes the key out of the ignition and turns to look at me, her dark eyes full of concern.

I want to tell the girl I'm fine. She's not Leonora and I don't want to need her. They're all strangers and they're nothing to me, and I know I must not feel this deep-rooted resentment at their fuss. A smouldering ember is banked deep within me. The need to lash out grows and is liable to burst into full-blown rage at the next bit of provocation. *Please don't touch me.* I shrink from their hands. I turn the emotion over in my mind, tasting it. I try to recall whether Lizzie carried any anger within her or if this is residue of Ashton's.

But I am Lizzie, am I not?

You are Nefretkheperi, my logic tells me. *Lizzie is but the* Ka, *the double. The* Ba *has taken a new residence. In the eternal cycle of death and rebirth you will have many Kas. You know this as a truth.* The blurring of identity makes my head ache.

Instead of protesting, I clench my fists as I'm guided down a dark passageway into a home where all the windows are covered with heavy drapes.

"Here is your uncle, Ashton. Do you remember my brother Stanley—Stanley Rodgers? We're staying in his house until Father can sort out the finances," Mrs Kennedy says.

Uncle Rodgers is older than his sister, bald and stooped, and it's glaringly obvious he despises Ashton—me. He stares at our party in the hallway before disappearing, into what I take as a study, without a word. I don't need heightened Inkarna senses to tell me what he thinks of his nephew.

We pause, Marlise drawing her breath with a hiss, her grip momentarily strengthening on my wrist.

Mr Kennedy stumps up the stairs ahead of us, as though this exchange never took place. From the corner of my eye I see Mrs Kennedy shake her head, an almost imperceptible movement.

"We have two rooms on the third floor," Mrs Kennedy continues, as though the air of dysfunctional relations doesn't weigh down the atmosphere. "You'll like your room. It overlooks the garden." It's as if she's insinuating that I *must* like this room, and this entire arrangement. Begging. Pleading.

Marlise's smile is grim.

I don't like this house. It is too old; harbours far too many echoes. It has presence, and I wouldn't at all be surprised if it is haunted. No, I *know* it's haunted. Something here is aware of us, but whatever shade has taken up residence slips at the edge of my vision, reluctant to allow me access to its past. Perhaps I should be glad I am sensitive still. As for my full daimonic powers... I need time.

The room I am given has a sloping roof and two

small windows overlooking a rambling garden. Below a rectangular swimming pool is visible between the boughs of a massive camphor tree. Marlise sits next to me on the narrow bed, watching me stare into the nothingness. Mr and Mrs Kennedy have at least offered us some privacy. Now if only the young woman would take the hint. I clasp my hands loosely in my lap.

"Ash?"

What do I say to her? "I'm tired. I'd like to sleep." I lean over to slip off the sneakers I've been wearing. The mattress offers little resistance as I lie down and study the ceiling. Anything is better than to suffer this scrutiny of strangers. Can none of them understand that I need to be left alone?

While this stolen *Kha* is tired, and my sense of dimensions warped, I can't help the sense of curiosity. For the first time since my awakening, I have an opportunity to be truly on my own. Marlise must understand that I don't need her pitying gaze, so filled with hunger, her hands constantly straying to touch, just like Mrs Kennedy's.

Marlise doesn't move from her position on the edge of the bed. Her worry extends into the environment. I can taste its bitterness. The girl shifts and leans down, brushing her lips against mine.

I stiffen against the unwanted contact and raise a hand to cover my face and turn my head to the side. "Just leave. Please. I need to rest."

An indrawn breath is my only answer before she obeys, closing the door behind her with nary a snick. God, I'm such a bastard. If it weren't for the accompanying claustrophobia and the fear of being eternally lost, I'd welcome the oblivion offered in the Sea of Nun.

CHAPTER THREE
No House to Call Home

THE FOLLOWING morning I wake early, just as the darkness bleeds out of the dawn and the world outside my window resolves into recognisable objects taking form out of the inkiness. From here I can see into the house next door, a bathroom window perhaps because the glass is opaque, a rectangle of gold. Occasionally a figure passes in a ruddy blur before this aperture.

Beneath me the house is as silent as a tomb, save for the insistent hissing of tinnitus in my ears. Is this further residue of the damage the previous tenant in this *Kha* incurred during his tenure? Like a thief I slink downstairs once I'm dressed, pausing on the landing to listen for any other signs of life. It is weekend. Most people sleep late, I'm assuming, except for me. I don't think I managed more than one or two hours' solid rest throughout the night.

The roiling nothingness of the Sea of Nun lapped at my awareness whenever I slid from consciousness, and each time I'd awoken on the verge of crying out in fear. Now I'm scratchy behind the eyes and my centre of gravity is ever so slightly off kilter. The ground keeps shifting each time I place a foot before the other.

It's as I make my way down the passage to the kitchen, my footfalls muffled by almost threadbare carpets, that I realise I'm not the only one awake. The static-filled buzz of a radio reaches me, shrugging aside the cloying silence pervading this old house. The kitchen door is slightly ajar, and I pause here. I'm thirsty. My stomach coils in knots because I didn't eat supper last night. I can't keep pretending I'm not here. At some point I have to face these people to whom I've become a stranger.

After a deep breath I push open the door, blinking in the sudden illumination of the kitchen. Mrs Kennedy, paused in mid-stir of her tea, is seated at the kitchen counter. She stares at me with big eyes. I glance instead at a photo stuck with magnets to the fridge. A young man with shoulder-length hair smiles at the photographer. That's supposed to be me, but the pieces don't fit.

"Morning, my dear. Are you feeling better?" Her smile is tremulous, like she's about to start crying.

I don't want to have this conversation. "I'm fine." The words come out more like a growl as I close the distance to the fridge. Part of me wants to beg of her for help, to share every lurid detail of my predicament, but instead I turn in on myself. No one must know. Imagine what this knowledge, the truth of my existence, would do to her?

"Can I make you some tea?" she asks. "Some oats?

It used to be your favourite when you were younger. You had it with honey and butter." Her words make me cringe.

The interior of the fridge is filled with an assortment of covered plastic containers, all neatly sealed, and I have no desire to rummage through them to find something edible. Vegetables in the drawers look more like wax replicas. My hunger evaporates yet I continue to stare before me.

"No. Thanks." I turn then, closing the fridge behind me, and lean against the appliance to watch the woman who would be my mother.

Mrs Kennedy lifts the mug, which depicts some orange cartoon cat with a too-wide smile, and takes a gulp of her tea, her gaze never once leaving my face. Her lips are too pale without lipstick, her skin ashen.

"Where does Marlise stay?" If one thing's for certain, I cannot remain another moment in this house, to be examined as though I am some sort of freakish exhibit in a zoo—a wild animal that has just been released from its cage to pad from enclosure to enclosure looking for a way out.

A visit to Marlise seems the lesser of the two evils. Plus it will give me something to do, a sense of progress. I can find a way to ask questions so I can reconnect with this new age.

"She's at fifteen Ophir Road in Plumstead," Mrs Kennedy says. "Would you like Uncle Stanley to lift you there?"

The thought of spending even five minutes, let alone a twenty-minute car journey alone with the man makes my flesh crawl.

"No." I brush past her to stomp down the passage and leave the house, glad that I thought to shrug into my leather jacket before coming downstairs, as though on some cellular level I already knew I wasn't going to go back to my room. Voices whisper at the edge of my hearing, shadows linger where there should be none. This *Kha* I inhabit is leaden with exhaustion and hunger but if I don't get out now, I'll go stark raving insane. That's if I'm not already a complete loon stuck in this nightmare.

What would the doctor say if I spilled my little tale of woe? I laugh at that thought and push open the gate's latch, and stride into the morning, envisioning padded walls and strait jackets. *Needles and pills.* A snatch of a tune ghosts on the edge of my hearing, but as soon as I strain toward it, it's gone.

It's winter. The day before Lizzie's death returns to me with full force now that I'm outside of the confines of the gloomy house. It stings thinking of my other self as some old dead lady. It's this body I now inhabit. It's changing the way I think and act. Too much testosterone? I've been avoiding mirrors of late. Looking at this stranger's face makes me feel as though the *Kha* doesn't fit properly. Of course it doesn't. Who am I fooling? I'm too tall, too broad-shouldered.

The sky is clear but pale, as though the blue is misted through a thin veil of gauze, but the air holds a chill that immediately nips at my face. It's Sunday. All the good people are going to church. Many years ago I'd walk with Leonora along the main drag in Simon's Town. We'd stop by a coffee shop for a slice of chocolate cake and a cuppa. Or occasionally scones laden with whipped cream and strawberry jam. A real English lady's treat. We'd watch all the Christians pull up outside the church for the first service before returning to the chapter house and our books. We'd wave at the Major, out walking his Great Danes.

Some say the dogs were descendants of the legendary Able Seaman Just Nuisance. Simon's Town was like that, always with one foot in the past, and stories behind stories waiting for the curious.

I need to get to the chapter house. I've been abominably foolish to alienate Marlise, the only person who might be sympathetic to my cause. There's no way in hell *Uncle* Rodgers is going to lend me his car. Not that I could drive it anyway. Ashton's parents are insipid, all too aware of their benefactor's displeasure. This prodigal son of theirs is an unwelcome inconvenience. Besides, there is nothing for me to do. The television bores me, the shows' presenters talking down to their audience. And, for goodness' sake, the only books on the shelves are either crime novels or decades-old hard-backed condensed books.

The most bizarre part of my situation at present is just getting used to this damned body, moving in it. Ashton's height measures at more than six feet. With proper muscle tone, he'd be damned intimidating. Today, however, is the first day I feel well enough to even consider walking. I shove my hands into the pockets of the old biker jacket I suspect was probably part of Ashton's "uniform." My hands now—so large, the fingers thicker. And the hair. I still can't decide whether I want to cut it. It seems better to scrape it back into a ponytail so it doesn't annoy the living hell out of me, like everything else is at present.

I have to pace myself while I walk to the station. My shortness of breath forces me to pause every so often so that the wiggling sparks stop flying in my field of vision.

People avoid me when I pass them on the sidewalk. Bent grannies observe me with great trepidation etched upon their features, and step away as I pass. This is a novel experience, to say the least. When I was Lizzie, I was content to be almost invisible, one of these self-same old ladies who now glance up at me with mingled fear and awe. I look *rough*. That's the understatement of the century.

Ashton had great power. People either gravitated towards him or lurched back in fear. In another age he might have been a general or a despot. That much is a certainty. I shudder to think how he wielded his natural charisma. And, it's no joke. He's a ghost of his former self with me in command, yet still imposing despite the ravages of the long infirmity.

If only I could remember what my old face should look like, the soft grey curls, the hands gnarled by time. I'm losing my grip on Lizzie's identity. This is as it should be, but I mustn't be in this *Kha*, not here, not now. The terrible wrongness is an ever-present gnawing at my heart.

Marlise was the one who looked after the *Kha* in the spirit's absence. She cared enough to keep the nails short, the face free of stubble. Now I resemble a bergie, a vagrant. *All the better to keep you at arm's length, my dear.*

What will Marlise say when I pitch up on her doorstep unannounced? I'll worry about that when I get there. I have no idea of what sort of reception I'll receive. Perhaps it is better this way. I've really been a right royal idiot, haven't I?

The dreams from last night seep through as I walk—night terrors I've tried to block since waking, without much success. A sticky grey limbo stalks me, the Sea of Nun sucking at my limbs and I shudder, as much from the cold as from this nothingness that threatens to swallow me whole. If only sleep would offer sanctuary, like it always did when I was Lizzie. Am I forced to dwell in torment in the realm of Morpheus? Will I have no rest in the waking world either?

The trains still run, but the carriages are vastly different from the wood-panelled beauties I recall. These are all hard plastic edges and grey vinyl. What possesses the youth of today to cover the walls and more with reams and reams of illegible scrawl in black or coloured marker? The trains have definitely gone backward since the old days...

Are these scribble-scrawls a stab at immortality? I watch a young couple at the other end of the carriage. They purposefully avoid making eye contact with me. That's fine by me. I can't be much to look at right now. The training and reassurances I had in Per Ankh have not prepared me for this, a naked, cold reality immersed in conflicting desires. If I could sink into the oblivion offered by sleep, to allow my *Akh* to untether from this *Kha*, to let the *Ka* and *Ba* fly loose, I'm certain I could bring this schism into being. Instead I'm the walking dead trying to make sense of a world gone mad. And I'm too scared to reach out with the powers I took for granted the last time I lived. What if I try and fail, yet again?

Plumstead station is tired. Weeds push up between the cement paving and a ficus sends its red, threadlike roots from a gutter. If no one takes care of that it may soon strangle the building. An aloe leans at a drunken angle, a dried candelabrum remaining from last season, with this year's new bloom shoving through in a solar-phallic outburst of inflorescence. It being a Sunday, not much is happening here apart from a bergie taking advantage of the lack of Metrorail security to chase her from the platform. She sorts through her shopping packets while muttering incoherently to herself. The crazy old woman is a stark reminder I don't have much further to fall before I'm like her. This is not a pleasant thought to entertain.

Marlise still lives with her parents, in one of the original homesteads in the neighbourhood. I remember visiting here once, in this very street, almost a century ago. It is a strange sensation to view a space in time from dual perspectives. Apart from the walls topped with razor wire and electrified fencing, and the silver streamlined vehicles parked in the road, little has changed.

I stand in the scant shade offered by a bare-branched syringa when I push the doorbell. About thirty seconds pass before someone answers.

"Can I help you?" a man asks.

"Um, Li-Ashton here. To see Marlise."

The electronic connection crackles.

"Oh."

I'm left outside for a long time, enough of a pause to watch a pair of laughing doves court above on the telephone wires. The male has his chest puffed out, his feathers fluffed, but the smaller bird keeps hopping away from him.

Footsteps slap on the paving on the other side of the timber fence. "Ash?" Marlise speaks from the other side of the closed gate.

I swear I'm about ready to slap the woman every time she says my name with that exact tone but I'm glad she's here. I don't want to be left standing out in the cold, for the chill bites at my bones despite the watery sunlight. I don't want to be turned away.

"Marlise? We need to talk." I'm just bloody relieved she's home and willing to see me, especially since I've been such a dreadful person to be around. *Bastard.*

The latch hums and clicks open, something else I must grow accustomed to—automated systems, the stuff of science fiction. Maybe, given enough practice, I could harness my daimonic powers to trigger electronics. Back then, as Lizzie, I'd developed some telekinetic ability, but then there hadn't been nearly as much to experiment on as there is now.

Once I push the gate open, I pause. Marlise stands right in the doorway, as though she would bar my entrance. She pulls the oversized maroon cable-knit sweater closer to her and blinks up at me with her dark gaze. "Ash." She looks even younger than I remember, and it's difficult to remember that this *Kha* I now inhabit can't be that much older than hers.

"Hello." I shove my hands deep in my pockets. She expects me to hug her.

She says my name with so little hope all I can do is stare at her wordlessly while I fumble for something to make this entire mess right. But nothing will be right, will it? It's a case of making do with the resources, of which there are pitifully few. I need to see the chapter house. I need to speak to Leonora, if she still lives.

"We need to talk," I say, "somewhere where we won't be interrupted."

"We can go to my room." She gestures behind her then steps aside so I can follow her up the narrow passage between the house and the garage. More than a physical distance yawns between us, the way she keeps looking over her shoulder as if to check whether I'm too close. It's as if the air between us buzzes.

The implications bother me. I don't want to be somewhere so private, so intimate with this woman but I don't have a choice, do I? She's not dumb either.

She can tell I don't want her to touch me, and she's wary, like a dog that's been beaten before, her eyes focusing anywhere but my face. Oh gods, Ashton, what the hell did you do to this woman's mind?

Marlise stays in a room that once must have been the maid's quarters. It's at the back of the house, off the veranda by the kitchen. The garden stretching out behind the residence is large, and is filled with a small orchard. Pear, peach or apple, I can't tell. The branches are naked. The house itself is locked tight, but a curtain twitches from the interior when my shadow darkens the panes.

The interior of Marlise's room gives off an essence of *darkness*. The windows are covered in heavy black-out curtains, the floor a deep mahogany. An unmade double bed takes pride of place in the centre of the far wall, the bedding a rich burgundy. She lives in a tomb. My blessed memories suggest adherence to subcultures, but all I can do is shake my head. Posters on the black-painted wall depict groups of long-haired men wearing sombre clothing, in various serious poses: in graveyards, desolate landscapes or decayed urban environments. One poster in particular captures my attention.

Ashton stands with three other long-haired males beside a mausoleum. My heart almost stops. It's Maitland cemetery, not far from where Richard and my previous *Kha* are buried. This is a poster for some sort of music group. The heading proclaims the band's name as Anubis rendered in Gothic type. Is this some sort of sick joke? Ashton here is a lot bulkier, a supercilious sneer playing across his lips. Muscles bulge beneath a tight black T-shirt, lustrous black hair framing his face.

"You don't remember anything, do you?" Marlise

has been standing right beside me the whole time, and I haven't noticed. The small hairs on my arms prickle at this proximity. Almost, but not, touching.

I can't help it. I start and spin round to face her, my back to the wall. "No." There's no point telling her I'm not even a *man*. Or I am now but I'm not quite sure what I must do about it. Or that the last I knew I was almost ninety, an old woman alive during the mid-1960s.

We stare at each other for a while before Marlise gives a loud sigh. "Look, do you want a cuppa tea or something?"

I nod. Anything to distract from the sheer uncomfortable situation we are in, at present.

"It's probably best you stay here and wait for me. The last time you were here, you weren't exactly welcome." Marlise shoots me a meaningful look before she turns and leaves, shutting the door behind her and plunging the room in gloom the bedside lamp doesn't quite dispel.

Ashton, what in heaven's name did you do with your life?

I seat myself on the edge of the bed, my fingers threaded together on my lap. What a fine mess. Part of me wants to get up and get the hell out of here. I'll walk to Simon's Town if I have to, but I suspect it could be so much easier if I look to Marlise for help. She's an anchor I'd be foolish to ignore. Just the thought of going back to where the Kennedys are lodged fills me with a vague sense of dread. To endure all that silent suffering...

What's worse is that I don't have a cent to my name.

When staring at my hands loses its appeal, I turn to study Marlise's bookshelves in an attempt to get to know her better. There's a lot one can tell just by being aware of a person's reading tastes. The titles appear to be mostly horror-orientated, and authors I don't know anything about: *The Awakening*, *Dead in the Family*, *Queen of the Damned*, *Interview with the Vampire*, *Twilight*... Clunky books featuring a boy-wizard on the front cover make me laugh. *Harry Potter and the Philosopher's Stone*, *Harry Potter and the Deathly Hallows*...

Such fanciful notions.

Her film collection reveals more of the same and I come to the conclusion that if a quarter of these titles were available when I'd been her age, I'd have amused myself to the point where I'd gotten nothing done. And I wouldn't be standing here right now. I'd be dead, as in *really* dead.

I grimace, putting yet another thin plastic case back on its shelf.

House Adamastor—immortal librarians. That was the running joke bandied about by some of our allies, according to Richard, though our libraries back then were nothing compared to what must be available to people today.

We are just lucky that, while we are out of the material plane, we can still access the memories of the Blessed Dead before they sink away in the Sea of Nun. Call the Inkarna of House Adamastor stodgy, but it's better to plunge into the unknown armed with knowledge rather than try to figure it all out after a few years have caused massive cultural shifts. And, hence, another reason why a young child's *Kha* was the better option. Catherine's *Kha* would have given me the time to grow into the culture, to not wander about like an alien recently arrived from another dimension. Essentially, that's what I am.

Marlise returns, and I help her with the tray. She

flinches when our fingers brush. I take the tea things from her and place them on her desk.

"You never used to drink tea." She watches me stir a spoon of sugar into the steaming brew. She's brought a small plate of biscuits too, and I take two Lemon Creams. My stomach growls ominously, and I hope she doesn't notice.

After I swallow the first bite, I speak. "I'm not the person I was. I'm a clean slate, and I need your help." There, that's about as much as I can say without spilling a story so bizarre and convoluted she'd no doubt run screaming.

I seat myself on the edge of her bed again, sipping at the tea while watching her watch me. She becomes conscious that she's staring and, after shrugging to herself, prepares her own mug. When she sits on the bed, Marlise makes it obvious that she's keeping a degree of space between us, so our limbs don't accidentally touch.

"What do you want me to do? You haven't exactly been forthcoming over the past few days. How's that supposed to make me feel about the situation *and* want to help?"

My face grows warm, and I stare into the cup, intensely aware this is not the kind of posture Ash would have held or the type of behaviour in which he'd engage. Even the act of finishing a biscuit is a poor substitute for giving an answer. For all I know Ash would probably have her on the bed and gasping for more; not nibbling on baked treats nor sitting here hunched like someone afraid of his own shadow. "Tabula rasa," I mutter.

"What did you say?" She leans closer and her minty perfume reaches me.

I straighten. Hell, why is a mere slip of a girl

making me want to cringe into myself? Maintaining eye contact is probably one of the most difficult things I've had to do in a while. "I'm completely lost, Marlise. You have no idea what it's like. Whoever I was before...before the accident... That man is dead. I find myself surrounded by complete strangers. I'm sorry if I was so rude to you when I first came to. You must understand how overwhelming this situation can be. Just stop and imagine yourself in a similar predicament."

The cup pauses halfway to her lips and she closes her eyes, her hand trembling so I worry she's going to spill her tea. A stray tear rolls down her cheek before she looks at me again. "I can't imagine, but what can I do to help you? I don't even know where to start. Everything has been so fucked up this year." She pouts as if she wants to add something to the sentence then shakes her head.

"I need to piece things together. I've had..." It's time to lie. "I've had some really peculiar dreams. I need to connect the loose ends. I may need to go to places that...seem odd to you, places I would never have gone before the accident, and concepts I'd discuss that are?"

Marlise frowns. "You don't even talk like you used to. You're using words in a way I've never heard. Hell, you're not even swearing." She shudders.

I laugh; cover my face with a hand. If she had any inkling... After a deep breath, I continue, "Can you drive me somewhere today? It's vitally important. I'll find a way to make it up to you. I feel awful having to ask you, but if you can't, I'd have to walk or ride the trains without a ticket."

"Not far?"

"Just out to Simon's Town?"

Her expression turns to one of disbelief. "Why there?"

"I can't explain, just that I need to see someone there, someone who may be able to offer me some answers as to why things are so messed up."

For a moment I think she's going to refuse, but she puts her mug down and stands. "Okay. Let's go. Now."

It's becoming clear why Ashton was able to treat Marlise like a piece of dirt. She's obsessed with him. She'll do anything to keep him happy. It's pathetic, really, and here I am, continuing with this sick, co-dependent relationship, yet I'm quite serious about finding some way to thank her. She's looking at me with such longing, however. How can I explain that Ashton really is dead?

She plays a recording of the band in which Ashton used to perform. The music is filled with heavy electric guitars, like the rock music of the sixties but just...*growlier, dirtier*—for lack of better description—and slower than what I'd heard before. I didn't like the contemporary music back then and I certainly don't like this *gothic metal*, as Marlise happily calls it. The lyrics sound awfully like the titles of the novels the woman enjoys reading so much. Ashton has, no *had*, a very deep voice and a definite flair for the melodramatic. I don't know if I could sing like that, though I'm grateful for its use. Some of the low notes remind me of the Tibetan-style chanting I'd heard at another House's open meeting. At least my present gender orientation would be good for something—the chanting, that is.

"You don't like the music?" Marlise asks. "You guys were fantastic! You were going on tour regularly and there was even talk about you going to the States. That was until..."

I sigh. "The accident, I suppose?"

"*Ja*, that. They got someone else to sing for them, though."

"That's good."

"He's not as good as you. Doesn't have nearly as much stage presence."

"I don't like the music."

That shuts her up. She sniffs and turns the volume down, keeping her eyes on the road. This state doesn't seem to please her either, and Marlise pushes another button. A radio station crackles into life with some awful music featuring some guy *talking* over an electronic beat and a woman wails in the distance as if she's being tortured on a rack.

I peer at the buttons on the car stereo interface until I identify the one I suspect may be the power button, which I promptly jab. Blessed silence reigns, underpinned only by the Toyota's rumbling engine.

My forehead pressed against the glass, I watch the landscape flash by. Marlise takes Ou Kaapseweg, a winding mountain pass that brings us into the far south. It wasn't here when I was last walking and breathing, though I did occasionally walk the trails winding around the peaks. Where have all the pine trees gone? I don't remember the summit so *naked*, so covered in heath. It's difficult not allowing my surprise to show when we come down onto the Noordhoek side. Where before there was mostly wilderness shrouded in Australian acacia an entire neighbourhood has sprung up, bounded on one side by windswept Long Beach and, on the other, a Fish

47

Hoek of monstrous, sprawling proportions.

"This place has chang—" I've said too much.

Marlise glances at me sharply. "What do you mean? You've been here hundreds of times. How can you say it's changed?"

"Nothing. Just a weird dream I had, okay?" If I could shrink into the seat, I would. If Marlise gains the slightest suspicion I'm completely unhinged, I'm absolutely lost. As it is, her worry is an almost-tangible presence.

We drive in silence for the rest of the way, shooting up a highway where no such road existed the last time I was here. So many houses... The Glencairn area, a narrow valley with a few homes near the river mouth where a dairy farm used to operate, now has houses that extend almost the entire length of the glen. How long will it take me to get used to the way things are?

"Some disorientation is normal," Ahmose had told me in Per Ankh. "Try not to dwell in the past. Give yourself time. You'll have a young *Kha* in which to explore." He couldn't have been more wrong.

Getting to know this present age is easier said than done, and this sense of dislocation bedevils me all the way to Simon's Town, where many of the original Victorian buildings remain. That much is heartening, but the soul, the very character of the place has changed so much I hardly recognise it. I frown at the shop fronts with their myriad African curios.

"What's with you trying to make holes in my passenger seat?" Marlise remarks. "Lighten up."

Without realising it I've been digging my fingers into vinyl upholstery. Instead I cross my arms over my chest and clutch the flesh of my upper arms. "It's nothing."

"Doesn't look like nothing, if you ask me."

"I'm not asking you. Just drive, will you?" There. The bastard is back. I'd dearly love to kick myself right now. If I could crawl into myself I would, and my face grows warm at my mortification. Lizzie would never have displayed such impatience. "Sorry." The word is glue on my tongue, barely audible.

She says nothing to that, and I direct her to the street running parallel to Main Road, a narrow, cobblestoned byway from my memories. Most people would never think to turn down into the nameless cul-de-sac terminating off Chapel Lane. It's not much, really, just enough space for someone to park a car.

That Marlise drives right past the entrance gives some credit to the compulsion I laid upon the turn-off all those years ago.

"Stop," I tell her.

She obeys but sits with white-knuckled hands clasping the steering wheel. Although I make it obvious that I'm observing her, she keeps staring dead ahead.

"Oh, for crying out loud," I mutter then get out.

I've forgotten about the wind in Simon's Town. It cuts me to the quick and takes me straight back to that last day in Maitland cemetery, when I paid my respects to Richard, Leonora at my side. When will these memories stop looping?

With a hiss I slam the car door and pull my jacket to me as tightly as possible. The zip must have broken ages ago, so there's no way I can close it properly, and I'm beginning to suspect Ashton was more concerned with *how* clothing made him look rather than any practical purposes, like keeping warm, for instance.

The chapter house is still here. I suppose I should be grateful for small mercies. To the casual eye it's one of many double-storey, semi-detached homes in the town. What is worrying, though, is that the place doesn't appear to have received a lick of paint for a decade and the bougainvillea has run rampant, swamping most of the veranda so I can hardly see the front door or the shuttered bay window for the dark foliage.

Leonora would never have allowed the property to fall into such a state of disrepair. Sweet Amun, let her not be dead.

I approach with halting steps, careful, and push aside the creeper's thorny branches, mindful of how one wicked hook could easily take out an eye. The boarded-up door stops me in my tracks.

"What in..." With my index finger, I wipe up a thick layer of dust coating the latch, which has been welded shut.

Moving to the window, I press my face to a crack in the louvers. The interior, or as much as I can discern in the dim lighting, is empty, and appears to have been so for a long time. The disappointment is bitter at the back of my throat.

"Leonora, where are you?"

"Who's Leonora?" Marlise has crept up to stand next to me.

"No one you'd know. And she wouldn't know me either, but I need to speak to her."

"Why?" Marlise's voice is brittle with suspicion.

"I can't tell you. Not now. And, before you start thinking along the lines of the obvious, it's not *that*." I'd like to add that Leo's much too old for any physical kinds of affection, but hell, she's most likely long gone.

This place feels dead, not just abandoned in the physical sense, but in an *other* sense. It could just be the chapter house's familiarity to that undefined daimonic extension of the senses Inkarna possess that allows me to detect this subtle difference.

"You're doing that thing again," Marlise says.

"What?" I turn to glare at her.

"Staring off into space."

"It can't be helped." I bite back an expletive. Some damnable impulse has me take a swing at the door. Such a stupid, futile gesture, but one that will offer me some outlet for this smouldering rage just beneath my skin. I expect my fist to bounce back, my knuckles grazed, but with a faint implosion of energy I punch through one of the horizontal planks. My fingers tingle and I fancy that small sparkling motes swirl about the fingers. I blink and the effect vanishes, followed by a sharp twinge somewhere in my sinuses.

Marlise squeaks and stiffens next to me.

"Board's rotten," I mumble, though I know that's not the case. Maybe my powers are returning after all, though not in any predictable manner. The beginnings of a migraine stabs at my temples.

I turn to Marlise and she steps back, her expression that of horror.

A horrible thought occurs to me. "Did he, I mean, *I*...ever lift a hand to you?"

She shakes her head, but the slightest hesitation before she does so suggests she's hiding something from me. *Temper-temper, Ashton?*

"Never mind." I turn and place both palms on the door. On a whim I trace a winged scarab in the dust coating the peeling enamelled paintwork. "I've got another headache starting up, Marlise. Can you take me home, please?"

Maybe it's out of guilt or a sense of wanting to

do something to please the woman, I ask her to play Anubis's music. While we return to Newlands, I close my eyes, not just to cope with my sudden photophobia but also to filter out the visual overstimulation. Breathing deeply also helps to keep the migraine at bay—slow, measured inhalations and exhalations, though my belly roils with incipient nausea. And I do try to listen to the music. I need to understand this man, this stranger I've become, but I can find nothing to relate to him. I'd like to rip out the remaining jewellery, shave this creature's hair, but it seems almost sacrilege, as if I may, too, be cast adrift without these reminders of another person's life.

While the semblance of Ashton walks and talks, I feel safer. There is an identity, however tenuous, to cling to.

⚱

It is some time after lunch when we pull up outside Uncle Rodgers's house and we sit still in the car.

"I don't really want to go in," I admit to Marlise. "I don't feel as though I belong here." It brings comfort to admit this, and I don't flinch when she places a warm hand over my own. The human contact feels good, right.

"You'll be okay, Ash."

"I wish I could believe you."

"Despite everything, they love you very much."

A pained laugh escapes me. "That's just the rub. I'm gaining the distinct impression I've done some pretty heinous stuff in the past, and I'm too scared to find out what exactly, just in case I die of embarrassment." I want to grab her by her shoulders and demand that she tells me every lurid detail, but I hold back. By equal measure, ignorance is bliss.

Marlise's eyes shine with unshed tears. Gods, does this woman just cry all the time?

After a deep breath, I say, "Whatever it is that I did to you, however horrid it is, you have my promise that it's not going to happen again. I'm not that person anymore." She can take that metaphorically or literally, it doesn't matter.

"Thank you, Ash. That means the world to me." She gives my hand another squeeze.

Our close contact grows uncomfortable. I don't want her to jump to the wrong conclusions, so I undo the safety belt and open the door. "Right, I must go." I pause. "Thank you, Marlise. I will speak with you soon. I just need...some time, okay? I've a lot to figure out right now and I...value your...*friendship*." I can only hope she understands that I'm not in any way interested in resuming a physical relationship. For the briefest moment I wonder what it must be like, to be on the other end of a sexual partnership, the one doing the impaling. I shove that thought far away.

Biting the inside of my cheek in the hope to somehow lessen my discomfort, I get out of the car and go to the house. It occurs to me then that I should have asked Marlise for her telephone number. Mrs Kennedy could give it to me but I don't want to ask her. I don't want to take anything from them. I am a thief. I am not their son.

Marlise waits for me to enter the front gate before she starts the car. It's when I'm standing before the front door that I realise I don't have a key.

"Damn."

There's nothing to do save knock, like the beggar I am, and pray someone will open for me. Three times

53

I knock before footsteps thud dully within, and the door swings open to reveal Uncle Rodgers's florid face. He glares with rheumy eyes and his hatred for me can be compared to a shimmering heat haze. It seems somehow incongruous that he is Ashton's flesh and bone, that we share some sort of genetic heritage. There is very little resemblance. Ashton may as well be a changeling.

"May I come in?" I ask when he doesn't move out of the way.

His lip curls as if he'd say something less than savoury and struggles to restrain himself. He does shift to one side to allow me to enter. Although my stomach rumbles ominously, I can't bring myself to go to the kitchen to fix myself something to eat. The sense of being unwelcome and unwanted is so palpable in this house that I slink upstairs to my room and lock the door behind me before collapsing on the bed. Two biscuits the whole day is hardly going to keep this body going. The headache digs its claws in deep, and it is better to lie back and let the pain surge through me. A bitter taste lodges on the back of my tongue.

No money. No job. No chapter house as sanctuary. No friends save an obsessive erstwhile girlfriend who no doubt hero-worships me for what I represent, not for who I am... "Damn, Lizzie, what the fuck?"

Now I'm starting to swear like a man, too, some part of Ashton no doubt impinging on my manner. Like a mould, the *Kha* begins to shape the *Akh*. Yet I can't help the bitter smile that twists to my lips. I stare at the ceiling, at the myriad cracks in the plaster and the progress a spider makes toward one of the corners. The migraine sends its tentacles down my spine, making me curl onto my side with a pillow squashed over my face.

☥

In an abandoned city, mist swirls between tumbled pillars, and forgotten gods crumble into dust. My feet crunch on the debris of a lost civilisation, each step loud to my ears. My pulse is a drum, marking time. I'm looking for something, a treasure that is important, but I don't know what it is or why it's so dear to me. All that is clear is the compulsion laid across my soul. I must find this thing, and time is running out.

I hear it then, a low moaning here among the ruins. When it starts, I'm tempted to believe it's the wind, but it grows louder, closing in, and I almost discern voices, calling my name, my *Ren*.

"*Nefret-Nefretkheperiii...*"

It's not just one voice but a rag-tag threnody, promising pain, hinting at sharp teeth and claws just itching to sink into flesh. I run, my feet catch on something and I trip—

☥

And fall... I jerk awake. It's dusk outside and a man and a woman are arguing loudly downstairs. Groaning, I pull myself upright. That migraine is still there, at the edges of my awareness. Damn. I wait for a few seconds to regain my bearings, to allow my pulse to settle. My stomach grumbles. To hell with feeling like vermin, this *Kha* is starving and I need to face whatever conflict is taking place downstairs and get something—*anything*—to eat. I'll worry about the dreams later.

Halfway down the stairs I pause, gripping the railing. Those two are still at it: Mrs Kennedy and Uncle Rodgers.

"Well, I can't have him in this house!" bellows Uncle Rodgers. "Look at him, no better than a drug addict."

"He's not like that anymore. Please, Stanley. He's a changed man. He almost died. He needs our support. Surely you can see that. Where else can he go? He's my *son*."

"I agreed that you and Mark could stay. That is the least I can do. I'm giving you until the end of the week to make a plan with *that*. And that's final."

"Please, Stanley! I don't know who else to turn to."

Despite my hunger, I'm not going into the kitchen. That would be about as wise as walking into a lion's den. Who am I kidding? I'm already *in* the lion's den. I want to barge into the room where Uncle Rodgers is haranguing Ash's mother and smash his face in. My right hand curls into a fist, but that's not going to improve my situation. Ashton would solve a situation by employing brute force, but I hold back because I fear my present physique is too confrontational. With the lingering headache still a ghost at my temples, I'm too reluctant to try any of the tricks Lizzie took for granted, such as using my daimonic powers to hold Stanley against a wall until he becomes more amenable.

It's quite laughable. The old lady could do so much more with her mind though her *Kha* was feeble. The man, on the other hand... I uncurl my fist and take a deep breath. I have to remind myself I'm taller than most of the people around me and will be stronger, too, in time.

The walls are becoming too close in this house.

From the lounge the television blares some sports match at such a high volume the speakers distort. Mr Kennedy is no doubt watching the rugby far too intently, in an attempt to block out the ruckus in the kitchen. Why isn't he defending his wife? He has the look of someone who's been dealt far too many heavy blows.

Should I ask him for cash then go out and grab a bite to eat?

But that's something a teenager would do, not a grown man, and he is not my father any more than I am his son. I can't be beholden to these people. I must get out of this mess on my own. Before I can make any further decisions, a door slams and Ashton's uncle storms down the passage. The glare he reserves for me as he brushes past on the staircase is so foul, so murderous, I have to turn my face away.

"Useless piece of shit," he mutters, low but loud enough for me to hear it and know it's meant for me.

Something within me snaps, and with a low growl I rush up after the man. Despite my weakened state, I grab him by his jersey and thrust him against the wall, almost succeeding in sending us both tumbling down the stairs.

He squeals, his anger and resentment dissipating to naked fear when I make eye contact and shove him again and again so that his head rattles.

"Don't you talk to me like that! You don't even know me! You don't know what I'm capable of. Do you think I want to be here, under your roof, taking charity from a spineless sod who'd rather rail at his younger sister than face the problem head on?" A venomous black anger boils within me, coiling up my spine. My hands tingle, energies roiling through my sinews, my vision tunnelling on this pathetic man's features. Stanley whimpers. I drop the frightened man and he crumples at my feet, scrabbling like a crab down the stairs in his attempt to get away from me.

Something ugly stirs inside me, and an ancient muscle memory of Lizzie's takes hold, impinging itself over Ashton's form. It's as if I'm pushing open a door or toppling a pillar. Daimonic powers whip from me, knocking the older man hard so that he tumbles the rest of the way down the stairs to fall in a pile against an imbuia armoire.

For a blood-freezing moment I think I've killed him, but then he stirs, twitches. His eyes widen as he stares up at me, horror stamped on his features.

What have I done? I had no control over that blast. It rode me, unleashing itself on a man who had no natural defences against an Inkarna attack. This is not the way of Ma'at.

The skin on my hands prickles, and the dancing motes aroun them are unmistakable. Daimonic energy, visible to the eye for those who know what they're looking at.

I need to get out of this house—*now*—before I end up murdering someone. The headache returns with crippling force and I grip the balustrade to stop myself from collapsing.

My rational self calmly suggests going upstairs to get my jacket first, and a scarf. My limbs are leaden, but I make it to my room to scratch through more of Ashton's things. I squint through the wiggling shapes worming across my vision and find a worn leather wallet with a few silver pieces, nothing more, and an ID document. These I shove into my jeans pocket. Not that I know how to use it, I pocket a butterfly knife. That's when I find the silver pendant—Anubis or Anpu Upuaut as I know the Neter.

Is this what drew me to the man in the first place? Some tentative esoteric connection Ashton established out of complete ignorance? As it is, he had a pair of jackal-headed figures tattooed on his back, one on either side of a flaming *udjuat* eye. I send a wordless thanks to the Neter for Ashton's unschooled interest in ancient Egypt, and I pocket the pendant. Anpu Upuaut, the patron of travellers and a proto-St Christopher, is clearly looking out for me if I've made it this far to escape the clutches of the Sea of Nun. These small hints at the Neter's interest in my situation are just too uncanny.

Mercifully the house is silent, the television switched off, when I make my way downstairs. I pause at the foot of the stairs, stretching my senses, but apart from an angry buzz of static on the edge of my awareness, it's as if every living thing in this dwelling has slipped into hiding—mice waiting for the cat to depart.

But it's more like a phantom that I slip into the twilight, walking quickly down the road to get as far away from the drama as possible. Each step sends a jarring blaze of agony through my frame. I honestly feel as though my head will explode. Although I don't want to have to depend on Marlise for anything, she's about the only option available to me right now. I'm not sure who else Ashton could turn to and, even if I knew a name or two, the devil only knows on what sort of terms the man parted company with those in question.

It takes me about half an hour to walk to Claremont station, and it's fully dark by then. Waiting for the next train doesn't seem like an option, so I keep walking, more from the need of having something to keep me occupied. A restless energy, now awakened, tangles within my gut, occasionally joining in tandem with my splitting headache. I have eaten next to nothing all day. This *Kha* I inhabit needs something more substantial than fresh air. Being lightheaded and filled with an unpredictable daimonic force is not a good place to be. It's like a bomb waiting to go off, with no way to tell when the fateful moment arrives. About the only blessing right now is knowing I have *some* of my innate resources at my disposal, unpredictable though they may be.

Not that I'd spontaneously combust, but *strangeness*, for a lack of more convenient term, tends to follow Inkarna, or so I'd been told in Per Ankh. Lizzie's life was stable compared to what I am going through now as Ashton.

The breathing exercises help somewhat, as does the walking, banking that edginess, slipping me into a half-meditative state. The pain in my head abates to a manageable undercurrent. I complete the calculations according to the train stations: Claremont, Harfield, Kenilworth, Wynberg, Wittebome then Plumstead. That's quite a walk, but it's better than cowering in a dark room waiting for other people to decide my fate. I don't want to take my chances of riding without a ticket like I did earlier today. Besides, goodness knows what sort of scum I'll encounter on the train.

The night sky is overcast, the clouds low and concealing Table Mountain's eastern slopes. Small pinpricks of drizzle fall on my exposed skin, and I adjust the scarf around my neck. I don't have far to fall before I'm on the streets. It's winter and, in my weakened state, I'll probably get pneumonia and die.

What if Leonora died without training another initiate? This would be a dark day for House

Adamastor indeed. What happened to all the books? These thoughts chase each other around in my head. What happened to the House's trust fund? There's no way I can seek that information without having some sort of legal representation.

The chapter house may be gone but Finlayson and Ericson, the attorneys, should still have a branch somewhere in Cape Town. So stupid of me not to have considered this before. All the more reason to get hold of Marlise, find a phone book, though if the House is collapsed, how the hell can I prove I'm a client? While I'm at it, I may as well see how many Van Vuurens are listed. I have to start somewhere.

A nasty little voice reminds me about another aspect of my new existence I've been avoiding. I will have to find work and earn a living wage if I'm to have a support base. What sort of qualifications did Ashton have? Somehow I can't imagine myself taking to the stage with a band again. That thought, as ridiculous as it seems, elicits a snort of derision.

Though the evening is chill with a nasty wind, I encounter more than one prostitute plying her trade when I walk through Kenilworth. By now my body has fallen into the rhythm of regular movement and that ember within me is tightly banked. Although I'm on the go, I'm still freezing. These luckless women stand about in nothing more than hot pants and crop tops that reveal more than they conceal. Their jackets, such as they are, do little in the way of keeping them warm.

They watch me walk past. One or two hiss something at me. I don't quite catch what it is, but right now I don't care. I know I look like death warmed over.

The Kenilworth I remember used to be quite

upmarket with its art deco apartment blocks. The place is now decidedly down at heel, but Wynberg, which in its day was quite the spot to get shopping done, is even worse. Dozens of Chinese stores line the streets. Many of these have protective trellis covering the windows, adding to the place's unfriendly façade. The homeless are numerous, huddling in their assortment of makeshift shelters on doorsteps, muttering and scratching and swearing at each other. As I pass them, I catch a whiff of sour grapes. Cheap late harvest, no doubt.

These people shouldn't scare me. I am, after all, bigger than they are, but I remember that doddery *Kha* of Lizzie's, where one hard shove from an unexpected quarter could have sent her sprawling. I can't help it. My palms are slick and my heart hammers.

One vagrant woman doesn't bother to get up. She simply pulls her pants down, shifts her buttocks slightly to the side of her shelter, and urinates there, in the street, as I step past. Though I'm disgusted by what I don't want to see, I can't help but be aware of her actions.

"Ek pis nou," she mutters before dabbing at her crotch with a crumpled tissue she wads then tosses onto the sidewalk before she straightens her clothing.

Too taken aback to say or do anything, I quicken my pace, revulsion bitter in the back of my throat. How is it that this city has gone to hell? While it wasn't unheard of to see the odd vagrant about most neighbourhoods back in the 1960s, the streets here in Wynberg swarm with them. I recall some Blessed memories of refugees seeking sanctuary in South Africa due to troubles farther north in the continent, but these people appear to be locals. They speak their jumbled Afrikaans patois, their features bearing the stamp of a Khoisan heritage blighted by years of alcohol abuse and exposure to the elements. Lips are thick, milky eyes lost in folds of wrinkled skin.

More streetwalkers lurk in corners, dark-skinned women who don't quite meet my gaze. Although many are pretty, their expressions are *hard* and I quicken my pace. The sooner I get through this area, the better. I'm the one who's the outsider here.

It's more a prickling at the back of my neck, the *sense* of being watched, that warns me I'm being followed. A cursory glance over my shoulder reveals two youths falling in step about five metres behind me, their focus very much on me; their arms too loose by their sides. Trouble.

One of them conceals an object in his hand. I'm so busy keeping an eye on them that I walk straight into a man approaching from the front. We collide hard, and we both stumble.

"*Ooof*! I'm sorry!" I hold my hands before me to show I don't mean him any harm.

He's skinny, all elbows and knees, and he glares at me through slit eyes. That's when I note the metallic flash of a blade in his hand. "Gee my jou geld." When he grins he shows a gap where his front teeth used to be. Scum.

"I'm sorry, I don't have any money. I don't want trouble." I back up into a lamp post.

"Wit poes, wat soek jy hie'?"

His friends reach us, the shorter one of the pair circling round to flank me while the other lends support to my toothless friend.

"Gee die geld."

"I don't have any money! Why don't you all just fuck off and leave me alone!" Darkness takes hold of me, flaring from within the deepest recesses of my psyche. I want to *hurt* this unfortunate trio. I lash out with my right arm, even as the other knife-wielding scum takes a stab at me. It doesn't occur to me that I should feel fear.

How can I describe the outpouring of daimonic energy? It's like taking a breath, reaching into the core of matter around one, borrowing from the humming wires, from the ground, from every available source, so the world goes a little dim for a few heartbeats. The path I opened earlier during my confrontation with Ashton's uncle has forced a breach in whatever blocked me until now. My body becomes a conduit for this force and, with a soft implosion, I release. My assailants drop, the glass of the nearest shop front filling with millions of hairline fractures radiating outward from a band of impact at about chest height.

A car alarm starts wailing across the road. A woman screams. That dull throb begins again behind my temples, the small zigzags of visual disturbances wriggling across my field of vision in my left eye. My mouth has gone dry and I swallow reflexively, my arms numb, my legs not quite willing to support me.

Now's about a good a time as any to get the hell out of here, before I need to pass out from the incipient migraine that will no doubt flatten me. Something tickles my left nostril. When I raise the back of my hand to wipe, the skin is stained with dark liquid, blood. Just perfect, I have a nose bleed on top of everything.

It's only when I've stumbled far enough to put a few blocks between me and the incident that it occurs to me I've started swearing like a thug. Lizzie never used to do that.

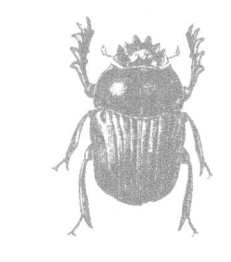

CHAPTER FOUR
Picking up the Pieces

HOW I MANAGE to reach Marlise's house, I don't know. The blessed thing is I don't run into any further trouble along the way. On a whim, I try my powers on the gate's mechanism—I don't want to be ringing the bell to alert the entire household to my arrival—but it remains stubbornly locked. This would never have presented a problem to Lizzie. For a while I stand in the damp night, staring stupidly at the barrier. There's nothing to it. I depress the button and pray Marlise answers.

The connection crackles, and a man's voice bleats through. "Hello? Who's there?"

Damn. "It's Ash. I'm sorry to bother so late, but it's a bit of an emergency. I really need to see Marlise." They're not going to let me in.

After about a minute the intercom crackles again. "Ash?" Thank goodness it's Marlise. She sounds as though she's been sleeping.

"I'm sorry to be doing this to you, but there's been trouble back home and I rea—"

The gate unlocks.

"Come 'round the back like last time," she says.

I don't need further invitation. A male figure is silhouetted in the warm light spilling from the lounge window, and I hurry around the side the house, away from prying eyes. Hell, I don't know what Marlise's parents look like or, indeed how many siblings she has, but I know I'm not welcome here. Damn you, Ashton Kennedy.

She waits for me on the veranda, and I have to stifle a smile at her cartoon kitty-cat pyjamas. It makes her look like she's a teenager, mussed-up hair and sleepy expression included. Her breasts strain against the fabric, and I look away, focusing on her face instead. I'm uncomfortably aware of my maleness, of how tall I am compared to her. I almost stumble on the top step.

"You look like you've gone through hell," she says. "Have you been fighting with someone?"

"No... I mean, there's been some trouble."

"Come inside."

I hesitate, and she offers me a sharp glance.

"You used to sleep over all the time. It didn't bother you going into my room then."

"Your parents..." I gesture at the kitchen door.

Marlise raises a brow. "That knock to your head's turned you into a real prude." She turns and vanishes inside, leaving me with no choice but to follow.

If it wasn't an issue for Ashton, it shouldn't be one for me and I'm more than just a little relieved to be out of the damp and the cold. My head throbs in time with the beat of my pulse. Her bedroom is toasty, but

I can't stop shivering and my extremities are numb. To my relief, she's pragmatic about the situation, bidding me use her en-suite bathroom while she disappears into the house to make me something to drink and, I can only hope, to eat.

Ashton had left behind a pair of old jeans and a long-sleeve T-shirt emblazoned with some metal band's name. It reads *Slayer* and features a heraldic eagle with a reverse pentagram. It smells faintly of Marlise, and I realise as I shrug into it, warm after a welcome shower, that she's been sleeping in it.

Ashton's reflection glares back at me. Almost a week without shaving has left the body with a beard. The hair is wet and tangled, and I twist it into a rope that falls across my left shoulder. My appearance fills me with revulsion, and I turn away, hating the way the stubble feels beneath my fingers and how nothing is neat and tidy, as it should be. At some point I need to do something about my appearance, but not now, not tonight. A bone-tired weariness tugs at me. The thought of having to do anything beyond eating and sleeping fills me with horror.

Marlise waits for me in the bedroom, seated crosslegged on the bed and watching me while I wolf down the toasted cheese-and-tomato sandwich she has made.

"Thanks," I say, wiping crumbs from my mouth. The food is nowhere nearly enough, but I'm not going to complain. The hot chocolate will give the illusion of satiety, and I lean back on the rickety office chair while I sip between giving Marlise the barest details of my recent misadventures. For obvious reasons I leave out any mention of knocking Stanley backward or stunning the thugs with a daimonic blast.

"I can't believe you didn't get injured with those

skollies." Marlise shakes her head. "Three against one, that's quite something."

I shrug, watching her watch me. It's not the recent encounter with lowlifes I want to discuss. "Surviving one altercation is still not going to help my present situation. I need to start rebuilding my life, and don't really know where to start. Hell, I don't even know if I can go back to what I did before."

She nods slowly at my words. "You used to work at a club called The Event Horizon. The money was okay. You didn't do too badly."

Does she mean for me to go back to being a barman? I pray my face doesn't betray my distaste. Still, it's a start. How difficult could it be? "Could I get my job back, or did I bugger that up as well?" Bitterness creeps through in the tone of my voice, and she flinches.

"You could try. You could go tomorrow. The place is easy to find."

"What do you do for a living?"

"I'm still studying." She brightens at my questions, her posture less tense. "I'm going to be teaching pre-schoolers next year."

Ashton no doubt teased her about this or made some sort of horrid comments from time to time. I smile at her, in an attempt to offer a genuine reaction. "That's really good!" Then I look away. This sounds stupid, me getting to know this girl when she already walked so far with Ashton, knows more about his quirks and misadventures.

"What's wrong?"

Facing her, I say, "I just feel peculiar, like I'm getting to know you as a person when you already know more about my history than I do. Everything is unfamiliar. It's that whole cliché of a stranger in a strange land."

She laughs. "It's kinda cool, don't you think? Getting to start over again."

I grimace. I can't help it. Is she implying that we're rekindling the relationship? I swallow hard, trying to imagine seeing her in a more than sisterly way. A shudder runs through me. I can't. She is pretty, though, a bubbly young woman. What the hell was she doing mooning over a bastard like Ashton? She deserves better.

I laugh with Marlise. "Baby steps, baby steps, hey?"

Her expression turns serious, and she gazes at me speculatively.

"I don't want to rush anything, okay? Friends?" I extend a hand.

Marlise squeezes my fingers, her grip uncertain but her sense of relief, love and joy all too obvious before she lets go.

We talk deep into the night and I quiz Marlise about Ashton. The picture I put together is even less to my liking than my initial opinion of the man. All that is certain is that she's pathetically grateful for this apparent change in attitude. I can only wonder how all his fair-weather friends at The Event Horizon are going to feel about his return, because before I can pick up the threads I dropped in 1966, I'm going to have to repair the mess this man made of his life before it reaches out to stab me in the back.

☥

"Ash! Ash! Wake up! You're dreaming!" Someone's shaking me and repeating these words over and over again. I'm wrenched from the clutching miasma of terror, where I'm mired in the nameless horror swirling in the Sea of Nun.

"Aaah!" I sit bolt upright, for the first time grateful for the warm arms thrown about me, for this softness of a woman's unconditional love.

"Hush," she whispers in my ear, rocking me as though I'm a child. Her hair smells like fresh herbs and I lean into her, allowing my body to slacken.

"What time is it?" I won't be going to sleep again.

"Half past five."

"May as well get up now," I mutter, swinging my legs over the edge of the bed.

"We could lie in if you like."

That old, horrible restlessness pricks at me. "I can't." It's bad enough that we shared a bed. It took me ages to fall asleep knowing another person lay next to me, a woman.

We haven't made any solid arrangements, but I'm grateful Marlise will help me. She's offered me a place to sleep until I've enough cash to find lodgings elsewhere. Anything is better than having to suffer the silent misery of Ashton's parents and their sacrifice to an ungrateful son. There's no way in hell Ashton's uncle is going to allow me to set foot over his threshold again. Not after what happened yesterday. The more I consider their predicament, the less I want to have anything to do with Ashton's relatives, though I do owe them a lot for having given so much to keep their son alive.

This particular guilt I shelve. One day, when I sort out the man's life and I'm back on track again, I must repay them. At present there is precious little I can do to ameliorate their troubles except stay the hell away from them until such time it's clear their efforts weren't wasted.

Marlise's classes only start at nine and she agrees

to pick up Ashton's things on my behalf while I wait in the car. It's pure prudence on my part that I don't set foot there, at least not for a while. I'm lucky they haven't called the cops on me. But then, how would Stanley explain me hurling him down the stairs without even touching him? When Marlise exits with the remainders of Ash's life packed neatly into one box, I suppress a shudder. He hasn't left behind much of a legacy.

He had a motorcycle, Marlise explains, but the Kennedys had to sell that. He'd been staying in a digs with some people in Observatory who couldn't have been the most honest around, because by the time Marlise and Ashton's mother had pitched up to collect his things, the housemates had nicked most of his CD and DVD collection and valuables, including what musical equipment he'd owned. So much for friends.

I walk with Marlise to her classes at the college in Rosebank. At the entrance she shoves two twenties into my hand and, when I protest, gives me such a hard look that I shut my mouth.

"I'm sure you can find the train station. Go speak to Gavin at The Event Horizon. It's in town on the corner of Long and Shortmarket. He'll be glad to have you back, I'm sure. You were good at what you did." She gives a soft laugh. "You didn't take any kak from the patrons and could hold your own if there was trouble. My classes finish at three. See you then."

She doesn't offer to lend me the car, which is a relief. I think she suspects I don't know how to drive or, rather that Ashton's forgotten. Before I can protest, she stands on her tiptoes and presses a chaste kiss to my left cheek before dashing through the doorway.

I'm too taken aback by the gesture to do anything more than raise a hand to my face and stand, staring after her departing figure for a few heartbeats. It's just a kiss. Why am I rooted to the spot? Then I shrug and turn, making my way back onto the main road to wend my way to the station.

The clouds are closing ranks again when the train pulls in at its platform and I join the hustle of passengers disembarking and shuffling through the what's to me an unfamiliar station building. Pigeons still flock in the eaves, their droppings making a mess of the super-sized white tiles that must be hell when wet. It's easier to allow the press of bodies to sweep me along, headed toward the subterranean part of the Golden Acre shopping centre. Some of what I see I recall from snatches of memories gleaned from the Blessed Dead but mostly it is complete and utter culture shock.

I don't think I'd ever truly understood that Cape Town was part of Africa. Richard and I had toured the central parts of the continent, but that had been more than a hundred years ago and always with a degree of separation between us and the masses. Now I am immersed, just one of many nameless strangers. Cape Town never seethed with so many different languages. I pick up smatterings of isiXhosa, French and Arabic, as well as the local Cape Coloured patois.

The only blessing I have is that I'm not completely ignorant of all that has changed since Lizzie's passing, although the accessed memories are often fuzzy and tinged by the opinions of the persons who passed. This experience can only be likened to visiting a new destination after having read about it in a travel guide. The only recollections I earnestly wish I could access are those that belonged to Ashton. If I probe, it's almost as if the missing information has left behind an imprint, a empty space in a gum where a tooth used to be.

It is with a sense of relief that I take the escalators up to the ground floor again, pleased to see how some of the old art deco buildings have had their façades preserved, though many of them have been painted garish colours. So many tall structures stab at the sky that were never here when I last set foot in Adderley Street. I watch as pedestrians ignore the lights at the crossing and elect to wait rather than allow myself to be flattened by a truck or minibus taxi. I'm surprised when I hit St George's Mall. This used to be a busy road but now it has been paved with red brick. Plantain trees and white stinkwood form an avenue along its length. Myriad stallholders peddle an assortment of African curios—beadwork, masks and ugly paintings, among numerous odds and ends I don't pause to gawk at.

Cape Town has become, in my mind, a veritable melting pot of cultures. Distantly I recall the times when it was unheard of for a black person to think of setting foot in the city centre without a passbook. Much has changed. Richard would have had a fit. He hadn't liked people of colour much.

I don't think I have a choice whether to like or dislike a particular race group. I'm just glad to be alive. Truly at the bottom, I'm no better than anyone else here. Richard's absence continues to chew at me. He would have loved to have returned in this time. The other Inkarna told me they thought he'd somehow become trapped in the Sea of Nun, in grey limbo. He could return to Per Ankh tomorrow or he could remain lost for another thousand years. Such are the perils of our existence. I can't help but shudder. It could have been me. Now I'm here.

The Event Horizon is unmistakeable, operating out of one of the Victorian-era buildings in a largely historical area off Greenmarket Square and its profusion of curio stalls. I pause outside the tobacconist opposite, just observing my destination. The last time I saw the place it had hosted a restaurant on the ground floor with offices on the first and second storeys. Now it's painted black with purple edgings on the windowsills. Even though it's early morning, loud music blares and a heavily muscled blond man, easily as tall as I am, stands at the door. He leans against the lintel, deep in conversation with an overweight biker who absently strokes the saddle of a motorcycle.

None of the Blessed memories recall this place. I'm on my own here.

After drawing a deep breath, I approach, my stomach contracting. I have to remind myself the people here see Ashton, not Lizzie, though the gods know I'm so far out of my depth here it's going to be murder giving the impression I'm a six-foot-something man on the inside as well—one with a bad attitude to boot and an ego the size of a small planet.

The blond man turns to face me as I approach. His scowl is enough to freeze lava.

I stop, close my eyes and inhale deeply before I make eye contact with him. He's slightly shorter than I am, though bulkier. We stare at each other for longer than is comfortable.

I clear my throat then speak, though I trip over my tongue a few times. "I-I've just recovered from a four-month coma and, as bizarre as it sounds...am suffering from amnesia. Whatever I did before the accident, I'm sorry. Marlise sent me here, said I need to talk to Gavin about getting my old job back." The words sound so pathetic I have to force myself not to cringe visibly.

The look the doorman gives me suggests I've just spoken the biggest load of horse droppings he's ever heard in his life. The fat biker starts laughing. I don't break eye contact, willing the blond to see the truth in my words. I *need* him to believe me. Something in reality shifts, a slight pressure at my forehead, and I pray this subtle twinge in daimonic energies won't result in another nosebleed. Not here. Not now.

He narrows his eyes, rubbing his stubbly chin with one hand. "You're not talking kak, are you? I heard they took you off life support and that you didn't croak it."

"I may as well have died for all the good waking did me," I say. Good, he's talking. I don't allow the relief to sag my posture. Be firm but non-threatening...

He raises a brow at my words, the biker next to him now silent. "You'll find Gavin on the first floor, the office that's in the turret." He points to a window.

I wish I had some memories of the winding stairwell I take so I'd know what awaits me at the top. The place reeks of overfull ashtrays and years of incense burning, and from below the beat of a rock band reaches me with the dim fuzz of male voices.

Gavin proves to be a weasel of a man in his midthirties, sideburns shaved to points to accentuate cheekbones and somewhat greasy brown hair scraped back into a ponytail. When he glances up from his laptop, it is at first with a grimace of annoyance. He pales when he registers who's standing at his door then all but falls from his chair.

"Ash! I thought you died!" The small man leaps to his feet and rounds his desk to stand before me. At least someone is happy to see me, for a change. He clasps my hands and doesn't let go until I'm seated before his desk on an office chair with only three wheels.

I give him the abbreviated sorry spiel I'm beginning to suspect I'll gain a lot of practice in retelling. Gavin listens without interrupting, until a sticky silence descends and I find myself gazing out the grimy window at the building opposite.

"Beer?" he offers.

This early in the morning? The man must be a loon, but I just shake my head and turn back to him. "No, thanks. Have to keep a clear head for a bit still. I'm still on medication." A lie won't hurt here.

Gavin nods but dials down and orders a beer anyway, for himself. He puts down the receiver and gives me a good once over. "You look like shit."

"Lots of people have been saying that lately."

"I'm assuming that if you're here, it's about getting your old job back again."

"Something like that." I keep my expression neutral.

"It's not a great time of the year to be doing this kinda work. It's not like I'm short-staffed. Why should I want to take you back? You caused a lot of trouble before you got hit by that car, and it's all very convenient for you to claim you don't remember, but not everyone's going to buy that story."

"It's all about easing back into life again," I tell him. "Something will be better than nothing and I hope familiarity with this place will help jog my memory."

He frowns at me. "You speak funny, Ash. Looks like that car accident fucked up your brains real good. Sure you haven't had a personality transplant or something?"

For a moment I freeze with the shock but then figure he's just trying to have me on. Damn. How the hell am I going to fool people who knew the real Ash? My foot starts tapping, and I struggle for words, trying not to squirm beneath this man's gaze. "I'm hoping you'd take me back because I don't know who else to turn to. My life's a mess. I need to put things together again." I put my hands palm down on the table, maintaining eye contact with the man though every part of me wants to jerk away.

"That's no reason for me to want you back."

"I've changed. I'm not going to stir trouble like I used to. How about just on probation? Let me prove my worth." It's difficult keeping a wheedling tone out of my voice. For some reason it's become extremely important to me to get back Ashton's old job, as if I can take ownership of the man by stepping into his shoes on a figurative level as well.

At that point a diminutive woman with pixielike features and a mop of rainbow-hued dreadlocks knocks and enters. She freezes when she sees me, her lips drawn into a taught line before she hands Gavin his beer. Without a word she turns and leaves the office.

Gavin laughs. "As you can see, Lisa's anything but happy to see you again."

I stare at him blankly.

"You don't remember her?" He quirks a brow, searching my face.

"Of course I don't remember her," I snap. "Look, Gavin, I'm at rock bottom. I'm trying to piece together my life and at least if I start here, it's in an environment I'm supposed to be familiar with, surrounded by people who can hopefully offer me some details about my past."

Gavin draws hard on his beer, all the while studying me. He presses his fingers into his temples, massaging so hard I'm sure it must hurt. "I'm going to regret this," he mumbles. Then he straightens, reaches for a pack of cigarettes and lights one.

I watch him blow a plume of lazy smoke, my knees dancing now as well. Is this even the right thing to do? Should I bother? What other options do I have? In the distance the throbbing beat of some heavy rock song filters through the walls.

Gavin coughs. "Fine. I'll give you three shifts a week. Keep your nose clean." He taps the side of his nose for emphasis, as if I should know what he's getting at. "Don't stir shit and we'll see where we can take it from there."

I let out a breath. "Thank you."

"You'll get Monday and Thursday day-shifts, with Saturday late-shift, which runs from ten at night until closing at two the Sunday morning. You'll be paid your wages on Sundays but keep tips split from the staff pool each day."

"That's fine."

Gavin starts laughing. "You should see your face, dude. You look like some kid that's sitting in the headmaster's office. Are you on drugs or something? You're more fucked up than I ever thought."

I frown at this. How the hell am I supposed to respond? I can only assume that the old Ashton would never have been so formal with this rat of a man. They must have some sort of shared history of debauchery I don't know whether I want to guess at.

"Fuck this. You'll come right, I'm sure." Gavin rises and holds out his hand. "It will be like old days soon."

This is easy enough. I shake his hand.

"Come downstairs with me so I can break the news

to Lisa. She'll be thrilled." He laughs again, wheezing on the last few cackles. "She's the manager. You'll answer to her, understand? No bullshit. She's your boss, after me."

I should be grateful, but it's with some dread that I follow him downstairs for the rounds of introductions. Lisa is anything but happy to have me here. Gavin vanishes back upstairs, I take time getting acquainted with the job. Although not officially starting today, I'm nonetheless given the rundown and introduced to the rest of the staff, and end up working anyway, since I've nothing better to do with my time.

The same questions dog me for most of the morning: "So, you don't remember anything? Nothing at all? What was it like being in a coma for so long?"

Those nightmares resurface, but I fake a smile and shrug, saying something along the lines of, "Oh, it's just like getting a good night's rest," which is absolute rubbish. They don't need to know what has me screaming myself awake almost every time I drift off.

And things do get busy 'round about lunch time, when student types come in to shoot pool, eat greasy baskets of fries and take advantage of the noon-'til-two happy hour. It's uncomplicated work. It's easy being friendly and turning on the charm. There's something to be said for keeping the hands busy so the mind doesn't go off on tangents leading to fruitless speculation.

When a curvaceous flame-haired lady comes around the bar counter to knee me in the groin, I'm caught completely unawares. Now I discover firsthand why men are so precious over their privates. The world turns bright white for a few heartbeats then contracts to a narrow point centred on the redhead's face as I slide down against the bar counter to land with my backside in a damp patch.

She stands above me, arms akimbo, her short black skirt not doing much to hide her knickers, though why my gaze is drawn there I'm not really too sure, maybe because from this angle it can't be helped. At any rate, it's not going to matter, at least not until the pain lessens enough for me to stand. That's if the crazy woman lets me get to my feet.

"I heard that you'd come back!" Her voice is tight with rage. She has the traces of a Russian accent I would have found beguiling under a different set of circumstances. "I had to come back and see that for myself because I couldn't quite believe it." She aims to kick at me, but Lisa, bless her little cotton socks, grabs the crazy redhead around the waist and pulls her out of range before she can deliver a fatal blow.

"Cut the crap, Isabelle. He doesn't remember anything." Lisa's voice is a beacon of calm and reason. "Don't you think he's gone through enough? Must I get Pierre to chuck you out and ban you? Again? You know he doesn't like manhandling chicks."

Isabelle struggles against Lisa's grip, but the tiny bar lady's size is deceptive. Although my assailant manages to take a step forward, Lisa holds her in check.

"You're a poes, Ashton! I can't believe you'd dare show your face around here again." Isabelle's voice goes up an octave. Tears shine at the corners of her eyes and her complexion has gone from snow white to flushed.

All I can do is gape at her, my mouth opening and shutting while I cradle my injured parts. The pain shoots its horrifying ache right through me, making it almost impossible to breathe, let alone speak. Whatever Ashton did to her, it must have been something horrid.

Pierre, my blond friend at the door earlier, comes to the rescue. With the struggling, weeping woman's arms pinned behind her, he guides her outside while she hurls insults, using the most dreadful expletives I've ever heard issued from a woman's lips.

"You okay?" Lisa helps me stand.

I lean heavily on the bar counter, aware of how my own face is warm. Too many heads are turned in our direction, patrons momentarily distracted from their drinks and staring at this little drama that has just played itself out.

"What was that all about?"

Lisa presses her fingers to her temples then shakes her head. "Oh, sweet Jesus, Ash. You don't remember, do you? It was a great big scene here about six months ago. You were shagging Isabelle. Everyone knew about it except Marlise, and she had to find out in the worst possible way when you knocked Isabelle up. You told her to go get an abortion and would have nothing to do with her after that. She went through with it, but something went wrong. She started bleeding really badly, and the doctors say she can't have kids anymore. She apparently pitched up at your digs asking you to take her to hospital, but you never answered the door." The reproach in her tone is obvious.

My knees buckle and I struggle to hold myself upright. It's a genuine horror story. This *Kha* has blood on its hands. "And everyone knows this except for me?"

Lisa's expression turns to one of pity and she nods.

I'm a murderer. By default.

"I think I need to go sit down." I stagger to the empty table nearest the bar and rest for a long while breathing deeply, my face in my hands. My skin alternates between hot and cold.

Of all the dreadful things this man could have done, this has to be the worst. It's murder. Some would like to reason about predestination; that a soul in the womb terminated before birth was going to die anyway. There are too many people, they argue. But killing is killing, whether it is a bundle of cells or a grown man. That Ashton could be so callous...

Unclean. This *Kha* is unclean and my *Akh* has fused with this dreadful man's flesh, bones and blood. I dig into the muscles of my upper arms as though I could somehow rip that terrible stain out of the body, but it's impossible. I try to conceptualise that poor woman's anguish, of standing there in front of a closed door, probably bleeding, weeping and crying out for him to help her, to show some understanding.

Bloody bastard. Conscious that others are watching me, judging me for the way I shake, I knuckle my eyes and hold trembling hands over my face. Murderer.

Lizzie never could have children. A hollow ache sucks its way up through my belly, a terrible sense of loss that threatens to pull tears from my eyes and I have to breathe deeply to maintain some possession over this reaction.

Some of the pain in Isabelle's glare flashes back at me, the way she snarled when she lashed out at me with clawed hands. I understand. I would have done the same, if not more in the same situation.

Bastard. How could you?

It stings even worse knowing that Marlise hasn't told me this horror story. What, did she think I'd come here and the tale wouldn't bite me in the backside? Or is this her little piece of revenge for the grief I've caused her? It's bad enough that Ashton cheated on her so openly, and worse, indicative of his callousness that he'd expect the woman to clean up his mess on his behalf. Then again, she could have used birth control as well... Or perhaps she had tried to trap him in some way, which was entirely possible.

What's even worse is that I'm stuck with his identity. It's surprising no one's tried to kill me yet. That car accident... What if it wasn't as accidental as everyone seems to think it is? Ashton Kennedy, what am I to do with you?

"You okay?" Lisa sits opposite me, leaning on an elbow. Her dark eyes are full of genuine concern.

"I didn't sleep with you, did I?" I blurt.

Lisa laughs so hard a bunch of people at the nearest tables turn to stare. "Do you honestly think I'd sleep with the likes of you?"

Should I be pleased at her admission? For a moment I'm affronted. "Well, that's a relief then. Is there anything else I need to be aware of, apart from the fact that I've been a monumental bastard?"

"I'm sure you'll still bump into a few of your old buddies."

I groan and grab at my hair. "Do I want to?"

She spreads her hands. "Hey, it's a small scene. I'm sure by now, especially after Isabelle's spectacular display, that word will spread."

"That's just perfect." I hang my head.

The rest of the afternoon passes without further incident, for which I'm grateful. Lisa proves to have a rare streak of humour, which bolsters what remains of my flagging confidence. Her attitude toward me has shifted since the incident with Isabelle. Later one of Ashton's friends and a fellow barman shows up and, once again, I end up repeating the Routine, as I'm calling the briefest summary of Ashton's saga of pain and woe. I'm gratified to note that Davy, much like Lisa, doesn't seem to care too much for Ashton's dirty past.

I knock off early, shortly after happy hour, with just enough time to catch the train back to Rosebank to meet Marlise. Lisa's kind enough to share some of the tips from the day's takings, though fifty rand is hardly enough money, by her estimation.

"Glad to have you back on board," she says.

"Really?"

"Just kidding. Now fuck off. I'll see you on Thursday." She's smiling, though.

By the time I arrive in Rosebank, I'm exhausted. Evidently this body isn't quite ready to cope with being up and about. I wait by the front gate of the college, allowing myself to breathe and be. My clothing stinks of cigarette smoke. This doesn't please me. The students exiting the building look so young and it's difficult conceptualising that I'm in inhabiting the body of a twenty-one-year-old male. I'm not that much older than them.

The looks the young people give me as they walk past tell me they think I'm disreputable, bad news. At some point I'll have to shave, do something about my appearance. I've been of two minds about the hair, but after spending the day inside The Event Horizon, I reckon I'm going to keep it. None of the men there had short hair, and Ashton fits right in. Now that thought elicits another shudder. What have I come to? I'm no better than a thug.

It's perhaps the sense of being watched that has me look up. Marlise stands at the front door of the college with two female students, but she has eyes only for me. She waves, her face alive with joy. I return the gesture. My heart twists at the knowledge that she's said nothing about what happened between Ashton and Isabelle. That knowledge weighs heavily, and I'll need to get it out.

After hurriedly saying goodbye to her friends, she trots along the pathway to stop a few paces before me. My expression must communicate my displeasure, because she frowns then tucks a reddish-brown curl behind her ear.

"Hey," I say.

"Hey." Marlise shifts from foot to foot. "You found out, didn't you?"

"You could have told me about Isabelle."

"I didn't know how to. Oh, Ash, I'm sorry."

"And I suppose sorry from me should do. You didn't have to help me, but you did. Thank you." I do mean exactly what I say. The mortification of knowing what the old Ashton is lead in my heart.

Marlise sighs then passes me to unlock the car. "We'd best go then. Tell me about your day while we're driving."

This isn't quite the reaction I was expecting. If she'd been angry, I could have dealt with this somehow, but the quiet resignation? This only makes it worse.

CHAPTER FIVE
At Loose Ends

THURSDAY AND MY first official day as a barman at The Event Horizon comes 'round a lot sooner than I anticipate. In that time I've gone through about a quarter of the Van Vuurens in the white pages. There must be close on two hundred in Cape Town alone, including Janse van Vuurens, whom I decide to call as well, just to make sure. So far, no luck. I've encountered one geriatric Katrina van Vuuren, who stays in a retirement village in Durbanville. An awful crawly sense festers at the back of my mind. Although my fellow Inkarna assured me the process should occur seamlessly, there was always a chance a *Kha* could perish before an Inkarna could take over.

Catherine van Vuuren was a near-drowning that left the body in a coma. All I had to go on was that she had been three years of age in 2007. Where was my *Akh* during those five years if I wasn't in Per

Ankh? Is there some sort of nebulous no-man's-land? For surely, if I'd been completely immersed in the Sea of Nun, I wouldn't be back, would I? Spend too much time there and one loses all sense of identity, returning to the primordial sea. How easy it would have been to be lost forever. Has that time left its mark on me? Is this why I have terrible nightmares? So many questions and not enough answers.

I resolve to finish working my way through the list of names first. Afterwards I can start checking newspaper archives and the like. If I can track down representatives of one of the other Inkarna Houses, I'm sure I'll be able to get their help. But it's a case of finding them. Each House guards the location of its chapter house jealously, and we're not the type one could look up in a telephone directory.

Worse luck is the attorneys. They're not listed, and Marlise helps me run a search on the internet— something about which I don't want to give away too much of my ignorance—only to discover the firm was liquidated two years ago amid some sort of scandal attached to a pyramid investment scheme.

"That's not good," says Marlise.

I have to agree, though I can't go into the finer details as to why this upsets me deeply.

Damn. I'm back to square one, and this isn't helped by the frequency and growing ferocity of my nightmares. I wake two or three times a night, gasping, as if something heavy is trying to smother me. If I'm not drowning in my sleep, I'm floundering through a grey morass, unable to see, hear or taste. And always the whispering of voices, calling my *Ren*, beckoning and hinting at tastes of darkness and despair.

By Thursday morning, Marlise threatens to sleep on

the couch in the house, but neither of us wants that. Her shadowy family, whom I'm yet to meet, would welcome that as a sure sign of a doomed relationship. Not that we're in a relationship, but right now I'm happier letting people assume things until such time I can afford to put a roof over my head.

We've done the best we can with my physical appearance. I only nicked myself once this morning. Shaving Ashton's face gives me the horrors, still so alien whenever I glance in the mirror. I sneer at myself, try to recapture that expression so common in the photographs of him, the man I've become.

Marlise tries her best to educate me, taking me to assorted social networking sites online to show me photographs, to try to illustrate some of the connections, but it's all a blur of names and faces. While to a degree, I'm more familiar with some of the most recent events in Ashton's life, I'm not entirely convinced it's going to help once I start making progress with my investigations. That's a big *if* I make any progress.

The man in the mirror gazing back at me is a haunted echo of who he once was. None of the former self-assurance remains. It is with great effort that I try to stand tall, pull the shoulders out of the slight roundedness that has beset them, and it is almost with a sense of relief that I show up for shift at ten on Thursday morning, to work through until six that evening when the night's crew turns up.

How Ashton could stomach this as a career is beyond me, because there's a fair amount of grunt work involved: stacking glasses, counting out the float in the till, tallying up stock and ordering more from the store rooms when particular brands run low. I learn all about some of the latest cocktails thanks to

Davy's cheerful education, and I find myself liking the young man despite his grungy style.

Damn, and I must stop making these comparisons. He's only a year or so younger than Ashton, perfectly happy with his lot in life working in this den of iniquity, where I watch people get increasingly sozzled during lunch hour.

Pierre remains aloof. Every time he passes the bar, he glares at me. Davy tells me not to worry, that the man's just full of shit.

I just find it difficult to fathom that this is what my life has been relegated to, a mind-crippling job that certainly isn't going to be easy to escape.

Shortly before we finish, Davy asks that I go to the store in the basement to fetch another case of Windhoeks—hardly a daunting task, and one that I should be able to manage. The subterranean room runs the length of the main bar area and carries that unmistakeable fusty scent underpinned with aeons of spilled beer.

Shadows are almost physical here, tenebrous puddles of darkness that shift and coil of their own accord. My hackles are up immediately. A buzzing hangs in the air, filling it with a peculiar heaviness. I've had an inkling this building is spiritually active on some level, filled with so many memories, of so many lives who have passed through, but it has never hit me so hard.

I pause on the bottom step and scan the gloom, reluctant to take that first step. Piles of crates lean almost haphazardly, row upon row of kegs lining the walls. My very being screams that I mustn't go farther into this space, my lungs tightening. The single naked bulb doesn't do much to provide illumination. It could be my imagination, but I'm pretty sure the thing has a slight swing, as though a breeze stirs the room.

All the breath is knocked out of me with such ferocity I can do nothing to protect myself. An invisible force sends me skidding onto my side into a pillar. I lie there, stunned after the impact, while my vision goes black. On a daimonic level I sense it: an implosion of power and an unearthly howl of rage so filled with dark torment I shrink into myself, half-expecting blows to rain upon me.

Nothing of the sort happens and I lie still, gradually taking inventory of my physical well-being, my ears ringing. An eternity passes before I can get up and stand, leaning heavily against the wall for support. My left side is ablaze, each breath screaming agony. I allow myself a low groan, nothing more. There is no need to draw unwarranted attention to myself.

This is how Davy finds me, with tears of pain wetting my face.

"You okay, dude?"

"I-I must have slipped on a damp patch of concrete." *Believe me on this one*, I will. The floor is damp, but it's not that dangerous. My head throbs in time with the ache in my side.

Davy frowns and pushes his shoulder-length brown hair from his face. "I'll chat to Gavin about getting that seen to." He narrows his eyes. "Your nose is bleeding."

"Oh." I swipe at the trickle of blood and stare at it stupidly. At this rate my brain will be haemorrhaging out of my sinuses before the body hits its mid-twenties. Lizzie never had this much trouble.

"You'd better go see a doctor tomorrow. Just in case it's cracked ribs or something. Lisa would have my hide if you're lifting and carrying in that condition."

"She will?"

"Ah, fuck off." He turns and walks back up the stairs, which makes me glad so he can't see me limp to the bathroom.

Cold water does little to ease my now-raging headache, but mercifully the bleeding stops. My reflection is paler than usual and I bare my teeth at Ashton's face. "Bastard," I mutter.

What in the Tuat's name attacked me? In all Lizzie's time as the mistress of House Adamastor, I never encountered anything quite like that, filled with so much violence. Ghosts, genius loci, inexplicable entities... Those I'd run across from time to time, but they are not central to the work of the Inkarna. They are mere curiosities that, as long as they don't impinge on our ability to work and study, are relegated to journal entries.

After all, it is our abilities to manipulate the stuff of our own souls, our selves, that requires primary concern. If we were to become distracted, we would lose the grip on our ability to pass through the Black Gate with our memories intact.

Lisa comes onto late shift shortly after I exit the bathroom. She takes one look at me and immediately figures out something's up, getting the bones of the small drama out of Davy with little effort. She's the one who, despite my pleas not to, calls Marlise to collect me.

"You're not going on the train looking like a wreck. If I find out you didn't go to the doctor tomorrow, there's going to be hell to pay." She tosses her dreads the same way an angry cat flicks its tail just once, warning me not to cross an invisible line.

"Sure, sure." I do, however, take an involuntary step back.

Davy snickers from the opposite end of the bar.

☥

Back at Marlise's place I find myself embroiled in a tug of war with the woman.

"No! I'm not taking off my shirt! I'm fine!"

"You look like you're gonna pass out every time you get up or sit down. At least let me look." Marlise has a death grip on my right wrist, but I'm hurting too much to jerk away.

"I honestly don't know what you looking at a few bruised ribs is going to do to make it any better."

"Ash!"

"Don't keep saying my name like that, woman!"

Marlise flinches at the anger in my words, lets go of my arm and takes a step back from where I'm seated on the bed.

My guilt nibbles, and I place a weary hand over my face. "Oh for goodness sake..." I lie back with a groan, my feet still on the ground. "I'm sorry. I'm just...in a lot of pain right now. If you want to help me, rather find me some anti-inflammatories and some painkillers, okay?" What would she say if I told her the bit about the homicidal entity? *Oh, I got sideswiped by an angry ghost, nothing serious, just a few bruises...*

That's the kind of humour in which Ashton would no doubt engage, tormenting the poor woman with a flippant attitude, despite the severity of the situation.

The mattress is pressed down as Marlise climbs onto the bed, once again keeping a careful distance between the two of us. Her eagerness to be near Ashton, to touch him, to be needed, washes over me, and I pull back on my daimonic awareness. The last thing I want right now, aside from a hysterical woman, is another nosebleed.

Softly she begins combing my hair with her fingers and I let her. When last did someone brush my hair? A memory of Leonora returns to me, of us sitting in the living room overlooking the bay, the southeaster outside whipping the sea into submission. I had been so secure in my knowledge back then, thinking that, despite my age, I was well off, and all was secured for the future—for many futures.

I lose myself in the recollections, Marlise's fingers deftly unsnagging tendrils and, with them, some of the worries that have been festering. Perhaps it is a good thing to rest a while. The entire situation may look less dire. I can call a few more of the Van Vuurens, get some rest and, it can be hoped, enjoy some dreamless sleep.

Soft lips close on mine, the kiss chaste. Reflex allows me to return the kiss, not quite so chaste, before I realise what's happening and shoot up amid a fresh stab of pain.

Marlise stares at me, fingers touching her lips, then I'm doubled over from the agony in my ribs in a fit of coughing.

"Oh sweet Amun," I say once I catch my breath.

"What's wrong?"

"In case you haven't noticed, I'm in extreme pain."

The mattress springs back as she gets to her feet. I remain in my hunched-over position.

"I'll get those painkillers," Marlise says.

"Please."

What the hell just happened? Not her kiss. That could be expected. After all, it's clear she's still madly in love with the ass Ashton. No. With *me*. I'd responded to that kiss and it had felt like…

It hadn't felt wrong.

I sit up carefully and raise my fingers to my mouth, tracing the skin lightly. This is wrong in so many ways. I'm supposed to be staying here for a short while only, until I can save enough money to find my own place, not take advantage of this poor gullible girl. She's so very innocent. Ashton has done enough damage. I don't want to contribute to that special brand of hell he must have put her through.

Marlise returns with the medication, but it's quite obvious something between us has shifted. We're too poised, too wary in one another's presence. When we go to sleep that night, we're even more careful about not touching each other accidentally. It's like those olden-day stories about young married couples sharing a bed with a sword lying between them. I'm tempted to go sleep on the armchair, but that would be a little too obvious, not to mention bloody uncomfortable.

☥

By Saturday afternoon I finish calling the Van Vuurens and have given a lot of my spare cash to Marlise to pass on to her father for the use of the telephone, accompanied by some cock-and-bull story about trying to get my life on track. It's a small mercy she has an extension here in her room, but someone's still going to get upset once they see the phone bill.

I've had absolutely no luck, although granted one or two of the names I called were no longer listed. A cursory search on the internet brings up no mention either.

"Why are you getting so worked up about this? Who is this Catherine girl?" Marlise asks.

"I can't tell you."

She's overheard the gist of my search, however, and eyes me with suspicion.

"Look, if it's any consolation, it's not what you think, okay? And it was a hunch I had to follow up and it's failed miserably."

"Ash, something very weird is going on here."

"You're telling me?" I laugh and try to imagine telling her the entire story. "I'm not myself, I know." Further laughter peters out when I focus on her expression. She does not find my attitude at all amusing.

☥

The great thing about working on a Saturday evening at The Event Horizon is that I'm so busy I don't have any opportunity to be maudlin. The beer flows, bottles clink into the black bin behind the bar counter and money changes hands. A week of good food and plenty of rest has imbued me with a sense of well-being as I get into the rhythm of continuing with the ruse of Ashton's former life.

How people can still manage to follow conversation above the din of what passes for music among this crowd is beyond me, but they seem to be having a good time. The dance floor is a mess of bodies as people propel themselves around on the black-and-white chequered surface. The strobe light is most likely sending them into a near-transcendental state. The best part is the confusion of those old friends of Ashton's, when they try to strike up a conversation and I end up looking at them dumbly with a puzzled "Do I know you?" expression. The only blessing is the music's too loud for me to go through the Routine.

Marlise arrives at ten, with two of her friends. I'd said I'd get a lift back, but she tells me she's glad to be out. She's dressed to the nines in a tight velvet corset and long, flowing skirt trimmed with scarlet lace, quite a transformation from the long jerseys and tights which are her usual uniform. I can't help but notice the swell of her breasts and the way she moistens her lips whenever she glances at me. That's another thing I need to get used to, the way women flaunt themselves wearing little more than underwear.

Why does it bother me that Marlise looks so unutterably gorgeous? My face warms and I feign interest in wiping down the bar counter.

Don't go down that road.

When the girl makes an effort, she's striking, and I can see why Ashton would have maintained a relationship with her. Maybe I'm just old-fashioned. I shrug away the thought. Serial monogamy seems to be the norm nowadays.

But the pain in my side is enough of a distraction every time I bend to open a fridge and liberate bottles of beer or cider, or reach up to pour hard tack. Lisa notices my hesitation whenever I have to move and she raises a brow in query. That look asks: *Did you go see the doctor like I said you must?*

I have not gone to see the doctor. It's not just the money issue. The idea of one more medical professional poking and prodding at me, asking all sorts of questions and probing into my past, is not one I want to entertain. My first days of wakefulness in hospital certainly delivered enough of that, thank you very much.

Gradually the place becomes quieter. It's half-past two when Davy turns up the house lights and the DJ kills the music. It's time for the stragglers to go home, and I'm so pathetically grateful, because each step I take brings fresh, blazing agony.

Marlise makes small talk with Davy or Lisa or the DJ—I think his name is Chris. I don't like the way he stands so close, leaning on one arm, a bit too near her. His teeth flash white; he smiles too much at what she has to say. Why does this bother me so much?

I'm only too glad when we lock up at half-past three and can get the hell out of this place.

"You're looking a bit grey," Marlise comments as we step into the night.

"All the better to go home." I feel the wad of cash in my pocket: this week's pay with a share of the tips. It's not much but it's something. More than I had when I walked in on Monday.

"You sure you're okay?" She looks up at me while we walk to where she's parked in Long Street. I don't protest when she links her arm with mine. I welcome the contact because it speaks of friendship, nothing more.

"I'm hurting a bit, that's all. Need to get some rest."

"You could ask for some time off."

"I can't. Need to get stuff done. Need to get my life on track."

"Jesus, Ash! You've just come out of a months-long coma. You were as good as dead. Give yourself time to recover!"

"I don't have enough time!" I say with more force than I intend, my tone harsh enough for her to flinch.

"Enough time for what?"

"I don't know." That much is true. Exactly why, I have no idea, but my daimonic senses prickle, tapping into some undefined awareness, of the way fate will play out if I can't disentangle the threads of wyrd trapping me in a knotted tapestry of destiny.

We don't talk until we get to the vehicle, where Marlise pays the car guard and unlocks. It is bitterly cold out, the clouds pulled away to reveal a spattering of stars. Not many folks are still out on the streets. A particularly nasty wind leeches the warmth from the world, and I can hardly wait for Marlise to start the engine so the heater can kick into action.

"Thank you for doing this, for coming to collect me," I say.

"It's nothing." She keeps her eye on the road. Not many cars about this time of the morning, but those that are, are headed mainly out of the city centre, much like us.

"I could have waited for the first train."

"Ash." Her voice holds a warning tone. "You'd have been sitting around waiting for the cows to come home for at least three hours. In this cold. And you're not well."

I let out a hiss. To be so helpless, to have to rely on others without being able to recompense them for their time... "I feel shit for being like this...that you're going to so much trouble for me when— When I treated you like rubbish."

"It's okay. Really. Things are better." Marlise squeezes my hand and holds onto me until she has to change gears. Her skin is warm compared to mine.

How do I explain to her? What if I never get to the bottom of this situation and I'm stuck like this, in this *Kha*, in a less than ideal economic situation? What do I tell my fellow Inkarna one day when this flesh goes the way of all mortals?

It's my duty to continue. If all is lost—and many libraries have suffered the same fate as Alexandria's—then it is my task to rebuild, to make sure that House

Adamastor endures. I sift through my memories of the past few years. Was I wrong in trusting Leonora? She passed the tests, seemed so earnest in her search for the mysteries. This is always the risk when taking on new initiates. Some fail the first time they pass through the Black Gate, to be lost in the Sea of Nun.

But then she stood me by so well, so attentive. I doubt any mother could claim a daughter so devoted. It can't be any fault of hers.

Of me, then? Did I somehow betray the House?

House Malkuth and House Montu both maintain a presence in the city but are as secretive in their business as House Adamastor. The former is too embroiled in worldly affairs and the latter with their philosophy and martial arts, as we are with our books and secret knowledge. Neither would seek the other's downfall unless a rogue House has intruded to upset the balance. That is a possibility.

How shall I seek them out? Details of postal addresses would have been kept at our chapter house, and that resource is no longer available to me. With so many options closed to me, I can only approach a library in Wynberg, run by the Rosicrucians, where we sometimes pinned messages on a board. That may well work... It's a slim hope, but it's better than nothing.

"You're awfully quiet," Marlise says.

"A lot on my mind."

"A penny for your thoughts?"

"Just tired. Trying to figure out what the hell I'm going to do about my situation."

"You'll get there." She places her left hand on my thigh, giving it a squeeze; such an intimate gesture. If only I could relax into the sense of allowing someone to care for me. I'm just using her—that guilt niggles—

but I won't hurt her like Ashton did. Or am I trying to justify my current actions? These thoughts shuffle through my exhausted mind, and I have no clear answers.

Marlise must feel my muscles contract from the touch because she removes her hand. Or maybe it's because she changes gears as we turn from the M3 into the Kendal Road off-ramp.

I want to apologise, say something, but words desert me and we drive the rest of the way in silence. The glass is cool against my forehead, my skin almost feverish. I'm overtired, that's what it is. Things will look better after a full night's rest and maybe, just maybe, this prickling restlessness will abate.

Marlise's scream jolts me out of my half-slumber.

"Get out of the car, bitch!" a man shouts.

"Huh?" I jerk upright.

Dark figures stand on either side of the car, half-parked in the driveway, the gate already closing without us driving through it. Marlise makes small whimpers and raises her hands, and that's when I turn to the man standing on the passenger side. He's holding an object, and it takes me a moment to register he's pointing a gun at me.

"We don't want trouble," this one says. "Get out."

Marlise is already obeying, her movements slow, exaggerated.

What else can I do? A ridiculous notion occurs to me. Who'd want to steal Marlise's old Toyota? It looks as if it would fall apart at the slightest hint of a sneeze. She shouldn't even be driving it at night.

Moving slowly, and with care, I obey the gunman. The wind shakes the trees, their branches forming crazy patterns with the street lamps' illumination on the tar. Just my luck. Our hijacker's English tells me a lot. He's Russian. This isn't an ordinary hijacking, my instinct screams. Unbidden, three Blessed memories assail me in a three-dimensional flush of images underpinned by fear. Screams. Voices raised in anger. Guns. Bullets. One victim died in a driveway not too far from this block. Isabelle's face contorted in anger completes the visuals.

"What do you want?" I keep my tone neutral, trying to memorise the man's features.

Of medium height, he's bulky and wears a leather jacket over a dark turtleneck sweater. At some point he had his nose broken and the orange light reveals the pits of acne scars. A beanie obscures his hair and is pulled low over his forehead to cover his eyebrows. He holds that gun rock-steady, aimed directly at my chest.

He gestures for me to join Marlise, our backs to them, facing the car's hood. She's trembling hard and I take her hand, willing her to be calm. Her fingers are cold. *Everything will be all right.*

I ask them, "What do you want?" A whining starts in my ears. A horrible crawling twists up my guts.

"On your knees," says the other.

They're going to kill us, executioner style.

Blessed memory or Inkarna foresight I know not and, at this point, there's no time to think, only act, in a last desperate bid to stay alive. I can't die again now, not when I've so much that needs to get done. It's not Marlise's fault that she's in this mess. If she dies now, that's it, and she's hardly had a chance in life to live it to the full. Unsure as to whether this will work, I draw on every available energy source in the vicinity, as if I still had half the ability of my previous incarnation. Above us, the street lamps flicker, an electric whine filling the air before the lights go out.

Time slows, every cell in my body expands, and my blood buzzes. The engine of the big black SUV idling just behind the Toyota gurgles then cuts out.

An explosion down the street sends up a fountain sparks amid an electric-blue lightning crackle. The entire neighbourhood is plunged into darkness, which is my cue to let go.

With a wordless roar I spin around, faster than these men can react, and lash out with the daimonic power thrumming through my veins. They fly back as though they've been flung from a moving train, falling like two bags of meat about a dozen paces from us.

At once all the dogs in the neighbourhood set up a frightful howling and yammering. The sound is unearthly, unholy, as if a pack of Dracula's hounds has been unleashed upon the world. For a few heartbeats I stand, arm outstretched, before I collapse to my knees. One of the men stirs, groaning. Blood runs out of his ears, his nose.

To my eyes, the night is as bright as day. I can see the auras of all life forms shimmering about me—the way the one man is faded, ragged at the edges, the other gone out. The world tilts sideways.

"Ash!" Marlise grabs me before I fall. Something salty and warm fills my mouth and runs down my throat. My vision turns hazy.

She lays me down carefully and I watch, numb, as she runs to the men, shrieking incoherently, a fury all tooth and nail, biting and kicking.

After this I don't know any more.

I don't recognise the room I'm in, but it has high ceilings. Shutters on the outside block whatever sunlight tries to slant its golden fingers through the slats. Posters peel off the walls, depicting a plethora of long-haired metal heads, Goths and their mascots: dragons, wolves, demons and more than one voluptuous half-naked female I assume is a somewhat naive rendering of a witch.

Clothing is strewn everywhere, almost completely covering the hardwood floor. The bed is a mess of linen and I start when I make eye contact with the man seated on the edge. Ashton Kennedy—in his prime.

He cradles his head on his arms, hair spilling loose over his shoulders. Ashton becomes aware of my presence because he looks up, sees me and jumps to his feet. I take a step back just in time, just before he jabs an accusing finger at my eye.

"You! You've stolen my life!"

CHAPTER SIX
What the Hell, Ash

A SHARP SLAP brings me to my senses, and I sit up, a man's scream still ringing in my ears. I'm in bed—Marlise's bed. Candles flicker on her desk, casting grotesque shadows on the walls and ceiling as the flames dance. A herd of elephants tap-dances through my skull.

"Ash! Please! No more!" Marlise straddles my chest, leaning over me so her hair spills over her shoulder. Her eyes glisten with tears.

"Where? How?" The road, the men, the attempted hijacking... Oh my gods, she saw me wield my powers. I fall back, my entire body ablaze, my head throbbing in time to my pulse.

"I got my dad and my brothers to bring you in. They're dealing with the cops. I'm sorry, had to call the cops. We didn't tell them about you. Didn't want any trouble."

"But they'll talk, the hijackers, I mea—"

"They're dead, Ash."

My world crashes to a standstill. We stare at each other for a good while. I hardly dare to breathe.

Eventually I speak. "Dead." I've never knowingly killed anyone before. Not even in self-defence. Yet I can't bring myself to feel anything for that one word relating to the fate of those two men. I should, but I don't. I raise a hand, study the fingers where blue-green motes tease me with their almost-visibility. Then I make eye contact with Marlise, unable to hide the frown that is the physical manifestation of my suspicion. "What did you tell them?"

"That there was an explosion by the substation that somehow coincided, knocked them out. All the cars in the neighbourhood for four blocks won't start, the substation looks like a bomb has exploded. The police think it's a terrorist attack or something. I've made out that I interrupted them while they were planting a bomb. Things are still very unclear. Did a good job acting the hysterical woman." Marlise smiles, but her lips twitch.

What the hell? The girl has more backbone than I expected. "And no one's mentioned me? Absolutely no nothing at all?"

She shakes her head. "But you've got to find somewhere else to stay. Soon. Dad said when you're feeling... It was my dad who suggested we didn't involve you. Said it was better for everyone concerned."

"I'm trouble. I know." A big cover-up. I'm sure this won't be the first time I'm pathetically grateful for the help of strangers.

"What's going on?" She shifts, and my body protests.

"Argh, if you get off me, maybe I can try to tell you."

Her eyes widen, but she slips off me then sits, feet tucked under her backside, on the other side of the bed. I push myself so that I'm leaning my back against the headboard. Where the hell do I start?

"Damn, no matter what I say, this is going to sound unbelievable."

"Try me. People don't just fly through the air when you point at them. Entire blocks don't just blink out with no power. Substations don't just explode." Her expression hardens.

My options don't look good. I don't have resources. At some point, if I continue involving Marlise in this mess my life has become, she's going to find out everything or, by the looks of it, suffer severe injury. Either I give her something to go on or I get up out of this bed now, put some clothing on and walk out into the night. Neither option's going to be pretty.

"Ash?"

"For Amun's sake! Give me a moment!" I don't mean to raise my voice but I do.

"I need answers." For once Marlise isn't cowering. She's risen to her knees and has placed her hands on her hips. "If I don't get answers I'm going to... Screw it! I don't know what I'm going to do with you but I think, after all that I've been through looking after you, I deserve to know what the hell is going on. How can you knock those guys back as if you've got Jedi powers or something?"

"Jedi powers?" I frown.

"*Star Wars*?" she offers.

My Blessed memories remain decidedly blank on that topic.

"Oh, never mind! What in heaven's name is going on? It's like you've stepped out of another era. You don't even talk like you used to."

"All right!" I draw a deep breath. "The short version is that Ashton Kennedy died just over four months ago. I'm some glorified disembodied spirit that has reincarnated in his body. Only I wasn't supposed to take over his body. I was supposed to take over the body of a young girl named Catherine van Vuuren, but as far as I can tell, either she's dead or her family isn't listed, or they've left the country. I don't know.

"I am a member of an esoteric order that uses the bodies of recently deceased people to return and continue the work of those who await in a…a sort of afterlife. But I've got problems. The chapter house where I should have been able to access my order's resources is gone, and I have no idea what happened." I hang my head. "And that is the truth. And you're not going to believe me. And I'm not really a man. I was a woman… Her name was Lizzie." This last part I mumble, and I'm not sure if she catches it. My story sounds like pure fantasy. I'm not even sure I believe myself.

Deafening silence allows me to concentrate on the ringing in my ears and the way my head throbs with each beat of my heart. I don't blame Marlise if she gets up to call the cops, or the men in the white coats. Nothing matters.

Marlise moves on the mattress, and I half expect her to get up, but she doesn't. She scoots closer, covering my hands with hers.

"Ash. Look at me. I'm not sure if I want to, but I'm going to try to believe you, okay? Because I can't see any other rational way to explain what I saw two hours ago."

I make eye contact. "You're going to *try* to believe me? How's that supposed to help? Look, if you can help me just get past this I'll clear out of your life. I'll try to find a way to pay you back for the trouble you've taken. I'm really, *really* sorry. I didn't mean for things to spin out of hand."

Her frown vanishes. "I can see you don't mean for things to be so crazy, okay? And if it's any consolation, I think I like this new Ash more than the old one."

"Um. Thanks. I'm not sure I know how to take that."

She laughs before sitting back again. "I'm not sure what's going on but I'm glad...for this." Marlise gestures vaguely between me and her.

"I don't know if it's safe for me to be around you."

"It doesn't matter."

"Yes it does. Why did you allow him to walk all over you? He was...not a very nice man."

"Oh, god." She buries her face in her hands. "I can't believe I'm having this conversation. One minute I want to believe you, because it makes more sense, explains so much more, but it sounds so crazy." Marlise looks up. "You're not joking about being someone else, are you?" Tears streak down her cheeks.

"No. I could tell you plenty of stuff Ashton couldn't even begin to fathom. I could show you places nobody alive today could possibly know about."

"Thing is, I don't know what I should do about this. Part of me wants to laugh you off as being delusional, that the time you had that accident you got brain damaged. People who've woken after long comas have been known to suffer personality changes. But your recovery, it's just so *uncanny*, as the doctor called it. We'd have expected you to be wheelchair-bound, with some loss of motor function, to have some sort of speech impediment at least. The doctor was very explicit about this. But you just recovered. Completely. Except for the total change in personality. It's just not natural." Marlise shakes her head.

I rack my memories for some of the knowledge. They had told me that Inkarna abilities do, to a certain degree, extend to facilitate rapid healing. Once established, our souls are tenacious, our ability to manipulate reality resulting in all manner of effects. To tell Marlise will bring cold comfort.

"I don't know what to say."

She looks so lost, so vulnerable where she sits, holding herself at what she probably considers a safe distance, though it's clear she wants to be closer.

Marlise laughs. "It's like something in one of the books I read."

I roll my eyes and can't help but snort softly. "It's not a game."

"What now?"

"That's my question. I don't know. I suppose I focus on getting better."

"We could move out. I've some savings from my tutoring."

"*We?*" She's clearly the one who's delusional.

Marlise nods. "You think I want to spend the rest of my life living with my parents?"

"What? Are you crazy? You hardly know me!" I want to tell her it wouldn't be right, but at this point words fail me.

Marlise crawls across the bed and kisses me, hard, on the mouth, her tongue flicking against my lips. I want to push her away, want to protest, but my body betrays me, giving in to her insistence. When last has someone kissed me with real passion? An answering fire in my groin should alarm me, but it's been such a long time to be without physical affection. Her body is so soft beneath my hands as I lift the heavy jersey she's wearing to cup her breasts. It's then that it registers: she's a woman.

I break away, pushing myself up with a groan, half in pain and half in confusion. "I can't. It's too soon."

She sits up, a hand to her mouth. "Oh! I'm sorry, I didn't mean to hurt you."

"Um, yes." She thinks I'm hurting from what happened a few hours before. I pull my legs up to my chest and turn to look at the posters on the wall. Anywhere but here. For the first time since I've awoken, I'm in a position to do something about having a hard-on. It's not something I want to consider, this aching hunger festering down there, and I know perfectly well how I can assuage it. Marlise certainly is no stranger to having a man in her bed, one man specifically. But I'm not that man anymore.

It hurts trying to think too hard on how I'm becoming Ashton Kennedy, slipping into his old life.

"You've stolen my life!" his spectre shouted at me in that dream. His features, contorted in rage, make me curl onto my side, a low moan of pain mingled with fear ripping from my lips.

"I'll go get the painkillers," Marlise says.

⚳

Marlise has taken the phone off the hook but, shortly after sunrise, someone knocks discreetly on her door, and she steps outside. I wake enough to register this but it's not long before she returns to creep into the bed, bringing the cold air with her.

"Ash?" she queries.

"Mmm?"

"I just got a call from a friend of mine who's friends with Isabelle."

This has me opening my eyes. "You're friends with someone who's friends with Isabelle?"

She shrugs next to me. "It's a small scene."

"What about Isabelle?"

"Her brother apparently got killed last night, in some freak accident here, in Plumstead." Marlise almost mumbles those words.

"What?" I sit up, immediately wishing I hadn't. A wall of pain smashes through my skull. A warm hand rests on my shoulder while I wait out the bright sparks flashing before my eyes.

"No one knows what happened to us, at least not yet. You may not know this, but Isabelle's brother reportedly had connections to the Russian mob, or so they say. The two of you were as thick as thieves, for a while, allegedly. It happened during a time when you and I weren't...close."

It doesn't take much of a leap of an imagination to do the maths. I ask her, "Do you think he had something to do with the accident, the first one that resulted in this?" I point at my head.

She nods then shakes her head. "Yes. No. I don't know. The guy Isabelle was dating a while back ended up on the wrong side of Alexei's fists. There was some sort of assault charge, but the case got mysteriously dropped, and Alexei didn't even have to go to court. Smells fishy. In all the confusion when we got back, I didn't recognise him. I'd only ever seen photos of him on Facebook. Not enough to recognise him in the dark with a gun pointed to my head, but it seems to be making some sense now."

111

"And you didn't have suspicions, listening to their cheesy Russian accents?"

She shakes her head.

This chills me, suggesting Alexei's activities may run higher than I'd like to consider. Pay-offs to cops. Ouch. "And I was fucking his sister? Sorry, Ash was... He almost deserved to be put out of his misery."

Marlise's expression is pained.

"Sorry, I didn't mean?" As if I'm doing a better job. "This is coming out all wrong." I need to change the subject. "What's the time now?"

"It's half-past eight."

"I need to go check something out."

"You look like you're about to keel over."

Gingerly I get my legs over the side of the bed. "I absolutely have to."

"Go where?"

"There's a library in Wynberg, run by the Rosicrucians. I need to get there."

"Um, Ash, the car isn't working."

"Damn. I'll catch the train."

She rises abruptly. "You're crazy! You just about kill both of us with that crazy stunt, and now you want to go out, when you can hardly stand?"

"Marlise," I warn. "I don't know what's happening right now. I'm clutching at straws. Someone's just tried to kill me. I need to do something. If I carry on lying here, I'm going to wind up dead." Or worse, because there is worse than dead, as far as I'm concerned.

That urgency has me on my feet despite the overwhelming nausea and dizziness that assails me. Marlise watches me for about a minute before she, too, starts dressing.

"I'm coming with," she explains.

"Don't you have studying you have to do or something? I don't want to be responsible for you wrecking your life on my behalf."

The look Marlise shoots my way is positively venomous. "I'm not a child."

I should feel guilty. In fact, a small twinge almost has the word *sorry* tumble from my lips. "Suit yourself." I shrug.

"Are you going to at least eat something before we go out?"

"Are you offering?"

A small hiss escapes her and something about her annoyance makes me flash a smile at her—*mother hen*. I'd be beyond foolish to say that to her face but if I can't find something to laugh at in this entire messed-up situation, I'd be buggered.

That smile works its charm. Marlise offers a tentative one in return.

"I was thinking, since I made some money yesterday, and since you're insisting on tagging along, the least I can do is buy you coffee and a muffin along the way. Is the electricity still out?"

She nods.

We make quite the pair as we exit her room, me limping as if I've recently returned from a prize fight and Marlise with her arm around my waist, as though she could somehow stop me from toppling over, should the occasion arise.

I catch my first glimpse of her father, who was enjoying his cigarette on the veranda until we come round the side of the house. Marlise doesn't look anything like the tall, austere man still wrapped in a well-worn blue dressing gown. His scowl is enough to curdle milk, and he vanishes into the house before I can bid him good morning.

"I guess I'm even less popular than I was yesterday."

Marlise's smile is more a grimace, and she tightens her grip on my arm to tug me through the front gate.

This winter's morning is crisp, the sky hazy and the sun not doing much to raise the ambient temperature. Of last night's drama, the only sign is a patch of blood, a rusty, gooey puddle where one of the men fell. We walk past quickly, but neither of us can stop ourselves from checking the smear and sharing a glance. Will the cops still question her? This is possible.

Moisture coats everything, the leaves turning to a brown mush in the gutter and, despite all the horrors, it feels good to be out, the air cold in my lungs and my breath pluming before my face.

We wait for about half an hour at the station. The only distraction to our mutual silence is a phone call Marlise receives.

She frowns when she answers. "Sorry, you've got the wrong number. My name's not Lucy. No. Not. Lucy. I've told you this before."

"Who was that?" I ask when she stuffs her phone back in her pocket.

"Just some old granny. She calls every other week. Insists on talking to Lucy." Thank the Neteru it wasn't the police. I can't help but glance about to check whether we're being watched.

Then the cables overhead start singing, and the silver Metrorail train pulls in. The office is still closed so we embark without purchasing tickets. At this stage, I couldn't really be bothered if the security guards decide to hassle us. I'm too tired. In fact, it's Marlise who nudges me awake as the train screeches into Wynberg.

"You should have stayed in bed," she mutters.

"We're here now." I shove my hands in my pockets but I can't shake that chill lodged in my marrow.

If Wynberg is horrid at night, it's worse during the day, when I can see how badly some of the buildings are in need of a lick of paint. Bins overflow, with garbage leaking noxious liquids onto the tar, and the blanket-shrouded forms of vagrants look more like corpses strewn outside shop fronts. I buy us watery instant coffee with day-old doughnuts from Joe's Milk Bar near the police station. I have to say "Excuse me" twice before the Indian proprietor deigns to notice us. He's too busy paging through a dog-eared copy of *Playboy* magazine.

Luckily, where we're headed is nowhere near this filth; it's a Victorian-era homestead set in the older, historical part of the suburb. The distance is far enough from the station for me to start seeing double, and I stop often to catch my breath while Marlise glares daggers at me.

She doesn't have to say, *I told you so.*

"Just wait 'til you get there," I tell her. "It's a stunning building."

"It's a Sunday. Who's going to let us in?"

"I'll sweet-talk our way in. Besides, there's always someone there, especially on the weekends. Not busy, but if I have a bit of time to speak to the librarian, they'll let us in. There's a fireplace in the study and they serve hot chocolate during winter." There are ways to allude to my being a member of House Adamastor, which the Rosicrucians consider some sort of obscure Hermetic organisation.

Marlise raises a brow. "How come I've never heard of this library?"

"Not many people do. Only the right people ever find out."

She offers a soft snort of disbelief then sips her coffee from the Styrofoam cup and grimaces.

The road is almost as I remember it from the last time I was here. It's a relief to know that people exist who value the historical integrity of some of the old stately neighbourhoods. Or maybe I'm just overly fond right now of clinging to anachronisms.

"So, um, where is this infamous library?"

This brings me up short and I look around, searching for familiar landmarks. The problem is, the library was situated in a row of almost-identical houses, The Alexandrian is shaded by two massive magnolias, but it's the missing trees that have thrown me. I've been looking for those gnarled trunks and have walked right past.

The trees have been reduced to stumps covered in pot plants. The house has also been painted a tint of lime. I turn back, quickening my pace until I reach the front gate, Marlise at my side.

The name plaque, with its ibis motif is missing. The place looks decidedly residential with its swing set and a children's slide on the front lawn.

"I-I don't understand..." Choking disappointment squeezes my throat.

"It doesn't look like your library even exists, Ash."

"It was here. Really. I still came here the week before...before I died. Leonora was with me. We were reading up on ancient Enochian chants. There had been talk of a meeting between..." It's all in the past. No use clutching at the memories.

"Well, it's not here now. This has been a waste of my time and you should be in bed, resting."

I stare numbly for a long while, ignoring Marlise's

fidgeting and sighing next to me. If I don't give myself this moment, she'll know how on the verge of crying I am, and it won't do for anyone to see Ash lose his composure. After all, men aren't supposed to show emotion, are they?

☥

For the rest of the Sunday I allow Marlise to fuss over me. I don't want to tell her I'm already feeling a lot better. Even my side doesn't ache so much, although it's still bruised. She mentions again that we should move in together, but I divert the conversation to a safer topic without hurting her feelings.

It's frustrating knowing she's right about me resting and I relax, drink the tea she brings and enjoy the food she prepares: the ubiquitous toasted cheese-and-tomato sandwiches appearing to be her forte. We watch movies on her laptop, film renditions of a few of the books on her shelves. I marvel at the detail of the special effects compared to the films I saw at the drive-in with Leonora. Not in my wildest dreams had I ever imagined this level of sophistication and, not for the first time, I find myself wondering what changes will have occurred the next time I return.

That's *if* there's a next time. And that's *if* the Inkarna of House Adamastor allow me to return. It takes a great deal of collective energy for us to punch through to the material world. I should feel honoured that I was allowed to return directly after my first departure, but they were adamant after their initial misgivings of my ability. I need to find out why Richard—Siptah—never returned to Per Ankh. But how am I to figure out what happened to him, if my own life is such a mess?

I must admit I had not been incredibly enthused to

discover that Meritiset had been his lover during two previous lifetimes, but she had reacted with grace at my arrival. Besides, we have an eternity. Ordinary folk don't. What are the attachments of a life bond, after all? Yet still, I sense there was some resentment on her part that I punched through to the material realm before her, that I was selected and not her. But we are not to go against the will of the council. Some of them have been knocking around since the age of Ramses.

And here I am, now, without any of my past resources, trying to solve a greater mystery than one missing Inkarna. While they conduct their searches in the Tuat and beyond, trawling for echoes, dipping even in the Sea of Nun, I am to sift through for clues here. Not an easy job at best and now, with the worst having happened, I'm not even sure I know where to start. My only qualification: the culture shock wouldn't be as overwhelming as it would be for one of the elders who had experienced an absence of a century or more.

I should sleep. I know I must. Exhaustion clings to me, dragging me down to oblivion, but to give in to that impulse is to surrender to the snapping nightmares lurking in the shadows.

"Go to sleep," Marlise says on more than one occasion when I nod off, only to jerk awake when I realise I'm losing the struggle.

"Can't," I mumble, rubbing at my eyes or rising to go splash water on my face.

I haven't spent any time on my meditations. This is a bad thing. I'm not thinking straight, the lines between my physical, emotional and intellectual selves blurring into a tangled mess. A simple meditation, that's all I need, but how do I explain this to Marlise without scaring her with the details of esoteric practice? This is the other problem with my present situation. I don't have a single moment to myself. I don't have opportunities for self-reflection. There is no chamber, no private space I can call my own.

The situation can't continue to stagnate.

"I know what will help me, actually *us*."

This perks her up, and she shifts on the bed so she can look me in the eye. With her hair in a loose ruddy wave about her shoulders, she seems so young.

"Part of our practice in the old days was to meditate. It helps calm the soul, put things into perspective. I need to start doing this again, and I think it would be…beneficial if you also partake of the activity, especially if you're planning on consorting with the likes of me." I give a dry laugh at that thought.

Her gaze becomes distant. Even if she says no, that's also fine, but it would help if I were able to recruit a willing partner. Is she initiate material? Should I tell her where this path leads? Am I being selfish?

I had not at first believed Richard. He'd caught me in the Inkarna snare with almost the exact same innocent suggestion. What harm can a little meditation do? I suppress the second laugh that wants out. At present I need all the help I can get, and Marlise has already seen more than ordinary folk should. It's already too late for her. If I don't school her, she won't be able to deal with any of the other strangeness coming our way.

And there will be further strangeness. Of that I have no doubt.

"Okay," says Marlise. "What do we do?"

This is a small step in the right direction.

"Oh, it's quite simple." I make my answer sound flippant, though I know it's anything but.

An hour later I've managed to get the room into some semblance of a ritual chamber. We've tidied away as much as possible. Ideally, we'd need a space almost bare of furnishings, but this will have to do. It helps that the room itself is plunged into darkness once the lights are off and the curtains drawn.

And there's no dearth of candles. For this I select two new, each in an identical holder—two crystal blobs that look like they belong to a fancy dinner service.

Marlise has taken the phone off the hook, as per my instructions, and she's put a *do not disturb* sign on the door—not that her family would disturb what's going on in this room. For all they know, we regularly engage in sordid acts of fornication and, right now, I'd prefer it if they think the worst and stay far away.

We sit next to each other on a blanket thrown over the floor, to keep some of the chill at bay. Marlise surprises me by having frankincense in stock, which I bid her place on her incense burner. Soon the fresh resin scent fills the room, and it's easy for me to slip into my past, recalling the beautiful chamber I maintained in the Simon's Town chapter house.

It's all still there. If I find out what went wrong, there's a chance I can re-establish House Adamastor's sanctuary.

Eager to please, Marlise settles, our knees almost touching, and easily follows my instructions to slip into rhythmic breathing. Soon we maintain the measured inhalations and exhalations that take one's body and mind into a trancelike state. Quietly, so as to not alarm her with the alien words, I begin to chant, words drawn from the Egyptian Book of the Dead, a hymn to Weser, or Osiris, as he is most commonly known.

It amazes me that Ashton's lips will form the Middle Egyptian words, "...thou sendest forth the north wind at eventide..." It is even more fantastic that I can draw upon these ancient phrases as though they are freshly scribed on my heart and tongue. That is our gift, to tap into the old words that hold the most power. There are benefits to being an immortal librarian.

I can recall the pylons of Per Ankh rising from the opalescent waters bathed in starlight. Lotuses add their sweet scent to the evening air and, for a moment, I can take those first faltering steps along the causeway. Sothis blinks low on the western horizon. Oh, Per Ankh! My souls' rest! Are you lost to me for eternity?

Static mars this vision and I falter, the scene dissolving into Marlise's room. We are not alone. A darker shadow forms in a corner by the dresser, to our right. At first I think it's a trick of the light, but the candles are guttering even though there's no breeze. It's as if the very darkness is trying to smother their fire.

That horrible, familiar buzz begins in my ears, the same I encountered beneath The Event Horizon. Whatever entity lurks with us, it gives off the exact same signature as the one that sideswiped me.

Marlise's breathing grows irregular. *Stay in trance*, I will at her, but she gives a small gasp next to me and I know she can see the thing, too.

"Ash?" Her breath mists. The room is a lot colder than it should be.

"Just sit perfectly still. Don't say anything. Let me

handle this." I try to sound more confident than I feel. I've not had many dealings with angry spirits, and my heart feels as though it will explode from the fear.

"I, Nefretkheperi of the Inkarna, of House Adamastor, demand to know why you trouble me," I say. It is best to speak with authority.

The shadow shudders when I speak. It bubbles and bulges until it forms a man-sized shape. The head and shoulders are clearly defined, but the rest of the features remain nebulous.

"*You stole my life!*" The voice echoes in the room, hollow. The thing raises an arm, the fingers unformed, and it points directly at me. Judging by the startled squeak that escapes Marlise, she's heard this as well.

"It is not your life anymore, ghost. You forfeited that. You must proceed to the Hall of Judgment. You are no longer wanted here."

A roar, as of thunder building before a lightning strike, fills the room. It's hard not to flinch. Any instant now this unquiet spirit will summon enough daimonic power to dash both myself and Marlise against the walls until we are reduced to a bloody pulp. This time I may not escape, and I certainly don't want Marlise to get hurt.

"Your pontificating and bluster doesn't frighten me," I say to the ghost. "And mashing us into a pulp won't work either. Say what you must then let us be done with this. Know this, however, you can't have your *Kha* back. You forfeited that right by bringing about great *isfet*, by going against the tenets of Ma'at." This last I state with great vehemence, the pain Isabelle and Marlise must have suffered adding weight to my words.

A distant wailing, as of winds speeding across a

desolate landscape, reaches our ears. With a soft implosion, the entity collapses in on itself and the candles flare briefly before settling into ordinary tongues of flame.

We sit in silence for a good few heartbeats before Marlise speaks up, her eyes wide and posture stiff. "If that's what happens when you meditate, I'm sure as hell not interested in any more of this hocus-pocus."

I start laughing. How else can I respond to what's just taken place? If I admit I'm scared witless, I'd be better off slitting my wrists or drinking poison, for all the good living will do for me. Marlise shivers when I pull her to me, but I need the human contact as much as she does.

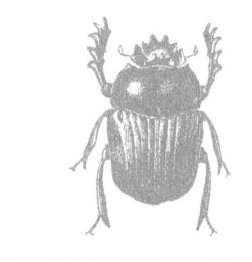

CHAPTER SEVEN
Ghost from the Past

WE HEAR NOTHING more from our unquiet friend for the rest of Sunday. In fact, I manage to have the first dreamless sleep since this entire drama started.

When we wake the following morning, not to my scream but to the pedestrian bleeping of her phone's alarm, we blink blearily but smile at each other.

"A full night without you waking the entire neighbourhood. That's a first." She doesn't just mean me waking and screaming. It can be hoped that the electricity department will come sort out the substation this morning. I'm beginning to miss not having a hot bath.

"Let's see if we can keep it that way."

It's bitterly cold out and the rain lashes the windowpanes and drums down hard on the tin roof. Other mornings like this, many, many years ago, Leonora would bring me my tea first thing, and perch on the edge of the bed drinking hers while going through the list of activities on our schedule.

Then we'd perform our first Adoration, have breakfast...

"You've got that faraway look in your eyes again."

"Oh, sorry. Just remembering," I said.

"What?"

"Stuff." How can I explain this other self? Day by day this past life I lived grows fainter, fuzzier at the edges, as if Lizzie's hold is gradually slackening. Who am I becoming?

I half sit up when Marlise pulls me back into the bed. "Let's snuggle, just a little. We'll have to take the train today so we can afford to leave a little later."

The protest dies on my lips as I allow her to snake her arms around my chest, as though I am some giant toy bear. How can I allow her to be so intimate with me? It's a gradual realisation, this situation between me and Marlise, something she may have taken for granted but because I have not resisted enough, she has slowly chipped away at my misgivings.

You're a man now. Act like one.

But she is so delicate, so soft. It's difficult seeing her as a woman with needs, someone who was used to Ash taking what he wanted, *when* he wanted. Hell, she seems to need us, like this. Here. Now.

"Ash?"

"Mmm?"

"Do you think you could love me?"

"I like you, if that's what you mean. It's a bit early to tell. I mean, this isn't really like a boyfriend-girlfriend relationship."

"No, love me as in physically. It's like you get scared to touch me."

"I-I don't feel that it is right for me to take

advantage of you."

"It wouldn't be wrong. It's not like we never fucked before."

"That was then. I'm not—"

"The same person, yes, you've said that a billion times."

"Give me time, liefling." I press a kiss to the top of her head.

It's almost with a sense of relief that I immerse myself in my Monday shift at The Event Horizon.

"Have you heard about Isabelle's brother?"

I play dumb and avoid getting drawn into any conversation concerning Alexei. It's too much of a coincidence—one that I would do best to avoid, since people talk. I get three nosebleeds during the course of the day making people forget. Lisa raises a brow but doesn't pursue the matter.

At the tired part of the day, when all the student types have filtered away and the evening happy-hour crowd hasn't yet arrived, an old man wearing a fedora and a brown suit dating back to the sixties enters, leaning heavily on his cane. The cane captures my attention. It is ibis-headed. A very similar cane used to stand at the front door of the Simon's Town chapter house. A chill creeps over my skin.

His face is heavily lined but his eyes miss nothing. I purposefully feign interest in polishing the beer glasses.

The man lays a twenty on the counter. "A Castle, please." His voice is weary, dry, as though he has had a thirst laid upon him that no amount of beer can slake. He stares at a point in the distance, much farther than the first row of bottles lining the racks.

"Coming right up," I answer, palming his money. I want to ask him about the cane but I don't want to make a total fool of myself because I *want* there to be a connection when there isn't.

The space around him shimmers, and I blink. The effect vanishes.

I place a bottle next to his hand with a chilled glass, trying to affect nonchalance while he pours the amber liquid and takes his first sip. What follows feels like a carefully orchestrated dance, each of us maintaining disinterest in the other. The old man is the antithesis of The Event Horizon regulars, yet he sits here as though he has all the right in the world to drop in for a pint, which he does, but his kind normally doesn't frequent this establishment.

He reminds me of a friendly uncle. His small round spectacles catch the glare from the television screens broadcasting the media's latest and greatest while some heavy metal track blares, incongruously, totally at odds with the swaying black bosoms on the screen.

It's as if time slows down; the other patrons pale ghosts compared to this man, this anachronism who's taken up residence at the seat right at the end of the bar. I turn to speak to Providence, one of the cleaning staff, and when I look again, the old man is gone, like he never was there.

I stare for a few heartbeats at the empty glass, the bottle that has been pushed an arm's length from where he sat. Dimly I'm aware of Davy chatting to the pale Goth chick I assume is his girlfriend—she looks barely legal, though I'm sure that's intentional on her part. They all seem so young.

A piece of paper has been tucked under the glass. I snatch it up and unfold it, my heart contracting when

I recognise the winged scarab of House Adamastor printed on the outside in black marker.

Upon opening the paper, which is a creamy yellow, almost parchment-like, I suck in air when I register the carefully printed words: *Richard Stanton Perry* with tomorrow's date and a time—noon. All the breath flees from my lungs and I crouch behind the bar, leaning against the fridges and not minding how cold the metal is.

Richard! Why is it so difficult to picture your smile, remember the scent that lingered on your clothing even after you were gone? I miss you, with my whole heart.

"Are you okay?" Davy looms above me, his expression concerned.

"I'm good," I say, though it's a bit of a struggle to rise to my feet.

"You're all pale."

"I think I've taken a bad turn, that's all."

"Lisa says you should take off early if you're not feeling good. She seems to say that every day, but you're too stubborn." His concern for my well-being is genuine. "I wish she'd do the same for me some time." Davy laughs.

"I'd appreciate that." My voice sounds tinny, distant.

I don't feel bad about leaving early. I pocket my share of the tips, shrug on my jacket and stumble into the murk of what's left of the day. It's early enough for me to catch Marlise before she leaves for home. She'd said she'd pick me up from work, but I reckon it's a pleasant enough surprise for her to get me outside her college, unannounced.

I shoulder my way through the throngs in the subterranean Strand Street Concourse. All the while some other part of me maintains alertness, constantly on the lookout for trouble. The piece of paper the old man left behind is folded, clasped tightly in my left hand. Tomorrow. Noon.

All I can think of is Richard's grave, the clean lines of the tombstone. Has the passage of time been kinder to his memorial than it has to the rest of my past? I'm filled with the burning compulsion to go there, now, but I hold myself back, threading between people who give the appearance of bumbling through this existence with little or no thought.

Marlise can see something's wrong the moment she steps outside. "You look like you've seen a ghost." She laughs, obviously referring to last night.

"In some ways I have," I say. We walk to the car, which she had fixed this morning, and I'm glad for her arm around my waist. I need the warmth, the reassurance.

"How so?"

I show her the paper once we're inside. Marlise turns it over a few times, tracing the scarab outline.

"It's a bug with wings. What does this mean?"

"That's the sigil for House Adamastor. Inside is the name of the man..." I can't bring myself to say *I was married to*. "The man who taught me everything I know. And the date he died."

"But you haven't answered my question."

"This was given to me by some old guy who pitched up at The Event Horizon this afternoon. It was all very strange."

"Why's the date there?"

"I think I'm supposed to go meet someone, at Richard's memorial."

She raises her brow at that answer. "Where's he buried?"

"Maitland cemetery."

"Eish, that's not a great place to go nowadays."

"How so?"

"It's not safe there. They've had issues with squatters and people are always getting mugged, or worse."

"After the other night do you honestly think someone's going to get the better of me?" I say this with far more bravado than I feel.

"And every time you do something that involves..." She shudders, and it's clear she doesn't want to consider the supernatural aspects intruding on what she considers to be our vastly improved relationship. Marlise glares at me before starting the car. "You wreck yourself." I had told her about the incident in the basement.

"I'll be fine. I'll take a knife."

"As if that's going to make a difference."

"I was fine against those two thugs, and they had guns. They didn't know what hit them." I don't think they suffered, and a small twinge of guilt knots my gut.

We argue about me going tomorrow, all the way home, but I don't budge on my decision. She's got a practical examination, otherwise I know she'd have insisted on tagging along. When I tell her she's behaving as if we're an old married couple, that shuts her up and, although some tension remains, we have a reasonably peaceful evening until I tell her I plan to meditate again.

"Oh no, Ash. I can't let you do that. Whatever it was that happened last night, I don't want to think about it. We can't go on messing with stuff."

"I have to."

"You're going to call that *thing*."

"Then I'll go meditate in a churchyard or somewhere."

Marlise gapes at me. "You'd never do that. It's not safe."

"Do you want me to wake up screaming again? You forget, I've lived an entire lifetime before this." This whole situation is beginning to work on my nerves. I should never have taken her into my confidence, but what other options were there? Go live under a bush?

"No."

"I could move out, I suppose. Davy told me about a pay-by-week lodge in Gardens. Sunrise Lodge. I'm thinking of checking it out."

"That's an even worse idea than going down to Maitland cemetery!"

"Well, I can't keep living here. It's a miracle your parents haven't turfed me out yet. By all rights, they shouldn't even have helped cover up the other night. They should told the cops about me."

"They wouldn't!"

"They're the fools then."

We stare at each other for a few heartbeats. Oddly, I am remarkably calm, though deep down I know I should feel somewhat angry because Marlise, as sweet as she is, seeks to control me and is enjoying this vulnerability in a man who previously manipulated her to his heart's content.

"Don't do that, Ash. Please." Her lower lip trembles, her chest heaving.

"I'm an adult. I need to take responsibility for my life, not shack up here indefinitely like some runaway teen. You just want a little of your own back because of what Ashton did to you when he was still alive."

Her confusion and inability to understand causes her to shake. These emotions are so intense I don't have to reach with my senses to taste them.

"B-b-but..."

I reach out and cup her chin. "You know we can't carry on like this. It's not right for you, or me. If we are going to have any chance of remaining on speaking terms, I have to have my own space where I can do what I need to. The way things are going, you will get hurt. I can't predict what's going to happen next."

Some of my daimonic senses slip free to read Marlise. She doesn't want to believe everything that is transpiring yet, on another level, she doesn't have any other explanation, and the one I'm currently offering, that I'm a transplanted soul in the body of her dead lover, offers easier answers. She wants to possess me. Marlise cannot and will not accept the most logical answer: that the bang I received to my head four months ago addled my brains.

She grips my wrist, tears now flowing freely. "Ash, I love you."

My lips twist into a sneer and I pull away. "You don't even *know* me, and you were purposefully blind to Ashton as the lying bastard he was. How could you let him take advantage of you? I should have stuck it out there with Ashton's parents."

Then you may not have gotten as far as you are now. You wouldn't have met the old man or have a job.

"Don't talk like that!"

"Then what must I say? Tell me! Because you know I'm not going to lie to you."

Her features scrunch up and she presses her palms over her face, sobbing.

"Crying won't help, Marlise. You're not going to get my sympathy."

"But you're making me cry!" she wails.

"No. *You're* making yourself cry. You're crying because you want me to feel sorry for you. You're crying because you want me to put my arms around you and tell you everything's going to be all right. I'm not going to play along and feed into your co-dependency."

To give her some credit, she rubs at her eyes vigorously, but the glare she casts in my direction lets me know she's anything but pleased with this turn of conversation. "Fine."

I take her hand in mine, squeezing firmly and *willing* a sense of reassurance over the link. I'm pushing it. Another nosebleed is the last item on my agenda at this point.

"You need to allow me to do these things. You need to let go of Ashton. That man is dead. Really. Whoever I am, I'm still trying to figure that out. I can't replace Ashton in your life. I am not that person. I apologise for taking advantage of your hospitality but I really didn't have anyone else I could turn to."

"You're going to leave me."

"No, I'm not. I'm still here, but you need to understand that I have to get my feet on the ground again. Let things develop. I need you to be my friend first, before anything else." There, that doesn't quite squash the idea that a proper relationship isn't going to happen, but I'm hoping to get it through to her that I can't just pick up where things left off.

"I don't understand why we can't do this together?"

"We are, but I need you to do some important things for yourself first, like finish your studies. And, when things settle down, then we can relook everything, all right?" I've been a fool. She's in too deep. She's not Inkarna material. Too trusting, not

133

curious enough, and scared of the unknown.

Just like you were way back then.

"Fuck." Damn, that word is tumbling off my lips far too often nowadays.

"What?"

"I've really made a hash of things, haven't I?" It hasn't been my intention to hurt her, not after what the real Ashton did. Hah! The real Ashton, as if I'm not any more real than he was.

At that moment, the lights flicker and look as though they are set to go out. We look at each other; Marlise has gone pale.

"That's not what I think it is, is it?" she asks, her voice quiet.

"I don't know." But that horrible whining starts on the edge of my hearing.

The sound system turns on full blast with a horrible burst of static that has both of us clutching at our ears. Marlise darts up to switch the thing off but no matter how she turns the dials and pushes at the buttons, the sound doesn't die until she pulls out the plug.

"What the fuck?" she asks.

I rub at my arms and glance about the room, trying to cast out with my daimonic senses. It's like hitting a brick wall. Something twinges in my sinuses and the itchy warm telltale trickle of blood starts out of my right nostril.

"You're bleeding."

How about stating the obvious? I wipe at my nose with my left wrist with a sense of inevitability. Crimson streaks my skin. "Just great."

Her eyes are huge. "It's *him*, isn't it? He's haunting us."

"Correction. He's haunting *me*, and I don't think he

cares terribly that you get caught in the crossfire."

The sash window rattles heavily in its frame, as though something is trying to batter its way in. There's no time to think too hard, or fall back on the myriad chants I have at my disposal. I stand, drawing myself up to my full six feet and four inches. The words in Middle Egyptian come naturally to my lips. "Ashton Kennedy, in the name of Amun, the Hidden One, and with the authority of Weser, the Lord of the Dead, I command you to cease and be quiet."

The effect is instantaneous. Silence.

We glance at each other. Marlise has bunched a section of the duvet into a bundle she clutches to her chest. "Is he gone?" The whites of her eyes show, like she's a spooked horse.

I offer a slight shake of my head, ignoring the renewed trickle of liquid running over my lip and into my mouth. The buzzing has started again, an insistent electric hum that is almost audible.

The sound grows in frequency, the lights dim and it is as if a giant vortex begins to swirl, threatening to suck all the life from the room. A deluge pours onto the roof, rattling at the tin, great gusts of wind howling against the side of the house with all the ferocity of a hell beast.

The shadows creep from their corners, stretching long-fingered hands towards us, a terrible hunger lapping at their edges. I reach across the bed to drag Marlise into what I hope is the relative safety offered by my arms. She shivers, presses herself tightly against me and wraps her arms around my waist before she buries her face in my chest.

The chant I choose is an old one, based on an example drawn from the Papyrus of Ani, of a man coming forth by day against his enemies. "I have divided the heavens. I have cleft the horizon..."

It is about establishing dominion over the spirit realms and, in this case, one angry spirit that seeks to impinge itself upon the world of the living. The world blurs at its edges. The room in which we stand is bled of colour, furniture and décor becoming a smear of grey shot through with blue-green streaks that could be motes of light attenuating into infinity.

"What's happening?" Marlise asks, but her words muffled, as though she is speaking through a pillow.

My response is to grip her tighter to me, to press a kiss to her crown in the hope to quell her shaking. "We're going into a space between worlds, to what purpose I can't fully tell. The spirit is drawing us partially into its realm, because it costs it too much energy to attack us in the material, which is what it's been doing up until now."

She whimpers. I can't show fear, not now. I don't dare admit now is the first time, in practice, that I've experienced this kind of phenomenon. Oh, I'd read theory until it poured out of my ears, and so many theories abound, and many of them conflicting. All paranormal happenings of this nature are highly subjective, coloured by the perception of the viewer in the objective.

The only way to describe our present environment is to compare it to being underwater, in some emerald-tinted lake, the water shimmering under the influence of miragelike heat waves. Our legs give the appearance of dissolving halfway beneath the knee, our feet invisible, though I can still feel that I'm standing on the floor, possibly still in Marlise's bedroom. It's impossible to be sure of anything here.

The entity takes shape, drawing in some of what surrounds us as it forms a semblance of the *Ka*, the spiritual double. It's like staring into a perverse mirror of myself, the sneering image of the old Ashton Kennedy coming into being before us. He flickers with bursts of static, suggesting that it is with a great force of will that he's making his environment conform to his vision.

Marlise's shaking grows greater as she realises what is transpiring and I hug her as tightly as possible without hurting her.

"Be firm," I tell her. "He can't harm you." Oh, how I wish that is the truth.

"*I want my life back*," Ashton says.

"You can't do this," I answer.

"*You have no right to my body.*"

"What is done is done. You must depart, go on for judgment."

"*No.*" He takes a step forward, hands balled into fists. His hair is a nimbus of shadow, surrounding his face in a cloud, moved by invisible currents.

"Don't come any closer." I hold up a hand, palm facing towards him. My daimonic powers come easily here, and I push at him, forcing the motes of energy to stream up from my feet, to flow through my chakra points as a beam of white that strikes him on his chest. "Come no farther."

He howls, the sound unearthly, tearing through my very core. Marlise's death grip around my waist strengthens.

"You've passed from this life, Ashton Kennedy and, by some twist of the laws of Ma'at, I am now the owner of your *Kha*. You need to pass to the Hall of Judgment. That is how it is. Even for those of us who come into being as blessed *Akh*."

For a moment the entity shimmers, flickers, and gives the appearance of dissolving, but some nasty, crawling thought suggests we won't be so easily rid of him. Our world darkens for a heartbeat before the spirit draws more solidity into himself.

"*I won't go.*"

"I have ways and means to force you into the Hall of Judgment," I say. This is a lie, if ever there was, but I'm sure as hell not going to let this thing know that.

He tries to rush me, and I pull hard on my daimonic resources, though I know on a physical level this effort taxes me hard, but if I don't try, I don't know if I'll have a body to which I can return. The powers flow through me, an electric current that singes my synapses, and it's all that I can do to keep Ashton from reaching us. The Neteru help us if he succeeds. I'm not sure what he could achieve and I do not want to find out, either.

He howls again, the sound shivering through me, and I grit my teeth, pushing with all the conscious force I can muster. Marlise twists around, letting go of me to stand squarely.

"Marlise, no," I mutter.

"Ashton." She speaks with assurance, addressing the angry ghost.

The being's attention shifts from me to her, and some of its intensity flickers.

"Don't," I say.

"Ashton, you're dead. You died that night when Alexei drove over you with his SUV. Why can't you see that? Have you ever wondered why he drove over you? Have you stopped to consider that you are a murderer? I know you didn't care, what you did to Isabelle, but you've got a stain on your soul because of that. Look at yourself. Consider my words."

A bluish glow envelops us, spreading from Marlise's exhaled breath. Weird.

"Leave us alone, Ashton! I don't want you in my life anymore."

Incongruously the spirit falters. Its expression turns from anger to something else. Remorse?

A sense of where I'd been wandering for the past five years reaches me. "If you don't go, Ashton, you'll be wandering in limbo for eternity. You don't want that, do you?" I try to convey some of horror of my nightmares, pushing out with thoughts of the endless grey of the Sea of Nun, of the sucking nothingness.

Ashton reels, as though he's taken a left hook, and he staggers back a few feet, holding his arms over his face.

"*You don't know!*" he wails. "*You don't know what it's like!*"

"That's where you're wrong!" I shout back. "You've only had this for four months. Try five years, you fool!" I surprise myself with the depth of my emotion. Here, in this world where the quick might touch the dead, a veil has been lifted. The memories wash over me, of the fitful searching, of being blocked at every opportunity by invisible barriers, an existence lacking in all aural, visual and tactile stimuli. If ever there was a hell, this is it.

At the same time a warm sweep of compassion moves me. How must it be for this man, no matter how despicable, to have been lost for any time, wandering, without knowing what has happened? In a way, the five years have been easier for me, one of the Inkarna, who has the strength of will to endure. Ashton Kennedy must be driven half-mad by fear.

His image folds and collapses, shrinking before us, spent. The environment blinks out, and we drop to the floor, our breath misting before our faces. The room is icy, a lot colder than it could possibly be, even in the depths of winter.

Marlise's teeth chatter, and I draw her close, enfolding her in my arms. Her flesh is so chilled I'm scared she's gone into shock.

"Marlise?"

"We're back?"

"We're safe. For now." Tentatively I sit up, only to be blinded by a fierce stab of pain that can only be compared to having a chisel wedged into my skull. Tears run freely down my cheeks, mingling with the warm wetness running from my sinuses. All I can do is cradle my head in my hands and rock.

"Ashton... Fuck. Whatever your name is. Are you all right?" Marlise places her hands on either side of my face, lifting so I'm looking up at her.

I blink at her, hissing at the brightness in her room. Concern and fear are etched on her features and she searches my eyes.

"I'll live. I think."

"I believe you," she says. "Utterly and completely."

CHAPTER EIGHT
Revelations

WHILE ASHTON'S SPIRIT might not be able to torment me further in the material world, he follows me in my dreams, where I walk through Wynberg. Every corner I turn, there he is, grinning at me, watching me to see whether his appearance rattles me. I won't allow him that pleasure and turn down a side street or cross the road. And, yet, he is relentless, and Wynberg grows into a combination of Maitland cemetery and a deserted train station where the sea crashes against a decayed cement and yellow-brick platform.

He is perched catlike upon a pillar, his cold grey eyes the same hue as the ocean tearing hungrily at the shore.

"Be careful," Marlise says when we get out of her car

in Rosebank. "I wish I could go with you. I want this all to end, so we can figure out where to go from here."

Her phone rings and she answers. Judging from the way she rolls her eyes, it must be Lucy's granny, as we've come to call the old bag.

"You've got the wrong number! This is not Lucy." Marlise kills the call, well aware I'm impatient to get going.

I clasp her hand in mine and give her fingers a gentle squeeze while trying to smother a smirk at her annoyance. "I'll be fine. No one's going to mess with me. I can guarantee that. And, if there's other trouble, I'm sure I can figure out how to deal with it."

She doesn't look convinced. "I care about you, Ash."

We've agreed that she must continue calling me by the *Kha*'s name. We both stand staring at each other for a few moments. Since last night we're back to being careful about physical contact. If it bothers Marlise that I was once a woman by the name of Elizabeth Rae Perry, she doesn't let on. Likewise, I'm all too aware of Marlise's gender, especially now that we've been so close to each other physically. I can't let these traitorous thoughts cloud my judgment: that I want to hold her, do things with her that...

"Ash?"

"Huh?"

She studies me with that slightly puzzled expression she seems to have so often nowadays.

"Sorry, I had a thought there for a second."

Marlise hugs me, her minty scent making me hold her tightly before breaking away to maintain a little more distance between us.

"Please be careful, okay? I'd suggest you look into

getting yourself a cell phone so you can at least call for help."

"I need to get that room first," I remind her.

"Ugh. We're not going to have this conversation right now."

"We're not," I agree but try to smile warmly to lessen the finality in my words. "You have a good day. I'll meet you back here at three, okay?" I turn and walk before our farewell grows any more awkward. I can feel her watching me as I stride down to the station. Today's going to be enough of a misadventure without adding extra drama.

I have to switch trains at Salt River, not the best of stations, but for once I'm glad for my height as I shoulder through the throngs. As always, I'm one of the few white people—and a strange-looking one by the coloured folks' cultural standards, what with the long hair and the piercings—and I receive more than one fearful look or muttered commentary.

But they leave me alone, and that is all I ask, even when a trio of disreputable gangster types sits near me on the carriage headed out on the Bellville line. I recall some of Ashton's nastiness and stare at them, half sneering, projecting *at* them on the verge of tapping into my daimonic self. Before anything can come of this, I disembark at the Old Mutual station.

Maitland cemetery is a lot larger than when I last saw it. It sprawls for hectares, bounded on one side by Voortrekker Road and the railway line on the other. Scraggly Australian acacias grow in thickets demarcating the different divisions. The brisk wind makes their leaves shiver. The good winter rains have gifted an urgency to the riot of weeds pushing between the plots and, while I walk, the red-orange mud sucks at my boot soles.

The sky hangs low, and small spittles of moisture prickle at my exposed flesh. I've arrived with an hour or so to spare, for what reason I'm not sure. I don't have a watch and, subsequently have no way of telling the time, but that's also fine. At this point in my existence, I have more time than I care for.

A murder of pied crows offers their peculiar high-pitched calls to the wind and takes off the moment I pass the skeletal umbrella pine in which they were perched. I resist the urge to count them, something I used to do when my name was Lizzie, and I was growing up on a wine farm in Paarl.

Is the farm even there anymore? What has become of Lizzie's family? I sift through those ancient memories, of the times leading up to the Anglo Boer War, and it all seems so dreamlike, unreal. I recall the day I met Richard, at a dinner my father had hosted, and how a dapper Richard had enchanted me.

Where is he now? Memories of the sucking grey nothing of the *inbetween* seep up. Is he also there in the Sea of Nun, wandering, lost? If five years are enough to have me jerk awake screaming each night, what must it be like to exist in limbo for more than a century? The forgetfulness of death would be kinder.

Why would Richard, who has lived two or more lifetimes before, fall by the wayside, lost to us, and I, a mere stripling in our kind's terms, endure? This question has been bugging me too often. When I consider the powerful beings I met in Per Ankh, I am humbled by the knowledge that they nonetheless pooled their powers to punch me through so soon after my initial arrival.

This hadn't been without some disagreement. They'd held meetings after meetings in the Obsidian Hall, meetings from which I'd been excluded.

Meritiset had been such a great comfort then, one of the few who'd spoken to me. *The Upstart*, some of them had called me.

Meritiset had told me of her previous life. Like me, this was her first period of long rest in Per Ankh.

"Don't you want to go back?" I asked her.

She'd gotten a faraway look in her eyes as she gazed out across our gardens. "I miss it, sometimes, but to be honest, the world of matter is too red in tooth and claw. I know Siptah will come, soon, and we can all be together."

The times I miss now are the ones where we'd chant the hymns, where we'd maintain the identity of ourselves as separate yet connected beings, the sound filling the Obsidian Hall with its glory, of feeling the daimonic powers thrum through our ethereal bodies.

For all the time spent in Per Ankh, we could clothe ourselves in any shape, yet we chose a facsimile of our last mortal life. Only the elders, who had returned numerous times, took on peculiar, almost sexless forms. Oh, they were recognisably human but they were—for lack of better description—perfect, beautiful. Too perfect. One could call them angelic, though they were anything but. When they looked me in the eye, I gained the distinct impression they gazed upon me as an object worthy of pity.

And here I am, wandering about in a *Kha* not of my choosing. How will this affect my return? Will I be simply Lizzie again, or will it feel right, natural to manifest in Per Ankh in some idealised form of Ashton Kennedy, change my *Ren* to Neferkhepera instead? Can one even change one's *Ren*?

These thoughts tumble about until I reach one of the chapels, where services had been held when Lizzie had last been here. I stand for a good while gaping at the tumbled red-brick and at the blackened arches pointing naked at the clouds. A ficus strangles one of the walls, its roots threading through the very structure of the ruin.

Then I see *him*. Ashton.

He watches me from the doorway, not quite venturing into the light, a thing of shadows not wholly of this plane. His clothing mirrors mine: black jeans ragged at the knee, leather jacket gaping to reveal a Slayer T-shirt, and hair tied back.

"What do you want?" If anyone is watching, they'll see me talking to thin air.

Ashton says nothing, just carries on watching me watch him, impassive. He lifts a cigarette to his lips and blows a ghostly plume into the air. So, he was a smoker. Why am I not surprised?

"Didn't know ghosts could still light up." I don't wait for an answer and turn to continue walking down to the older part of the cemetery.

I don't need this, not now, not when I'm trying to figure out what the hell is going on. How do I convey to this spirit that I never meant for any of this to happen? If I hadn't taken his *Kha* he wouldn't have had any links to the material realm, he would have had no choice but to pass to the Hall of Judgment. Does this mean I have to take responsibility for him?

Maybe.

But right now I don't want to think about Ashton. Now it's time to pay respects to my dead. As I approach the graveside I try not to take in too much of the disrespect shown to the memorials, the graffiti scrawled on walls, used condoms, broken bottles and discarded clothing, among other things. I step over piles of human excrement.

It wasn't like this when I was last here. If this is the

way people treat their dead, it's no wonder society is in such a state. Our propensity for human misery is insatiable. When I think of how the people are packed in the townships in their rusted tin shacks, of the faces of the bergies sleeping fitfully on their cardboard beds, I'm not so sure if returning to Cape Town is such an honour. A wry laugh escapes me. Maybe it's a prison sentence, for losing Richard.

Like House Adamastor would just pack up and leave because they knew *I* was the next one incarnating? My return a joke of cosmic proportions?

I don't at first recognise Richard's grave. Someone knocked down the pylon and thoughtfully piled rubble over the marker. An old Wellington boot obscures the cartouche bearing his name. Who in their right mind dumps here? Moss creates a vivid slash of green where the slab has cracked.

Nothing is permanent, even those who court immortality. Even those who have completed the round trip once, twice, three times, can fall by the wayside. Richard, where are you? Do you still think of me? How would you think of me now if you could see me? A man.

Would you still put your arms around me and tell me you love me?

"It's all fucked up," I mutter. I don't even feel the initial horror at saying the word *fuck*, like it's a word I would have used every day had I been Lizzie. Had I been Lizzie… I'm not Lizzie anymore. I stopped being Lizzie the day I first passed through the Black Gate. Then I became some disembodied, sexless being. It's not supposed to matter what we return as yet we cling to that initial gender. Once a woman, always a woman. Purity. Men are fire, air, active. Women are water, earth, receptive.

What does that make me who partakes of both? The all, the nothing?

And what's the point anyway? What's stopping me from walking away from all of this, giving up now? Play the barman, maybe study something and get a real job as a doctor or a soldier or a mortician? Then, one day when I die, I'll die. I'll forget any of this ever happened. This would be the easy way out.

How long I stand there with my hands balled into fists, I don't know. It's cold. I breathe. I lose myself in the forlorn mourning of the wind through the ruins. None of what has been, is and will be, matters. Everything hangs suspended in this bottomless moment, the sky darkening with an incipient storm, loose pieces of hair whipping across my face to get stuck in my mouth.

That's when I feel my angry ghost. I can't see him but I know he's here, with me. He frets at the edge of my awareness. Maybe making himself visible earlier at the burnt-out church cost him too much of his daimonic power, but he's not leaving me any time soon. Can I face the next forty or fifty-odd years with this sort of daily interference?

"Yes, Ashton, I've taken your life, through no fault of my own. I did not steal your life. I'm as much a prisoner here as you are."

I stand a while longer but then, out of nowhere, the anger bubbles up, and I start yelling. "Do you think I asked for this? Do you think I saw your fucked-up life and wanted it? Come on! Be real! Look at you! Look at me! You were in a hole, and you knew it, but instead you didn't stop digging, did you?"

The last syllables die away, echoing on not only off my surroundings but on an aetheric level, and a small twinge of pain deep in my sinuses reminds me it isn't wise to lose my temper. He's just a damn ghost, and I'm the one who's here, now. If anything, the sense of Ashton hanging about has gone. It's just me and this empty place. Angrily I dash away the small trickle of blood that forms in my left nostril.

People always say cemeteries are full of ghosts and spirits. Their preconceptions couldn't be further from the truth. These fields of granite and marble markers are sterile. A person's *Ka* may hang about a bit until the *Ba* is reborn, but I don't pick up anything here. Not at this moment. Apart from the troublesome ghost that appears to have latched onto me, that is.

With nothing better to do, I clear a granite slab of pebbles and sit, weaving chains from grass stems. I close my eyes, opening myself only to the beating of my heart and the incidental sounds around me. It's a gradual spreading of awareness, the gentlest of our daimonic abilities. Slow. Breathe deep. Feel the earth upon which I sit; the exact temperature of the air and the way my muscles tense when I shift ever so slightly. My emotions, a welter of anger, desperation, fear. These act together on my intellect, making it difficult for rational decisions.

I appraise my environment. Here a rat rummages through the remains of a discarded sandwich. The creature's entire being is focused on the mouldy bread, and I soon lose interest. Two stray dogs trot along the railway line, intent on the scent trail of a bitch in heat. Nothing is amiss.

I was drawn here by the old man but for what reason? Am I a fool? What if this is a trap? Hunt the Inkarna of House Adamastor down one at a time, they're easy pickings, they just walk right into a situation without considering the dangers. After all, they're immortal. They'll just keep coming back.

I break my meditation with a muttered curse, wiping experimentally below my nose. The skin on my wrist comes away clear. Good. I cast about, checking my environment, but there's no sign of human life save for me. The thick cloud cover won't reveal the sun's exact position but I reckon it's as close as it will get to midday.

This has all been some sort of cruel joke, a misunderstanding. Maybe I wanted to read too much into the old man handing me that paper. I wanted something to happen today, some clue that I've not become completely deluded. What if I really am Ashton? What if the Inkarna are all just some fever dream made up during four months of being comatose?

That doesn't explain why I have these powers, or why Marlise shared my experience of Ashton's pitiful attempt at striking fear into me. My laughter sounds bitter to my ears as I rise, jamming my hands deep in my pockets.

Stupid. This whole episode is a glorious waste of time. What am I doing here?

I'm five paces away, intent on returning to the train station, when I grow aware of the human presence not ten metres behind me, standing at Richard's memorial. It's slight, on the edges of my senses, but it's there, nonetheless—the barest whisper of watchfulness.

An older woman speaks. "Seeker, what do you desire?"

All my muscles freeze. It's *her*, Leonora. I'll never forget her voice.

Slowly I turn, my heart clenching, to face her. I can't equate the bent old woman dressed in a khaki army-issue parka and jeans before me. Still the same, round face but her skin is so lined. She clutches an ibis-headed walking cane, much like the one yesterday's messenger possessed.

Her eyes, however, these are still the ones I remember, the last vision I beheld before Lizzie closed hers for the last time. She has a beanie jammed over her head, and a few white strands escape to blow about her ears.

"Leonora?"

"This isn't right." She shakes her head vigorously. "This cannot be!" She's suffering from the same denial I had.

"Lizzie's dead. This is who I've become. I'm sorry. Something went wrong."

She sways and, scared that she'll collapse I rush forward to support her, uncomfortably reminded of that day in 1966 where our roles were reversed. The dichotomy of our present physical states strikes me hard. Her frame is so light, her bones birdlike as she clutches at my jacket.

"You came back. I'm so glad."

"What's happened?"

"We can't talk here." Her eyes are bright, searching mine.

"Where can we go?"

"I've got a car in the parking lot not far from here. We must leave immediately. I've taken a massive risk with this meeting. *They* might be watching." She glances about, and I feel a hum of daimonic power, so strong compared to my fitful attempts.

I don't ask who *they* are, intent only on helping Leonora to the car, an ancient Volkswagen Golf so rusted I'm surprised the engine purrs into life when she turns the key in the ignition. Once she's behind the wheel, some of her old resilience becomes evident as she noses the car into the bustle of Voortrekker Road. A minibus taxi almost ploughs into us from behind, but the old lady rolls down her window to pull a zap sign at the speeding vehicle. The driver hoots and gesticulates wildly before he roars ahead.

"Damn taxi drivers. They think they own the roads."

"What's happened?" I try to hide the smile at seeing her give as good as she gets on the road.

Leonora spares me a glance then keeps her gaze fixed ahead of her. She's so tiny she can barely see over the wheel. "Goodness, where do I start? In brief, you passed away, and I carried on. I studied, nurtured the investments, took on two initiates. Things were looking good. Those were golden years. It really appeared that House Adamastor was going to grow, become something.

"We of course didn't know when the next Inkarna would return. I mean, how could we? A new incarnate every fifty or so years, that's what the journals recorded. We hoped if we worked hard we could somehow grow that knowledge and power base. After all, the other Houses have greater strength. House Adamastor has always been so precarious in its existence."

"Our strength has always lain in being beneath the radar," I interject. "We are scholars, watchers." Gods, it feels so good to speak to her again, to be myself, no matter what my physical state of being.

She raises her brow at me. "Things are shifting, or rather, have been. During the eighties, when our country was going through some of its worst turmoil, the local Houses had their last annual general meeting. There were...tensions. House Malkuth severed ties with its chapter houses in Europe and the States. They went underground. I haven't heard from them since. It's like they never were. I suspect they may be founding a new House, but they have not resurfaced.

"House Montu..." She sighs. "House Montu started making overtures, stating that with the coming troubles, House Adamastor should align, meld even. Although tempted, we did not like it at all. That's when..." Leonora goes silent, biting her lip while she indicates and noses us into the stream of traffic heading south on the M5. "To make a long story short, I had a visitation from a man about five years ago. He called himself Siptah."

A cold claw of shock tears through my system. "Richard! Did he say anything, tell you where he was?"

"He came one night and warned me about a stele hidden in our ritual chamber, beneath a false tile before the altar. 'Don't look at it,' he told me, 'just hide it in a very safe place. They're coming. Tell the Inkarna—' Then he vanished, just like that, as if his daimonic powers gave out before he could pass on the rest of the message, but at the same time I picked up on his fear. Very great fear.

"I was, naturally, rattled, but followed his instructions to the letter. I made arrangements the next day to shift some of the finances into an account not linked to the House's, and took rooms outside of the chapter house, close by. While Siptah had not been able to communicate the full message, that deep, gut-wrenching fear like I've never known spurred me on to greater caution.

"They came for us a week later. House Montu. We were no match for them. They are warriors, after all."

"How did you escape?"

"Quite by chance, really. A bird had flown into

the window, one of those red-eyed pigeons. I went outside to see if it was all right, and there I was, crouching in the back yard behind the lavender bushes prodding at a dazed bird, when I heard the first sounds of commotion coming from inside. I drew upon concealment and snuck back in, but it was hopeless. Three of them, one Inkarna, I'm sure, and two initiates, had forced open the door.

"They made quick work of William. Sara still put up a fight, but they took her down within seconds." Leonora's sigh is bone weary. "They hadn't even attained full initiate rankings yet. I don't hold out much hope for their souls once they've passed through the Black Gate into the Hall of Judgment."

"You mean to tell me they came in killing?"

She nods. "It's like they knew exactly where to go, where to find us. More than a century of compulsions laid on the chapter house, and they swung through as if none of that mattered one whit, as if someone had provided them with insider information. What I don't understand is the sudden change in attitude. I mean, it's not like we were ever sitting with an open-door policy. To attack out and out…"

A chill passes through me. "I was supposed to punch through five years ago, into the body of a young girl by the name of Catherine van Vuuren." I give a wry laugh. "It's obvious that there has been some sort of miscommunication somewhere along the line."

Leonora glances at me. "Yes, not quite what I was expecting, but it's good to have you back."

"Not quite the blink of an eye, though. What else can you tell me? Obviously the chapter house is standing empty, so someone must have laid claim to the library and all that."

"I watched..." Leonora sighs. "It was terrible, what happened to our attorneys. I tried to get hold of them, but they were placed under liquidation the same day of the attack. It was like it was all orchestrated before the time. I was too scared to call them after that but followed in the news. It was all over the papers. All our assets were seized and a company called Maverick Enterprises bought the chapter house."

"But it's still standing empty."

"They've left it empty. Bait. A trap. They know one day one of the House Adamastor Inkarna will come. Like you did."

"That means..." News of the attack hadn't filtered through to us in Per Ankh. Leonora would have had no way to communicate it to them because her link hadn't been established yet.

She sniffs. "They've grown slack. They expected a reprisal early after the hostile takeover. When all answer to their action was a deafening silence, they now send a chap 'round maybe once or twice a week. He casts about for clues but then he leaves. Ha! They used to practically camp outside, as much good it did them."

Five years in limbo. Five years wasted while all this transpired. Of course I'd have no way of knowing and, it would appear, my brethren have given me up for lost.

"What do we do now?" I ask. "And where are we headed?" We've reached Sunrise Circle in Muizenberg, and Leonora has the car pointed toward the mountain again.

"Well, Simon's Town, of course. They'd never have expected me to hole up right under their noses." She gives a wicked cackle. "But you may as well tell me what your story is, so we can be up to speed. Where were you?"

"I don't know. It was a nothingness that may have been Nun." Even recalling the Sea of Nun gives me cold thrills of fear.

"You can't remember anything?"

"Just complete absence of any sensory input and a terrible need for…physical manifestation. Remember those times during the mid-fifties when we experimented with isolation tanks?" She nods. "It was like that, but it never ended. The next I knew, I woke in a hospital bed. It was two thousand and twelve, and I'm here, in this body."

"What did you say the name of the *Kha* was? The one you were supposed to inhabit?"

"Catherine van Vuuren."

Leonora gives a low whistle. "This is not looking good. I've done some careful investigations when the almighty paw-paw hit the proverbial fan. One of the men on the board of directors for Maverick…his name is Christopher van Vuuren. It's too uncanny."

"How old is he?"

She shrugs. "Late forties maybe. I've looked at all the major players in that company. They've connections to government arms deals. They're not small fry."

"Sounds like something House Montu would be involved in."

"Just the fact that of late the government's been sending in more troops to central African countries, the hostilities there… There are other Houses there, as warlike as Montu. Everything's in turmoil, all the trouble in the Middle East, South Africa sending so many mercenaries up there. I fear it's all connected."

"Shit."

She gives a soft chuckle. "You know, you've changed, hey?"

At this I laugh, possibly the first genuine laughter that's escaped me in days. "Oh, hell, I know that."

For the rest of the drive I fill her in on Marlise, Ashton's parents and his angry ghost. Leonora's concerned about my continued nosebleeds and we both agree it must have something to do about the *Kha*'s maturity. It's not natural for Inkarna to take over a body that has never, until now, been forced to lean on daimonic powers.

"I suggest taking it slowly. Practice a bit. Remember those exercises you made me do?" Although Leonora hadn't ended up with nosebleeds, her migraines had been legendary as she had learned to access her daimonic powers. She had been eighteen when she'd started.

She pulls the car up inside the subterranean parking lot of a three-storey apartment block directly behind the old chapter house. Eschewing the archaic lift, we trudge up three flights of stairs and make our way along a walkway to the apartment overlooking the chapter house.

"Right under their noses... Or should I say over..." I stare down on the back yard. Where our outdoor ritual area was, a mess of wattle strives, tangled with verdant weeds.

"Sometimes the most obvious hiding place is the best." Leonora leans on the railing, gazing down.

She unlocks the security gate, and then the door, and a frisson of a compulsion tingles through my being as we enter. Leonora is not without her defences. If I had not been accompanied by her, I'd probably have walked right past this apartment.

Her home is cramped, a one-room unit. Every

available bit of wall space is filled with books, some new, some clearly ancient in their leather bindings. Her neatly made single bed is almost hidden behind crates. A small table stands near the window, also piled with books. The only life form here is a giant peace lily, its bladelike leaves spilling over its terracotta pot.

"It's not much," Leonora says. "A bit of a come-down from our previous illustrious quarters, but at this point in my life, I feel it would be better to err on the side of caution."

"Who was that man, the one who came in to The Event Horizon to deliver the note? And how did you know to find me there?"

"Oh, that was Bill. He lives on the first floor." She gives a conspiratorial wink. "I think he has the hots for me."

"He carries the same walking cane."

"I lent him mine. Thought it would catch the eye. As for finding you, I did a bit of snooping after I wrote down your car's registration number. I may not have material wealth but I still have a few contacts here and there in various departments. Doesn't take a brain surgeon, you know. Some of those students at Marlise's college are quite chatty. It's not that hard to find someone if you know what to look for and what questions to ask the right people. You're just lucky I covered up the evidence of your visit. If House Montu knew you were back..." The warning is abundantly clear.

I try not to let my surprise show. "And now?"

"And now we have tea. Earl Grey?"

I nod, a small smile tugging at my lips. If there's one thing that's certain, Ashton would sooner curl up and die than drink tea. "Two sugars."

CHAPTER NINE
Carved in Stone

"WHERE'S THE STELE?" I ask Leonora when she brings the tea tray from the kitchenette.

She sets her burden down with a clink of Willow Pattern china but doesn't at first look at me. Her eyes are large. "I was afraid you were going to ask after it."

"And you have not looked at it in all this time?"

"I didn't feel...*worthy*. I kept it wrapped in the cloth in which it had been stored. It, *tingled*, for lack of better description, when I touched even the fabric. I'm too scared to take it further. I don't think I'm qualified."

I run a hand through my hair, which has come loose from its binding. "And you think I'm qualified?"

"You've passed through the Black Gate, you've had your heart weighed in the Hall of Judgment; you have resided in Per Ankh and have walked the path of Ma'at. You have returned and you are worthy."

"How can you gauge that I'm worthy? I have spent a few decades biding my time, raiding the memories of the Blessed Dead before they sink into rebirth and forgetfulness. What I know is patchy at best, and the skills I took with me when I died are rusty from disuse. I don't have a fraction of the skill, the control you have over your daimonic powers. I have vague knowledge of world events, popular culture, that's it. I'm lucky I can even recall half of the hymns and chants."

My revelation stuns her and she sits heavily on her chair, hands cupping the teapot. Richard had never told me what it was like. *Study hard, you'll find out*, was all he'd ever said accompanied by one of his enigmatic smiles. And here I was now blurting the mysteries as if they were worth nothing.

"I'm sorry if this wasn't the glorious afterlife in the Tuat they led you to believe. There are about two-dozen Inkarna of our House. Most are content, after several sojourns on the mortal plain, to remain in Per Ankh, to advise, meditate and machinate. The eldest barely acknowledge our existence and eventually, they just…" I wave my hand, half amused by the memory. "They're simply not there anymore. And no one knows what becomes of them, save that they are less and less keen to involve themselves in affairs that they give the impression of being somehow beneath them.

"Even there, in Per Ankh, there is back-stabbing and in-fighting. I almost didn't come back, and I'm suspecting they sent me back because they blame me for Richard's—Siptah's—disappearance.

"And, you know what?" The bitterness flows forth with my words. "I wasn't even the love of Richard's life. He had another before me." I cradle my head in my hands and stare at the steaming cup of tea Leonora pours.

"Well... A cup of tea will give you more perspective. Have you eaten yet? I have some soup I can warm up and then we can look at this stele everyone's got their knickers in a twist about."

I shake my head, a dozen conflicting thoughts striving for dominance over each other. "It would have been better if I'd never made it to Per Ankh."

"Don't talk like that!" Leonora sounds angry, but I don't look up. "Do you honestly think one of the others would have done half as well despite the circumstances?"

"What if I did something wrong somehow? I mean, it's my first time."

"Look at me, Lizzie."

"That's not my name anymore. Call me Ash. Only the *Ren* matters, not the name of the *Kha* and, besides, I'm getting used to it."

"Fine. Ash. Look at me."

I obey, allowing Leonora's concern to wash over me. Now that she's taken off her beanie, it shocks me to see how thin her hair is, how white it is, how *old* she's become. "And now that I've found you I'm going to lose you soon, won't I?"

She doesn't break my gaze. "My death is waiting around the corner, *Ash*. There's nothing I can do about it." Leo says the name carefully, as though she doesn't quite want to pronounce it, as if it makes things final.

"Will you tell them everything? Tell them that we tried?"

"That's a stupid thing to ask, but yes. You know I'll do everything in my power for the truth to come out."

It's almost pathetic how our roles are reversed. She

places her hand on top of mine, the skin rough from age, liver spotted. I reciprocate by placing my free hand on hers. For a moment our daimonic selves stir, mingling essences. We know each other on a deeper level, siblings. There is love here, the peace of knowing another individual understands completely.

"My *Ren* is Ankhakhet. Will you scribe it on my memorial?"

My throat grows tight, warmth prickling at the corners of my eyes. "I will."

"Now, down to business." Leo withdraws her hand and rises. "You have your tea, I'll set the soup to warm in the microwave, and we'll look at this stele. Mind you, my Middle Egyptian is not what it was, but we'll see what we can do about this."

She vanishes into the kitchenette where I hear doors open and shut, and the clink of crockery. The microwave hums. I stare out the window, half-listening to her busyness until Leo brings a steaming bowl of what smells like pea soup and a thick slice of brown bread smothered in cream cheese. While she kneels by the bed to withdraw a wooden chest, I busy myself with the ritual of tea drinking. It strikes me then, with a frightening pang of nostalgia, that I recognise this exact cup. This tea set dates back to the early 1900s. The humour doesn't escape me.

"What are you smiling about?" Leo sets the box on her lap as she sits.

"This tea set..."

"I used to bring you your early morning cuppa in that exact one. See the little chip there on the ear?" She beams at me.

"Oh gods." I sit back, staring.

"Eat your soup. It's going to get cold."

I have eyes only for the chest on her lap.

"I will not open this thing until you eat and have at least three sips of tea." There's no arguing with Leonora. Her tone is firm and, for once, I feel like a scolded child, and it's comforting to have someone in charge like this, telling me what to do.

Although the tea is divine, the food is tasteless, the sick expectation of wanting to see the object that has caused so much hassle, keeping me from fully appreciating anything else.

I push the plate away once I've eaten enough. "All right, show me what's in the box."

Leonora raises a brow, her gnarled hands caressing the highly polished wood. Without a word, she flips back the antique brass latch and reaches within to pull out a cloth-wrapped bundle.

Gingerly I take the burgundy velvet from her and the moment I touch the fabric I can feel a buzz emanating from the object. "It's old but it's not *that* old. It has presence."

She nods, her tongue darting out to wet her lips. Her inquisitiveness is almost tangible. How did she manage to live for half a decade with this thing under her bed and not suffer the curiosity of wanting to examine it? She is stronger than I am, for sure.

With reverence I untie the leather thongs, fumbling at first with knots until they loosen under my insistent tugs.

I hold a slab of fine-grained serpentine, the hieroglyphs carved in a delicate hand. This was no ornamental stele, with the typical figures of the Neteru parading across the surface. The artist was intent only on imparting information, carving both sides of the stone. Permanence, not aesthetics—this in itself is highly out of the ordinary when considering ancient Egyptian artefacts.

"This wasn't carved during the pharaonic age," I tell Leonora. I close my eyes and hold the stone to my heart, reaching into it, *reading* it. Jumbled visions reach me. It's like trying to push through putty to get to the heart of the information.

A young man cautiously carves in a dimly lit chamber. I can hear sonorous chanting, and he curses when his chisel slips, and he cuts his finger. A man asks in a stilted form of Middle Egyptian, "Are you done yet?"

The young man answers in French-accented English, "Almost, sir."

I open my eyes. "I think if anything, this dates back to Napoleonic times. It's hard to tell."

We spend the next half-hour reading the stele. The ritual it illustrates frightens me beyond anything I've ever encountered, including the five years in limbo. Simply entitled *The Book of Ammit*, it imparts the knowledge of the permanent destruction of the heart, or *Ib*, so that the *Akh* cannot form, which results in the destruction of the *Ba* and *Ka*.

The words burn themselves on my heart and souls, indelibly painted. Once this knowledge is taken in, it is impossible to forget. For a long time, Leonora and I sit and stare, unable, at first, to fully comprehend the implications.

"I shouldn't have read this," she says.

I straighten, nod and wipe at the cold sweat that has formed on my brow. "We've been sitting on this knowledge now for all this time? And Richard didn't tell me." Now *that* stings. How many in Per Ankh know this terrible secret?

Leonora gulps and pours herself a cup from the teapot's dregs, her hands shaking. "I don't want to know this."

"This thing is too dangerous to just lie around. I can't believe you kept it in a box under your bed. We should destroy it."

"Sometimes the most obvious places… What can we do? I don't advocate destroying it. This is something we could one day use to our advantage."

To destroy another's immortal soul… This goes against our very nature, yet at the same time I can't deny that while this knowledge must never slip into the wrong hands, we cannot simply let it be lost. There was a reason why this was laid down in stone, why it was kept hidden. How many others know of its existence?

We sit in silence, simply staring at each in horror while the cuckoo clock ticks off the empty minutes. The stone tablet rests between us, innocent in its speckled green-and-black surface until one reads the text. Where the hell can I hide this thing? Many years ago, Richard had spoken of a ritual he'd enacted in a cavern in Table Mountain. Perhaps…

"There are caves up in the mountains here," I tell her.

"I've never been to any of them."

"Neither have I." The thought tantalises me, however. I glance out the window into the gloomy afternoon. "What's the time?"

"It's after four."

"Shit!"

"What?"

"I was supposed to meet Marlise outside her college at three. She must be worried sick."

"Want to call her?"

I nod. Small mercies be praised, I've memorised the woman's cell phone number. With a sigh Leonora rises and retrieves her phone from the bedside table.

It's clunky and old, more like a black brick compared to the slim silver device Marlise uses.

Staring at it dumbly for a few heartbeats—I have to suppress a laugh for this is the first time I'm using one of these—I punch in the digits then the green button Leonora gestures at. She smiles indulgently at my fumblings as I hold the thing up to my ear.

Marlise answers on the third ring. "Hello?"

"It's me. I'm fine. I'm sorry I didn't call earlier."

"I've been freaking out on this side wondering if you've been kidnapped or something!"

"I'm safe. I'm fine. I'm sorry I didn't call earlier. Can you come collect me, please? But stop in Jubilee Square in Simon's Town. I'll meet you at the statue of Just Nuisance."

"Ash, what's going on?"

"I can't talk to you about it on the phone, okay? It's absolutely vital you don't tell anyone where you're going."

"I've seen *him* again."

I don't want to hear this, not now, and my blood turns to ice. I know exactly who she's talking about. "Where?"

"He's in the room here with me, just watching me. He won't leave me. He's been here ever since I got home. Every so often he gives me this filthy look."

"Just tell him to fuck off and finish with the rest of what he needs to be really dead. Will you be there? Then we'll sort out our troublesome ghost." My growing paranoia stops me from saying more. Would I really consign this man's soul to true oblivion?

"It's gonna take me at least half an hour to get there, but I'll come," says Marlise. "I'm not happy about this."

"Neither am I. Now stop talking and get going." I

don't mean to be abrupt but a growing urgency nags at me. I kill the call.

Leonora gazes at me. "Can she be trusted? And the ghost? This should be dealt with."

"She's in the thick of things, thanks to me. I don't have a choice. I'd rather keep her close than have her jumping to all sorts of the wrong conclusions. As for the ghost..." I give a noncommittal shrug.

"An innocent, dragged into this." Leonora doesn't sound happy. "It would be best if she weren't."

"You know that's not possible. She's seen too much already." I don't have to add that it's all my fault.

She sighs and lifts a tired hand to her face before glancing at the stone. "How do you know the stele will be safe?"

"I'll lay a compulsion over it."

"What if they somehow gain the information with regard to its location? Wouldn't it be better to keep it with you?"

"And if I get caught? What then?"

We spend the next thirty minutes making plans. Although I protest, Leonora gives me a wad of money saying it's the least she can do until she passes through the Black Gate. For all I know this is the last time I'll see her in a long time. That thought sends a dark fear coursing through me to snatch at my heart.

Eventually, we make our way down to Main Road, Leonora once again stuffed into her army jacket. The wind is blowing in earnest, a black northwester. It will be dark soon, the low clouds gobbling up what little light remains. Cars are already driving with their headlights on. The sea here in the bay is a dark olive slate puckered with every squall. The moisture on my face is salt-laden, whipped from the ocean. We reach the statue of the Great Dane, Able Seaman

Just Nuisance, and I look anywhere but at Leonora. Nothing has gone according to plan. I need more time with her, and yet I know this won't be the case. Her calm surety is something I've only realised I've missed this much now that I've found her again, only to realise she will be taken from me too soon. Once I was the one who guided her. Now it's the other way round and I want her, *need* her in my life. The stone I carry is heavy, its evil words whispering through my memory, indelible.

"Don't cry, Ash." She turns me around to face her, lifting a hand to caress my cheek. Her touch is electric, that instant recognition between Inkarna.

"It's not fair," I tell her. "Things should have been better, different circumstances."

"Life is cruel, my dear. Surely you, who have lived through three wars and now this, should know."

I clasp her hand in mine. "We were sheltered from so much, both here and in Per Ankh. I never dreamt I'd see the day when everything would be stripped from me, and now we've been robbed even of the short time we would have had in each other's company." It is at that moment that I realise how much I'm about to lose again—my truest, dearest friend.

"We'll meet again. You told me that so many times when we knew of your time. It should be sufficient that we could see each other and that I could help you, as you helped me when I was younger."

A memory of that forlorn streetwalker returns with recollections of my crazy whim to take her home with me. I'd seen something in Leonora back then, even beneath the tawdry clothing and cheap make-up.

She smiles, squeezes my arm then turns and starts walking. "No goodbyes. You know I've never been big on those. I'll see you soon."

That's it, no long embraces. I half raise my hand to wave farewell but she doesn't turn around. Who knows, maybe she doesn't want me to see *her* cry. It's impossible to tell in this weather, with the fat droplets now pattering with greater frequency. I watch Leonora's bent form disappear up a lane, until she's swallowed by the gloom between the old Victorians facing the road.

Although I suspect the time that passes is only about ten or so minutes, it feels like an hour, and when I see the familiar beat-up Toyota hatchback pull into the square, I'm soaked, my teeth chattering so much I'm scared I'm going to bite the inside of my mouth.

Marlise throws open the passenger door and I slip in, grateful for the hot blast of air from the car's heater.

"I'm sorry I'm late," she says.

"And I'm sorry I didn't call earlier," I reply. If I can pre-empt any lectures before they get out of hand that would be better. "I discovered some things, and had a lot of catching up to do."

"Well, your disappearing sucked, okay?" Marlise shifts the gears with far too much force, and we're headed north again. "Will you tell me what's going on?"

"Essentially, I've met up with one of the old House members. The woman I mentioned, Leonora. She's given me a...relic of some sort that I need to hide somewhere safe."

Marlise gives a soft snort. "And what are we going to do about the spook?"

"We'll sort that out tonight. Finally," I reply, not liking the tack my mind is taking: a final solution, for

Ashton Kennedy's unquiet soul—not nice. To destroy his *Ib*. Even as I consider my intention I realise what a burden this knowledge is, not something to be considered lightly. Already it is corrupting me.

But what to do with the stele? I need a place no one would know about, or as few people as possible, a most unlikely spot. Closing my eyes, I tap into Blessed memories of Cape Town and its hidden places, along the lines of Richard's comment. Structures are too impermanent until a sudden flash hits me: *a view of False Bay from a kloof. A boardwalk runs through a forest—the Amazon Forest—Kroon se Bos—it's called nearby, more toward Kalk Bay, a path snakes up to where sandstone cliffs rise. Cliffs filled with caves. Long, winding caves. A damp cleft where the folded sandstone has cracked to drop away into the earth through a narrow slot...* I silently thank the Blessed memory and open my eyes.

"Marlise?"

"Um?"

"How well do you know the caves above Kalk Bay?"

"Oh no, I don't like the direction your thoughts are taking."

"I need to hide this thing, and burying it in your parents' back yard won't be enough."

"You're crazy!"

"Better crazy than dead. Do you know about the caves?"

"Sort of. Not quite. Never went there, but my brothers did."

"We're going there. Now. The place I need is about half an hour's walk from the hairpin bend."

"Jesus, Ash! You're crazy! That's not half an hour! That's at least two hours up and two down." She glances away from the road long enough to give me a death glare.

"Fine. Then stop the car. I'll walk."

Marlise clutches the steering wheel, over-revving the engine when we take off from the traffic lights outside Simon's Town. "I'll wait for you in the car." Her tone is resigned, tired.

"Thank you. That's all I need."

Her only response is a deep sigh, and I can't help but smile to myself, allowing my eyes to go unfocused as Marlise takes the corners too tightly.

It's almost fully dark when we arrive at the parking area at the hairpin bend curving up Boyes Drive. By now the rain sifts down in a steady downpour and the windscreen wipers do little to improve visibility.

"Are you sure you want to do this?" Marlise says as she pulls up the hand brake. A particularly heavy gust sideswipes the vehicle. "We could go home, sleep on it, then I'll take tomorrow off from college and we can do this together, with proper gear."

"Do you want us to get killed?" I can't take chances with this thing. All the small hairs on my arms prickle at the stone's proximity.

"What is this thing? It's just some antique, right? No one knows you've got it?"

"I don't know." I clench my fists. "If Leo could find me, it means *they* can, too. Anyone could have seen me meet with her today."

"Ash, you're scaring me. Who's looking for you? What have you done?"

"Stay in the car. It's safer." With a low growl rumbling in my throat I step out of the vehicle into a raging tempest. The contrast from the warm interior and outside knocks the breath from my lungs, my skin screaming at the cold. This is not a time to question my judgment. Marlise has sense suggesting we sleep on this and return tomorrow but, by equal measure, if I don't lay this thing to rest, now, who knows what sort of trouble may hound me. House Montu could be after us already.

I've gone about a dozen steps up the steep path, tripping over rocks and tree roots, all but blind, when a torch beam pierces the night. Whenever I slip, I press my burden tightly against my chest. Pain slashes through my knee when I skin it on some obstacle. Damn Ashton for wearing jeans with holey knees.

"Ash! Ash! Wait! I'm coming with!"

Relief and concern wash through me, and I stop and wait for Marlise to catch up.

I hug her to me, feeling how her hair is already plastered to her skull. "Thank you for coming."

"You're a fool. I don't know why I'm tagging after you."

"Neither do I, but I appreciate the company." My laugh is choked. By all rights I should get her to turn back.

Hand in hand we make our way up the narrow footpath, stumbling more often than not. Where the one slips, the other saves. Marlise wields the torch only when it's necessary. We have to conserve the batteries. I silently bless the woman for keeping the device in her car's glove compartment. No other sounds reach us, save for the steady patter of rain through the bushes, our occasional oaths and the clatter of moisture-loosened stones.

We lose track of time but eventually reach a point where the path flattens, the stone steps giving way to sodden sand that gleams whitely even in the low light. Below us, to our left, Fish Hoek shines, a festive scattering of white and orange lights, the cars small moving points of illumination. Here we pause, shivering in the incessant wash. Marlise presses herself to me, and I offer what shelter I can, positioning myself so that I have my back to the wind.

The Blessed memories suggest taking the right turn soon and, satisfied that this is the correct choice, I give Marlise's shoulder a squeeze. "You okay?"

She's shivering so much her nod looks like a shake of the head. I should never have allowed her to come, but I worry also what would happen if she'd remained in the car. Boyes Drive at night is never the safest of places. Here I can still offer some protection.

There is something I can do. I've never tried it, and it's dangerous at best, but I can channel some of my daimonic essence into her. It's there, not far below the surface. All I need to do is nudge a little, visualise the power blossoming in my heart. It's a slow fire I can push, willing it to travel, to spiral down my arm where we make contact.

I have no idea if this will work as I imagine her essence flare in sympathy with mine. I nuzzle her hair, drawing strength from the scent of her, a sweetness beneath the mint that is the first to spring to mind.

"What are you doing?" I feel her look up and our lips graze accidentally.

Pulling back, I say, "I've just tried something I've only read about. Feel better?" In this rain, I have no idea whether I'm suffering another nosebleed but there is no pain, so I assume I'm doing all right.

"I feel... Not so cold." The wonder is evident in her words.

"It should last for a while, until we get there. But it won't last forever. We'll need to rest at some point."

Although the rest of the climb is taxing, it's almost as if this exertion doesn't matter as much because we climb in concert. Yes, the Inkarna are tougher than ordinary people. We are more in tune with our environment and how our bodies react to stimuli. Mind over matter, they say, but my answer to that is synthesis, the daimonic self which lies hidden within all mankind for those brave and foolish enough to reach beyond the limitations of the flesh.

Each step we take is carefully calculated in the darkness, more a sense of when and where our feet will make a connection with the earth. At first Marlise draws heavily on my essence but, after about ten minutes we reach an equilibrium. It pains me to know that I'm forcing her into a heightened state. She has no conception of what it means to be Inkarna, to number among Those Who Return.

This won't be permanent. Later I can discuss this with her, to see whether she wants to take things further, but right now this could mean the difference between her freezing to death or making it through the night. Let this rest on my conscience for allowing her to tag along.

Our path grows steeper, and the first scrambles begin, the cliffs looming as a darker patch against the cloud, which reflect a weird orange glow that could only be light from the town. Light pollution, but for once I'm glad for it, for offering us some visibility on this mad quest.

Another small mercy is that the rain lets up once we near the top and are plunged into thick brush. Here it's not always easy keeping to the path, and we have to double back a few times until we pick up on subtle cues, a branch rubbed smooth from countless hands here, a boot print preserved in the relative shelter of an overhanging rock. Droplets *drip-drip* from foliage and the muted rumble of traffic reaches us from Boyes Drive—the remainder of the evening rush from the city centre. Above, ragged holes are torn in the clouds that, before closing, display a faint sprinkling of stars. I'm glad the wind has died down. It's not going to be as pleasant when we get to a higher elevation.

"Tell me about your other life," Marlise says when we pause before a particularly nasty scramble.

"I don't really want to. That person is dead." The torch's beam illustrates a precipitous series of hand- and footholds.

"What was your life like?"

"I lived through the Anglo Boer War. My name was Elizabeth Rae, but everyone called me Lizzie. It kinda stuck."

"A woman?" Marlise's laughter rasps in her throat.

This salient fact obviously didn't sink in the first time I told her the story, and I snort softly. "You laugh now, but you never know, if and when you decide to come back…"

"So, what did you do?"

"I was a schoolteacher for a while. That was until the man I married swept me off my feet and into his very bizarre world. Believe it or not, we travelled a lot, and I even met Aleister Crowley once while he owned Boleskine House on the shores of Loch Ness."

"Who's Aleister Crowley?"

"Never mind. I'll educate you at some point. Besides, the man was a buffoon, so full of himself he pretty much lost the plot."

"Right."

The talking helps keep my mind off our goal, because once we reach the cave, I still have to find a niche or some hidey-hole slightly off the main path. Spelunking is the last thing I'd have considered myself involved in, especially on a night like this.

Marlise whimpers once or twice during the hairiest climbing but otherwise doesn't complain. We have a heart-stopping moment when she slips, and it's only because I'm right behind her that I stop her from taking a nasty tumble. Dense bush screens us from the view of False Bay, but the mountain before us looms, a forbidding presence. I can feel the weight of the sandstone. It's as if the mountain watches us, aware of the puny humans clawing along its flanks.

If I listen carefully, I can hear whispers of the hundreds of souls who've tramped here before us. Marlise uses the flashlight for the last stretch. The beam cuts through the murk to eventually illuminate a dark slot before us once we reach a flattened area. The reflection off the frowning folded stone lends harsh shadows, and I can't help a flutter of trepidation at the yawning blackness waiting for me.

"Wanna switch that thing off?" I ask.

Both of us groan as we collapse just within a metre of the opening, the night's cold beginning to seep into my bones for the first time since I drew upon my daimonic essence. A little voice of self-doubt niggles, suggesting I'm going to pay for this expenditure come dawn. Right now I can't care. The hand clutching the stele has gone numb, the stone far too heavy.

"What now?" Marlise says. A tremor passes through her body, and I pull her to me, willing more strength from my reserve into her. Her voice echoes down into the throat of the mountain.

"We rest a bit then we go in a little way. We don't have to go far, just until we find a suitable crack so I can stow this thing."

"Good, because I don't like the dark."

"That's a fine time to be telling me this now."

"People have died up here in the caves."

"We're not going to die." I hope I can reassure her. "But you don't have to come in. In fact, I need you to stay here, to look after the entrance for me. I will be about half an hour at most. *Don't* fall asleep. If you hear anyone come, call my name and get the hell out of here."

"Who'd come up here at night? Besides us? This is crazy."

I sigh. "Things are about to get a lot crazier, especially if I don't sort out this stele."

After I give her my jacket—though it will do little good as even the lining is soaked through—I rise, wiping first one hand then the other on my jeans. In this impenetrable night, Marlise is reduced to just one more blob of shadow moving against the darkness, silhouetted against an inky background.

"I'm scared."

"Don't be. I won't be long. I'll only go about twenty or thirty metres into the cave. Will you give me the torch?"

She hisses, but I feel the object batting against my legs, and I take it from her. I should do something, make her feel that this is somehow not the end of the world, that the shadows won't eat her.

"While I'm gone, I want you to visualise that you've got a coal in your stomach. Every time you breathe in, I want you to imagine that it flares a little brighter. You know, like when people are starting up a fire that's down to embers? I want you to imagine the warmth radiating off that coal, that you keep it at the point where it's just about to burst into flame but doesn't. Breathe regularly, in for three, hold for two, out for three, hold for two, okay?"

"Why?"

"Just do it. It will keep you warm. But don't forget to listen out for anything unusual." On a whim, I kneel and hug her, placing a kiss on her cold cheek. She's so brave. I'd never have had the sheer guts to do what she's doing now, following a madman into danger. The gods know Richard never expected anything like this of me when he went off on his jaunts to Rhodesia and central Africa.

I feel her nod then I rise. She should be fine, I hope. The exercise I've given her is one that's used to train initiates when they hold vigil for a full night. The body rests but the mind falls into a calming trance, and the daimonic powers are nursed, warming the *Kha*. It's one of the ways we learn to control our bodies.

Taking the first faltering steps, I switch on the torch long enough to discern the tunnel with its slowly downward-sloping roof, rounded rocks convenient stepping stones. Previous visitors have painted in scrawling white letters the name of this slot: Boomslang. Tree snake. Soon I'm crouching, feeling my way forward, my nose tickling from the mustiness of centuries of damp. I try to move without disturbing the ground too much. The constant drip of water tells of continuous moisture. My hands come away slick with a rusty grime. I switch off the torch to preserve the batteries.

The problem with inching along in darkness so thick is that one's eyes create disturbing visuals to compensate for the lack of light. Violet and silver blossoms keep forming, exploding then starting all over again. My breathing is loud to me, ragged gasps that echo just ever so slightly to make me think I'm not alone. Every few metres, or what I consider a decent distance, I flash the torch briefly, checking that the ground doesn't plunge into some bottomless abyss. Wouldn't that be a joke? I make it this far and manage to hide the stele by plunging to my death?

Blessed memories tell me there's a cave, one of many in this mountain, where a chasm opens so abruptly that people have slipped to their deaths in such a hideous fashion. Luckily none of the recollections I access involve such a drama here, but I'm not about to take any more chances—other than already being a colossal fool for going through with this tonight, of all nights. We're here now. No point in turning back without completing the mission.

Presently a narrow gap opens to my right on ground level, a small indentation that seems suitable. The cave's ceiling is so low here my back is pressed against it while I crawl, and I try hard not to think about how much rock squeezes down. That leads to a tightening of the chest and an intense need to turn and scramble out. The torch reveals that the slot continues at least ten or so meters into the rock, and I probe carefully with my hand, feeling for a spot that will be right for the stele.

Is it such a wise thing to be leaving it here, hidden? I don't know. Carrying it with me seems a worse option, for if I'm caught, this knowledge will belong to someone else. The method of the ritual remains etched in my subconscious. I understand now why Richard didn't want Leonora to read it. This knowledge makes her almost too dangerous to continue existing. I pray she remains safe when she reaches Per Ankh.

The fewer who know about this the better, and it

makes sense why House Adamastor wanted to keep beneath the radar.

With a flat shard of stone, I scratch a depression in the earth, far into the lateral tunnel. It's not easy work, and I bite back a few choice curses when I skin my knuckles. While I intend laying a compulsion on the stele anyway, it's important the thing is buried, that it doesn't look as though anything is hidden here.

A peculiar reluctance overwhelms me when I place the damned thing in the hiding place I've created for it. I want to unwrap it, gaze over those hieroglyphs one more time, trail a finger along the edge and feel how soap-smooth the serpentine is. Some objects of power hold compulsions of their own. No, it's safer that I let this thing go. The chances of anyone ever coming up here are slim, even more so finding this thing with its dire words.

With a sigh I place it, feeling in the dark for small pebbles to pack over the cloth, followed by handfuls of dirt until the soil is flat. For good measure, I pack larger fragments of stone on top, as randomly as possible.

The real work comes at this point and, cross-legged, I crouch before the opening. Terrible shivers wrack my body. Only now am I aware of how this evening's physical abuse is taking its toll. Biting the inside of my cheek to quell the chattering of my teeth, I draw deep breaths, pulling at that ember within me. I will this into flame. Hell, I'm going to pay for this tomorrow but first I need to get through tonight. If House Montu is becoming more militant, I cannot, in good conscience, allow this information to slide into the wrong hands. As it is I'm taking a risk having Marlise with me, involving her in this debacle. My thoughts slip to those fateful words inscribed on the tablet. Once read, impossible to forget.

You could kill her now, a nasty whisper suggests. *If you kill her now there won't be any loose ends.*

The thought is so appalling I grimace, because, unbidden, at least three or four methods come to mind. I could push her down the mountain. I could bash her head in with a rock. I could stalk back and strangle her and hide her body where it won't be found for a long time. Or, I could use the knowledge I've gained from *The Book of Ammit* and separate her souls and send them hurtling into the Devourer's slavering jaws—bypassing the Hall of Judgment so no one need know of my crime.

At this moment I realise something with a horrible, sick certainty. I'm not capable of bringing about such an evil. *Isfet*, that's the word for it. I would deviate from the path of Ma'at and I would become a twisted parody of all that Per Ankh stands for. Such an act would place an indelible stain on my *Akh*.

But why hold onto such knowledge? To what purpose? Surely it would be better to destroy these words. Knowledge is power, that much I know, but even more powerful is he who holds power and chooses to withhold it.

House Adamastor could rise to become the most eminent of the Houses, but we haven't. The Houses at the top are constantly jockeying for resources, for power. Even in the Tuat, during my short sojourn there, I'd been witness to three attempted coups between the larger players. Granted, we'd kept to ourselves, largely ignored save by those seeking knowledge, but it had still been frightening to know that even there, the Inkarna were apt to play games, sometimes sending their brethren howling into Sea of Nun's limbo for goodness knew how long. No one emerges from that unscathed. The lapping waters too easily swallow the unwary.

A war in Heaven, only not in the terms average humans would understand. And all the time, those who returned would bring back first-hand knowledge, developments in psychology and science to refine the ones observing...

This all becomes too much, distracting me from the matter at hand. *The Book of Ammit* must lie hidden a while longer, until such time as we would need it. It makes me wonder how many in Per Ankh are aware of its existence or hold the knowledge to wield the power scribed on stone.

I don't want to know, not now.

Nothing is permanent in Per Ankh. That's the rub. We hold dreams and memories, but each time one of our kind Ascends, he or she takes something with them, diminishing those who remain behind to continue the cycle of death and rebirth. What lies beyond Ascension only those masters know, and they're certainly not telling us anything. We whisper of them among each other in awe. The world of matter and the realm of the Tuat are polar opposites, the one existing because of the other, what lies beyond exists only in conjecture.

With a shake of my head, I push all these meanderings as far back as possible. Now. This is important, this is my burden until such time someone follows to lift it.

At first it is difficult to still my mind, to find that inferno within and make the soul-fires flare. It doesn't matter whether I close my eyes. The darkness here is absolute.

It begins with a faint susurration at the edge of my hearing, my skin tingling and the sense of the ground opening beneath me, and my physical self tumbling end over end. The words come to my lips unbidden, words of binding, of forgetfulness. Aset, Mistress of Magic, will turn the eye of the casual viewer, make them grope farther, overlooking this unimportant slot that leads nowhere, holding nothing of interest. After all, she turned Set's murderous eye when she hid the child Harwer in the papyrus beds of the Nile Delta.

She comes to me, crowned with stars, caresses my face and presses cool lips to mine. In her eyes shines the light of distant constellations, and the sweet scent of the lotus offers succour. A soft glow illumines her skin, the many braids of her hair falling to her shoulders in a rush.

The vision cuts off abruptly, the pressure in my loins unfamiliar and, somehow, frightening. But my limbs are leaden, and I would like nothing more than to close my eyes and rest my head against the rock.

"Ash?" Marlise's voice reaches me as though from a distance, shaky.

"I'm coming," I tell her, stifling a groan as I shift around. Perhaps it is a good thing she is here. I'd rather sleep, but this would only result in a slow slide into death.

The woman meets me halfway, her skin feverish compared to the tomblike chill clinging to me. I stagger into her embrace and, for once, she is the one who lends me strength. The Mistress of Magic's features blur in my mind over the memory of Marlise.

"Aset!"

"What did you call me?" Marlise's voice is muffled as she speaks against my chest.

"Sorry," I mumble. I've called her by the wrong name. "Caught up in the moment."

"I'm cold, I'm hungry, and I want to go home." She

sounds like a little girl lost.

"So'm I, babe." Is that something Ashton would say?

"Can we go?"

I look over my shoulder, to where I've come from, but it's a futile gesture. "Sure." My bones ache, and we stagger out, back to the mouth of the cavern.

The clouds have pulled away completely, such is the capriciousness of Cape winters. On any other night I may have been enthralled by the view, but now all I can dream of is a warm bed and sleep—dreamless rest.

While we were driven during our ascent by wind and falling rain, the descent is hell as we battle gravity and a treacherous slope. By the time we reach the stairs, we've slid and fallen so many times I've lost track. Marlise takes this abuse stoically, but whenever either of us loses our footing, she grips my arm hard enough to hurt. All sense of intelligible thought is lost in the slow placement of the next step, the pause before we shakily put our weight down.

Neither of us is shivering but I've not claimed my jacket back from Marlise. I can no longer feel my extremities and, a few times, stray tears trace their way down my cheeks. Ashton wouldn't cry, but then I'm not the bastard he was. Shame at my earlier uncharitable thoughts towards Marlise makes me overly protective of her now, her silent agony a beacon during this ordeal.

It is almost with a complete sense of disbelief that we reach the car. While Marlise fumbles in her pocket for her keys, I look back up at the mountain, bathed as it is in the glow from the streetlights that lend it an eerie orange tint.

Keys jingle and Marlise says, "Thank fuck. I thought I'd lost these."

If I'd been glad to get into the car earlier this afternoon when Marlise collected me in Simon's Town, I'm doubly grateful now when the Toyota starts. We have to wait for the engine to warm first before the blessed hot air from the heater strips the cold from us.

Marlise looks tiny, huddled in my jacket, her curls now wet rats' tails dangling on either side of her face, her hair band lost somewhere during our misadventure. What bothers me is that she doesn't look at me and keeps her gaze firmly on the road. I can't tell whether she's angry. Whatever connection we had on the mountain has fled, and judging by the way her lips are set in a thin line, her state of mind can't be all that happy.

"Can I buy you coffee or something to eat along the way?" I suggest. As if in answer to my suggestion, my stomach rumbles.

"I just want to go home. There's food there. My parents are probably freaking out that I've missed supper." Not *we*. That's bad.

"I'm sorry, okay?"

"You're always sorry, Ash. I...don't know what to think anymore. I need to sleep. We can talk about what just happened tom—"

She hits the brakes, hard, and if I hadn't been wearing my safety belt, I'd have gone through the windscreen. As it is, I'm jerked hard against the restraints.

"Shit!" she screams as the car slews diagonally along Boyes Drive. Tyres squeal.

Not that it would make any difference, I hold my hands up to protect myself, expecting the connection with something solid, but the car skids to a halt, half turned on the wrong side of the road. I open my eyes gingerly, a metallic taste in my mouth. The inside of my cheek throbs dully from where I've bit it.

But that's not what scares the living bejezus out of me. Ashton, the cause of our almost-accident, stands in the middle of the road. In this dim light he glows, almost ethereal. He raises a hand, like he's greeting us, before he dissolves like snowflakes.

"We've got to do something about him," I say.

Marlise doesn't answer. Even in the low light of the console, which gives everything inside the car a greenish cast, I can see her knuckles are white. Her teeth chatter.

"Marlise. Are you okay?"

"I'm. Not. Okay."

"Can you drive?" I place a hand on her shoulder.

She jerks away from me and fixes me with a glare that would kill me ten times over.

"Marlise," I begin as calmly. "We're sitting on the wrong side of the road. If a car comes 'round that corner fast, they're going to hit us."

This snaps her out of her inaction, and she starts the car with an angry twist of the key in the ignition. With a squeal, the Toyota returns to the correct lane. I just pray we make it back home safely.

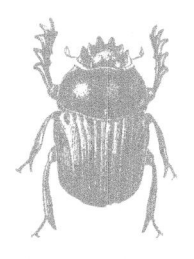

CHAPTER TEN
We Gotta do Something about that Ghost

WE DON'T STIR from the bed until noon on Wednesday. At some time during the early hours of the morning, Marlise forgets she is furious with me, because when I wake, she's snuggled into the crook of my arm, her hand stolen beneath my T-shirt to lie palm down on my chest. Warm breath tickles the underside of my chin.

I can't say this situation is wholly unpleasant, though any discomforting thoughts of the other things I could be doing with this woman are somewhat dulled by the polarised hurt seeping all the way to my very heart. Bruising had already bloomed all over my legs and arms in the hot shower I'd had when we arrived at two this morning. My skin is a latticework of scratches and, in some places, abrasions. Marlise hasn't fared much better. What a pair of invalids we make.

Thankfully no one has enquired about our status today, no phone calls from the main house or concerned queries on the cell phone. They probably think we're dead drunk or something. Somehow I'll have to haul this body out of bed tomorrow and go to work, but I'm not going to dwell on that just yet. This situation with Ashton's ghost cannot continue in this fashion. Someone's going to get hurt. I don't so much mind if it's me catching the fallout, but Marlise didn't do anything to deserve this, other than love the wrong man.

I've yet to see how much money Leonora gave me. Tomorrow I will go see about renting a room in Sunrise Lodge. It's the least I can do to offer Marlise a degree of sanity and, it can be hoped, safety. I'll deal with the troublesome Ashton, one way or another.

In the meanwhile, I need to look for Christopher van Vuuren, online at least. A man who has so much say in such a massive company can't be invisible. It's too convenient. Catherine van Vuuren must be his daughter. Treachery has an ugly smell. Can all of House Adamastor even be trusted? What of Meritiset? I hope she's all right and not caught up in the mess, or that the others I was close to, beautiful souls such as Ptahotep and Thothmes, are not in any danger.

Careful, so as not to disturb her, I ease Marlise off me, pausing when she mumbles incoherent words. I'm of two minds as to what I should do about her. Logic suggests I should cut myself out of her life completely, but I don't know if that will be enough to keep her safe. Then, there's the possibility she may well prove an invaluable ally if I continue initiating her in the mysteries.

That thought doesn't rest easy. Richard had made

it quite clear what was at stake when he started my initiation, though at first he'd been a little sneaky about it. Just meditation exercises, my foot. Leonora, of course, had been a different matter entirely. I'd seen something in her, some desire to be loved, and she'd been receptive to my suggestions, although I'd first taken her on as a librarian's assistant. She'd been eased into the whole Inkarna business, while Marlise, on the other hand, has been dumped headfirst through no choice of her own.

My stomach rumbles, but I ignore the physical discomfort of hunger. The sandwich and coffee for which I was able to make Marlise stop last night barely touched sides, but waking her now is not an option. She needs the rest more than I do, or at least the way I look at it I owe her the rest, especially since she's skipping her classes today. I'm sure as hell not going into the main house looking like I've been attacked by a pack of wild animals.

After relieving myself and splashing water on my face—I try not to look too closely at the haggard mess staring back at me in the mirror—I power up Marlise's laptop. If anything, I should use this quiet time for research, uninterrupted because I won't have her hanging over my shoulder watching which pages I open. It's not easy thinking when someone *tsks* over my shoulder when I keep using the drop-down menus on these stupid machines instead of knowing the shortcuts. I'll gain my proficiency in good time.

The internet is still a source of wonder to me, a vast Akashic library of sorts. The problem isn't the information. It's rather being able to sift through the vast quantities of rubbish and dead ends to find the gems.

First I look up Maverick Enterprises. The website

is slick, all cool whites and blues. The organisation appears to be a holding company for a number of interests, mostly medical development, information systems and military research. Typical House Montu. Everything they do is geared towards warfare. I'd bet there are a bunch of departments not listed on this site.

They have branches in Cape Town, Joburg, Durban and Port Elizabeth, with a satellite office in Bloemfontein, like a canker spread through the country. It makes sense that they'd control the road, ports and air. A cold shiver of foreboding passes through me. I'm uncomfortably reminded of the way a strangler fig will use its host for support until its roots strangle its victim.

Under the image gallery I pick up a number of corporate social responsibility events in which Christopher van Vuuren has made a public appearance. In his mid-forties, he looks exactly like the kind of man I wouldn't want to meet: tall and broad about the chest and shoulders. In most of the photographs he's wearing chinos and a golf shirt emblazoned with the Maverick falcon logo. His dark blond hair is cropped close to his skull, military style, but his light blue eyes give the appearance of dancing with merriment. He's always smiling when he knows the camera is pointed in his direction. Christopher is everyone's favourite uncle. Maybe it's just typical House territoriality that's coming to the fore, but this entire company and its people reek to the high heavens of House Montu. If Maverick Enterprises isn't House Montu, then the sky isn't blue.

Images show Van Vuuren shaking hands with Nelson Mandela, donating oversized cheques to children's homes and digging the foundations for

RDP housing and medical clinics in townships. He's a people's man. He's always at all the glittering events, hob-knobbing with the top brass from the ANC *and* the DA, always cheerful.

In all the right places at the right time, my nasty little voice informs me.

His life is charmed, it would appear: head of the rugby team, eight A's for matric, two years' military service and a masters degree in civil engineering. And, another thought chills me. Catherine van Vuuren, if she is his daughter, was who I'd be right now. This would have placed me right in the heart of House Montu affairs, if they are indeed behind Maverick Enterprises. The falcon head logo is so obvious it burns me, but unless I can uncover definite proof, this could also be happy coincidence that an ancient falcon-headed Neter associated with warfare can be echoed in a logo chosen by this company.

Is it coincidence? I don't think so.

Am I paranoid? Better paranoid than dead.

Would House Adamastor knowingly place one of its own in the lion's den without first informing the individual? Especially someone who's been a wife and a glorified librarian having tea parties before she popped off? The council had been adamant, so sure of the decision, but no one had informed me of any particular dangers. What's going on?

Nausea sends out its questing tentacles, and I'm so not hungry anymore.

The search engine delivers numerous other links related to this illustrious man and his projects. The *Opulent Living* magazine website shows an exclusive gated neighbourhood Van Vuuren developed in Noordhoek: his flagship enterprise, he calls it. Kakapo Mountain Estate is set in the natural amphitheatre formed by the mountain slopes in the area. The properties are priced way out of the range of mere mortals, offering security in these troubled times for discerning homeowners wishing for privacy. Advertising spin. I grimace while reading.

In an interview, Van Vuuren states his confidence in his work as he, personally, has chosen to reside here. *Gotcha!* There's a photograph of him with his family, a beautiful blond trophy wife, ex-super model, of course, and their daughter, who isn't mentioned by name.

I can find only the one image of her, taken two years ago when she would have been six years old. She is the picture of innocence, with cherubic features. White-blond hair hangs in twin braids, making her look like Pippi Longstocking. This would have been me. The thought makes my breath catch.

Who are you, Catherine van Vuuren? Who are you *really*?

Someone has stolen my life, and I intend to find out who the thief is.

Marlise stirs and mutters, and I close the browser windows and go to her side.

"Hey." I take her hand in mind. "How're you feeling?"

She blinks up at me sleepily, but her features are relaxed. None of last night's anger remains. "Like I've been out all night partying."

"Thank you for yesterday."

She wets her lips, a slight frown creasing her forehead. "It sucks, Ash. No matter how hard I try, I can't stay mad with you. Not like the old days."

I have to laugh. "I can only try, hey?"

"What are we going to do about the ghost?" She says 'ghost' so quietly it's almost a whisper.

With a groan I allow myself to collapse next to her, breathing in the comforting scent of the linen, her lingering sweetness. "I honestly don't know. I'd thought to destroy him, but that's just going to make me as bad as the people who've messed everything up. I don't want to wield such power. Trouble is—I can."

"That's the thing from last night, isn't it? That thing you buried. So, what are we going to do? He almost killed us both, in case you hadn't noticed."

"In theory, I could come up with some sort of binding, but it would be better for all of us if we could somehow convince him to let go of this existence, and I'm beginning to come to the horrid suspicion that he's somehow tied to me." It makes sense. I'd need to sever his ties with the *Kha*. But how will this impact on my current state?

"Then why don't you?"

"It's not that simple. His ties are obviously strong. If I sever them I may also end up severing my own ties. The body might die, or he might get back into it, and then where will we be? We can't both inhabit this body, and he clearly wants it back. We're headed into uncharted territory here. House Adamastor doesn't place emphasis on necromancy the way House Thanatos does." I shudder, recalling the pasty individual Richard and I encountered in Paris so many years ago.

"Can't you speak to one of them?"

"I'd rather not alert them to my existence. At least not until I've sorted out this current mess. You don't know what the other Houses are like."

"Well?"

An idea begins to form. "We could call him to us, bind him in my body. That way I can control him."

"You mean like being possessed? That's just sick."

"I can't think of anything else, save destroying him. I can't cut him from me but I need to bring him more firmly into my control."

Marlise sits up quickly, pinning my arms so she's leaning over me. "That's crazy!"

"The last time I checked, I was the one with more experience in these matters." A weary resignation floods me. "I doubt appealing to his good will is going to help, and he's not going to stop until he has some sort of spectacular success killing us, or me at least. And, even then, do you really want him back? He'd hurt you, worse than before. You know that. He's *dangerous*." I don't add that we're equally dangerous, the way we're going.

She stares at me for a long while before her expression turns from one of horror to something more neutral. "I'm going to go get us some breakfast."

I exhale harshly through my mouth, as if I'm breathing my last. "You do that. I need time to think things through."

Marlise rises and shrugs into the threadbare purple dressing gown she's hardly without when home. She's all businesslike, and I can only fathom this is because she draws comfort from familiar activities. Pausing by the door, she glances at me before vanishing into the house.

The cold leeches into my bones again, and I pull the duvet over me, huddling into the downy warmth while I close my eyes. Surely my *Akh*, which has passed through the Hall of Judgment and returned, would be more resilient than Ash? He is but a fragment that hasn't had the benefit of years of meditation and training. I know my *Ren*; he doesn't. The true name is stronger, and if I can somehow stamp that over him to create a binding, he has to be subservient to my will. The man with two souls—it has a strange, prophetic ring to it.

By the time Marlise returns with our lunch of ubiquitous toasted cheese-and-tomato sandwiches and a mug of tea each, I've made up my mind.

"I'm doing it," I tell her between bites.

She shakes her head, takes a sip of her tea.

"I don't want anything bad to happen to you. When I've neutralised the ghost, I'm going to move to Sunrise Lodge. It's close to my work and I won't be a burden to you. It's not right that I, a grown man, shack up with my girlfriend in her parents' house." I realise what I've said the moment the words leave my mouth. Girlfriend? I've just admitted it.

For a moment I'm afraid she's going to spill her tea, but Marlise regains her composure quickly. "You've not even seen the dump. How can you be so sure you'll stay there all that long?"

I shrug. "It's temporary."

"I qualify at the end of the year. I'll be able to look for work. We could find a place together..." The wild hope etched on her features is almost too much to bear.

"Let's see how things go." Is it so bad that I'm with her? I can't see myself falling in love with a man, not in my current physical state. That thought makes my lip curl in distaste.

"What's going on between us?" Marlise asks.

"It's complicated."

She laughs. "It's like those Facebook status updates. But, really, what future lies ahead for us?"

"I don't know. All I can tell you is that I'm sorry I dragged you into this mess. There's no going back for either of us."

"How do you feel about me?"

I glance at her then look at the half-eaten sandwich on my plate. "I really like you very much."

"As a *friend*." It's impossible missing the reproach in those three words.

"I don't know... It's confusing. There's an undeniable physical attraction but I've been trying to avoid it."

Marlise's laugh sounds bitter.

To hide some of my discomfort, I take another bite, but the bread is like clay in my mouth when I chew, and I have to swallow hard to get it down.

"Am I that unattractive? Are you also going to fuck other women again?"

"I don't know!" I cry. "By now you must have some sort of understanding about my dilemma."

"You're not Lizzie anymore, Ash. She's dead. This is where you are now."

"I know this! But it doesn't make it any easier!" I get up from the bed and put my plate and mug down on the table with too much force. The walls close in, and the air tastes stale in the back of my throat. The old Ashton Kennedy glares down at me from the poster on the wall, all attitude, balls and a big dick.

"Ash, please. I know I was stupid for running after who you used to be, but the entire situation has changed. Come to me, please. I love you, no matter who or what you are."

"You're mad!" I round on her, my hands balling into fists. "You're insane! Look at me! Look at what I've become! I'm not human! Not in the terms you'd understand. I'm *Inkarna*. I will live many lives. I will die many times. How can you love some *thing* that doesn't fit into the natural order? How can you still want me knowing what you know now, that you'll never have a normal life if you hang around me? Trouble will always follow us, and we will know no rest."

"Don't you believe in fate?"

"I believe in myself. I follow the path of Ma'at, or I try to. I make my own fate, though the gods know I'm making such a hash of it right now."

"I believe in fate, Ash. I believe that for everything that has happened, it's happened for a reason. I sat for days when you were on the respirator. Many times they wanted to switch off the machines. So many times I convinced your mother otherwise."

"She's not my mother."

Marlise blanches. "She cares about you. So does Mr Kennedy. You need to let people into your life. After everything I've gone through, those months of not knowing. I sat there one night and I prayed, I prayed to anyone or anything that might be listening to bring you back. I haven't told you this one because for a long time I thought I was just dreaming, that it was just wishful thinking, but I saw something, someone." She whispers the last two words.

"What?" This piques my interest.

She grips her mug as though it contains some sort of precious elixir. "It was late. That was the night Mrs Kennedy came to tell me that they couldn't afford to keep you on life support anymore. The doctor had already agreed to switching off the machines. You couldn't breathe without them. They tried before. They were going to give you morphine to make you comfortable, and they were going to turn the machines off the following day. There was nothing I could say or do about the matter.

"I decided to stay that night, and I sat there a long while, holding your hand, watching your chest rise and fall, knowing that this was the last time."

"And you did this despite the previous tenant treating you like dirt." I snort, but something about the utter defeat in the way she rounds her shoulders, makes me approach the bed and sit next to her. Removing the half-empty mug from her clenched fingers, I put this aside, under the bed where it won't spill, and take her hands in mine. "Speak. Finish your story."

"Thank you." Marlise's smile is tentative. "I must have nodded off, but I jerked awake. I wasn't alone. There was a man in the room with us, only he wasn't like any man I've seen before. He had a head like a dog or a wolf, and he stood on the other side of the bed, resting a hand on your chest. Here." She places her palm on my chest, above my heart. "He said something in a language that I now think sounded like the one I've heard you use, and a scent like incense filled the ward. Then he looked up at me. He had the strangest eyes, like I could see stars reflected in them, all luminous and dark. I heard him say a word, something like *keffer* three times. At least that's what I remember."

"Anpu Upuaut." I breathe the words, all the small hairs on my arms and the back of my neck rising. Though we work with the Neteru, it's incredibly rare that we connect with them. Hell, some Inkarna state flatly the Neteru only exist because it's easy for us to package certain ideas in pretty forms, that the Neteru are extensions of ourselves that have gained a measure of autonomy in the shared human subconscious.

While I'm not that progressive in my thinking, this is nonetheless chilling that one such as Anpu Upuaut will take personal notice of me. It's just too uncanny, with all the small clues that have been doing the rounds of late.

"You're not saying anything," Marlise prompts.

"What can I say?"

"Was I dreaming?"

"I don't think so."

Her face pales and a tremor passes through her. "These things are real…"

"As if I haven't been able to convince you yet." I laugh, because it's the only reaction I can give.

"You can choose," I tell her. "Either we part ways here and now, and you can try to forget any of this happened, forget about me. And you'll be safe. Or you can remain part of this craziness, but I can guarantee that you'll see many strange and wondrous things, and your life will not take a path that you can predict. It will be dangerous." The selfish part of me wants her to come with me, to follow where I walk. I have so little in this world and one other person who understands, who cares enough to want to help, is better than none, for Leonora won't be here forever, or not for another few decades or more.

"Ash, you know I'm in far too deep to turn around now, but I can't do this if you're going to break my heart."

I look at Marlise then, really observe her. She is not a classic beauty, is too short and a little round in figure, in a way that makes me constantly want to put my arm around her, to feel her near me. Rich brown eyes burn with an inner fire, never leaving mine. If she were cast in a film, she'd be the slightly geeky girl next door, the one who's good with children and constantly has her nose in a book, who loves receiving Valentine's cards and single red roses wrapped in cellophane. But it's that spirit in her that has me reach out to tuck a ruddy curl behind her ear and cup her face just below the chin. I graze my thumb over her slightly parted lips.

"You've shown me such kindness, Marlise. How can I not feel some sort of love in return?"

"But you're too scared to take it further, aren't you?"

"Yes. I don't know what I want."

"Yet I sometimes catch you looking at me in a way Ashton never did."

"Why did you hold onto him?"

"I just couldn't say no to him. We started dating when we were both in school. He became cruel, or maybe he always had this nasty streak to him. When he knew his own power…" She shakes her head.

"Why didn't he just leave you? He seems like the kind of guy who'd just stop visiting once he tired of you."

"Oh, he'd meet someone new and he'd call, tell me we're breaking up. Everyone would be talking about it for about a week or two, then the girl would get too clingy or do something to annoy him. Then he'd start seeing me again. Just friends, right? And next thing I'd know, he'd be taking me out to dinner or buying me a CD or something, and we'd be together again. A month or two, things would be fine. Then some girl…" She sobs. "They were always the same, some barely legal, hanging out at The Event Horizon. And he could be so damned charming. You couldn't say no to him even if you tried, even though you knew he was poison."

I pull her into my arms and hold her while she cries. Years of pent-up sorrow shiver through her, and the only comfort I can offer is to crush her to me. How must it have been for her when the new and messed-up-in-other-ways Ash woke? An uncertain Ash, hesitant, always apologising?

Could I love her? I turn my feelings over. I'm vulnerable right now. She's the first person, apart from Leonora, I can bare my soul to, but what will happen two or three years from now if I meet someone else? Or what if Marlise decides she tires of me?

Logic screams at me to not do anything stupid by committing to anyone right now, but another, selfish part—my carnal side—delights in this soft gentle creature that has opened herself to me. Is it so wrong to draw physical comfort from another person? Especially if it is freely given? I'd never play her the way the old Ash seemed to delight in tormenting the people who loved him.

Marlise wants a physical affirmation of a bond between us, and I can't deny I'm curious. What's it like, this interchange between man and woman when I'm no longer on the receiving end?

"Do you really want me?" I ask. It's a stupid question and a foolish notion now, while there is so much at stake.

She lifts her head to look up at me, her eyes wet and wide. "Was there ever any doubt?"

I let her kiss me, losing myself in the softness of her lips, her insistent tongue that flicks into my mouth, gentle, almost apologetic. It's easier to respond, to return this offering and, despite the beating my body took the night before, a steady answering warmth spreads from my loins.

Her breasts are pleasing in their weight. When I run my palms over the nipples they peak at my touch. We fall back on the bed and Marlise shifts so her thigh presses against my crotch and the growing tightness.

I have a bad moment, or should I rather say an unfamiliar moment, when I feel my shaft harden at this pressure. But it's good, so good, this ember within me stirring into life, causing the blood in my veins to quicken.

Her hands roam over my belly, tugging at the tracksuit pants I'm wearing to slip inside. Nice, warm hands that trail torturous fingers along the sensitive skin of the inside of my thighs, close but not touching the erection straining against the fabric.

With a grunt I push her T-shirt up to expose her breasts, burying my face in the flesh, licking, tasting and drinking in her scent that, beneath the mint, is almost milky sweet. A terrible hunger consumes me, and I take her nipples into my mouth, experimenting with the texture of sucking at them, teasing them in circles with my tongue the way Richard used to torment Lizzie. It has the same effect on Marlise. Her hips push against me, the sweet torture of her riding my leg.

She breaks for air with a gasp. "I can't wait anymore!" Marlise tugs hard at my pants and pushes me onto my back. I'm too lost in the way she grabs my phallus, massaging it in ways that make me dizzy, helpless and lost to the sensation.

Marlise straddles me, holding the tip to the warm folds of her cunt. This is sweet agony as she devours me, her muscles accommodating my girth as she grinds down hard. I can't help but cry out, grabbing her thighs as I do so and thrusting into her.

"This. Feels. So. Good!" is all I can manage before I'm lost in the push and pull, her small gasps of pleasure doing things to my mind so that I white out.

It's not enough that she rides me. With a growl I roll her over so I can thrust deeper, harder. I'm pushing at a barrier, a build-up of pressure that needs release. Dimly I'm aware of her wrapping her legs around my waist, somehow changing the way her passage enfolds me.

The explosion of my orgasm rockets through me, out of this strange pulsing organ that is now mine. Infinitely sublime. We lie back in a tangle of limbs and clothing, our breath rasping in our throats, our skin moist where fabric doesn't separate.

Marlise is the first to move, shifting so that my now-flaccid phallus slips out. The intensity of our intercourse returns to me in scattered visions of frantic pumping, my back stinging from lacerations I wasn't aware Marlise was making when she dug her nails into skin.

"I didn't hurt you?" I ask.

Marlise's laugh is throaty. "He never used to ask me that."

"Am I supposed to take that as a compliment?"

"Take it any way you want to but I'm going to go have a shower now. You're welcome to join me, but don't expect a blowjob 'cause I can't handle water getting up my nose." She pecks me on the lips and on the forehead then launches off the bed, laughing as she disappears into the bathroom.

This must be my cue to follow her. Lizzie played similar games with Richard. His memory elicits a sharp pang of guilt. When will I stop these comparisons? Will I always hold Marlise next to him? I shove these uncharitable thoughts far away, wincing from latent aches as I rise. Pulling the T-shirt off over my head, I head to where Marlise is, already under a hot stream of water.

It feels so good, so right to hold her, all warm, wet and slippery while the water cascades down on us, washing away sweat and old anger. She pushes into me when I run my hands down her belly to tangle in the short fuzz of her pubic mound.

"For someone who claims to be uncomfortable with getting down and dirty, you seem to know exactly what to do," she murmurs when I slide my fingers inside her cleft.

"I'm a fast learner," I reply.

I love the way she grinds against me, entirely too intoxicating, and my phallus quirks at the thought of what untold pleasures reside within this diminutive woman who has opened herself so willingly to me.

Now's not the time to think too hard, to consider all the implications of our actions. With the water still jetting over us, she turns and I explore her lips, sliding my hands down the small of her back to hold her buttocks and pull her against my already stiff phallus. I could get used to this. All the cares, the worries, fade to distant recesses as I press my mouth to Marlise's in the shower, somehow satisfied with the way she feels so abominably good writhing against me, opening her legs to my insistent, questing fingers.

When I press her against the wall of the shower, however, she lets out a small shriek. "The tiles! They're freezing!"

At this point we both break down into helpless laughter. Something tight within my heart snaps and I realise it's good to be human, to be clothed in flesh and to indulge in the senses. The Inkarna of Per Ankh are too uptight.

☥

Much later, after allowing our carnal natures free rein, Marlise and I lie, half-drowsing in her bed. I must have nodded off, replete, when a faint buzzing starts on an almost subsonic level. All the hairs on my nape tingle, and Marlise senses it at the same time. Her hand, which had been lying so casually on the soft skin above my hip, tightens, the fingernails digging painfully into my muscle.

We lock gazes simultaneously.

"Ash?" Ragged fear tinges my name.

I sit up, Marlise mirroring my movement but pressing herself to my side. The clock's digital display tells me it's twenty past six, after sunset, and I don't like the way my breath mists before my face. The room hasn't been that cold naturally, despite it being midwinter. The bedside lamp's illumination doesn't quite push aside the murk. It's as if the air is denser, not just with the cold but also a tangible darkness that seeks to extinguish visibility.

"Marlise, I want you to put on your clothes and go to your parents. Go make tea or watch TV or something. I don't want you to see this."

"No. Don't try to cut me out. What part of 'we're in this together,' don't you understand?"

A sound like fingernails scratching down a chalkboard starts, a sound that crawls down my spine. Marlise's death grip on my upper arm hurts.

"While I appreciate your loyalty, I don't want you—"

Faint laughter rings out, as if from a great distance, lending the sense that the room is, in fact, an illusion, and we're situated in some giant cavern.

Extricating Marlise's fingers from my arm, I rise and face the corner where the darkness seems to be the most tangible. I stretch out my arms, palms held up. "You miss this, Ashton? This flesh you didn't seem to care enough for when you still inhabited it?" I need to make him angry, so his emotions will cloud his judgment.

The laughter stops, and instead, an icy wind begins to sough outside, the branches of the plantain scratching against the window.

"Oh, you think you're so clever. That time beneath The Event Horizon, when you gathered enough energy to knock me flat with your first pitiful attempt. You think I'm scared, Ashton? Think again. You're trapped here, and the way I see it, I'm quite enjoying your body without you in it. I get to taste food, feel warm or cold. Hell—" I laugh, even though I don't feel it. "I can go take a piss or a crap whenever I want to. I get hungry, I eat food. And, you know what? It feels really good. You can't do that, can you?"

The air grows thicker. Marlise is still behind me, and the shadows in the corner bulge and distort. An intense longing reaches me, tendrils shooting off from the darkness, but stopping short about a metre or so from where I stand.

What's the worst thing I can say to this disembodied spirit? A slow smile spreads across my lips, and I close my eyes, to rather feel where Ashton is. His presence is an angry buzz, like a hive preparing to swarm. I am ready for his attack. The ember within me flares, increasing my pulse and my breathing. Slow fire crawls outward from my belly, igniting my blood, making my phallus harden.

"Even better, Ashton, is that I fucked your woman today. I fucked her long and hard, three times already, and she was more than willing. In fact, she says I really know how to make a woman feel good about herself." I cringe inwardly as I speak these words. They are how I imagine Ashton to be in this very situation, cocksure and arrogant, enjoying someone else's torment for the pure kick it lends his ego.

These last few words have the desired effect, though. With a roar more like a storm wind than that of a man, Ashton launches himself, his fury concentrated on me. Every inch of my being screams at me to shove up some sort of shield or at least jump out of the path of such mindless fury, but I hold.

Ashton hits me, a tsunami of daimonic force, and I stagger back to land on the bed. An intense polar chill invades my limbs, and my flesh quivers and jerks spasmodically.

"*I've got you now*," Ashton whispers. His triumph is abrasive.

And I let him penetrate to my core, right down to that little ember I always nurture as my essential concept of *Akh*-hood, that which makes me Inkarna.

In the distance Marlise cries out my name. She shakes the *Kha*, but all sensation is dulled. The angry ghost floods through my veins like a shot of morphine, and everything grows unimportant.

Hold on in there! A wash of memories tries to override my own.

The lights are bright in my eyes, and I cavort around on a stage with a host of writhing bodies before me. My voice is thunderous as I let loose into the microphone, my black hair a banner as I throw myself around in time to the music, the grinding guitars—a dirty sound that sends my pulse racing.

A line of white powder leads me down to a glass-topped coffee table, the rolled-up fifty rand note in my hand damp from my fingers. My stomach clenches in painful anticipation as I stick the paper tube in my right nostril and Hoover up the white powder. Tonight's going to be great.

So what if I don't remember her name. I glance at the blonde comatose in the bed next to me. Where the hell am I? I get up, pull on my jeans and part the curtain. Fuck. How the hell did I end up in Panorama? Table Mountain is blue in the distance, its characteristic "tablecloth" boiling off its flat top. How the hell am I going to get back to Obz?

The motorcycle roars between my legs, and I give the bike more juice, taking pleasure in watching the speedometer creeping up from a two hundred and twenty to two-sixty. The world blurs past, and it feels like I'm flying. Nothing can stop me now.

Memory after memory spills over me as Ashton tries to overwrite me. Hot and cold flushes grip me, and I'm aware of ragged breathing—my own—my muscles cramping. All the while Marlise calls my name, and I would reply if it weren't for the occasional strangled moan I offer her instead.

It would be easier to let go. I'm aware of that. I can slip into limbo, cut loose my ties, and none of this would hurt anymore. *Let go, it's easy, c'mon man, you've got the wrong body.* The grey Sea of Nun beckons.

I'm privy to all Ashton's memories, of him growing up in the relatively affluent suburb of Claremont, of him going to school, getting bullied until he got his first growth spurt and started beating up on the kids who'd tormented him. It's surprising that he did love Marlise, because those first tender emotions bloom. Only with time did the rot set in, that arrogance of a man who believes he is immortal, infallible. The problem with Ashton Kennedy is he believes the world owes him something.

His anger flashes when I maintain this thought,

holding up a dark mirror.

You're a child, nothing more than a spoilt brat everyone's been pandering to, humouring because you're so god-damned charming. And when you don't get what you want, you have the sulks, throw a tantrum. Grow up, Ashton. You've messed up one time too many, and now it's too late.

It grows darker, and a great pressure pushes down on my chest so that I'm gasping for air. I've got to rally against this spiral into oblivion, and it really does feel like I'm a leaf caught in an ever-decreasing eddy, spinning faster and faster to reach the singularity where I'll...

Memories of grey limbo reach their clammy hands to envelope me. Perhaps I was a fool for thinking I could welcome Ashton back into his body. After all, I'm nothing more than a rider at the end of the day. He's had a score of years to really know every inch of how this *Kha* works. But that nothingness! How can I return there, especially with so much unfinished?

I stand in a maelstrom of cloud and air, my feet firmly on frozen shale, the rock sending its chill through me. This can't be it? It's heartening to know I can visualise an actual setting, though now I'm cut off from the sense of being in the *Kha*. Something tugs at my chest, above my heart chakra—a silver cord. The hand I reach out to pluck at this string glows, long fingers—not quite male or female. Translucent skin shimmers, like that of an Inkarna resident in Per Ankh. This is a good thing. I smile with grim determination and tug. The rope isn't slack; it vanishes into the boiling cloud a mere five paces from me.

Pulling harder, I meet resistance. I grip with both hands, centre my will and yank, hard. The world turns black, and it's as though I'm dragging myself through a viscous liquid, and all sense of holding onto a physical form vanishes save for the determination to progress, to return to the material.

A terrible wailing rises into a high-pitched whine until all blurs into a rush of falling through an endless void, great bursts of electricity buzzing through me in a longitudinal explosion.

With a snap I'm back in Ashton's *Kha*, straddling Marlise, pressing her down into the bed, my hands wrapped around her throat.

"Shit!" I fall back as though I've been trying to throttle a live snake.

Marlise scuttles to the edge of the bed, gasping for air, her face pale. She coughs.

A wall of pain smashes into me, and I curl into a foetal position, as wave after wave of pure agony blazes through me. My head wants to explode, and for a moment, I entertain a morbid vision of my skull bursting, spattering my grey matter all over the bedding.

This doesn't happen. As abruptly as this attack started, it ends, and my body uncoils. Only a terrible ringing in my ears remains. My skin is slick with a cold sheen of perspiration. Then the shivering starts, my teeth chattering. But after this violent decompression of daimonic energy, it's just me here in this room with Marlise, whom I've just tried to kill.

The horror of that outcome chills me, and I sit up gingerly. Marlise watches me, everything in her posture screaming wariness from the other end of the bed. The duvet is kept pulled around her as she massages at her throat with her left hand.

"Ash, is that you now or is it..." She shudders.

"No, it's me. Or at least the 'me' that I hope you

prefer." I knee-walk toward her, slowly holding my palms toward her to show I mean no harm. "I'm so, so sorry."

Marlise bites her lip. "He said the most terrible things, Ash. He said he was going to kill me."

She allows me to pull her into my arms, and I hold her, pressing kisses to her neck and the top of her head. "It's okay now, I think. I'm so very, very sorry."

The depths of my shame at this unfortunate turn of events makes me wish I could curl into a tiny ball, that Marlise would at least be angry, that she'd lash out at me, kicking and punching. She doesn't. Instead she pulls me closer, as though we could somehow meld into each other. The storm has passed. I hope.

Tentatively I push with my daimonic self, slowly increasing my awareness to fill this room. Nothing. Not a whisper. Ashton Kennedy's unquiet spirit is either locked deep within me, or I've sent him howling back into limbo. I can only pray he stays there. It's too soon to tell.

By unspoken agreement, we drop any discussion of the Inkarna, the now-hidden stele and Ash's attack. We share silent moments where we stare into each other's eyes, haunted by what we've experienced, but we focus instead on the mundane world.

My return to The Event Horizon on Thursday morning is an anticlimax, to say the least. Lisa's off, so it's just me and Davy, and we fall into easy banter. If he notices that I move with care, he says nothing. I wear long sleeves to cover any of the scratches on my arms. Once or twice he hints that Marlise and I are keeping each other up late nights. I let him think what he will, even playing along with a few sly winks.

Of Ash's spirit there is not a whisper, though if he expended so much energy in his attempt at a hostile takeover it's quite possible he's biding his time until such point that he can unleash another attack. For now it's blissfully quiet.

Smiling at the patrons is easy; concentrating on their drink orders gives me a focus. So too is calling up to the kitchen for another basket of fries or just losing myself in such tasks as packing bottles into the fridge. I don't have to think too hard. I have one bad moment when I go down to the basement to fetch a crate of beers, but it passes after I take a deep breath and force myself to take that first step into the gloom-ridden area.

Marlise comes through to The Event Horizon after her classes finish, and Davy raises a brow when I embrace her and plant a lingering kiss on her lips. It's clear to everyone that something has changed in our relationship. The old Ash's memories, I find, wriggle just beneath the surface, hinting that he may not have been so demonstrative in his attentions.

And that is odd, because if I push just a little below the surface, something gives, some sort of pliant barrier, and I can access the barest whispers of a past that isn't my own. It's not like when I access Blessed memories, which only requires a slight shift in perception to that part of me that is Inkarna. No. If I think about what has changed since the past night, it's almost as if I'm *superimposed*. It takes a little more effort, but the old Ashton is very much there, just dormant. Exactly how dormant, I don't know.

Marlise accompanies me to Sunrise Lodge and it's the dump she said it was. She's thin-lipped as Karin, the owner, shows us a few of the rooms that are available. The place reminds me of the stories I've heard of California's Winchester Mystery House, with obscure rooms, angles that are slightly off and passages that terminate for no logical reason. It appears that bits of the lodge were tacked on over the years, without giving much consideration to architectural aesthetics or practical considerations. Though the place is hardly as grand as the old lady's eccentric mansion, Sunrise Lodge certainly dates back to a similar age.

Two storeys tall, it boasts scuffed and often holey Oregon pine floors and high ceilings. The carpets, where the place still possesses such luxuries, are threadbare and covered in unidentifiable stains. I assume it was built initially as an upmarket boarding house, but whatever grace the property once had is long gone. Where the paint isn't mouldy, it's peeling in great swaths. The other tenants, such that we do pass while clomping down the echoing dark passages, all hail from central Africa, if the snatches of overheard French suggests anything. Contrasting cooking smells compete for dominance, here braised meat, there a curry of some sort, or burnt toast. None of it, however, can mask the underlying old house smell, of dust and something darker and somehow sentient. Here be ghosts aplenty, and worse.

Karin, a dowdy woman with short curly white hair, seems oblivious to the state of the premises, marching determinately ahead of Marlise and me. Every so often, between viewing available rooms, Marlise shoots me a doubtful glance, raising her brow as if to say, *I told you so and you wouldn't listen.*

At least half a dozen of Karin's mangy canines follow us, nearing to sniff at our shoes only to shoot back with bared teeth when we turn to look at them.

I have severe misgivings about making a decision, my hand often travelling to the bundle of cash Leonora gave me. There are better things I could spend my money on, my inner critic chides. Yet if I stay longer with Marlise in her parents' house, I may also put them in danger, should House Montu cotton onto my return. That's if they haven't already.

Perhaps Sunrise Lodge is a good enough option. Here I'd be anonymous, in a place where no one asks too many questions. As for safety? Who'd want to mess with a man who's more than six feet tall who, although he doesn't carry a gun, still packs enough punch to put someone through a wall, literally. The way I look at it, Sunrise Lodge is the last place on earth anyone who knew of Lizzie, or Nefretkheperi, would look.

Eventually I settle for a room near the fire escape on the first floor—I have to remain prudent, after all—that is more an afterthought than a room. Technically, I suspect, this used to be a stairwell leading down to the ground floor, but was walled off, creating an awkward space featuring an extremely high ceiling, and a spot where I can make my bed beneath the stairs. A little additional cover never hurts. Anyone entering by the top won't see me around the curve, which gives me time to react.

Another reason I've chosen this is the door on the ground floor which, although it has been boarded up, can be broken through at a moment's notice. It's always good to have an emergency exit. It's too bad for the person who lives in the unit next door if that eventuality occurs. I pray it won't.

The only major problem with this set-up is that I don't have a bathroom. I cringe at the very idea of having to use the communal facilities in this building.

I'd already spotted six massive roaches during our tour.

With Marlise rolling her eyes, I pay the deposit of four hundred rand plus a week's rent of four hundred, and we leave after Karin gives us the key. I still have about six hundred left, and plan to purchase a few assortments before I move in tomorrow.

"Is this really such a good idea?" Marlise asks the moment we step outside the gate and into the night and a thin drizzle. She stands more than an arm's length from me, her shoulders hunched.

"No, but neither is the current status quo." The streetlights paint her face in a wash of orange, and I can't help but consider how young she is. "Come here, silly."

Marlise obeys and I draw her into my embrace.

"I'm going to miss you at night, but let's get through the mess, okay? Then you and I can think about something better."

I can't quite make out her murmured response. It feels so right holding her, another of Ashton's memories of a similar night bubbling up from the depths. The gods know I don't want any harm to befall Marlise. Some deeper connection tugs at me, an echo of Ashton's older feelings for this woman mirroring my own.

Her phone rings then. She answers. "No, ma'am, I'm sorry. This is the wrong number. My name is not Lucy."

I have to laugh, and it feels good to lift from the heaviness of my meanderings.

☥

By the time Marlise drops by Sunrise Lodge late on Friday afternoon, I've done the best I can to set up my new living quarters. Granted, the institution-grey walls need a lick of paint, but I've scrubbed the pine floor until the wood's true colour shows once I remove decades of unmentionable grime.

My earthly possessions now include a mattress, two blankets, two sheets and a pillow. I've added two tin mugs, so I can make myself tea in the squalid excuse of a communal kitchen.

"It's better," Marlise says, while appraising the room from her position at the head of the stairs. "I can't say I like it, but at least it's clean...er." She wrinkles her nose.

I fit her beneath the crook of my arm, where it feels she's always belonged. "It's gonna have to do for now. I won't be having any tea parties here, that much is for sure."

We don't stay long at all. She's not comfortable in this creaky old building and, besides, we've got work to do. I give her the last of my money for fuel, and we head out to the far south, to Noordhoek. It's a good three-quarter hour drive and we don't say much. Marlise plays a dirgelike album by some band whose rambling name I forget the moment she tells me. It's all dirty noise to my ears, the lyrics so gloomy I wonder about the lead singer's past. Something must have happened to him. But that small part of me that is Ashton likes the sound, and that's enough for me right now.

Kakapo Estate sprawls across a large section of the mountainside. The sun's on its way down, and all we can really do is pull the car up a hundred metres or so from the main gates.

"It's pointless," Marlise says. "You've just wasted a lot of my fuel."

"It's not pointless. I need to see the place for myself." The problem is a guard manning the entrance. Six-foot palisade fencing with jagged edges encloses the sacred land of the filthy rich. It's going to be all but impossible to get in. Not to mention the security cameras at regular intervals. Maverick Enterprises wants to make damn sure no intruders breach the perimeter.

"What are you going to do about it?" she asks.

"Dunno yet. I need time to think about it." At the back of my mind I know this isn't going to be easy, especially when examining the disparity in resources. Me, go up against House Montu, and all *this*? Still, there has to be a way. "Let's go see Leonora. I'd like you to meet her. She was a big part of my life before..."

"You sure it would be okay?"

I ask to borrow her phone, cursing when I can't get the right buttons to work, but I'm glad to see we can look back to the received calls list and retrieve Leo's number. She answers almost immediately and, despite the short notice, is happy to see us.

We don't have much time, and that damned hour glass keeps emptying. Although I worry that Marlise won't get on with Leo, I'm gratified that an instant connection is forged the moment they meet each other. It's a completed circle, and I sit back listening to the two most important women in my life. Even now, looking at the younger woman, I can hardly believe I've allowed her to creep into my heart. *She's not Richard*, my doubt reminds me. But it's better than being alone, and if I could be grateful for anyone with whom to spend time, it's Marlise.

Naturally, Marlise is in awe and, like a child, asks so many questions, rising often to peer at books, take them off the shelves to page through them. Maybe there is hope for her future among the Inkarna after all.

"I just never thought there was this kind of stuff out there," she admits later.

"You were too busy ruining your mind with that vampire crap."

Marlise shoots me a glare that would strip paint.

"Perhaps you can start with this?" Leonora rises and hobbles to her bedside table where she retrieves a slim, leather-bound volume, which she brings to Marlise.

She flips through the pages then looks up at Leonora. "I can't! This book is a hundred years old!"

"Keep it," Leo says. "I have no use for it anymore, not where I'm going."

I'm painfully reminded then, of Leo's age. The candlelight softens some of the lines marring her features. We were together for such a short while, Inkarna and initiate. Ten short years compared to the lifetime she's had without me around. Do I even know her anymore?

As if aware of my thoughts, she makes eye contact over the table, and the sense of love and gratitude she feels washes over me, one of the gifts between Inkarna that grows with age, the ability to project. Marlise picks up on something, because she glances between us, her expression unreadable, before she continues paging through the book Leo gave her.

Leonora's energy signature is visible in the low light, a bulbous glowing oval shimmering just at the edges of my vision. It is ragged at the edges, struck through with dark veins that tell me her end is near.

This first time is always fraught with uncertainty. Leo will be asking many of the same hard questions I did when standing upon the cusp of the first great passage through the Black Gate.

But if I were to meet with some unfortunate accident, and had opportunity to consider this final journey, I'm sure the second time wouldn't be any easier than the first. So much can go wrong. Granted, I know what to expect, and this time, I'll bypass the Hall of Judgment.

"I'm going to arrange for my things to be placed in storage once I'm gone," Leonora says. "The estate should be wound up within three or four months. I spent time with my attorney this morning and have changed my will. You should find your life far more comfortable once what remains of the trust fund is in your name. Though I daresay don't give up your day job anytime soon if you're wanting luxuries." She gives a dry laugh.

Marlise gasps. "You mustn't talk like that, Leo! You can't die now."

"My dear." She clasps one of Marlise's hands. "It's going to happen soon. Death comes for each of us. We can choose to embrace the day and look back upon lives that have been full, or we can go kicking and screaming, causing unnecessary pain for not only ourselves but the people we love. It is the way of things. And, besides, you'll see me again soon. It will be like the blink of an eye." She winks at Marlise.

Marlise casts about wildly, first looking pleadingly at me before turning back to Leo. "But… But…"

I place my hand on Marlise's thigh, giving it a squeeze. "I know it hurts, but the consolation for our kind is that death is merely a portal, a catalyst for a transformation." Now's not the time to discuss the dangers. "Be glad for Leo that she has an opportunity to start afresh. Her *Kha* is tired and old, and her soul needs to complete its journey. She will progress to Per Ankh, where she will meet the other Inkarna, to be welcomed in their midst. There are many wonders for her still to experience." Gods, I sound like I'm reciting some sort of holy scripture.

I don't remember much of what transpired between my passing through the Black Gate and attaining Per Ankh. I don't think the human mind can comprehend the Hall of Judgment and bring back a clear recollection. *Ammit the Devourer lies there...*

When Marlise excuses herself to use the bathroom, Leo turns to me. "She is so young, Ash. Is this wise drawing her into our world?"

"Don't remind me," I murmur. The apartment is small. I don't want Marlise to overhear our discussion.

"You've forced changes in her. The daimonic powers are starting to awaken. Wouldn't it be better if you see a little less of her, at least until this mess with House Montu, Maverick Enterprises and the Van Vuurens is clarified? She will make a good Inkarna. She just needs time and encouragement. Much fear is lodged in her heart. You will need to tread carefully with her."

"I don't know if I can keep her safe. I may well be the most dangerous person in her life." I decide not to worry Leonora with talk about Ashton Kennedy's angry ghost. As if in response, something deep within me stirs. I push that thought away. "I'm afraid she already knows too much and it's a case of either leaving her in ignorance to get hurt, or preparing her so that she at least has a fighting chance."

Leonora nods. "*They* were here again yesterday.

This time they renewed their compulsions but also set traps. I fear they may be alert to shifts in the aethers. What happened with the stele?"

The toilet flushes in the bathroom, and I glance towards the closed door before turning to Leo. "It's safe, hidden. I'm more worried about the knowledge you hold."

The old woman laughs quietly. "Oh, I'm quite adept at keeping secrets. After all, one doesn't hide away from one of the most eminent Houses for so many years if one isn't capable of playing the game. Don't worry, it's crossed my mind as well that this isn't the sort of knowledge our brethren would want out in the open. I'll keep mum. We can discuss this when we meet again." Leo speaks with so much confidence I *want* to believe her.

At this point, Marlise exits the bathroom, pausing before she sits, searching our eyes. "My ears are burning," she says.

"What you don't know can't hurt you," I say, knowing it's going to drive her crazy.

"You know that's bullshit, Ash." She settles back in her chair and lets out a small annoyed huff.

Leonora's expression is troubled.

We stay until after ten, but it's clear Leo is tired, and we say our farewells.

I don't say what's on my mind, that this may be the last time I see Leo for a long time. Likewise, she remains cheerful, though I gain an affirmation from her daimonic self whispering up against mine, almost like someone brushing lint of a jacket.

Marlise, clutching the thin volume Leo gave her to her chest, natters about us doing meditations soon, now that we've dealt with the spiritual annoyance, stopping short of blathering about Ashton when she catches a sharp glance from me. I nod, and reply on autopilot. Although I'm glad I've seen Leonora, I can't help but feel I'm up against insurmountable odds, and I'm not quite sure how to proceed from here.

Maybe it's safer letting Marlise imagine this whole Inkarna business isn't as dangerous as it is, that it's just some old girls' and old boys' clubs that occasionally have disagreements. And it's not the first time that I curse allowing Marlise to see where I've hidden the stele. That's the sort of knowledge that can get her killed, even if she has no idea, in truth, what the issues at stake are.

House Montu is already nigh on unstoppable. It still bothers me that House Adamastor would have placed me in that House's midst, but equally disturbing is the thought, however unlikely, that they weren't aware. Who voted on the placement of Inkarna who punched through? Is it possible House Montu has a spy in House Adamastor's Per Ankh?

Usually the Houses keep each other balanced. What would happen to human society if House Montu were to pull together all its threads? A world dictatorship? Surely not? But then I've heard of their skills in combat, their almost superhuman speed, the ability to heal, to kill. Although House Adamastor's arsenal of talents is not to be sniffed at, we're essentially useless in hand-to-hand combat with House Montu's people.

House Montu with the ability to send souls howling into Ammit's slavering jaws? Now *that* is truly frightening.

Marlise asks that I spend the night with her, just one last time. She's hurt when I decline but nonetheless drives me back to town.

"You can always come in," I tell her. "Just for a

short while." It would be nice to spend time with her, even if my lodgings leave much to be desired.

She shudders and sits back in her seat. "Ugh. I'd rather not. It's Friday night. Some of those people are seriously dodgy. There're drug deals going down in there."

"Guess that's it then, for today." I lean over and kiss her, keeping it businesslike.

She doesn't look at me when I get out of the car. It's when she drives off that I realise we never did make plans for Saturday. But the prospect of solitude doesn't upset me as much as it should. I can use the time to meditate, an act I've neglected for far too long. Regular spiritual practice is important to Inkarna, as a way to strengthen the apprehension of the daimonic self.

☥

Ashton Kennedy sits opposite me at The Event Horizon, while I polish large medallions with the sigils of the different Houses stamped on them. *It's just a dream*. He seems thinner, somehow, his eyes hollow and the skin around them bruised.

"I suppose you should feel pleased with yourself, reducing me to this." He gestures around the club. The overhead screens broadcast nothing but static. There are no other patrons, and our faces reflect into infinity off the mirrored walls.

It's quite disconcerting seeing both of us at the same time, repeated over and over again into an eternal curve. I realise with a start that I'm the one who's firmly in control of this vision.

A small smile tugs at my lips. "I'm just glad there's peace and quiet, and we can talk without you throwing the kind of tantrum that would put a two-year-old to shame."

"I didn't ask for this to happen."

"Neither did I." I put down the cloth and lean over the bar counter so our faces are only inches apart.

He flinches and looks away, crossing his arms over his chest.

"What now, Ashton? You're now relegated to a sub-personality in your old *Kha*. I can destroy you if I want, but that would make me no better than the people who put both of us in this situation."

He faces me, his eyes boring into mine. "What the fuck are you? Your memories are...alien."

This catches me up short. It means he must be able to access my thoughts the same way I can dip into his, a disquieting realisation and even more reason that we need to come to some sort of an accord.

"What do you make of it?"

"I don't know."

"What do you want?" I ask him.

"I just want my life back."

"You know that isn't going to happen. This is the closest it's going to get to you having your life back. Through some bizarre accident of fate, we've been bound, you and I. There's no going back. There's no point fighting it." It must be horrible being a permanent passenger inside one's old body, able to perceive and feel and think what a dominant *Akh* does, but unable to do anything about it. And an *Akh* will always dominate an immature being. It's like a flea trying to move an elephant, as far as he's concerned.

Granted, I took a chance letting him in, being unprepared for the depth of his rage, but although he's always going to simmer beneath my *Akh*, I'm mostly certain he will stay there, beneath my thumb, unless I do something monumentally stupid. Just what exactly equates to monumentally stupid, I don't know yet, and it doesn't really bear consideration.

He looks so broken, genuinely contrite as he cradles his head in his hands. A surge of pity floods me. I may take drastic measures when I have to, but I'm not cruel.

"You can make this easier for yourself," I tell him. Ashton knows things about people and the present era I can access like I do with the Blessed memories. "I'll allow you more to the fore if you co-operate with me. Help me, and I won't keep you suppressed." That's taking a gamble, but I'd rather have him on my side than risk his later resurgence. "I've proven to you that I can force you to do my bidding whenever and however I want to. If you help me, and prove your use, I won't allow you to exist in this state." I gesture at my surroundings.

"Freak," he mutters, but wild hope gleams in his eyes when he looks at me.

I hold up my hand. "The moment I feel you're out of control, I'll push you back here. Understand?"

We stare at each other for a long time, a battle of wills. Ashton is the first to look away.

We shake hands on this. Whether this hare-brained arrangement of mine will work, I don't know. One thing is certain. I'll be watching him for one false move.

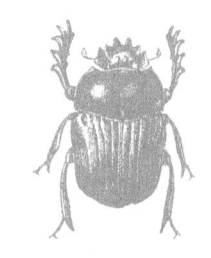

CHAPTER ELEVEN
A Scarab Pectoral

THE DREAM about Ashton ends, and I sit up in a room so shrouded in cloying darkness I don't at first know where I am. As my eyes adjust, the street lamps make two rectangles high against the wall that provide just enough light for me to see in the gloom.

Tentatively I prod inwards with my daimonic sense, much as one would test to see whether a fruit is ripe. The analogy makes me snort half in laughter. That alternate awareness is still there, and it stirs at my touch.

"*Are you going to make good on your word?*" Reproach is evident in Ashton's voice.

"Sweet Harwer." I fall back on the bed. He's still there, *in* me.

Dry laughter echoes in my mind, but I sense no anger in it. He's tired, spent.

"We'll see," I reply. "I will allow you to see what I

see, and hear. For now. We can share. But don't get any ideas of any more than that."

"*Fuck you.*"

His awareness brushes against mine, but I repel him. Instead I visualise my daimonic double opening its eyes and ears, two points of congruency for me and my angry ghost. "That's all I'm giving you, you bastard. One wrong turn, and I'll lock you in darkness. I won't even give you a simulacrum of a familiar place."

I don't pick up on any strong emotion, just a sense of relief. Pity for Ashton that I go back to sleep, so there's no exploring the world of matter for another few hours. I project the sense that it's not a good idea to disturb my rest, and sensibly, he backs off. But he's there. He agitates just beneath my skin.

A sharp pain in my chest and a crushing sense of loss have me gasping from my sleep shortly before dawn. If this was as the result of a dream, I can't say, but I can't get back to sleep. Instead I sit cross-legged on my bed, unable to shake the terrible sorrow that has tears rolling down my cheeks as I sob.

It's as if a bright light has been extinguished, something connected to me has passed from this world. I last felt something like this when Richard died. The sadness settles in my chest, and though I lie down again, I cannot sleep.

Ashton draws away from my inexplicable grief, his distaste for my show of emotion palpable, which doesn't help in the least. I am so *alone*, so very, very alone.

☥

"You're early," Lisa says when I arrive at The Event

Horizon shortly before lunch. Today her mostly blue dreads are bunched up on top of her head, so I assume she's had new extensions. It brings out the cornflower of her eyes.

I try my best smile, not sure it looks genuine. "I'm at odd ends today, not much to do, was wondering if I could start earlier, that's if you don't mind."

Lisa narrows her eyes and leans forward on the bar. "Are you okay? A problem with Marlise?"

"No problem." I could have called her, *should* have called her today, but I haven't. "Just moved into my new place and it's a real dump. Couldn't really deal with watching the roaches scrabble up the wall, and Marlise's busy, so I reckoned I'd come down here."

Lisa raises a brow. Clearly she doesn't believe me. "Sure, whatever. Reckon it's gonna be busy. There's a rugby match on at two, so we could probably use the extra hands."

"So long as I can keep myself occupied, that's fine. They could march a brass band through here so long as something's happening."

She shrugs, and I go drop my jacket in the broom closet in the fire escape that doubles as a staff office. The sorrow has tinged my day grey, leeching all my will. So what if I'm Inkarna? Right now I don't care. Or, if this is Ashton dragging me down into seeing life from his point of view, I'm too bummed to do anything proactive. Unaccountably I feel like smoking a cigarette, but that must be my angry ghost's impulse for comfort.

The weather outside the big arched windows matches my mood, with a steady sifting inundation. It is midday but already it's twilight. I bless the fact the rugby match draws its prerequisite crowd of bikers and backpackers, all seated happily cheek by jowl to cheer on their favourite team.

The venue's interior is soon muggy and beery, the noise level high enough to drown out the commentator. Gavin invested in a projector a while back, and the sports match glows on the white wall by the stage. If there's one thing where Ashton and I are in accordance, it's that rugby is possibly one of the most boring games ever invented, just a bunch of guys wearing tight shorts grappling at balls.

During another lifetime, in another era, Richard dragged me to a match while we were visiting in England. It was wet, cold and a score of men were running about on a field so muddy I couldn't tell who belonged to which team.

The shouting and rumble of voices are so overwhelming today I don't notice the old man with the brown suit until Ashton pricks at me.

"*Look. There. You know him, don't you?*" Bill.

The old gentleman stands by the far corner of the bar where the aquarium flashes with the *red-gold-red* of The Event Horizon's geriatric goldfish. He holds his hat, turning the brim while he stares directly at me. My stomach contorts, and for a terrible moment, I suffer the urge to vanish into the bathrooms so I can throw up.

The terrible sadness... Leo's messenger... How could I *not* have known? I have been in denial, haven't I?

I come out from behind the bar and stride to the old man. His eyes are red-rimmed and he swallows hard when I stop before him.

"Go outside?" Not sure if he heard me, I gesture for the front entrance.

He nods and follows me. We stand just by the door, sharing space with Viking, who looks none too pleased to be handling door duty on day where the heavens piss down nonstop. The din from inside fades to a tolerable ruckus, though my ears ring at the sudden shift to relative quiet.

Viking gives us the eyeball then crosses his massive arms over his chest. No one wants to mess with almost seven feet of muscle and attitude.

"What is it?" I ask my visitor.

Bill shakes his head and takes a crumpled kerchief out of his breast pocket, which he uses to noisily blow his nose. "She…" The man can't seem to bring himself to finish the sentence. His hands tremble.

I half-raise my hands because I want to shake his words out of him in case they aren't what I expect them to be. "What's happened to Leo?"

"She passed this morning." From the inside pocket of his jacket he retrieves a crumpled envelope. "She came to…see me last night, very late. She said— She said to give you this first thing today, no matter what happened."

My hand stops just before I take the proffered item. Leo knew all along, and she didn't say anything. It was purely by chance that we went to visit her. Lucky coincidence or my instincts as an Inkarna? She knew. She didn't tell me. At least not outright. And I suspected and hadn't done enough. A hot flush of anger courses through me only to fizzle out into that heavy sorrow. With a shake of my head, I accept the envelope. It contains an object of weight, and the slight clink of metal on metal raises all the hairs on my arms.

"She wanted you to have this," Bill says.

"Thank you." My voice is thick in my throat. The nausea contracts my stomach again, and I swallow hard, wiping at my eyes with the back of my wrist.

"I'll be going, then. Need to catch the trains before they become too dangerous." With those words, Bill turns. He opens a black umbrella and quickly vanishes down the road, his rapid strides belying his age.

Lisa frowns when she sees me coming back in. "You look like you've seen a ghost."

"In a way I have. Do you think you could spare me a cigarette?" If any circumstance requires a smoke, this is one event. Ashton fair wriggles within me at the prospect of subjecting this body to a nicotine rush.

"Thought you stopped." Lisa reaches below the counter and slides me a pack of Camel Blacks with a box of matches.

"I've just had some bad news." Smoking a cigarette is something Ashton would have done at a moment like this, and right now, anything that brings comfort to him is a better option than facing the full extent of the setback.

I'd wanted to meet with Leo again, to at least discuss strategy. It's too late now.

Back behind the bar, I stand pressed against the fridges and unfold the envelope, wincing at the tobacco taste and the oily smoke I draw into my lungs. I don't cough—testament to this *Kha*'s familiarity with the action.

Ashton Kennedy is printed in Leo's neat script in indelible marker. Although I already know what I'll find when I slit the envelope's flap, I nevertheless flinch when the winged scarab pendant falls into my palm. The metal is warm to the touch, still carrying the residual body heat from the old man. I turn the thing over to see *Nefretkheperi* inscribed after *Siptah*. It's up to me to have *Ankhakhet* added to this.

The tears want to come, but I blink them back. It

would do Ashton's reputation no good if I'm caught snivelling in public. I could stomp out into the rain and walk, for hours, in the downpour. My sensible self suggests it's better to stay busy here, among the beer-swilling throngs.

"You loved her very much, didn't you?" Ashton sounds mystified.

"You wouldn't understand."

Lisa turns to me. "Eh, did you say something?"

"Nothing," I mutter. I quickly fasten the chain around my neck and tuck the pendant beneath my T-shirt, where it clinks against Ashton's Anubis. It feels oddly familiar and incredibly comforting to have this touchstone of my previous existence against my skin. Another circle has been completed, with fresh current for the future—fresh current I'm not certain I'm ready to follow.

The rest of the afternoon spills into the evening, and I allow more of the old Ashton Kennedy to surface, to give him some enjoyment of work he knows so well. We're like a team of horses pulling the same carriage and, for once, it feels good to not have to be in control. From time to time I pause in my work, pushing Ashton back so I can touch the scarab pendant through the cloth. It's there, warm, pulsing almost with a life of its own.

⚱

Sunday dawns overcast and miserable. After my dawn adorations I dress as warmly as I can then set out for the train station. It bothers me that Marlise didn't come to The Event Horizon last night. It bothers me a lot more than I'd like to admit. With Ashton relegated very much to the back seat, I take over full awareness of the *Kha*, allowing him merely to see and hear.

"*You should get a motorcycle*," he tells me when I pay for a ticket out to Plumstead.

"Hell no," I say quietly, so the other people can't see me talking to myself.

The ride out is mercifully uneventful, save for the teams of beggars who seem to co-ordinate their turns on the train. A supposedly blind and rather overweight black woman is led by a young boy brandishing a tin cup. I reckon the few passengers this morning most likely give her coins to make her move on instead of having to listen to her plaintive wailing. Her voice is awful, high and reedy, and she can't hold a tune. Whatever hymn she belts out is relegated to an unrecognisable caterwauling. The young boy looks directly ahead, his expression wooden.

I shift to let them pass, wrinkling my nose at the stench of sweat and wood smoke. Within me, Ashton shrinks back from any accidental contact with the pair, but I tamp down his annoyance.

Perhaps it would have been better to call Marlise first, but I entertain discomforting visions of her either not answering when she sees an unknown Cape Town number, or putting the phone down on me when she realises who's speaking.

Some of the murkiness lifts by the time I step out at the station and, though yesterday's sorrow is mostly tucked away, I enjoy the walk. This *Kha*, despite the beating Ashton gave it with drugs and alcohol, is a marvel. I'd forgotten how it feels to be young again, to still believe I'm immortal. Functionally immortal, that is.

A rumble of discontent simmers below the surface. Ashton.

Marlise's mother answers the intercom when I buzz the house. "She's not home," the woman tells me.

It would take a bulldozer to get Marlise up on a Sunday morning. The woman is lying. It would be so pathetically easy to force the gate to open, but I refrain from doing so.

"I think you're not being truthful with me," I tell Marlise's mother. "She's still in her room."

"How dare you!" The connection dies.

"Bitch!" I say, and stop myself just in time from smashing the gate with my fist.

Closing my eyes, I reach with my daimonic senses, shivering at the eddy of power that now flows so much easier each time I employ it.

"Marlise, I'm outside," I whisper, visualising her curled up in her bed or reading a book. A slight pulling sensation at my temples suggests I've suceeded my sending. Whether Marlise hears is another matter.

"Her parents are full of shit," Ashton remarks drily. *"They used to pull these stunts all the time. You should just use your Jedi mind tricks to open the gate."*

"What, and get myself arrested? I'm not you."

He laughs, sending a burst of uncomfortable energy running down my spine. The spirit somehow offers a flash, some omnipresent viewpoint of me standing before the gate, annoyance written all over my face.

Not for the first time I wonder whether this union with my angry ghost is such a wise thing. A stab of my anger quietens him, and I turn, intent on walking back to the station.

I'm about to round the corner when Marlise calls my name. She's running down the road in only her pyjamas, her bare feet slapping on the tarmac.

"Ash! Ash! Don't go!"

A foolish grin creeps onto my lips, and I open my arms to envelop her. "So, you still talking to me? I thought I was in the dog box when you didn't call."

She smiles and looks up at me. "I will admit I was being a bit pissy, okay? I'm sorry. Besides, you could have called me."

"True. It's just been..."

Her smile fades. "What is it? I woke yesterday morning, and I was crying. I don't think I've ever felt so sad in my entire life. I phoned Leonora because I didn't have the number for Sunrise, but no one answered."

Crap.

I sigh, rubbing her back in small circular motions. "How do I..."

"It's Leo, isn't it?" Marlise's lower lip starts trembling. She knows.

I nod. "Let's not stand out here in the road. It'd be better if we go back to your room. There's something we need to do. We can mourn Leo later."

Marlise leans into me, and I refrain from commenting that she's out here in her nightclothes. Silent sobs wrack her frame, and all I can do is put my arm around her. She is so young, so vulnerable. It's unnerving that she's already so in tune with our connections as Inkarna. What have I done?

Although we don't meet her family on the way in, I can feel their stern disapproval through the windows. They're watching us, but I keep my gaze focused on what lies ahead. I won't dignify their hostility with any of my own. Ashton shifts, wanting to comment, but I clamp down hard, shoving him into the deepest recess I can find.

Marlise and I sit for a long while in her room. She

curls half her body onto my lap and I stroke her hair while she cries herself out. She cries for both of us. What tears I had dried long ago.

Fare thee well, Ankhakhet. I'll see you soon.

Presently, Marlise straightens, pushing errant tendrils from her face. Her eyes are puffy, the skin around them red. "Let me make some tea." Her hands on either side of my face, she kisses me lightly on the lips.

"At least go wash your face before you go in looking like I've been beating up on you."

She jumps up with a strangled cry of indignation. "You beast!" Marlise rushes into the bathroom, emitting a short shriek when she views herself in the mirror.

Laughter is the best response to tears. Despite the clinging sorrow, I still need to convince Marlise to take me to Noordhoek. I've given my next course of action some thought. I'll need to get into Kakapo Estate and find the house where the Van Vuurens reside. And, to do so, I'll need to employ those "Jedi mind tricks" I've been teased about again and again.

☥

"This is crazy," Marlise says.

We both stare at the gated estate, parked far enough down the road where I hope we won't awaken suspicion. My stomach roils, as though I've eaten something bad, but I need to do this thing. Marlise has the book Leonora gave her, a title published by House Pandora many years ago, detailing methods of psychic defence and shielding for beginners. I suspect she considers the book a talisman of sorts. I don't ask.

If it makes her feel somehow safer, then it's a good thing.

"I've got to do this."

"By just walking up in broad daylight and asking to be admitted? It's not going to work."

"Just because I haven't done this using this body before, doesn't mean I won't remember. Besides, I'm not getting any nose bleeds or darned headaches, which suggests I've settled in." I don't tell her about the other aspect of my plan, which involves letting Ashton loose. I spoke to him while Marlise was making us tea. While he didn't exactly agree to any of this, I pointed out our continued survival depended on his co-operation, hinting that I could lock him so far away he might as well have been sunk in the Sea of Nun.

He crackles below the surface, like a current in a seemingly placid ocean. And I can feel what he's been doing, slowly siphoning energy from the world around us, building and growing until my entire body feels too tight. Like me, he's becoming stronger.

Marlise reaches for my hand, squeezing hard, her eyes mirroring the concern prickling at my awareness. Despite the day's gloom, everything feels too bright. "Be careful."

"You, too," I tell her. "If anyone approaches you, I want you to drive off. Go drink coffee at the mall or something. I'll find you."

"And if you don't?"

"Go home. Forget about me."

Her expression is pained. "What about House Adamastor?"

"Then the House fails until they send someone to replace me. Study. Meditate."

"You're not expendable."

"Yes, I am." We stare at each other for a while, and I swallow hard, drinking in her face. I kiss her softly then press her against me. "I'll be fine. Really. They don't know who to look for." How I crave for a time when we don't have to keep glancing over our shoulders.

Getting out of the car is possibly one of the most difficult things I've had to do this entire day. I don't look back. Instead I breathe deeply, drawing on my daimonic self amplified by my angry ghost's writhing.

Ashton is frightened when he sees the extent of the forces at my command. While he can tap into the material world and steal, vampire-like, my powers goes deeper, to the earth, from the sun—not just from the electrical wires and the wind, the slow growth of the poplars bending in the wind. Given time, I'm certain I can reach all the way to the Tuat, like the elders.

"Do exactly what I tell you," I say to him, my voice low.

"*You're going to get this body killed.*"

"I won't."

"*I can tell when you're lying.*"

"Well, obey me, and that won't happen."

We reach the gate, the wind whipping my hair loose from its ponytail. The man seated in the glorified security shed looks up from the western novel he's reading. Not the best at his job if he's distracted from his duties by visions of lone rangers on silver steeds.

Hastily he shoves the book behind his chair and rises. An older man, in his fifties, I estimate. A subtle shift of perception pulls at my awareness when I quest out, a tightness at my temples. My daimonic self brushes against the man's mind. He is cold and bored, has been thinking about what he'll have for lunch soon and whether he should have coffee or tea.

"Good day, sir," I say. "I've an appointment to see Mr Van Vuuren."

The man's eyes become glazed when I apply pressure, imagining him seeing Leonora's messenger instead of a six foot something thug dressed completely in black. The last time I'd tried this kind of influence had been in the early 1960s, when I'd tangled with a particularly annoying spy from House Montu and his human associates.

For a moment I suspect this won't work, but the security guard nods. A nasty, wriggly pain begins in the back of my sinuses, and I pray I'm not overtaxing my abilities.

"You... Have an appointment with Mr Van Vuuren," the man parrots.

"Correct. You don't need to call him. He is expecting me. You will forget I was ever here."

"I will forget..."

"What are the directions to his house?"

"Twenty-two Protea Drive."

"Go make yourself tea."

The man shuffles around, a sleepwalker.

Smiling grimly to myself, I continue through the pedestrian entrance. The smile becomes a grinding of teeth as my head throbs with the release of energy, and when I wipe at what feels like moisture from my right nostril, there's a light smear of blood. Not a lot, but enough to warn me to go slow.

"*You gotta teach me to do that*," Ash remarks.

"I'm sure you'll pick up tips," I say. "But you've got work to do now. We can talk about some sort of reward if we survive this encounter."

He doesn't reply, but his keen anticipation is clear. He flashes me a vision of Marlise writhing beneath me, my cock hard as I thrust into her.

Annoyed, I push that thought away. "You need to scout ahead. I need an idea where Protea Drive is situated." Now's not the time to worry about Ashton's escape biting me in the rear. I have something he wants. I loosen the connection between us, pushing the old Ashton Kennedy from the *Kha*. He releases with a soft sigh, and I'm alone in my mind. A gust hits me at that precise moment, bringing with it cold droplets from the low-hanging clouds.

The pictures I remember from the website about Kakapo Estate suggest the Van Vuurens live near the top. There were tall date palms in that photograph, and I scan the area. Right on the mark, the trees are a few blocks farther. The estate is rather lovely, I have to admit. All the roads are cobbled in uniform grey, the terraced gardens perfectly manicured and consisting mostly of a collection of indigenous cone bushes, heaths, pincushions and proteas interspersed with a few silver trees nodding in the wind. The houses are all large, built mostly in a mock Cape Dutch style with its characteristic white gables, only most of them are double-storey, with far more plate glass windows than a traditional architect would allow.

Such cars that I do see parked in driveways are the usual gamut of expensive German brands. I don't want anyone taking note of my walking along their roads, so I wrap my *Kha* in a sense of *I'm not here— it's only a quirk of the light.* It's one of the first real uses of daimonic power House Adamastor teaches. How best to convince one's enemies there's no threat? The threat simply is not there.

This doesn't fool the dogs. I get barked at by a range of breeds, from Huskies to Great Danes. Once or twice puzzled owners emerge to squint out over their yards, but by then I'm already past.

"You need to take a right quite soon," Ashton whispers.

I follow his directions. It would appear that the increase in elevation also results in houses that are far more splendid than their brethren downslope. Number twenty-two is built on three successive tiers, with imposing Grecian columns on its veranda and a king's ransom in quiver trees out front that I assume must have been freighted in from the arid Northern Cape. How they survive our wet Western Cape winters is beyond me.

The property also has a six-foot wall topped with spikes. Despite its situation in a secure, gated neighbourhood, Christopher van Vuuren is security conscious to anal degrees. I pause for a few minutes, making the effort to draw harder on my daimonic self. No one must see me now, and it is difficult maintaining this level of concentration for long.

"Is there anyone inside?" I ask Ashton quietly.

For a moment I think he won't answer, and I worry at the obvious absence of his regard, that prickling sensation I have when I feel I'm being watched but can't see the observer. My palms are damp, and I wipe them on my jeans.

Just when I'm about to try my hand at breaking and entering blindly, Ashton's clammy awareness brushes up against mine and I have to repress a shudder. *"There's a forty-something-ish woman who's working on a computer in her study. She's writing something while listening to some classical crap. That's a window to the left from where you're standing. Other than that, there's a young girl in a playroom at the back of the house. I wouldn't worry about the black woman in the maid's quarters. She's watching soaps. Looks like she's off duty. Cleaning staff.*"

"No sign of Christopher?" I project an image of the father.

"*Nothing.*"

"Good. I need you to remain aware of the comings and goings. If you see that man, or anyone else, for that matter, warn me."

"*What makes you think the girl will talk to you?*"

"If she's Inkarna, she will." At least I hope she's Inkarna.

Ashton's presence evaporates, leaving me once again on my own. It's quite simple breaking into the pedestrian gate. The lock snicks open at the slightest prompt. We never used to be able to do this so easily in the past with purely mechanical access points. Maintaining a strong sense of *not-being-here*, I dash up the stairs, taking great pains to tread lightly. I may be all but invisible to those who are aware, but any incidental sounds I make will most certainly be audible. People won't know to look for me unless they have some clue I'm there.

The back area of the house is paved in smooth yellow travertine, and is more a narrow passage, because the residence is cut into the mountainside. A thick bank of ferns spills over into this area. The back door is unlocked—so much for all the precautions—and it doesn't take much effort to prompt the security gate to click open.

I'm in a joint scullery and laundry area, all the appliances matching in darkened stainless steel hues, giving me the impression that I've dropped into a space-age setting. The adjoining kitchen is larger than Marlise's bedroom and bathroom combined, all the surfaces finished with black granite and equally intimidating appliances, if I consider the humble stove-top ovens Lizzie used during the 1960s.

"*Down this passage,*" Ashton prompts when I exit the kitchen. "*Her door's open. I suggest knocking.*"

One of Mahler's symphonies wafts up from the stairs leading down to what I assume to be the living areas, where Catherine's mom is surfing the net or chatting online. What the hell am I going to say to an eight-year-old girl without scaring her half to death? Should I find some way to incapacitate her and carry her out? What if Catherine isn't Inkarna?

And if she is? What then? What if she's not House Adamastor but House Montu?

I've gone all cold, my stomach churning so much I don't know if I want to go take a shit or vomit, what with the cold sweat trickling down my brow and no doubt making my T-shirt's armpits damp while I hesitate outside the girl's door.

In the end, Catherine is the one who forces my hand. "Is that you, Cynthia?" she calls out, her voice girlish and sweet, which sends another cold spike of terror down my spine. How on earth will she react to seeing a guy framed in the door leading to her playroom? I'm not Lizzie, not some mild old granny who *looks* harmless, but isn't.

I steel myself then step into the doorway, affecting nonchalance by leaning against the frame. "Catherine van Vuuren, do you care to explain why I didn't reincarnate in your *Kha* five years ago?" I may as well take the proverbial bull by the horns.

For an eight-year-old, she's remarkably young-looking, her white-blond hair cut into a sharp-pointed bob framing a heart-shaped face. Eyes like cut emeralds return my stare, a few golden freckles sprinkled across her cheeks.

Her mouth drops open for only a moment before she regains her composure and draws herself up from the heavy leather-bound tome she's reading while sitting cross-legged on a scattering of multi-coloured cushions—bright, cheerful colours contrasting with the sombre tones of her clothing.

"*Neffie?*"

That one word slices right through me and I drop to my knees. Only Meritiset called me by that shortening of my *Ren*.

"Merry? What's happened?"

We stare at each other for an eternity of silence. Catherine's eyes go all glazed for a moment, as though the memories are too much, until she speaks. "There was a complication..."

My chest tight, I rise to my feet on shaky knees. "What sort of complication?"

Her gaze is pitying. "House Montu..." she whispers. Something's wrong.

An arm snakes around my neck and I am thrown against the wall, all the breath knocked out of me. Bright sparks fill my field of vision.

"*Nefretkheperi!*" Ashton yells.

"Wha—" I croak. For some reason I'm lying on the floor, the carpet gritty with sand grains pressing into my cheek.

"*I'm so sorry, I misjudged...*" He flashes me an image of the supposed maid rising, as if to a silent summons, and stalking out her room. "*I didn't realise until...*" Until she was almost upon me.

I gaze up into the face of the black woman Ash mentioned earlier. She's no cleaning lady or cook. Her hair is braided and falls medusa-like to her shoulders, and her eyes are far too alert. For her size she packs a considerable amount of strength. My daimonic self crackles, questing outwards to meet my assailant's signature: initiate. Thank goodness only an initiate.

The only problem is I'm at her mercy, and she kicks me the moment I try to rise, hard, making it all but impossible to draw breath or think straight.

"Wha—*ooof*!" Another crack to the ribs has me curled into a foetal position.

Dimly I'm aware of Catherine rising, small pink sneakers padding on the floor until she stands by my face. "Oh, Neffie, you disappoint me."

"What. Is..."

"I underestimated you all along. Anyone else would have had the good sense to stay hidden."

"I need to know what's going on." I claw at reality through the haze of pain. Something warm and sticky tickles my left nostril and drips salt into my mouth.

She kneels before me to peer into my eyes, her expression so innocent I want to curl up and die from my stupidity. The betrayal's wound has yet to register fully, a rusty blade that will still be twisted again and again. "Oh, my dear Neffie, don't you know? Haven't you been paying *any* attention? But I must commend you. The remaining Adamastor initiate has proved most wily." Her smile is chilling. "I'm enjoying the challenge."

She doesn't know Leonora's identity, that Leonora is full Inkarna. Or that she's passed. It's incredibly difficult to not let my relief show. "What have you *done*?"

Catherine sighs, her expression that of studied boredom. She stands and snaps her fingers. "Get him to his feet, Cynthia. Keep him from making any trouble."

The woman hauls me into a standing position. Still dazed, I lean against the wall, watching the pint-sized terror study me.

"How unfortunate. I'd at least have considered that you'd choose a more appropriate *Kha*."

"I didn't have a choice," I say through gritted teeth. "You try five years drowning in the Sea of Nun and you take what you get."

"I should have had you cast deeper. No matter. I must thank you for this opportunity to cut all House Adamastor's games short. Where is *The Book of Ammit*?"

Talk of cutting to the chase. I keep my expression neutral. "The book of what?"

The child flies at me so quickly I don't have a chance to flinch. In fact, Cynthia braces me so I take the full brunt of the girl's punch, straight to the groin. The pain blossoms from my loins upward, making it impossible to breathe as I double up in an attempt to contain the agony.

Cynthia chuckles then says something in isiXhosa that sounds vaguely insulting.

"Ash, what the fuck?" I manage beneath my breath. He's betrayed me in all this as well. What if he's in cahoots with Catherine? I've been foolish trusting anyone in House matters.

"*Talk kak, idiot*," he replies. "*Double-crossing lying bitch.*" His hatred for the girl surprises me with its intensity, a wave of pure loathing that washes over the room from a point directly above my crown.

"Then do something," I say quietly.

"What are you muttering about, Neffie?" The cold, calculated cruelty in Catherine's voice stuns me.

"You've betrayed the House."

"Which House?"

A flood of memories assails me, of times Meritiset told me of her life with Siptah during Elizabeth's reign, of meeting Dr John Dee and getting to grips with his angelic script, of moonlit trysts, of madrigals and magick with a K.

I wasn't Siptah's first love. That much I discovered when I passed through the Black Gate into Per Ankh the first time. It always struck me as odd that Meritiset had taken my arrival so calmly, without any rancour for having been his partner during the twentieth century. I'd thought I could name her *friend*.

"What did you do with Siptah?" This turn in questioning from her is surprising. She had ample opportunity to ask me this in Per Ankh. Why did she hide behind a mask of sisterhood then?

Cynthia's fingers maintain their squeeze on those pressure points, and I struggle to speak. "I didn't do anything with Siptah. Why bother with this now when we established that I was not guilty of any crime when I appeared before the council in Per Ankh?" That meeting had been so tense. For a long time I'd thought I'd be outcast, forced to wander the Tuat without a place of safety, at the mercy of the bigger Houses who could enslave me.

Still doubled over, I look up into her face. We're at eye level. There's nothing young or girlish about her expression now. Slowly I straighten, Cynthia moving to accommodate my motion. Please let them not aim for further physical damage. The way Cynthia has my arms pinned back at an unnatural angle suggests she could snap bones with little effort. The buzz of power through her tells me she's on the verge of coming into being as a full-blown Inkarna.

"*The Book of Ammit the Devourer*, Nef. I don't

believe you don't know where it is. Siptah knew, and he's gone. Where has your other initiate been hiding these past few years?"

"I can't tell you," I say. "I couldn't find her."

"You're lying. You always were a useless liar." She nods at Cynthia.

"*Asssh*," I hiss as Cynthia digs a finger into a fresh pressure point that sends a blaze of agony spilling from my arm down to my feet. What's keeping the spook? I can't think straight for the pain, and if I can't gain my composure I can't gather my daimonic self enough to lash out.

As if on cue, the lights start flickering, and a subtle hum begins right on the edge of my hearing. The temperature in the room plunges so quickly my breath mists before my face.

Catherine twists her head this way and that, craning her neck to see something that, technically speaking, isn't truly there.

"*You're going to owe me for this, motherfucker,*" Ash says. "*This is going to hurt me more than it will hurt you.*"

Cynthia's death grip on me doesn't slacken, and she does something horrid with her daimonic powers. Half-cocked as she is, she sends short bursts of static through me. I can only compare it to being electrocuted—once, twice, three times, until I'm bent at the waist again, a terrible whining starting, building with intense pressure in my skull. It's impossible to figure out whether Ashton is responsible for some of this phenomenon or if it's Cynthia's special brand of torture.

Catherine gives a small scream, beating at me with her fists, striking indiscriminately at my bowed head, chest and arms. "Make it stop! Make it stop!" A waft of her panic reaches me through the haze. I need to run, get the hell out of here.

That's the problem of starting out young: the insecurities, of not having grown into one's full powers. Granted, it's been hellishly uncomfortable coming into Inkarna powers in an already-adult body, but a child's would mature with the fresh *Akh*. I don't want to know how powerful Catherine will be by the time she reaches her majority.

The stench of ozone fills the air and fresh blood trickles down my nose. Ashton's drawing on my daimonic essence to fuel his slowly growing vortex of power centred round me. The power coils, a deliberate movement adding to the dawning horror of the coming release.

"Ashton?" He's going to blow himself into shreds of aether.

As if with the explosion of a small thermonuclear device, I'm flung across the room, Cynthia's fingers sliding from contact.

"*Run!*" Ashton wails at me. He sounds very far away. "*You don't have much ti—*"

Like a drunkard I stumble out of the room, away from the prone bodies of Catherine and Cynthia. Whatever psychic attack Ashton orchestrated, I was at its epicentre, and although dazed, I'm perfectly capable of escape, though my limbs don't quite obey my intentions. My ears ring, and I fight against the double vision swamping my eyes.

A woman calls from downstairs as I dash down the passage. I don't stop to find out how dangerous Mrs Van Vuuren is. Mercifully, the back door is open, the security gate swinging on its hinges. I pelt down the back of the house, down the terraced stairs to the front gate. Without bothering with my daimonic powers, I spend a handful of agonising seconds looking for the gate's release button, which I eventually find on a pillar near the exit.

The barrier clicks open, and I run, hardly caring who sees me at this point in my mad rush out. Please, oh, please, let Marlise be there when I escape this benighted place. The neighbourhood canines don't even have a chance to register my passing as my boots thud hard on the cobbles. The insane yammering starts after the fact, while my breath sears pure fire through my lungs. Any moment now my *Kha* will just seize up, and I'll collapse like so much meat on the cobblestones.

Only once I reach the main access control point do I slow, my lungs contracting painfully with each inhalation. With great effort I draw upon my *I'm-not-here* state, and even while I walk, I'm not certain whether my ruse will function, not after the massive expenditure of earlier.

To my gratification, the gate guard doesn't look up when I trot through the pedestrian gate. He has his nose buried in his western novel, most likely expecting trouble to approach, not leave the estate.

Every moment now I expect to hear shouts ring out behind me, but I've only the low mourning of the wind shaking the trees as accompaniment, the beefwoods lining the road slithering and fretting.

Marlise is bent over her book, her lips moving slightly as she reads. She starts, and almost drops the book when I rap on the glass, hopping from foot to foot. "Open! Let's get the fuck out of here!"

She complies, reaching over to pop up the doorknob, her concern at my appearance clear from her expression. "What happened to you?"

"Just drive!" I fall into the passenger seat, scanning

the top of the road for any sign of pursuit.

Something in my bearing succeeds in communicating my extreme urgency in getting the hell out of here because she twists the key hard in the ignition, the car jerking into gear the moment the engine roars into life. She pulls a hard U-turn, and we careen down the road.

Only once we're on Ou Kaapseweg does Marlise ask, "So, what's happening?"

I keep looking back, checking for any cars racing to catch up with us. Nothing. Satisfied for now, I straighten in my seat. "It's worse than I thought."

"What is?"

"We've been betrayed by one of our own." Even as I say the words they seem unreal.

"Who's betrayed you?"

"Someone I thought was my... A friend."

"What are we going to do?"

"I don't know. I need to get cleaned up. We need to go into hiding, preferably where they won't think to look. There's a chance they may trace your car back to your parents' house. I want you to come stay with me at Sunrise for a while."

"Ash, that place is—"

"It's terrible, I know. But you're going to leave your car at your parents' house, and you're coming to stay with me. You haven't told them where I live, have you?"

"No."

"Good." On a whim I flip down the shade on the passenger side and glare at myself in the mirror. Good gods. I really do look like I've been worked over well by someone with a unique understanding of how to cause pain. My skin is pale, the day-old stubble dark, and the blood streaks its crimson gore over my lips and down my chin. Ashton's eyes are wide and staring, the eyes of a madman.

"Why would one of your own betray the House?"

"She never was all that popular. Siptah brought her into the fold after finding her sometime during Queen Elizabeth's reign. Meritiset came to House Adamastor with almost all her Inkarna abilities intact, without having been mentored by anyone or belonging to another House. It's rare, but it happens from time to time, I'm told."

"What if she already had been with another House?" Marlise asked.

"It's possible. At the time House Adamastor was a part of House Alba, one of the main Houses of the British Isles. We broke away suddenly during the late seventeen hundreds, quite abruptly, apparently. The House has remained almost invisible since then. Now I know why."

Although Marlise pesters me to share more, I refuse to tell her. The less she knows, the safer she is. It makes sense. An elder Inkarna of House Adamastor had possibly gained *The Book of Ammit* then already, and had sought sanctuary as far as possible from the heart of intrigue. What better place than a far-flung European colony at the tip of Africa?

I wait in the car while Marlise goes inside to talk to her parents, informing them she's just found out about a weeklong outing for her class and that a friend's picking her up. It's a load of bullshit, but we can't think of any better reason of why she needs to vanish. When she returns with a damp towel for me to wipe the blood from my face, we lock the Toyota and start walking to the train station. She's packed herself a small backpack, which I pry from her fingers and sling over my shoulder.

Her face is tight with fear, and she maintains a death grip on my hand. "What would they do to us?"

"Whatever they'd do, it'd involve a lot of pain." Where do I even start?

"But what can we do?"

"I don't know yet. I'm thinking we need to lie low for a bit. They don't know who I am, yet, apart from who I used to be. We need to get out of Cape Town with that thing."

"The artefact?"

"I need to help you forget about it."

She looks up at me. "Is that possible?"

"To a degree. It's impossible to make you forget completely, but we can lock that memory away or disguise it with something else. That book Leo gave you?"

"Yes?"

"I want you to study and practice the techniques in there. They're basic but important. They'll offer some protection. They will come for us, of that I have no doubt."

Am I even doing the right thing, though? What are the chances that I'm being overly paranoid? No one would have thought to take a second glance at Marlise's car parked down the road. Or maybe they have cameras facing the approach to the gate I wasn't aware of. That's just the point. I don't know. I have nowhere to turn to.

Any way I look at the situation, Marlise is a weak point. They can use her to get at me. If House Montu is worth half its salt, they'd have traced Marlise right now, even if they didn't have the number plate. There are only so many Toyota Tazzes in Cape Town, especially ones with such idiosyncratic paintwork. Even now they could be running searches. My stomach contracts at the thought.

"We need to leave the city," I say.

"Ash, we can't. You're talking like a crazy person."

"You don't understand. It's not a case of 'can't'. It's a case of 'have to'."

"That's madness! I'm right in the middle of my practical exams. I'll be starting at a playschool in Gardens soon. I can't leave now."

"What don't you understand about 'we're in deep shit,' Marlise?" I glare at her for a second but keep our pace relentless. "You don't know what we're up against. We're talking one of the big militant Houses that can trace their lineage back to the Eighteenth Dynasty pharaohs. We're talking a global network that dates back not hundreds, but thousands of years. Some of these guys have been knocking around since before Jesus Christ was even a figment of the Christian imagination."

She laughs. "You make it sound like the Illuminati or something."

"These guys make the Illuminati look like toddlers. This is the real thing, not something cooked up by some so-called guru addled on LSD."

"What are we going to live on?"

"I don't know, but I will continue with what House Adamastor stands for, which is remaining as unobtrusive as possible. I just wish I didn't drag you down with me today. I've been really stupid about this."

Marlise stops dead in her tracks, a gasp escaping her. "What am I going to tell my parents after a week has passed?"

Sorely tempted to yank her down the road as though she were a child, I stop and turn, fixing her with what I hope to be the most penetrating stare I can muster. "If you contact your parents, we are both as good as dead. And so are your parents."

Her bottom lip quivers. "But I didn't say goodbye to my brothers…"

I feel like saying, *Well that's too bad*, but I stop myself. "It's not safe. Not for us, not for your family. We're going to leave Cape Town, *both* of us, because I don't want them to hurt you. And they will use you to get at me. I'm not such a heartless bastard that I'll just walk away from you. I know of a place where we may be welcome." At least I hope the Wareing family is still in existence. I'd encountered one of their Blessed Dead once, and the white-haired witch clan seems a slender hope. I purposefully keep the pertinent information from Marlise. Just in case.

In case of what?

The idea that we might be captured and tortured stings. I have some confidence in my own abilities, but Marlise…

"I don't like all these maybes, Ashton." She only ever calls me by my full name when she's pissed off with me. Her nostrils flare slightly, making her look ridiculous.

I tug at her hand and start walking, half-yanking her off her feet. "We must hurry."

"Ashton!" Marlise gives the slightest bit of resistance then stumbles after me, almost tripping.

Backward and forward we argue until we reach the station, where a sullen mother with two kids under the age of five shoots us death glares. Marlise is momentarily distracted by the children, and I'm glad for the relative peace as she engages the mother in conversation. She's adept at chipping away at people's ice, and I watch Marlise with half a smirk. Right now I've got a short reprieve before we no doubt start arguing again. The woman's like a bloody pit bull when she wants to be.

What would she be like if she were to come into full Inkarna powers? She isn't conscious of her power, of disarming people by seeming naive.

While we wait for the train, and the sun sinks lower behind its thick bank of cloud, I consider my angry ghost. Where is he? Has he inadvertently destroyed himself through a massive act of self-sacrifice? That definitely isn't his style. Perhaps he, too, needs time to gather his strength after creating a physical manifestation.

The Inkarna in Per Ankh can't punch through to the material realms without some massive expenditure of power, hence the dubious honour of being elected to go through, carrying all the hopes and dreams of the disembodied ones for the next generation.

What happened that day in Per Ankh? There had been talk of sending another, an Inkarna by the name of Besnakt, a taciturn elder who'd never had much to do with me. To say he'd ignored me would be too kind. He *unsaw* me. But the elders had been in many meetings. It was decided that Besnakt had been in isolation for far too long. Although powerful, he kept himself apart even from trawling the Blessed Dead for news of contemporary affairs.

How they settled on me only Apep knows. Meritiset had been the one swaying the council, I'm sure. For her own ends, no doubt, because there was no way in hell they would let her return. Some of the elders had been watching her closely.

I fought long and hard for you, she'd told me. *Only you will have the most up-to-date knowledge of the times. And it is only right that you solve this mystery.*

Oh, that I should have seen the barbs in her words then. Me, relatively inexperienced, making that first dangerous journey through the Sea of Nun, to be reborn in a new *Kha*. What a travesty. And that she had rushed me, come to my sanctuary to all but chase me to the Opal Gate. She must have followed after, using her greater knowledge to somehow shove me aside, sinking me in the Sea of Nun where she'd surely expected me to languish for aeons due to my inexperience.

The horrors of limbo return to me, the endless miasma of Nun, of no form, of no sensation. A terrible fear clutches at me, and I moan softly.

Marlise turns to me, frowning. "What is it?"

"I'm remembering something horrid, that's all."

Expecting her to turn back to her conversation with the woman, I'm nonetheless gratified when she slips her hand into mine before she natters on to the stranger.

While we ride the rest of the way to town, I try to keep my thoughts positive. We escaped Kakapo Estate. That is a good thing. We've made it this far, one of many slipped into the nameless throngs. It's headed towards early evening. After a good night's sleep we can pick up and make a dash for it first thing in the morning. I don't have much in the way of money, but we can hitchhike.

I curse the fact that I've not yet been contacted by Leonora's attorneys; they'll have Marlise's cell phone number. But it's a device we'll have to get rid of... Damn, damn and damn again. I don't have their details, either. None of this is going to be easy. What of the stele? Should I leave it where it is? Perhaps. Rather let House Montu think we've run with the thing than drag it with us halfway across the country.

They'd never think to look in Boomslang cave, unless they catch either of us.

So much plagues me, and I'm tired and bloody relieved when we arrive at Cape Town station. This late in the day the place is almost deserted, crisp packets skittering in the disconsolate wind that raises eddies of chill air.

Marlise has mercifully lapsed into silence, and she fits perfectly in the crook of my arm as we make our way through a dead city centre. The few people we encounter hurry past. Above, pigeons flap to roost in eaves, their wings clapping loudly in the stillness. Today Cape Town looks tired and dirty, most of her storefronts covered by heavy metal grilles.

No one gives us any trouble, but then I wouldn't expect that. The security cameras posted at intervals maintain their vigilance. It would be so like Montu to own shares in the company that supplies these to City of Cape Town. Where else do they have fingers in pies?

They could be watching us now, marking our progress. My gut twists at that thought.

I'd like to think I'm being silly. After all, they don't know this *Akh*'s name. They don't know where he stays. But how long before they do? It won't take much of a stretch of an imagination to start asking around alternative clubs or poking around assorted social networking sites featuring subculture haunts. After all, Ashton used to play in a reasonably popular band. Ask enough questions, and I'd be easy to find.

And if I can think of these avenues of investigation, it won't take Catherine all that long to jump to the same conclusions. Either way, my whereabouts will come out.

It being Sunday, however, The Event Horizon is

closed, so ostensibly they'd get round to dropping by there only by tomorrow. We have so little time, and a knot of constriction tightens around my throat.

Marlise buys us each a box of noodles for supper from the Asian place near Sunrise Lodge. We sit in gloomy silence in the dank chamber I now call home, eating while listening to the incidental sounds of the other inhabitants.

Voices ring out in the passages, and it is difficult discerning from where exactly people are calling to each other in this warren. Marlise hunches over her meal, her eyes darting from corner to corner, as though she expects a spectre to appear out of thin air.

Then again, after all the drama of the past few days, I don't blame her for coming across so hunted. It's not likely to become easier, either. She seems to be under the impression that we'll hide out here for a few days before returning to normal. There is no comfortable normal anymore.

"Ash," she says. "I'm cold."

Tonight may be the last night we'll know any peace, and I draw Marlise to me, revelling in the softness of her body. She shivers at my touch, slipping cold hands beneath my shirt. We don't need words right now. Words just get in the way, leading to discord and, with so much amiss with our lives at present, this physical closeness is a communion of sorts to ease some of the horrors.

Her lips are soft, and I taste them, probing with my tongue then planting small kisses down her jaw line so I can nuzzle at her neck, breathing in that underlying mint scent I've come to associate with her.

She teases my nipples with her chilly fingers, tugging at the rings piercing the sensitive skin before trailing down my belly, stroking with one hand the hardness of my phallus, which is already straining against the denim.

We push into each other, but the cold keeps us fully clothed during most of this desperate dance of flesh. I can never get enough of the fullness of her breasts, so soft, the flesh so pliant in my grasp. And I love the way she moans softly in the back of her throat when I run my thumbs over her nipples, which I tease erect before squeezing hard, rolling them between finger and thumb.

Her thighs grasping mine are a particular brand of hell, and though I want to finish this and gain my satisfaction, I hold back. The sweetest pleasure is the one that is withheld until the final moment, when one cannot conceptualise lasting one minute longer without giving in to the impulse.

I find that sweet spot at the apex of her legs, that secret moist cleft that invites me in, and I sink my fingers between the folds, rubbing at the nub. Oh, how glorious it would be to sink in my entire length, feeling that tight passage clench around me, but not yet. Marlise's scent is a delicious musk, all but driving me insane with the need to touch, taste and explore.

I enter her with two fingers, feeling the way she contracts at my intrusion. Wildly she clasps at my shaft, trying to unfasten the jeans one-handed, the nails of the other digging into my upper arm. Her hips grinding at me are too much. With a groan I raise myself onto my knees so I can unzip and release myself from the constraints of clothing.

Marlise's eyes glitter in the dim light and she reaches for me. "Come, put it in. I want you inside me." She spreads her legs, revealing herself to me in a way she knows I can't resist.

She is so warm, so wet and tight, and her muscles

squeeze pleasantly tight around my shaft when I enter her. Again and again I thrust, every instance building a fierce need to drive in harder and harder. Her legs wrapped around my waist, Marlise raises her hips, deepening her passage and shifting the angle to increase the pressure.

There is something so peculiar and so devastatingly sexy about feeling where my phallus enters her, pulling out far enough to have the head poised outside her opening before I ease myself back in. All the while I massage her clitoris, feeling how she rises to meet me, faster and more frantic.

And when I spill my seed in her, it is as though all my essence flows into her, the other half of this magical union, to create a sense of oneness. We can take on the entire world, the two of us together. Nothing can stop us. We are two halves of one. With a few final, shuddering thrusts, it ends, and we lie still for a while, a tangle of limbs and half-shed clothing.

Marlise's face is pressed to my neck, her breath tickling the skin and her fingers coiling through my hair. We could lie here for an eternity, but the moment can't last forever.

"Ash?"

"Mmm?"

"Where's the nearest bathroom in this place?"

I groan, burying my face in my pillow, which is liberally strewn with her hair. She shifts beneath me, pushing me off her so she can sit up. Wordlessly I pass her some tissues. I should have used a condom, but we don't discuss this as we straighten our clothing. I haven't asked her if she's on the pill, during all this time we've been together. The guilt nags at me. Surely Marlise isn't stupid enough to... Uncomfortably I recall Ash's times with Isabelle. He never bothered asking either, and see where that got him. Those memories with that woman, and more than a few others, crowd me. Strange faces and experiences tumbling over each other like a river over stones.

I shove these thoughts aside and go with Marlise down to the communal bathroom. The lights here don't work, and the only illumination comes from outside, the streetlights' glow filtered through thrashing tree limbs outside.

I glare at the wild man in the mirror, his hair loose and falling in ragged black skeins on either side of a too-pale face. How easy it is to have slipped into this other life. Did someone reckless always hide beneath Lizzie's prim exterior? That other life exists like a storybook I read a long, long time ago, that has little bearing on the present.

A gleam in the passage catches my eye, a pale figure that shivers into existence—a carbon copy of the *Kha* I inhabit. Ashton.

I step out of the bathroom, towards him. Behind me Marlise starts running the shower, the plumbing groaning as the water spews in bursts through the ancient pipes. Ashton is almost transparent, his appearance an idealised version of him in his heyday. Not this burnt-out wreck I am now.

"*What's it like?*" he asks.

"What?"

"*Screwing a woman when you were a woman in your past life.*" He sounds almost wistful.

"I- I don't know. I guess I don't really think about it anymore. I've grown used to having this *Kha*." Nevertheless, I rub at my arms, half-stunned by this realisation. And it's true. I haven't really given inhabiting a man's body much thought of late. Much like one would wear in a shoe, I've grown comfortable wearing this *Kha*. If the shoe fits...

Ashton flashes me a wicked leer. *"I'd bet you didn't expect to see me again."*

"I'd wondered. I did worry." I hadn't wondered nearly enough, but I keep that thought buried deeply.

"You'd hoped, hadn't you? You can't lie to me. I know you haven't given me much thought since I blew myself to yesterday."

I lean my head against the door frame, feeling how the splintery wood rubs off against my skin. If it weren't for Ashton, I would still be in House Montu's clutches, or worse. *Go back to go the beginning, do not collect...* "Thank you." And I do mean those two simple words.

Ashton whispers through me, into me like a cold wash of water. He says nothing, but I can pick up on his spidery sense of relief, lodged in flesh again, albeit as a passenger. On a daimonic level, something snicks into place, some sort of rightness...wholeness. Ma'at could not have foreseen such a peculiar association.

Sometimes it's better not to question too hard. This day has been fraught with danger, and the body is tired, the mind unwilling to puzzle through all the loose ends and half-formed, dog-eared thoughts. Tomorrow will bring its own troubles.

Presently Marlise exits the shower, once again dressed in the clothing she wore earlier, drying her hair with the towel. "Are you okay? You look, dunno..."

"Like I've seen a ghost?" I laugh at my own joke. It's better not to bother Marlise by sharing anything about my truce with Ashton.

Something's wrong. I sit up with a gasp, Marlise mumbling in her sleep next to me, her hand clenching at my side. Before I can pinpoint exactly what the matter is, the light in my room all but blinds me.

Cynthia stands at the head of the stairs, her teeth white in contrast to her dark skin.

"Molo umlungu," she says while she leers at me.

Oh, shit.

CHAPTER TWELVE
House Montu

CYNTHIA'S HAND moves so quickly, I don't have a chance to recognise what she's holding before a wasp-sting of pain flares on my neck. My vision washes into a muddy blur, and it's impossible to remain upright, let alone gather my daimonic powers. By the time I fall back on the bed, Marlise barely has the opportunity to emit a squeak. After that I gain the sense of hands pulling and pushing, and my body shoved and knocked about. People mutter in low tones. The cold air does little to revive me. I struggle to open my eyes, but when I do I focus, it's on inconsequential stuff, like the way a shadow paints the brickwork or a fifth-storey window in the apartment next door that has red curtains.

The black Hummer we've been bundled into is driven by a thin man wearing round spectacles and a pinched expression. Hardly House Montu material,

265

but then who am I to judge? The only idiosyncrasy in the vehicle is the small ivory bull's head hanging from the rear-view mirror. I've seen that before, an insignia used throughout the ages—another symbol for the ancient Egyptian war god.

Mesmerised, all I can do is watch the small object jiggle about, most of the rest of the trip blurring into blazing car headlights passing and momentarily blinding me. Cynthia sits between me and Marlise. Symphonic music plays on the vehicle's sound system, Schönberg's *Verklärte Nacht*, I think. It's been a while since I've listened to that sort of material. It adds to my sense of dislocation. My thoughts dart like frightened fish.

For some reason I recall the time Richard and I attended a performance in Cape Town's City Hall. It had been an early spring evening, and we'd spent the night at a business acquaintance's home in Oranjezicht afterwards, in a stately home with a large garden. The scent of late-blooming jasmine is lodged in this era, and I recall the way we stood on the balcony, and I felt so safe and warm with his arm around me. Nothing could go wrong.

Reality returns with the dull thump of car doors. Marlise and I are hauled out into the rain-swept darkness, but everything is so blurred I can't really tell what's happening around me.

Like a fool I watch my bare feet pad and tangle with themselves on the paving. My muscles are so uncoordinated and everything keeps swimming in and out of focus. Tilting my head up, I catch a glimpse of tall pillars from which ornamental wrought iron lamps hang, their warm light separating into blues, reds and greens at the edges. What the hell have they drugged me with?

We trade the cold outdoors for an imposing hallway clad mostly in marble, the air surprisingly warm. The bluish veins in the stone pulsate in a most disorientating fashion. A glance to my left reveals a massive floral arrangement, mostly roses and lilies. Are lilies even in season during winter?

Our journey ends in a lounge, the creamy wool warm beneath my soles, suggesting that whoever lives here has far too much money to burn on under-floor heating. A fire crackles merrily in an oversized hearth, the red-orange tongues doing strange things to my eyes, their after-burn lingering on my retinas.

A man sits silhouetted on a large corner suite, next to him a smaller figure I can't immediately focus on until too-familiar white-blond bangs send a shock of recognition through me.

Catherine!

My lips move of their own accord, and I realise it's Ashton who's in control this time, evidently able to overcome the drugs they've pumped into me. "Isn't it past your bed time, little girl?" He twists my mouth into an ugly leer. His dislike of her is clear.

Granted, he slurs the words, but Catherine's expression turns to one of pure disgust, as though she's just discovered that she's stepped in a dog's droppings.

She hates me.

A blow smashes into my skull from the side, the impact blinding. Whoever was holding me lets go, and I collapse on the floor in a boneless heap. Laughter tumbles from my lips.

I look up to see the tall thin man holding a semi-comatose Marlise upright. The way her head is lolling—whatever drugs they've administered have hit her far harder. When I turn my head slightly, I make eye contact with Cynthia, who stands above me, hands on hips. Her expression mirrors Catherine's. I'm not popular with the ladies today. Then again, that's hardly news.

The man on the couch coughs delicately, dragging my attention back to him. I blink owlishly, somehow unable to wipe a foolish grin from my face. Deep inside I know I should be scared shitless, but it's as if I view this entire sorry scenario disassociated from the true peril.

"I am told you are Inkarna Nefretkheperi, whom we used to know of as Elizabeth Rae Perry, of House Adamastor." His voice is curiously free of any emotion, and the way he annunciates his words suggests a British upbringing.

"And if I am?" I shoulder past Ashton's control of my *Kha*. There's no point in denying anything, is there? A small stab of alarm sends its insistent warning through my system.

I peg the man to be in his eighties, his face deeply lined. His white hair is combed neatly back and almost touches his collar. But his posture is that of one who is much younger, his eyes reflecting the light of the stained glass lamps casting pools of ruby in the room. It looks as though embers are lodged in his face, embers that strip away all attempts at subterfuge.

House Montu has its own tricks. I must be aware, but it is so difficult keeping my thoughts in order. They keep shooting along tangents.

"Who are you?" I ask when the man's regard grows too uncomfortable. "It's a bit rude for everyone to know me without me having the pleasure of your acquaintance." This is the old Lizzie speaking, the slightest hint of a colonial accent slipping through.

He laughs at this. "You may call me Jonathan. Jonathan Binneman. For now, that is. We are not in the business of handing out our *Rens* in this lifetime."

I choose this moment to glare at Catherine. Our *Rens* are something known only to those of one's House. To have a *Ren* known by an enemy can open one to all manner of mischief—enough to last several lifetimes. Names may change, but the *Ren* is eternal. And if one destroys the *Ib*... No. I must not think of the stele.

Catherine appears far too smug, a tiny smile obvious. Her attitude is triumphant. Only the fingers clenching and unclenching at the upholstery betray her tension.

"Should you be associating with the big people, Inkarna Meritiset? Your *Kha* is so young, so inexperienced, even if this isn't your first ride through the Opal Gate." I put all of Ashton's supercilious attitude into my manner, recalling that poster in Marlise's room, though how much of that arrogance I can communicate from where I'm sprawled, I'm not certain.

She stiffens and opens her mouth, but Jonathan raises a hand to still her, and the warning look he flashes at Cynthia behind me suggests the woman was about to give me an almighty wallop for my bad attitude. What else do I have left to me? Bad attitude and balls. More than what Catherine had.

The tall skinny man holding Marlise speaks. "What do we do with the girl?"

Jonathan turns to gaze at the man. "Put her in the guest bedroom. Dose her up again with more tranquilisers and have one of the initiates keep guard out front. Have him keep his cell at hand, should we offer further instructions to terminate her." He says this so casually my muscles spasm, as though I could leap at him to throttle the last life out of his *Kha*.

Cynthia's hand clamps down on my shoulder, and she pinches a pressure point hard between forefinger and thumb, buzzing me with a jolt of her power. If this is what an initiate can do, I really don't want to know what full-blown members of House Montu are capable of.

All I can do is hiss through my teeth as the cold paralysis sends its tendrils down my body.

Jonathan rests both liver-spotted hands on his knees and leans forward, as though he would gain a clearer view of me. His daimonic power brushes up against mine, a bubble of menace I'd shrink from if I had full control of my limbs. The last dregs of the tranquiliser wear off all too quickly as I stare back into those burning eyes.

The man's irises are brown, but not any shade I've ever encountered before, verging so close to red ochre I'd swear he's wearing special contact lenses. Jonathan, however, doesn't strike me as the kind of man who'd indulge in such an affectation.

"You do understand, Nefretkheperi, that we can and will do anything we want to your woman?"

"She's just an innocent. Let her go." My words sound pathetic.

A half-smile twitches to Jonathan's lips. "No one is truly innocent, and everyone has their uses. You of all people should know that."

Shame burns through me at the memories of my awakening, of how I so callously manipulated Marlise, justifying this as a means to an end. I didn't mean to start *loving* her. That stunning realisation makes my breath catch. She's not just a friend. Given time she'll mean more to me than Leonora ever would have. A true life partner through the ages. The thought of her dying, of suffering, makes me squirm.

The man leans back against the couch, his half-smile now full. He's scored a tactical victory, making me understand exactly how much I stand to lose.

"What do you want?" The words stick in my throat.

"You have something, an item of interest. We would like you to retrieve it from wherever you've hidden it. Then we'll let you go."

"You're lying."

He'd destroy me. Armed with the knowledge locked in the hieroglyphs carved upon the serpentine tablet, he'd finish me. Marlise and I are as good as dead.

Jonathan's laughter makes my gut contract, and I suddenly, overwhelmingly, feel like I'd soil myself. Not just the Sea of Nun. It would be as if I simply stopped existing. Even years spent wandering in limbo pale in comparison. At least in limbo there's still a chance to return in one form or another.

Catherine giggles. "You've gone all serious, *Neffie*!" How she manages to make the shortening of my *Ren* sound so pathetic is beyond me. Like I'm the one who's a child.

"Don't call me by that name!" Even as I turn to face her, Cynthia's fingers claw into my neck.

The tall man returns at this point to whisper something for Jonathan's attention only. Whatever's said makes his grin even broader. Those teeth of his are too perfect, too white and even.

When Jonathan turns to me, a slight smile tugs at his lips. "Right, well that was easy enough. Why you chose Boomslang cave is beyond me. Really, I expected far more from you. Can't even give you points for originality."

The skinny man—obviously Paul—stands behind

Jonathan, his hands clasped loosely before him. He watches me with cold, dead eyes. This man has extracted the stele's location from Marlise. If he's done anything to hurt her...

"I, ah..." I hang my head. My entire existence narrows to a pinprick. That's it. Game over.

"*We're fucked, aren't we?*" Ashton asks.

I daren't answer.

"*That knowledge provides eternal death, doesn't it?*"

I visualise someone from House Montu somehow getting past the compulsion I've laid on the cave, decimating entire Houses.

"*Oh.*" Ashton's horror matches mine, a spiralling blackness of the soul.

Yet a seed of an idea springs from these maudlin thoughts, and I look up. "Even though you know where it's hidden, you won't find it. I've laid a compulsion on the spot. Anyone else tries, and the curse it contains activates."

"*Clever.*"

I hold Jonathan's gaze without flinching. It's easier staring at the centre of his forehead, giving the impression that I'm making eye contact, because if I feel the full force of his penetrating gaze, I may well start whimpering.

"I'm not sure whether you're lying," he says.

"Do you want to take a chance?"

Although I can't muster any of my daimonic powers, I can summon Ashton's attitude, shoving his futile bravado in the face of the danger. While I won't risk speaking to my ghost, and so far no one but I am aware of his existence, I have an ace of sorts up my sleeve. No one knows about my angry ghost. They would assume that I act alone in this, that by incapacitating me, they have me under their control.

Ashton follows my chain of thought because I catch a whiff of his approval, and while I have absolutely no idea whether it's going to work, I hope I'm giving off that arrogance of his that drove people nuts. It's bugging Catherine—that much is a certainty—because the girl fidgets, knocking her sneakers together while she shifts about on the seat.

She's too young to be in this deep. No matter the wisdom of returned memories of a mature *Akh*, a chance at a second childhood should be grasped. Not for the first time I wonder how it would have been for me had I punched through in the child's body.

In the midst of House Montu...

I would have been privy to the machinations of a warrior cult, passing on valuable information to House Adamastor. Or it could have been that it had never been intended for me to get in, that it had been Meritiset's plan all along, to make us trust her so she could find out that one secret that would give House Montu the upper hand.

We'd been guarding a secret we'd kept in reserve, in case of what? Some things were better left undiscovered. Richard's disappearance may well have had something to do with House Montu.

Or not. He'd still somehow managed to warn Leonora about impending violence. Could it be that they had captured him before he passed through the Black Gate? No, if any House could do that it would be House Thanatos, who are anathema to all Houses, though I wouldn't put it past House Montu to use all tools available to them, if the end justified the means.

Jonathan looks away first, rubbing at his eyes. "Sedate him. It's too late now to be haring up the mountain. Cynthia, you'll go with him on the morrow.

You, too, Paul. I'm sure that between Catherine and myself and the staff, we can handle our friend's female companion. Perhaps given time she may even see the light of reason. We could have uses for her here in House Montu."

Jonathan smiles at me, and it takes all my willpower to not make some attempt to lash out at him. Paul steps forward, reaching into a back pocket for a small leather wallet, from which he retrieves an ampoule of clear liquid. There's a look of grim determination to him as he closes the distance between us.

Ashton makes an attempt to get me to my feet, and for a moment, we war with each other—Ashton obviously wanting to make a run for the door and me trying to keep the *Kha* in one place.

Paul fits the ampoule into a cartridge that looks like a pen, his hands cold and clinical as he pushes aside my hair to hold the pen to my neck. Cynthia's fingers dig even deeper, the pain excruciating for the split second before the drug kicks in and my world tumbles into a comfortable oblivion.

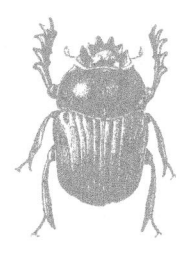

CHAPTER THIRTEEN
Striking Back

MOST PEOPLE would also have a sixth sense, an awareness of when they're not alone in a room. I wake groggily, disorientated, but completely sure someone's standing at the foot of my bed.

For a moment I thrash about on the narrow cot, uncertain as to where I am before the past night's occurrences flood me, and I strain doubly as hard against my bonds. My hands have been cuffed behind my back, chained to my feet so I'm effectively hog-tied. Ashton stands by my feet, more solid than ever before, his arms crossed over his broad chest so the muscles bulge.

"What the fuck are we going to do?"

I groan, my head thumping in time with my pulse.

"Feels like the mother of all hangovers," Ashton says. *"Now you know why I've stepped out."* He gives

a low chuckle. "*I guess there are advantages to this arrangement.*"

"First off, I'm going to get out of this." I strain back to get a good look at an intricate assortment of padlocks and chains. They obviously think I'm a fire starter, but they've done me a favour. Now rope may have presented a problem. Closing my eyes, I concentrate, shrugging aside the foggy after-effects of whatever drug they've given me.

The mechanism is easy to spring, run by a combination of interlocking parts, and it's almost like a puzzle, the small wheels spinning until, with a *snick*, the thing comes loose. It's easy enough grappling at each padlock in turn in order to unhook it.

Ashton stands there, watching, and I glare at him. "What?"

"*You're giving me ideas.*"

"What, you going to open doors now, too?"

He shrugs. "*Hurry up, hey.*"

"How is Marlise? I assume you've checked up on her."

His expression becomes pained for an instant, and he evaporates in a burst of snowlike static.

"Bloody hell," I mutter. The chains unravel and fall to a clinking pile on the bed. Gingerly I rise, massaging life into my wrists and legs, which are cramping something awful after being tied in this position the whole night.

What is the time, anyway? I rise and hobble to the window. The light spilling through the heavy maroon drapes is buttery, but heavy bars put paid to any thought of escaping via the window. At least the sky is blue. Beyond the glass is a rolling expanse of lawn running down to a thick stand of oak, and after that, the first rolling vineyards of Constantia, the vines bared this time of year to expose the red-orange soil. I must be near one of the original historical homesteads.

"*She's awake,*" Ash says as he envelopes me in a cool mist that seeps into my *Kha*. "*But you must hurry. I think they've got a camera or some sort of motion sensor in your room, or you've just had the rotten luck of waking as they were about to fetch you.*"

I nod, shoving at the dullness of my mind, just damned glad my daimonic abilities are working better, and sans the nosebleeds. Placing a trembling hand on the door handle, I breathe deeply, trying to *see* inside, to figure out how this one works because it's not the usual run-of-the-mill mechanism one would purchase at a shop.

The chains I'd been bound with earlier were just a tool to make me feel helpless. With the lock I encounter circuit boards, like one would find inside Marlise's computer, and some sort of recognition software linked to... Something—something that is almost sentient. I pull back with a gasp.

"*That's pretty close to AI,*" Ashton says. "*Like in the movies.*"

"Shut up. I need to concentrate."

As I put down my hand, there's a beep, and the door is flung inwards. I jump back in time to come face to face with Cynthia, too curvy in her black, tight-fitting tracksuit and running shoes. Her defensive stance is decidedly unsexy, however.

For a moment her expression is that of surprise but then she relaxes, looking me up and down. "White boy thinks he's being clever getting out of the chains. We'll just use rope next time."

Trying not to show my dismay, I smile. "Good morning to you, too." I bunch my muscles, trying to weigh up which would be the better course of action: to try shove past her or to yield. Paul appears behind her. The gun he's pointing at my midriff has me raise my hands immediately.

"Okay, okay." I step back. I may be Inkarna, but I can't dodge bullets, and I'm not sure I can sabotage the weapon before he pulls the trigger.

"*Don't make any holes in this body,*" Ashton says.

I bite my tongue, in case I answer him out loud.

"Bind his hands behind his back," Cynthia says to Paul. She takes the gun from him and motions for him to enter the room. Then she looks at me, holding up a plastic object, some sort of remote control. "See this? If I press the red button, it sends a signal, and one of the staff will know they have the instruction to terminate your pretty girlfriend. Paul has one, too. One false move... And I'm not totally dense. I can feel when you're drawing in power."

I swallow hard, yet turn my back from Paul as he advances so I'm pressed against the window. "You don't need to bind me, okay?"

"Don't take me for a fool."

Paul advances on me, the tranquiliser pen clutched in his right hand. A thin film of moisture beads his brow, small runlets trickling down his temple in slick dribbles. The man is close to shitting himself because of me.

"*You aren't just going to let them tie you up?*" Ashton asks.

"I don't have a choice, do I?"

Cynthia, her eyes never leaving mine, laughs, shaking her head. "*Aikona.*"

"Look, I'm going to need shoes where we're

headed." I glance pointedly at my bare feet.

Paul turns to Cynthia. "Binneman didn't say anythi—"

"Don't be such a wimp, Paul. Go get him a pair of your old running shoes. Looks like you two are of a size."

Paul scowls at her but obeys, turning his back on me. For a moment I consider drawing my powers, lashing out, but Cynthia's finger is twitchy, the ball of her thumb caressing that fateful red button.

How many other staff members patrol this estate? Do I want to take the chance to find out? Cynthia and Paul I may be able to take on once we're away from the property, though this in itself may prove tricky.

Cynthia walks behind me, the gun jammed into the small of my back. One false move and Marlise will be dead, this *Kha* with its spine blown out. Now's not the right moment.

My stomach growls ominously. "Can I at least have something to eat?" I ask.

Cynthia hisses. "You don't deserve food."

"It's quite a way up the mountain. You don't want me fainting before I can undo that compulsion."

"Very well." She walks me down several long passages where I recognise a few Claerhouts and even a Siopis adorning the walls. Jonathan is loaded.

Once in the kitchen—a typical modernistic affair clad in vast quantities of black and red granite—Cynthia unties my hands long enough for me to wolf down a bowl of corn flakes and a banana. This is hardly enough to fuel the body, but right now I can't expect any better.

By the time I'm done, Paul returns, holding an old, scruffy pair of running shoes as though both were covered in excrement. I try not to cringe as I slip my feet into them. They smell none too fresh as well, and I elect not to ask when he last wore them. The shoes are too small for my feet, my toes horribly scrunched up at the front, but it's still better than having to attempt a climb barefoot and during winter.

All the while they watch me, fingers conspicuously on the remote buttons as I do up the laces, gritting my teeth against the fusty smell.

"You could have brought me a pair of socks, you know," I say to Paul.

He offers me a silent snarl in response.

"*I'm so going to get him for this*," Ashton says. "*I would never be caught dead wearing crappy Adidas takkies that look like they've been used to run one half-marathon too many. If you get a weird, fucked-up fungal infection or something after this...*"

"What you grinning about, shithead?" Cynthia asks.

Carefully I school my face. "Nothing." I watch them warily, waiting for the cues that suggest I can rise to my feet.

Paul jingles keys in his pockets. "No point in waiting; he's done."

Cynthia gestures with the gun and I get up slowly, watching both of them watch me.

We file out into the driveway, and I get my first real glimpse of the house—a rambling faux-Tuscan edifice that sprawls, no doubt with a number of hidden courtyards. Palms shiver in the stiff breeze, eliciting a tremor in my *Kha*. It's bloody cold, and I'm wearing only a thin T-shirt and a pair of jeans with shoes in which not even a dead man would want to be buried. After a brief discussion, Cynthia has Paul restrain my hands behind my back with one of those plastic ties the cops use. The bindings quickly cut off circulation to my hands.

I don't need eyes in the back of my head to know we're being watched, from one or more of the dark-tinted windows in the house. My imagination suggests it could be Catherine, staring at me with her little hate-filled heart pumping fit to burst.

An old Egyptian saying warned against one eating one's own heart, lest one's hatred becomes all-consuming, like Apep trying to eat the sun-disc. I can only begin to imagine the centuries of feuding that are culminating in my present situation. A pawn, that's what I am. A pawn. Nothing more.

Ashton's angry ghost is my only advantage right now, also that I'm fully Inkarna. Give Cynthia another month or two, and she'd be more dangerous. Her daimonic powers sizzle just beneath the surface. She can call some of them forth, that much I've seen, but our kind can sense those who are lower in the scale. Both Paul and Cynthia would, no doubt, have had some experience with combat training and weapons. That goes without saying.

Ashton was, or rather is, a brawler. Him going up against these two? I'll have to catch them unawares, which may prove tricky. I don't doubt they'll go through with the threat of killing Marlise. Potential or no, she's a risk to them. What's it going to be, our lives relegated to a newspaper report about two decayed unidentifiable bodies discovered in some remote area?

I shudder. Not only at the thought of having to pass through the Black Gate again so soon, but also facing the ire awaiting me in Per Ankh should I fail. That's if House Adamastor is still recognisably a collective of Inkarna. I don't know.

My head pressed against the glass, I watch the world go by. Cynthia sits next to me in the back, her eyes never once leaving me as she watches every small gesture, every tiniest twitch of muscles. Paul handles the driving—a big black Mercedes sedan with tinted windows like our government officials sometimes drive when they leave their SUVs at home.

The car is so quiet I don't feel the slightest vibration through the floor, though I sense the power of the engine as the vehicle slips between the early morning traffic. Pushing my senses further may just alert Cynthia to my curiosity. Outside it's a beautiful day, the trees' stark branches catching the sunlight, the sky that special winter aquamarine I'd find especially beautiful if it weren't for the certainty that today may well be my last on the material plane, for a long time.

Even Paul's taste in music has a funerary mood, or at least I've always had the opinion that the music of Thomas Tallis verges on the maudlin. A motet has been arranged for a string quartet, and while the music is pretty, it only serves to increase my burden of sorrow.

I'm not ready to die again. I've had so little time. Today hangs on such a slender thread. My stomach lurches and I wonder idly if I'll get sick. Let me not think of the stele—a stone accusation. How the hell am I going to keep *The Book of Ammit* out of House Montu's hands?

We arrive in Kalk Bay sooner than I want, the risen sun glinting off the calm blue-green waters in the small harbour where colourful fishing boats bob. Cynthia motions for me to get out of the car, and I obey. Here on this road above Kalk Bay the cars passing below seem almost like toys, and I look anywhere but at her in an attempt to feign nonchalance.

Cynthia zips up her leather jacket, and I turn to

see her eye me speculatively as Paul fiddles inside the car. She waits for him to climb out then speaks. "We're going to have to untie his hands. Can't have people getting suspicious. I want you to have the house on speed dial." She glares at me. "One false move from you, and Paul calls to let them know that your girlfriend bites it. If I so much as even feel you tapping into the reserves around us, I will get him to make that call. Do you understand?"

I incline my head, not deigning to answer because I don't trust myself to prevent a snappy retort.

"Fucking bitch, I'm going to stick that gun so far up her pussy she'll have to get it surgically removed," Ashton says.

Paul unties my hands, and for that I'm grateful. I rub the feeling back into fingers gone numb. There's nothing left but to start climbing, with the two of them walking behind me. I don't have to turn to know that pistol's trained on my back. All the small hairs on my nape prickle—Cynthia keeps some of her daimonic powers cocked as well, like the gun. I can expect a physical backlash and more if I'm not careful.

The path up the mountain is ridiculously easy during the day. The stairs that tripped me and Marlise the last time are now only a pleasure, but my pair of goons doesn't give me a chance to admire the view. Paul gets out of breath easily, and so do I. This *Kha* doesn't want to stumble up the mountain at such a pace, but Cynthia is impatient. Every time I stop to catch my breath, her lips thin and her eyes glint dangerously.

With each step we are closer to the goal. While we walk I envision the scramble near the top. This would be an ideal spot. They will have to let me go on up ahead. Cynthia may have her pugnacious attitude as an advantage, but her limbs are much shorter than mine, and combat training or not, she's still going to have to put a lot more effort into clambering up that vertical spot.

I think long and hard—pointedly *at* Ashton—of how loose rocks can make someone slip, how he or she can fall at that particular spot where I'd been doubtful of getting Marlise to succeed at the last section.

"*On it.*" His awareness leaves me with a sigh.

"What was that?" Cynthia asks.

Damn. I stop and turn slowly, hands held up. "What?"

"I felt that. What did you do?"

Paul blinks at us then mops his brow, but that cell phone remains clutched in white-knuckled hands, thumb on the call button.

Summoning what I hope to be a puzzled expression, I look her square in the eye. "There's some daimonic activity here. I should have warned you. Someone or several someones died in a cave here a few years ago, or so I've heard. I felt that too when I came here the other day."

"If you're bullshitting me..."

I bite the inside of my cheek, maintaining a façade of calm. Bloody hell. She felt Ashton leave me. That means she could feel the build-up of daimonic energy if he were to try anything. If I attempt projecting, to tell him to back down, she'll probably detect that too.

The woman stares at me long enough for me to shift from foot to foot. My heels and toes burn with the icy fire of skin rubbed raw. My stomach is rumbling, and I'm desperate to take a piss.

Our path forks from the main track to cut through the veld to the low peak bulbing above us to our right. Pale lichen-encrusted sandstone folds grimace down on us, the cone bushes and fynbos verdant after so much winter rain. All so pretty and impassive compared to the small drama playing itself out here on the mountain's slope. Tomorrow I may lie here decomposing, and the bushes will still nod in the slight breeze. Only flies will be buzzing about my unmoving flesh. A deep shudder runs through me. I can't let any of this happen.

Soon we're climbing in the shade, and I can't help the way my teeth chatter. Ahead the scramble looms, two vertical bits where it's tricky to climb, especially if one is concentrating hard not to put a foot wrong with twitchy, combat-ready almost-Inkarna.

They argue briefly between them at the foot of the first ridge, and it is decided that Paul will go first, the icy barrel of Cynthia's gun pressed under my chin. Her hand clamps down hard on my shoulder as we watch Paul ascend. The man may look awkward, but he moves with surprising grace over the rocks, seeking hand- and footholds with great efficiency.

It's my turn thereafter, and I don't have to look back to know that damned pistol is trained on me, on some point targeting my spine to rip a bullet into my flesh at the slightest error in judgment. A whining starts in my head, like some sort of electric current, just as I pull myself over the lip of rock. Cynthia is already at my heels, her hand nudging my shoes when, with a sharp crack, soil loosens a stone above us.

In slow motion the trickle of soil starts running like a miniature river, the rock—about the size of a football—surfs down the small avalanche, bouncing off boulders. With a grunt I pull myself out of the way as the thing launches into the air. I'm almost certain Ashton was aiming for Cynthia, but the stone offers Paul a glancing blow to his thigh that sets him dancing on the edge.

For a moment I believe he'll overcome gravity somehow and re-assert his balance, but he falls. He doesn't plunge far, but the sound his head makes when it impacts with the edge of a boulder—and the angle of his neck when he lands—makes me turn away, the back of my skull aching in sympathy. A wet, meaty thud. I'm uncomfortably reminded of the term *like an overripe melon*. It's a cliché but, in this case, all too apt, the pulpy reddish matter splattered about.

His limbs twitch spasmodically, but his eyes stare into eternity. Oh, he's dead all right. I don't have a chance to feel any triumph at the matter. The cell phone emits the tinny words of a man saying "Hello, hello?" over and over again.

The call has gone through. House Montu knows something is amiss.

Marlise.

Her death freezes through me.

"Bastard!" I try to descend, only to have my world explode in a blaze of agony so that I fall back. Something large and heavy has just side-swiped me. Vaguely I'm aware of Cynthia crawling over me to finish her climb, but my ears ring so much I'm not quite sure what the hell is happening.

As I regain some of my composure, I'm able to piece together what occurred: Cynthia somehow smashing me with the pistol, the stock connecting with my temple, which throbs in such a way to suggest I'm leaking a steady flow of blood into my hair and onto the ledge.

Raising a shaky hand to touch the wound, I'm

stopped midway by Cynthia's boot smashing into my ribs.

"You fucking asshole!" she shrieks. "You've killed him!" Her grief lashes out with a secondary almost-physical blow.

For a moment my world constricts to the narrow band of pain, my inability to draw breath rendering me into nothing more than a crumpled bundle of quivering limbs. All I see in my mind is Paul's face, his lips parted and the steady spread of crimson dripping. In the distance is the tinny crackle of the cell phone call that has gone through…

What must the person on the other end of the connection be hearing?

Marlise.

I've killed her.

Deep within me an ember flares. They've killed her, an innocent. Whether the fury stems from a genetic quirk of this *Kha*'s make-up, I don't know, but I manage to curl onto my side and lunge at Cynthia. My fist meets only thin air before a heavy object smashes into my groin, and has me back in a foetal position faster than I can gather my scattered senses.

Cynthia strikes again, this time jabbing fingers into the soft flesh of my neck, half paralysing me. Jolt after jolt of daimonic power flashes through me. This is what someone who's accidently come into contact with an electricity cable must feel like.

The only mercy is that my awareness cuts out, dropping me into blessed nothingness.

☥

Birdcalls, a soft, insistent *swee-swee*, lure me back from the dark. It seems odd that I am outside, lying on damp earth with rocks prodding into my ribs and limbs. The events preceding this predicament hit me at full force, and I sit up, wishing immediately upon getting upright, that I'd been more careful.

I'm on the mountain overlooking Fish Hoek, the houses like some sort of malignant crust between the tarmac ribbons threading through the town. The golf course below to my right has tiny matchstick figures crawling about like ants. Breathing is only possible if I do so slowly, wincing at the sharp stab in my left side every time I move. An insistent dull pressure in my skull makes me wish I didn't have to open my eyes to a too-bright world.

The dark figure watching me from a rock about two paces to my left resolves into Cynthia, holding vigil with that damned pistol pointed directly at me. "Your woman is deceased, whitey." Malice glitters in her eyes.

All of this is so unreal I can't quite conceptualise what Marlise's death must mean. It's all insubstantial in the face of my current situation, which involves somehow ensuring that Cynthia...

I must kill her. A life for a life.

Yet somehow the idea of taking an active hand in another's death doesn't hold much appeal to a part of me that's rapidly being drowned out by another baying for vengeance.

"*She must die!*" It's Ashton.

Pressure builds up in me, a maelstrom in my heart centre, coiling up and down my spine. My fingers close around a fist-sized rock. Ashton's doing.

Cynthia smiles, gestures with the gun. "You can put the rock down, *Neffie*. You won't need that hand to undo the compulsion, and I'm quite happy to ensure you're in a lot of pain." The way she speaks a corruption of my *Ren* communicates layer upon layer of contempt.

"You killed her."

"No, you did, doing whatever it was that killed Paul."

"It wasn't me!" I shout. A searing fire within my heart says *Marlise is dead, Marlise is dead*, over and over again.

"Get up, filth. I don't have time for 'he said, she said', conversations after the fact."

"And if I don't?"

"I'll make you get up. You choose. Either you do it the easy way, of your own volition, or I make it extremely painful. And dampen your power or I shoot you where you won't bleed to death immediately."

"*We could die, both of us, and they'll never get that damned stone*," Ash whispers.

That's a vain hope. House Montu would never give up. Even if it takes them decades, they'll work here until they find the stele.

Cynthia rises, and by the way she moves, it's clear she's wary. She keeps her free hand loose, almost as if for balance. Her right hand clutches the pistol, which doesn't waver. Unshed tears glint in the corners of her eyes, and I wonder exactly what her relationship with Paul was. Lovers? A small stab of guilt niggles at me but I make an effort to ignore it. This woman is partially responsible for Marlise's death, and if I escape here today, I will go back and make the rest of them pay as well.

Near me Ashton surges, a bright fire of malevolence.

"Your powers," Cynthia says. "Dampen them."

It requires effort, but I close my eyes long enough to visualise a squaring away of my energy. I do this in a way that suggests to Ashton that he needs to make himself scarce. But he's outside of the *Kha*. There's no way of telling how much he's aware of.

With a groan I stumble to my feet, having to reach out for support offered by a boulder. The sandstone is rough under my fingers. My skin looks waxen against the lichen, the tone almost yellow, like that of a corpse. A sudden wave of nausea floods my system, and I have to swallow hard to stop myself from vomiting right there in front of the damned bitch who has her gun trained on me.

Cynthia motions for me to lead the way, and I hobble past her. I'm certain she's well aware I'm only biding my time, looking for that one chink in her armour so I can lash out. After all, I don't really have anything to lose. Each limb protests my ascent, and I have to pause often to catch my breath, bright sparks wiggling in my field of vision. If I stretch my awareness beyond my *Kha* with care, I detect her daimonic essence, which flares around her, questing, drinking in her environment and searching it for anything that may present a threat. Ashton had better tread with caution if he wants to prove himself as the ace up my sleeve.

Two false tunnels gape at us out of the wall of rock, looking far more innocent during the brightness of day than they did on that night when I was up here with Marlise. Nothing here strikes me as untoward.

I pause long enough to straighten my spine with an audible clack-clack of vertebrae sliding into place, pretending to ignore the death glares Cynthia offers me as I take my time. Where the hell is Ashton? I can't capture a whiff of his presence, not even the slightest sense of being watched.

"You gonna stand there all day and flex your

muscles, big boy?" Cynthia asks. "We don't have time."

If there's one thing I know for certain, if I find this stele and hand it over this hell-bitch, I won't be descending from the mountain. I pause, mid-stretch, and regard her as mildly as possible. There's no point in aggravating the woman any more than she already is.

"Do you want me to deactivate the compulsion, or do you want to fuck up your mission more than it already is?"

Cynthia emits a low hiss, her agitation reaching out for me so that I am forced to take a step back. "Stop playing games. Let's end this as soon as possible. The thing isn't in one of those two, is it?" She inclines her head towards the larger of the two gaps.

I gain the distinct impression she has no great love for enclosed spaces.

"It's around the corner." With a theatrical sigh, I trudge to the left of the largest of the two entrances, around a bulge of rock that hides the crack in the mountain where the cave's narrow slot gapes at me.

It's not just that I'm going to die at the hands of some psychotic madwoman. Something isn't quite right. I pause at the initial climb, just before the maw. The air here is damp, the kind of moisture I associate with stone that has never had a chance to fully dry, like one would find in basements. The air washing against my face holds a chill, not unlike that of a fridge.

It's the silent expectance that has me balking. How the hell did I manage to enter this place at night, during a storm? Perhaps it was because it already was so dark, it didn't bother me as much to fumble my way over the tumbled stones down the throat of this particular location.

"What is it?" Cynthia asks behind me. "Go in, will you."

"Wai—" I don't get a chance to finish my sentence.

I think we both hear the sound, a bone-deep *chunk-clunk-chunk* of loosening stone—a large rock—rough surfaces tearing and squeaking against each other and releasing a small shower of pebbles that rattle down the walls on either side of us.

We both look up at the exact moment that a dozen rocks varying from fist- through to coconut-sized bounce down, their descent almost cheerful.

A force crashes into my side just as a particularly large fragment shatters where I stood only moments ago, and I am flung against a wall, the breath knocked out of me. I'm sprawled half into the mouth of a dark hole that wends its way a few hundred metres through a mountain, with goodness knows how many lateral passages and pits for the unwary. This mountain is honeycombed with tunnels, cracks and abysses. It can swallow me, and no one will ever find my remains.

Cynthia's shape is silhouetted against the sky as she staggers towards me, her skin slick with blood flowing freely from a wicked-looking gash on her forehead.

"You don't quit, do you," I mumble.

The crackle of her indrawn daimonic powers is staggering. Nothing like a knock to the head to awaken one's full magical ability, eh? I don't have time to react. Whatever Ashton did, he's got her on uneven footing, and we're down to combat, Inkarna style.

Her teeth bared, Cynthia lashes out first,

attempting to punch me in the face, the strike reinforced by a gathering of power. Her fist misses me but the daimonic blow slams me so hard into the wall my head cracks against the rock, and all I can see is bright sparks wriggling across my field of vision.

Already I can feel the pull of daimonic essence being gathered, the same way a fisherman would drag in a net. Two can play at that game, though I'm so dazed, my own process takes off in fits and starts. She's going to release before I can.

But she's not ready for this kind of fighting. The air is heavy with the icy tang of her fear, and she's got the nosebleed to end all nosebleeds. Whether this is from the bump she took to her head earlier, courtesy of Ashton's poltergeist activities, or her efforts to fight on a full Inkarna level so soon into her awakening I don't know. It won't matter if she can keep me off centre. She's going to incapacitate me easily enough.

"Don't you want the stele?" I ask.

She answers by rushing me, displaying her uncanny strength by shoving me against the wall, her fists bunching my T-shirt so hard fabric tears. The small mercy is she hasn't fully grabbed her powers.

When I try to pull at my own abilities, it's through a haze of pain. Damn. Where the hell is Ashton? Has he expended himself in that spectacular rock fall? If so, I'm so royally stuffed it's going to take a miracle to get me out of this predicament. I may be taller than Cynthia, but her muscles are toned, and she knows exactly how to hit the most sensitive spots.

Though I snatch her wrists, her knee comes up to connect with my groin. There's no way in hell that I'm going to let go, so I twist, and we both fall the few steps down into the slot. Maybe it's the adrenalin or my jumped-up awareness, but I don't feel any pain from the impact. At least not yet.

Cynthia lets out a small whimper but brings her head down. I save myself at the last moment, but she still clips my right temple. For a few heartbeats, all I can do is lie back, my cheek pressed to slick damp stone and try to clear my vision of exploding star bursts.

There is another way, though I don't want to do it. The words of *The Book of Ammit* would be easy to recite. Those evil words would sever her connection and plunge her immortal souls into the slavering jaws of The Devourer. She has blood on her hands, this woman. Her *Ib* weighs more than the feather of Ma'at. Even now Marlise is possibly dead. Cynthia had had the power to stay the executioner's hand, and she didn't.

Marlise never asked for any of this, yet she gave, and in her own way, she tried to understand. She could have been so much more, given the opportunity, and now we are both tangled in House Montu's machinations.

This understanding, my fiery sense of Ma'at perverted, lifts a growl from deep in my chest. Where I get the power from, I'm not sure, but as I rise, I push Cynthia from me so hard she smashes into the wall opposite, her limbs almost boneless from the impact.

What dim light still reaches this far into this cave outlines the woman's fluttering lashes as she tries to open her eyes, her breath whistling in and out of her mouth. Where the gun is now, only the devil knows, but I have to finish her because she would not extend me the courtesy of walking away alive.

"I can't do it," I whisper.

Even now she stirs, her limbs twitching as she tries

to regain control of her faculties.

"Then we'll all die. You. Me. Marlise." It's Ashton, his presence a nebulous mist swirling about me, raising the small hairs on my arms. *"They haven't killed her. Yet."*

He must have gone back. There's no time to thank him. Cynthia lurches into a seated position, her muscles bunching as she prepares to fly at me. The inrush of power whines on the edges of my awareness, verging on audible.

I don't have time to negotiate. I strike. Where the power behind my blow comes from, I don't ask, but my senses blur as though I view the scene through two pairs of eyes—mine and Ashton's, who is slightly superimposed upon me, adding his force of will to mine.

My fist connects with Cynthia's skull, and something crunches upon the impact of knuckle to cartilage. A rush of energy so intense it burns through my tendons flows outwards. The world grows dimmer, the light from outside fades, and a terrible ringing starts in my ears.

Cynthia drops with a meaty thud. Where her face was is a concave hollow, her features collapsed inwards. No human fist should be able to offer so much damage. Sheer blazing agony envelopes my hand, and I blink stupidly, holding my arm up to the light. Already the skin is bruised, and I flex the fingers experimentally. Nothing's broken, but I'm going to be hurting for a long while yet. That's if I make it through the next day or two. Blue-green motes flit about my extremities, the residue of our altercation.

It sinks in then when I glance down at Cynthia's corpse. I've taken yet another life. The horror of that is dizzying, and I have to sit, unable to look away from the woman's corpse.

No one should be able to devastate like that.

"What have I done?" I murmur. Shadows wriggle at the edge of my vision.

Ashton's voice rings hollow in my head. *"What should have been done a long time ago, sweetcakes. I thought it was kak having to hang out with you in the same body, but I've grown quite fond of this deal."*

"You tried to kill Marlise that first time." My words echo off the stone walls.

Cynthia has been reduced to so much meat. How long before the decay sets in? That being a fact, should I even bother doing anything about the body?

"Wouldn't you have an extreme reaction after regaining your body?"

"No." Well, maybe. I can't tell anymore.

I woke in that hospital ward. So recently... Yet it feels as though months, even years, have passed since that first moment. My heart goes out to Ashton's parents. I don't ever want to see them for the shame of disappointment. They're a million light years from where we are now.

"They're ineffectual."

"They're your parents."

"We're a danger to them."

I can't disagree with that observation. So many loose ends. Groaning, I rise, pointedly looking away from the woman's body. "So, they haven't killed Marlise. Why?"

"I didn't stick around long enough to find out. The little girl was having an argument with the old man. Didn't pick up all the details, but whatever was up the old man wasn't budging."

They must have suspected something would go

wrong, but then why let a half-cocked Inkarna and an initiate handle something for which they were clearly not ready? What I do know of House Montu is that they have a high turnover among their initiates. Most of them don't make it past their trials. Could it be that this was a trial for Cynthia? Survival of the fittest, and now her error in judgment has taken her out of the game? It's doubtful whether she'll get her second opportunity, although she was so damn close there's always a chance I've just ensured myself an immortal enemy. And Binneman knows I'll come back for Marlise, no matter what transpires here on the mountain.

I shudder.

Of the stele? Should I take it with me, stash it somewhere temporary and try save Marlise? Or should I do the sensible thing and run, run as far as possible without looking back until such time that I can build up House Adamastor's resources?

I can't leave it where it is. So long as Marlise lives, she'll be able to lead them here.

Torn, I rock back on my heels, leaning my back against the stone, which immediately soaks through the thin cotton of my T-shirt to chill my skin.

"Screw it," I mutter and turn, fumbling my way in the darkness deeper into the cave. If I fail in my mission, it won't matter whether I keep the stele hidden here or carry it with me back into the belly of the beast. Thing is, they won't expect me to bring it with me when I pay them a visit.

They're banking on my return: Marlise was always intended as bait. They never meant to kill her. At least not yet. Knowing them, they'd find a way to corrupt her, to use her against me somehow in the future should I choose the coward's way out. No matter what I do, I'm being played. Ashton would punch a wall to vent his frustrations. Instead, I flex my muscles, work some of the kinks out of my system.

No torch illuminates my descent into Boomslang this time, and it's purely by feel that I inch my way back to the cavern. Each time I reach out, I worry about touching something that moves, that slithers out of my hand when I make contact. The air is frigid, and soon this cold seeps right into my bones. The only accompaniment to my journey is my ragged breathing and the occasional drip-drip of moisture. Round about now I could do with powers of illumination, but that's not a daimonic effect House Adamastor is known to cultivate.

When I arrive in what I assume to be the small space that is the chamber where the lateral shaft segues off, I worry for a few minutes when I don't immediately find that side passage. Is my own compulsion working against me in this situation?

The worst part follows when I do find it and pull myself along the lateral tunnel without knowing exactly what I'll find. Dust makes me sneeze repeatedly, and shards stick into my chest, arms and hands as I drag myself forward.

When I've gone far enough, I begin to chant the words to resonate with the compulsion. At first I feel the fool, worrying that this thing isn't going to work, but soft blue-green motes dance a metre or so in front of me, and I drag myself closer.

My hand meets resistance the moment I begin groping among the stones, much like when the same magnetic poles are brought together. The covered stele comes away in a shower of dirt, and I can begin my retreat, conscious of the warmth emanating even through the covering protecting the artefact from the elements.

The wash of light from outside forms a white-blue patina on the stones, drawing me ever out to the aquamarine sky. I don't look at Cynthia's sprawled form. The stench of blood and shit hangs heavy in the air. Let House Montu come care for their dead. I'm too broken to give a flying fuck.

We can't leave this place quickly enough. I lean heavily on Ashton's presence, drawing strength through him from the environment to bolster the burning in my knees and ankles as we all but tumble down the mountain.

It's better to pick my way carefully—I certainly can't afford a sprained ankle or worse—but a terrible sense of urgency grips me, driving me to get to the bottom of the mountain as soon as possible. The only blessing is that I encounter no other hikers here this day. I'm sure I'll give them the fright of their lives if they were to see me in this condition, my clothing ripped, smeared with gore and dirt. In many ways the journey down takes more of a toll than its opposite. I'm fighting the compulsion of gravity every step of the way.

In my mad rush to get off the mountain, the last thing I'd considered was the obvious. How the hell am I going to get from Kalk Bay back to Constantia? No one in their right minds would pick me up looking like this. I can't drive.

Although the sun is shining, and the last of the mist pulled away, I shiver nonetheless, exhaustion drawing at me, making me yearn for the comforting oblivion offered by sleep.

I eye the car we arrived in. The Mercedes—modern, sleek—most likely electrified. It shouldn't provide a problem, if Ashton were to play along.

"Feel like driving?" I ask Ashton.

"*That? Hell yeah!*"

I close my eyes and take a deep breath then tug at my surroundings, feeling the stone beneath my feet, the electricity humming in cables beneath the ground. I borrow this energy, take it into myself then extend my daimonic awareness. The thrum of power feels good, superimposing itself over my nervous system so the small hairs on my arms rise.

The car's system beeps back at me after I send a query, the doors unlocking.

"*We should go into business,*" Ashton says. "*I can think of a dozen benefits to this arrangement.*"

"Well, let's get the hell out of trouble first. We have to get near that place in Constantia, find some clothes and food then get in and save Marlise." I consciously pull back my control of the *Kha* while maintaining some semblance of a grip. I can never stop being vigilant with my ghost.

It's almost like walking a very big, powerful dog on a leash—and right now the leash is slack—but I keep a firm hand on Ashton as a reminder that if he were to try to jerk completely free, I can and I will, bring him to heel.

I catch a sight of him grinning like a fool in the rear-view mirror, his features rendered all the more ghoulish for the smears of blood. If the cops stop us now, we're going straight to lock-up with a hell of a lot of explaining along the way. There's no way either of us would be able to bullshit our way out of this sorry mess without making a greater hash of it.

The leather is smooth beneath fingers, the interior of the vehicle a warm comfort after the ordeal up on the mountain. It takes Ashton about a minute to absorb the car's layout before I lend him the rush of daimonic energy to start the engine. We nose into the midday traffic quickly, the engine almost inaudible.

"Where to?" he asks.

"*Just get us to Constantia. Find a quiet side road nearby the estate to park the car, somewhere where we can make a quick getaway if need be. Then some breaking and entering, get supplies, then complete this sorry mission.*" It feels strange to be the one who is remote, the body no longer under my control but all its sensations mine.

While he drives, I tug at the energy around us, siphoning it into the *Kha* in an attempt to promote healing of some of the damage. Ideally I'd need to rest so this process can take its time to work its magic, but we simply don't have that kind of luxury. Even now they could be subjecting Marlise to torture. The wrapped stele rests on the passenger seat. Impossibly heavy in its presence.

Ashton finds us a quiet lane, a panhandle, where four or five hidden driveways are tucked away from one of the main thoroughfares. If we're in luck, the home owners will think our stolen vehicle belongs to someone visiting one of their neighbours.

What must it be like to live here in splendid isolation? The gardens are big, lush, filled with a profusion of vegetation. Tall beefwoods create a susurration when the wind stirs their boughs, an almost sleepy sound. I reel Ashton in gradually so all he does is give the slightest whimper of disappointment when he's pushed into the background.

I lean back in my seat, exhausted, my body leaden. Every muscle burns, and it would be so easy to succumb to the need for sleep.

"Ashton?"

"*What?*"

"I need you to go do your thing again."

A faint flush of his annoyance washes over me.

"We need food, clothing. I need you to go find out which of these houses have no people in them, whether there are dogs or household staff. Pick the one that's got the least amount of people. I'm sure you'd like to enjoy food and a shower as much as I do."

This suggestion is all motivation he needs, and he pushes from me so hard my ears pop with the decompression. How much is he learning from me, from sharing my thoughts? Certainly during the drive, with him at the fore, I was privy to some of his past. I sort through some of the memories: of him at school, his favourite music, movies and times he'd performed on stage. The ghost of that exhilaration is foreign to me, someone who has always preferred to live a quiet life.

Would he have succeeded in his dreams if he'd not suffered that near-fatal accident?

No, it *had* been a fatal accident. One way or another, his arrogance would have resulted in misfortune. The man was only twenty-one, and he'd already made himself mighty fine enemies.

I must have snoozed a little, but Ashton's return brings me to full wakefulness.

"*The house right at the end. No one's home. Think you can handle two Labradors?*"

"They'll be more prone to licking me to death than biting once they're done barking. Besides, dogs have always loved Inkarna. Something to do with them walking between worlds to a degree themselves."

Ashton's doubt is obvious, but I shrug it aside and

get out of the car. This road has been deserted since I've pulled up here, and I pray no one comes by.

"I need you to keep checking whether the owners come back." I can't wait to get these running shoes off. It is my fondest hope I will find something more appropriate in the footwear department.

The front gate is a big black wrought-iron barrier trimmed with a stylised leaf motif. These people must have money. The house is set back quite a way from the road, along a dirt track overgrown with weeds. On one side is a paddock where a sleepy-looking palomino grazes. The horse lifts its head when I get the gate to slide open a fraction then continues with its grazing, its tail swishing while it lips at the grass.

Richard had told me a few tales about times when he'd had to leave places in a hurry, with the utmost secrecy. Once or twice these had involved his amorous conquests, which he'd known annoyed me, but he'd shared nonetheless, just to wind me up. If he could see me now, sneaking into someone's property. The laugh would be on me. I could almost imagine his face crinkling in amusement.

I don't go far before the pair of black Labradors detect the intrusion and storm the gate: two males; their glossy fur catches bright highlights. They rush down the driveway, barking madly as they bound towards me.

I stand still and wait for them to reach me, their hackles settling the moment they've had a good sniff of my hands, which I hold relaxed by my sides. Their wet noses press into my jeans, and they sniff at my feet, the smaller of the two sneezing when he gets a whiff of something on the running shoe that is not to his liking.

"Hey boys..." I speak in a low voice, reaching out

with tentative hands to pat each of them.

Expectant eyes gaze up at me, and my canine entourage follows me to the house, tails wagging. The place itself isn't as big as I'd have expected. Although it has a thatched roof, it appears to have been constructed out of previously existing outbuildings. This whole area used to be farmland, and this must have originally been the stables.

A rusty Land Rover that looks as though it's seen better days stands under a shadeport. An assortment of succulents and cacti grows in profusion out of old wine barrels cut in half to create planters. The brickwork of the front porch is greened with moss.

"*They may have a security system inside*," Ashton comments as grip the front door's handle.

I nod then reach out with my daimonic senses, feeling the buzz from the electrical current in the place. One frequency jumps out at me, linked to a telephone line. It's quite easy finding its complementary signal. Something beeps twice, loudly inside the empty house.

"*You never cease to be fucking amazing*," Ashton remarks.

"Flattery won't get you far with me, ghost," I reply.

The people who live here are definitely the old-school, over-the-top horsey types. Old prints of the animals adorn the walls, with more equine statues littering the area than should be legal. Apart from that, the dogs' heavy scent is imbued in the rooms. Ugh. Animal lovers. No doubt they cuddle with their pooches in bed.

"You keep a good watch, Ashton. I don't want people to walk in on me here."

He doesn't reply, but I feel his awareness spread out, away from me.

I hit the kitchen. Flies drone from the piles of dirty dishes and crockery in the sink, at least two days of washing up here. Although I don't see sign of the cat, crusty old fish still spills out of one of the food bowls. No way I'd live like this.

The fridge—one of those big, double-doored, family-sized numbers from the late 1980s—reveals a cornucopia of edibles. These folks do all their shopping at Woolworths, and I stuff myself with cooked chicken strips coated in a honey-mustard sauce, cheese and some pasta salad. There's so much food here it's doubtful they'll notice any of it's missing.

Family photos are stuck to the fridge door with an assortment of magnets. I study the portraits while I munch—a mother and father, both blond and in their mid- to late-forties, and two daughters, equally blond. Happy faces, sun-browned skin, they are the epitome of a family that functions as a unit. Most of the photographs show them riding, some show-jumping. Rosettes adorn nearly every available surface.

No doubt they'd be talking horses from breakfast to bedtime. I suppress a shudder then make my way to the master bedroom. Fortune smiles. The father of the family is pretty much the same size as me. Another bonus is the pair of hiking boots I find at the back of his cupboard. They fit with two pairs of socks, which help with the nasty blisters already formed on my toes and heels.

Feeling much more human after donning a fresh long-sleeved T-shirt and a dark corduroy jacket lined with sheepskin, I pause in the bathroom to clean myself as best I can with the limited time available. The shower would have been bliss, but I'm too on edge, imagining a daughter walking in on a strange thug using the family bathroom. A little bit of searching reveals a gun safe in the study. The combination lock offers up the contents after only five minutes' concentration.

I could grow used to a life of crime. Most burglars would give their right hand for my abilities. All the while I move about to leave as little sign as possible of my passage. With luck the family won't even notice they've been robbed until they think of looking for these specific items.

Ashton will most likely know how to use the pistol and ammunition I help myself to. I couldn't bring myself to search for the gun that was lost when I took out Cynthia. Gods, I don't know enough about these weapons but anything that will give me an advantage at this stage will be better than going into trouble without any preparation. The gun is heavy in my hand, its weight filled with portent. It seems strange somehow to consider how one little bullet can cause so much damage.

Richard had guns. He knew how to use them. I should have paid more attention back then but I hadn't considered that one day I'd have to look out for myself.

The Book of Ammit presents another problem entirely. I stow it in a small daypack I find in the same cupboard as the gun safe. Not knowing when I'll have food again, I filch muesli bars from the kitchen, as well as chocolate. No news is good news, as far as Ashton is concerned, but the hairs on the back of my neck prickle. I need to get out of this house before I push my luck further.

Ashton reconnects with me as I stride down the driveway. The shadows are growing long, and the air has a bite to it.

"I assume you know how to use guns?" I ask him when his presence settles on me like a chill mist.

"*You got a gun? Oh.*"

I touch the thing I've strapped to the holster I wear beneath the jacket, more so he can feel the slick metal. His wordless approval is apparent.

We leave the car where it's parked. Even if we don't use it as a getaway vehicle, I couldn't care what happens to it. It takes half an hour to get near Jonathan's compound, as I'm beginning to think of the place. *The Book of Ammit* burns a figurative hole in my back. It's foolish to stride into House Montu's territory with this thing. By now they should be well aware that something has gone wrong with Cynthia and Paul's mission, that I'm now at large. But by the gods, I can't hide the damned stele anywhere, especially if I have to make a run for it in a hurry. Any human stumbling upon it wouldn't know the worth of what they have found. Or the danger.

In the dimming light I view my enemies' stronghold from the relative safety of a low-spreading wild olive, which provides a modicum of cover should a vehicle approach along the road. Six-foot palisade fencing surrounds the property—topped with electric wiring no doubt linked to an alarm system should I short the current.

It would be best to wait for nightfall, to gain a small advantage offered by the darkness. There's nothing for me to do but wait, and I hunker down, resting my back against the wall, the pack containing *The Book of Ammit* cradled in my arms as though it were some malignant offspring.

Though I don't intend to, I nod off, my dreams an unsettling welter of nameless faces, voices accusing me. Someone shoves me hard against the wall and I lurch into a half-crouch only to be thrown down to the ground by an invisible force, soil and leaf litter filling my mouth.

"Someone's leaving the property, fool!"

For a moment I'm unable to place where I am, then it all shifts into stunning focus: I'm outside the House Montu headquarters; it's fully dark, I'm fucking freezing, and a large vehicle is exiting the property. Its headlights all but blind me while Ashton's angry ghost keeps me pressed into the dirt.

The large car shifts gears, and the sudden fear takes hold they've seen something that they'll stop, but it continues on its way, rumbling down the road, and Ashton lets go of his death grip.

"That was close. Thanks."

"The way you were sitting there with my mouth hanging open like you were passed out from smoking too much zol... How could anyone miss that?"

"How many people still in the compound?"

He departs in that unnerving way that makes me feel as though part of my essence peels off like a second skin, leaving me hunched behind the wild olive. It's best to fuel my body, so I eat one of the muesli bars, this sad substitute for a meal sticking in the back of my throat when I try to swallow.

The wind gusts, but so far no clouds have pulled in, and the temperature has plunged to a bone-chilling cold. What are the chances of this hare-brained scheme's success? It's easy for despair to set in when so much is unknown and I'm relying on the word of dead man.

He has served me well, but how far can I push this association? What entrapments lie in wait? For surely House Montu has much, much more in its arsenal than for which I can prepare at such short notice.

Ashton's whispery presence caresses my face. "*It's not a complete loss. It would appear that they've sent half their staff to find out what happened to Bitchface and the Beanpole. There are about six guys. I can show you where they are, if you want.*"

"No other option, is there? Where's the old man?"

"*He's in his study, reading.*"

"Marlise?"

"*Asleep or drugged. I don't know.*"

"Dare I ask about..."

Ashton's dry laughter brings cold comfort. "*It's way past that chick's bedtime. She's watching the History Channel. Fucking hell, I tell you it's unnatural. Shouldn't she be playing with dolls or something?*"

A surge of anger pushes past my worry. All this is Meritiset's fault. If it weren't for her I'd have... Damn. It would have been me there, now, watching television, in the heart of a great House. Would I have had the sense to play dumb, be an agent for House Adamastor? I don't know.

With a shake of my head, I rise. "Okay, stupid ghost. Lead on."

I stifle a chuckle, thinking of the military applications attached to my working relationship with Ashton. Certainly not ideal, and it astounds me I've managed to keep a handle on his fitful presence. Hugging the shadows, I pick my way along the side of the road until we near the front gate.

It takes only the briefest amount of concentration to freeze the security cameras, which, when I visualise them while using my powers, appear as blips of static when I focus on their aetheric *feel*. Then it's simply a case of matching the signal to get the gate to open and close behind me. Not all the way, of course, but enough space to slip my frame through a gap.

"*The first guy's over there in the office.*" Ashton directs my attention to a small room adjoining the garage along the side of the house, where a light casts yellow rectangles in the gloom. "*If you hurry, the patrol guy won't be round here for another three minutes. He's busy taking a piss in the rose bushes by the koi pond.*" The ghost's smirk is tactile, and my own lips tug in response.

"I'm glad someone's having fun." I pitch my voice low.

My footsteps sound unnaturally loud to my ears, but I'm glad for the wind in the trees, though it sends tendrils of hair into my mouth. I've no idea whether the man silhouetted in the window is an initiate. At any rate, House Montu would ensure that all their employees are highly aware, sensitive to their environment, so I begin to draw slowly, deliberately from a wide footprint around me, borrowing more from the wind than anything else.

Nothing like a bit of a flicker in the household power to distract someone's attention from whatever it is he's doing. Questing for the door mechanism, I'm glad to discover it is unlocked, and one of those regular mechanisms. House Montu obviously doesn't consider that someone would succeed in breaking into the property, or get this far.

"*Hurry,*" Ashton says. "*The oke is just around the corner now.*"

It's now or never. I grab the handle and barge into the small office, where a man turns around from a bank of screens, his eyes wide and mouth opened in an *O* of surprise. He doesn't get a chance to make a sound. The force of the daimonic power I smash into him is the equivalent of getting hit by a car. The man is flung into the wall opposite, taking most of the electronic equipment with him in a shower of breaking glass and sparks. His limbs twitch, and for a moment, his *Kha* shimmers as the souls depart.

"That was a little too spectacular," I say to Ashton.

"The other goon is running. He must have heard."

I spin around, gathering from the energy around me as I recharge for the next shot. A young black man, who can't be older than twenty, bumps right into me, most likely not expecting me to rush outside with the same force of his arrival.

Stunned, we both fall to the ground in a tangle of limbs. He has my jacket gripped by the lapels, and it's with great difficult that I bring my knee up to get him in the groin. The man lets go, but he's yelling his head off. Rising into a half-seated position I sideswipe him, hard. There's an audible *crack* as vertebrae in his neck disintegrate from the impact, and I scramble to escape the now-jerking corpse.

Killing is too easy and I stare stupidly at the body, another human reduced to so much meat in less than a minute—by my bare hands and daimonic potential. Then I'm knocked sideways by an invisible force.

A loud bang shatters the night, and something whines through the air near my left ear as I struggle to regain my feet. My lungs wheeze painfully.

"Motherfucker's got a gun!" Ashton yells. *"Run!"* He gives me another hard shove, in the direction of the back of the house, and I can hear the thud of at least two pairs of feet behind me, men shouting at me, but their words are an unintelligible jumble over my own ragged breathing.

The back of the house is paved, pillars supporting vine-laden beams as I dodge past wrought-iron furniture and a covered lap-pool. Another explosion shatters the night, and hot fire rips through my left arm, sending me sprawling against the wall. The blaze of agony is exquisite, each tendril coiling through my nervous system. At first I look about to figure out what I perhaps bumped into but then it dawns on me that I've been shot.

"*Bugger it!*" Ashton screams in my head.

It's through the haze as I manage to turn to face my aggressors that I see first how the one flies through the air to plunge head first into the pool, the second falling hard to come skidding to a halt five metres from where I'm half crouched.

Even as the one on the ground tries to rise, I release a blast of power that flips him over backwards. He does not get up again, his limbs contorting in final paroxysms of death and blood oozing out of various orifices.

The one in the pool thrashes to the side. I don't have any daimonic reserves for him, but I stagger forward to kick him hard in the face as he pulls himself over the lip. Cartilage crunches and he falls back. I almost follow him, swaying dangerously over the edge.

"*That's four down,*" Ashton says. "*You don't have long. The other two are coming down from their quarters. They've heard the ruckus.*"

"And the old man?" Warmth flows down my skin, soaking into the T-shirt and jacket.

"*He's gone to the girl's room. He seems far too chill.*"

"Save the best for last," I remark. "Let's get the annoying minnows out of the way."

"*Hardly annoying minnows. Look at how you've fucked up my body. If it weren't for your Jedi mind tricks I'd have taken over the steering again. You kill this body, bitch, I'm going to—"*

"What?"

"Never mind. They come. Kitchen door to your right."

Dragging at the aethers, I pull more power into me just as the two men shove through the door. The air around me crackles, and a sharp twinge in my sinuses warns me of an incipient nose bleed to accompany my efforts. Even Lizzie never had to draw so hard on her daimonic powers.

The men stop to stare at me.

The power hums through me, the wind whipping at my hair. For a moment I gain an impression of what I look like from Ashton's almost omniscient viewpoint, disorientating to have more than three dimensions, and an increased sense of the spirit world howling at the edges.

The creature these men face seems lit from within, the skull gleaming through a thin layer of skin spattered with blood flowing freely from the nostrils. Goulish. Hair flowing against the gusts of wind. Eyes wild, white-rimmed.

One man reaches in slow motion for the gun holstered at his thigh. This is all the prompting I need to release the gathered force. My aggressors are pummelled, the kitchen door splintering from the impact.

I lose my footing, thrown back by the recoil to smash into the ground, a devastating suddenness. Blackness swallows everything.

☥

The first thing I'm conscious of is the ringing in my ears. Then the crushing, polarised pain. Tentatively

I flex my arms, my fingers; my left arm chilled and numb in the blood-soaked jacket. Above the trees' limbs lash at the starry void.

"*Get up! Fool!*" Ashton says, his voice sounding in my head as though from a great distance.

An awful groan rips from my belly and I strain, my muscles at first not obeying me. "What?"

"*It's a mess. The kitchen. It looks as though you've microwaved them or something. Dunno. Bits of...*" Fear laces his tone. Ashton is deeply afraid. Of me, my powers.

I reach with my daimonic senses, but only the slightest trickle curls into me. I pray I haven't fried my synapses. It is with great effort that I manage to pull myself into a seated position, a wave of nausea bringing a sweet trickle of semi-digested vomit up from my stomach to trickle from my parted lips.

"*Get up, bitch!*"

"I'm...not...your bitch."

"*You gonna be the old poes's bitch if you don't pull yourself together.*"

"Wha—"

"*He's moving from the study. Coming this way. And I think he's fully loaded. You're not.*"

"Fuck."

It's one thing coming up against a rabble of initiates and almost-Inkarnas. It's quite another matching my strength against a man in the latter years of his power. While the *Kha* may no longer be as resilient as that of someone in his prime, the mind of an Inkarna, after years of meditation and workings, is a truly frightening thing to behold, especially in concert with an experienced *Akh*.

Lizzie would have packed some serious punch, controlled and efficient, but my grip over Ashton's

Kha seems to result in a bit of a hit-and-miss situation. Now I'm running on empty. When I stretch my senses, I can feel the vast presence approaching, a man who heads up the local chapter of one of the most powerful militant Houses in our society.

The first impulse is to turn tail, to try for a better day, but the backpack containing *The Book of Ammit* is a heavy burden. I will run and run, and every time I try to go to ground in order to lick my wounds, my enemy will grow stronger, wiser to my ways. I have a few seconds at best to prepare.

Anpu Upuaut, open the way for me, Set stand before me and lend me strength, Harwer behind me, give me dominion over the negation of Apep, Ma'at, let the just prevail…

There. I can sense a trickle. It's not much but something, a filament of strength flowing into my body as though I've broken a barrier holding me from tapping into the aethers. It's nothing like the build-up of power I used on the two unfortunate employees bare moments ago, but it's better than nothing.

"*The gun, idiot. Get your gun.*"

"I'm not sure?"

"*Let me guide you.*"

This means allowing Ashton a modicum of control over this *Kha*, which in this dire situation is less than ideal, but what option do I have? I've never used a gun before.

"*We're pretty fucked, either way.*"

"Scum it." I let slip some of my control—not everything, but enough for Ashton to move the *Kha* with some degree of autonomy. The all-too-real fear of obliteration, or eternal slavery, has me in its grip, though Ashton's handling of the slim black pistol is reassuring, especially the way he knows just how to toggle off the safety.

I recall something Richard said many years ago, about not having qualms about using any resource at one's disposal, that so long as the results are congruent with Ma'at, the way would be right. However, each action comes with consequences, and it is understanding this delicate balance that allows us to sometimes circumvent disaster.

It isn't right holding Ashton here, making him dance at my beck and call, yet without him I wouldn't have made it this far. Let the man have his hour, perhaps redeem himself for all the evil he has done to others.

Ashton bares my teeth in a bitter snarl as Jonathan steps out the kitchen door. The man has the same almost-supernatural presence about him, his white hair standing on end with the static of daimonic powers.

While Ashton lifts the gun, I do what I can to draw hard on the available sources. Damn, Jonathan is good, better even than Richard in his prime, and all energy—even mine—is sucked towards the impossible vortex spinning about my opponent.

The old man appears impassive, almost bored when he looks upon me. I'm not certain whether I detect a faint flicker of disappointment, even.

"You gonna die, old man," Ashton says. He pulls the trigger, but it's as if time itself slows down. I feel something click in the gun before a protracted roaring starts, the bullet crawling from the muzzle at a snail's pace.

Before me Jonathan has his hand raised, the projectile slowing until it glows white-hot before dropping to the ground with a metallic *plink*. True hearing returns, and reality resumes its mundane pace. The old man smiles at me, his features reminding me of someone more benevolent, a Benedictine monk perhaps. The wind falls oddly still, and in the garden beyond the first line of trees, a frog starts a hesitant call before falling silent abruptly.

"That wasn't a very intelligent way to approach this predicament, Inkarna Nefretkheperi." Jonathan shakes his head slightly.

He doesn't know about Ashton's angry ghost. He doesn't know who really is in charge of this body.

"*Please don't do anything stupid*," I beg of Ashton.

I may as well be asking a bull elephant to stop in mid-charge. Ashton bunches the muscles and storms forward before I can grab control of him. Jonathan doesn't do more than twitch his hand slightly. It's like colliding with a wall, and I fall back. While Ashton gasps for air it's easy to push him into the back, though the inversion of control for this *Kha* doesn't come without a price as the flesh surrounds me once more. *I'm* the one who now struggles for breath.

"*I'm going to fucking kill him!*" Ashton rages, rendered safely impotent.

I'm too busy trying to shake off the overwhelming pain to reply, dimly aware of Jonathan stepping forward to stand over me, peering down with concern stamped on his features.

"I must admit, I did underestimate you somewhat. I shall have to call in reinforcements from Johannesburg and Durban now, thanks to you. More than thirty years' training undone tonight with the amount of death and carnage." He sounds almost quizzical, as though everything that has transpired is a mere glitch in his well-oiled plans.

The grumble of an engine tells me the vehicle has

returned with its complement of staff. Whatever advantage I had is gone. The man gets a faraway look in his eyes, and he must have a mind-meld with one of the goons who has returned because it's not long before I hear the thud of boots coming around the side of the house.

I'm powerless to stop this, and tears of frustration form, running cold streaks down my cheeks. That's when I feel it, and so does Jonathan, because he stiffens where he stands, casting about wildly for the source of power whining.

The wind stops shaking the trees. The lights flicker in the house, dim; go out. The air plumes in front of my face, so cold my skin is instantly chilled. All is darkness, pale faces etched in starlight and the green gleam of emergency lanterns switching on to bathe everything in a chthonic glow. *Ashton, what in the hell are you doing?*

The men run up, half a dozen of them, but Jonathan holds up a hand in signal: *wait*.

"I can tell this is not you, Inkarna Nefretkheperi. It is too polarised. What is this thing you have brought upon us?"

My lips won't shape any words, and I blink up at him. Ashton, having learnt by example—having seen me in action enough times to—has figured this out himself. Only he has no body to act as focus. There's no telling what could happen. This trumps his previous manifestations by mega-Watts.

The whine grows into an ear-splitting hum, and I have to clap my hands over my ears in a vain attempt to shield myself. The vibration crawls through my core, wriggling in my collarbone. A man cries out and drops. Then another.

"What are you doing?" I ask, but I look straight at

Jonathan while mustering an expression of abject fear. I may as well confuse the hell out of him, but I can't deny the fact that I'm scared witless. Paralysed.

Ashton doesn't answer, but then I hadn't really expected he would.

One of the soldiers screams, flung like so much meat against a pillar. He doesn't move. While one of the remaining men freezes, his gun half-lowered, and looking about him with confusion stamped on his features, the two others run, uttering gibberish.

This is too much for the last guard. By now the air feels thick around us. I watch with dawning horror as the young man lifts the pistol to his own head. He turns to face Jonathan, a frightening too-wide grin splayed across his lips.

"Die, motherfucker." He pulls the trigger.

I close my eyes, but the sudden release of pressure and the thud of flesh and bone hitting the paving is unmistakeable, as is the iron tang of blood and something else, organic and wild.

Jonathan's groan has me summon the courage to look at the old man fallen to his knees before me. He stares glassily at the remains of the man he's trained for years.

Without waiting for Ashton, I stagger to my feet and throw myself at Jonathan, using all the power in my limbs. Although he is a slight man, Jonathan manages to flip me onto my side, but I grab him by the throat, eerily reminded of that night I fought Ashton off Marlise.

I straddle him, using the advantage of my height and bulk to keep him pinned to the ground. Whatever resources of daimonic power he had earlier he's lost. Words are wasted on this man. I'd dearly love to know why he's gone this far in his plans, but something ugly in me just wants to choke the life out of him. A sudden electricity flows through me, a raging torrent. Then a snap and everything spins into real-time, the wind crashing the branches overhead, Jonathan making a strangled gargling.

His skin turns blue, his eyes bulging as I apply more pressure, drawing on what slips of ambient power still occur in the area. Jonathan's hands snatch at my sleeves as he tries to grip my wrists, but each time he bucks, in a vain attempt to unseat me, his efforts grow weaker.

I'm doing it again. I'm taking a life, and each time it becomes easier and easier as I feed this core of hate that fuels my actions. The stone I carry in the backpack grows heavy and warm, as though it gains from this dismal activity, and snaking lines of life force drag from Jonathan to spiral through my arms and through my heart centre, and into the stele.

The fateful words inscribed upon the stone come to my lips unbidden—evil, forbidden words—and I stop in mid-incantation the moment I realise what it is I'm doing. I will not send someone's souls howling into nothingness.

With a choked cry I stumble backwards, my heel sending a gun skittering. Whether it is my own or the one the unfortunate guard used on himself, it doesn't matter. I snatch it up.

Jonathan lies gasping, pale now, a hand raised to his throat. He sees my intention and raises an arm. "Nnn—"

I don't give him a chance to finish. *Bang!*

The gun's recoil jars my arm, and I step back, a fresh ringing, this time more physical, marring my hearing. A dark blot spreads like an accusation from the centre of Jonathan's chest. Fascinated, I watch how the souls coalesce just on the edge of my vision, a soft, shimmering, almost humanoid shape that dissipates quickly, so that when I blink, the after-effect seems more something that I'd have imagined.

The lights in the house flicker then turn on, bathing this entire area in so much brightness that I have to squint for a moment to wait for my vision to adjust.

Feet planted wide, I stand, arms loose at my sides, still clutching the gun in my right hand. Warm blood drips from my left hand, but this *Kha* is so battered, so numbed from shock, the pain hardly registers.

Ten dead. All by my hand.

I sway, catching myself against a pillar, a wash of exhaustion making it seem a good idea to sit, rest and regain my breath. I have killed a powerful Inkarna. There will be hell to pay when I return to Per Ankh. I can only hope Leonora made it that far, that she can intercede for me when this almighty shit storm, as Ashton would call it, breaks.

"Ashton?" I murmur.

Nothing but the wind, that has renewed its raging, answers.

There is still Catherine, hiding somewhere in this house, no doubt guarding Marlise or poised to kill her. I know I would be with the hostage by now, holding some sort of power to threaten or cajole my enemy to slip up.

She's just a girl. How can I kill a young girl?

She betrayed me. That bitterness sinks its venomous stinger in deep, a scorpion I don't see until I step with a bare foot on the carapace. All those years that she must have been plotting this, machinating behind the scenes under the guise of sisterhood, so House Adamastor would send its weakest link—*me*—someone whose deepest secrets she'd pried out. All my fears. My hopes, my dreams. I'd told her so much, made myself naked to her.

And, on the outside, how ridiculous this situation, that a grown man in his early twenties should fear a confrontation with a young girl much weaker than him. The blurred identities are enough to raise a wave of disbelief.

None of this is real, is it? I'm just trapped in a wild nightmare.

What if Jonathan called the police before he came out? Or buzzed some private security company? Even now the chapter houses farther upcountry must be trying to raise them on the phone. What if Jonathan wasn't the only full Inkarna of House Montu in Cape Town?

This snaps me out of my miserable reverie.

I draw a deep breath and look about me. "Ashton?"

Still the angry ghost doesn't reply. Right, then I'm on my own for this one. Allowing myself three deep and calming breaths, I centre myself as well as I can, visualising a flaming serpent flaring its hood behind me.

"Wadjet protect me," I utter, pulling hard on what tatters of energy are available in my immediate surroundings.

Where I'm going now, guns won't help me, and I'm not entirely sure what I face. How would I feel in Catherine's position? Scared? Most certainly. How powerful is she? Is Marlise all right?

"Ashton, where are you?" I mutter.

I've come to rely on the angry ghost far too much, to the point that now, without his presence, I feel half-blind, exposed.

The house is eerily quiet, the only sound the impassioned voice of a television presenter discussing

Hitler's preoccupation with the Aryan race, orchestral music in the background. My boots crunch on broken glass, and I look up to see where a number of light bulbs have shattered from their fittings. I walk gingerly, so as to make as little noise as possible, and continue to tug at the aethers and drag more tendrils of power to me.

The energy is not nearly enough, but what little I gather thrums through my veins, pale in comparison to the might of earlier. This *Kha* is just shy of being a shambling corpse, and I must push it beyond its limits.

Damn you, Ashton, where the hell are you?

I hear it then—sobbing—from upstairs. The stone tablet I carry grows heavier with each step. I tread quietly up to the first floor. Stern-eyed portraits glare down at me from beneath bushy brows. I assume these to be previous masters of House Montu. Not a woman in sight. For them to have accepted Catherine so readily…

But then a horrible thought occurs to me. If Catherine's father already is so deeply entrenched in House Montu…and one cannot predict when the right *Kha* is available… Christopher van Vuuren must have drowned his own daughter to make way for the next Inkarna. A sacrifice freely given.

"Damn." I say the word softly, more for my own comfort than anyone else's.

The Oriental carpet with its tree of life design muffles my progress, a clock ticking quietly on the landing telling me it's a quarter to eight. The television presenter's voice drones on about the defences on the beaches of Normandy, of Allied and Axis powers. How apt.

A door at the end of the first floor passage is ajar, a

flickering blue light hinting at action occurring on a screen. I don't want to go any farther, fear of what I may find making my feet adhere to the carpet.

I have to face her.

Each metre feels like more than ten, my heart hammering and my throat tight. Paused by the door, I flex my fingers and swallow reflexively. Should I knock? A hysterical giggle wants to rip itself out of my belly, but I tamp it down. Another breath.

"I know you're there." Catherine sounds tired, resigned.

To hell with this. I step over the threshold into a small study. A desk and chair with a flat-screen computer monitor stands by the window. The television is against the wall facing the door, where I stand. Catherine sits on a massive pile of cushions, her back to me.

It's as if she says, *I know you wouldn't try to hurt me*, but her shoulders are hunched and she has pulled a blanket around her—an old tartan affair that looks as though it has seen better days. She doesn't turn to face me.

How can I possibly hurt a child?

But this is Meritiset, whose deception has cost me so much, has cost House Adamastor almost everything. *The Book of Ammit* weighs even heavier.

I reach with my senses and try to ascertain whether the child has pulled any daimonic energies to her— nothing. About two metres behind her I stop, my reluctance holding me from laying hands on her. What am I to do?

"Are you going to look at me, Meritiset? So we can talk, face to face?"

"She's in the spare bedroom. I suggest you take your woman and leave."

The child sniffs, and for one wild, brief moment I want to reach out to place a comforting hand on her shoulder. The impulse dies in an instant when I recall Cynthia's features twisted in hatred. Meritiset, Catherine... How the hell do I differentiate?

"Why me?" I pitch the words low.

"Why you?" She starts laughing, rises to her feet and turns slowly to face me.

A cold sick jolt passes through my stomach, the duality of looking upon the face of a would-be murderer inhabiting the body of an innocent.

This could have been me.

Now I am the murderer.

Try as I might, I can't meet her gaze, which remains steady and focused on my features.

"How do you think I felt, discovering Siptah courted you? He promised me forever, that we would find a way to punch through *together*. How do think I felt when you pitched up, alone, claiming Siptah trained you, *married* you? And that he never came back? Only you?"

Her words send barbs straight to the core of the matter, to memories that have lost some of their ferocity because, encased as I am in stolen flesh, a new life has come to me, my long-ago acceptance of Richard's death so far in the past it's reduced to an occasional dull ache.

"So you betrayed the House? I heard the stories, of Siptah finding you fully fledged. Don't you think it's just too convenient? Especially that you were supposedly the one who selected this child's body. What, is House Montu now sacrificing its younglings to keep it in the family, so to speak?"

She has the good grace to blanch before her expression hardens. "We are all pawns in this game,

Nefretkheperi. You. Me. We do what we must."

"Then why insist that I punch through? You could have persuaded the elders to send you instead, if Siptah's rescue was foremost on your mind. If you could get them over their initial distrust of me then surely you could undo what issues of trust still remained between you and the council? Or was it always your intention that I am lost in limbo for ages, just out of spite. You're as childish as that body you inhabit." I shake my head.

She laughs. "Oh, you don't know the half of what you're up against. I must admit you've done pretty well for someone who knows so little. Yes. I admit it. It's petty, but you really played into it. And yes, I took a *childish* delight in my machinations."

"You underestimated me," I say.

The child shakes her head, her eyes alight with mischief. "Oh, no. It's you who underestimate me. You may be bigger, daimonically stronger, but you don't have this."

Before I can move, she reaches out and grabs my left hand. Her skin is cold to the touch, her grip crippling. The world blinks out, and I lose all sensation of what's up, down, warm or cold. Just the deepest darkness remains, great gouts of daimonic power ripping through me as though I'm caught in the midst of a thunderstorm.

Falling...falling...tumbling end over end. This motion speeds up, and a roaring fills my ears. I snap into a completely different scene. My viewpoint is remote, as though I'm watching a scenario play out from multiple observers. There's a garden. Lavender bushes line gravel pathways. Although the sky is heavy, overcast, the air is warm, and lazy bees swarm drunkenly among the bruised purple heads of the fragrant shrubs, which have been sculpted into continuous hedges formed into the intricate pattern of a labyrinth.

High walls surround this hidden garden where a stately oak holds each quarter. A three-tiered fountain stands at the centre of this landscape, a stylised dolphin that looks more like a fish spouting a trickle of water into the successive bowls. The sound is music, singing of joy, the beauty of being alive.

Laughter then. I modify the focus to see a young man and woman rush into the garden, the man shoving shut a heavy door and leaning against it while his partner plants a dozen kisses on his lips, cheeks and forehead.

Judging by their dress I estimate them to belong to the Tudor era: all sombre-hued brocades and velvets, the woman's bosom straining out of her stomacher. Milky-white skin, auburn curls loosened from pins to drape seductively over a shoulder.

He is bearded, but there's no mistaking the lively glint in his eyes—Siptah, *Richard* in another life. It's the way he turns his head, the tilt to his lips. Those gestures are immortal.

She...

Meritiset.

The world shifts with a sickening lurch.

A chamber, its walls draped with heavy tapestries depicting hunt scenes. A four-poster bed and upon it two people writhing in the throes of lust. The woman sits astride the man, her auburn hair loose and spilling down her back. She raises herself and grinds down hard on her partner, whose fingers dig into the soft flesh of her buttocks as they strain together in their carnal dance.

The woman—Meritiset—throws her head back,

her eyes closed in obvious passion, and Siptah's hand trails up from her back to cover her breast. The abandon of this scene digs its knife deep. He's loved other women, possibly with more passion than he ever reserved for me, each thrust sending the blade further. Jealousy is an ugly thing, and though I want to rage at the pair, I'm held rooted to the spot, unable to move forward, my cries of anguish unheard.

The scene shifts again, and I'm standing on the mossy bank of a stream, green willow fronds dipping into the crystalline water. Meritiset lies on her back, her thighs spread wide, her voluminous skirts hitched up to around her waist while Richard crouches between her legs, offering her oral pleasures. The way she bucks her hips to his probing tongue leaves nothing to the imagination, and I wish I could look away from how he massages his straining phallus, his thumb rubbing at the head of his shaft, his hands slick with his emissions.

With a long groan of pleasure he straddles the woman on the ground, thrusting into her once, twice, hard before he shudders in climax, Meritiset wrapping her legs around his back.

I don't want to see this, don't want to know about a past that happened long before I even figured as a sentient being.

"This is not necessary!" I rage. "Why are you doing this to me?"

Scene after scene unfolds, and to my horror, I feel the backlash of Meritiset's desire burn through me. There seems something so perverse now in having a man enter my body with his phallus, of the peculiar aches and wants unique to a woman.

"Stop it!"

Laughter—Meritiset's—fills my head, and the

current scene of passion blurs into a smear of colour, revolving about me in a vortex, a thundering inferno of need. I don't have to brush my hand against my denims to know I'm hard, and for this I am furious, that Meritiset can manipulate me. If anyone were to walk in on this scene, of the child Catherine gripping Ashton's arm...

Yet I'm not even sure where I am.

Dimly I'm aware that my *Kha* in the material world is forced to its knees, the girl's paralysing hold on me having driven me to kneel before her.

"You're pathetic, Nefretkheperi, you know that? You really have mired yourself in this fool's past. Now look at you. Men were always weaker, didn't you know that?"

I want to struggle against the barrage of memories, all foreign, but it's almost as difficult as fighting the nothingness of limbo, the opposite really, like having one's finger shoved into an electric socket and being unable to pull away.

"Don't..." My voice sounds distant, as though it no longer belongs to me, while all my senses are hurled about in this maelstrom of Meritiset's memories.

A small hand pat at my jacket, my jeans pockets and a sudden realisation hits me when she pulls the butterfly knife from the back pocket—the butterfly knife the House Montu initiates never found in their arrogance. Hell, even I'd forgotten I'd had it on me. She means to end this here.

I try to jerk from her hold, both physically and mentally, but the meld of our two memories is so hard, so fast, it's as if we've become one person, with her *Akh* dominating. Is this how it has felt for Ashton when he tried to take over our shared *Kha*? How is it that Meritiset can still maintain so much control?

She's going to stab or gut me, or slit my throat, and there's nothing I can do about it. While she maintains her hold on my arm, keeping up this meld, I hear her flick open the knife.

But there is one thing that I can do, and the thought frightens me beyond anything I've ever considered. The words of Ammit. It's not so much the words, it's the knowledge of what I can do with the intention, especially now with my body incapacitated and my ability to reach through is paralysed.

One thing Meritiset hasn't banked on is my ability to wield these words like the knife she now holds. My other option is to give up, allow *The Book of Ammit* to fall into the hands of the House of Montu. Or I could take one more life to spare many.

The way of Ma'at must be served no matter how badly I stain my eternal *Akh*.

I don't need to speak the words with my lips and tongue, but I send them from me, shaping each one with care in my mind and directing them through the link with the girl. She pauses, and I'm assuming in mid-lunge, as the first import of what is transpiring hits her.

"What are you doing?" Her suspicion is a heavy cloud settling over me, an attempt to muffle my attack.

Then the realisation dawns upon her and she utters a small shriek.

"...and into the abyss your *Akh* shall be flung, after Ammit has devoured your *Ib*..."

Each syllable is a blade twisting through my *Ka* and my *Ba*, my *Akh*, my *Kha* responding. Then my voice is loud and echoes in the room as I open my eyes to stare into the face of the child. I've never noticed it before but her eyes have light flecks of brown embedded within the almost-crystalline green. The pupils become large as she registers that I'm actively returning her gaze, those fateful words dropping from my lips.

"*No*," she mouths, but no sound comes out.

This is not a child, I have to keep reminding myself. This is not a child. Meritiset would cheerfully have relegated me to an eternity of drowning in the Sea of Nun for a perceived slight. How was Lizzie to know Siptah had had another lover before me? Why judge me after the fact?

I was just a victim, collateral, someone who got in her way. I mean nothing in the larger scale of things, yet Meritiset's fit of pique has cost House Montu its victory at last gasp.

A single tear runs down the child's cheek. She is frozen, her fingers trembling where she clutches to me, now more for support than anything else. A cold fire blooms through my veins, thrumming through the floor, pumping through my heart to seep from the point of contact into Meritiset's frame. With each heartbeat she shivers, the frequency growing until, of a sudden, she stiffens and her eyes roll back to reveal the whites.

With a small gasp she lets go, topples over backward to land on the nest of pillows she'd made for herself earlier, when she'd been pretending to watching television.

"...what the Axis forces had not been prepared for was the tenacity of the French resistance, for the..." The television presenter drones on with his clipped British accent, and my gaze momentarily shifts to the occurrences on the screen, to grainy black-and-white images of Paris when the Nazi banner is torn down from a monument.

The child's body twitches spasmodically, glowing violet-blue at its edges, as though a spectral shape is superimposed for two or three heartbeats. She stills, and the stench of urine pervades the atmosphere.

I scrabble backwards with an oath, gazing in horror at the slow-spreading pool of liquid puddling between her thighs. She's dead. There's no sense of any spirit fleeing, only cold silence; *The Book of Ammit* is even heavier in the backpack, drawing me to sit hard on my rear while staring at the small corpse.

I've killed, *really* killed. I've destroyed someone's immortality, cut off any soul's energy from returning to the Sea of Nun. The realisation is crushing and my chest closes, tears prickling at the corners of my eyes. Those fateful words flash through my memory, etched indelibly. It is so easy to say them again. Too easy.

Is Ma'at satisfied? Was there any other possible outcome? If I'd killed the *Kha*, the *Akh* would keep returning, keep bedevilling me.

On the screen the Nazi insignia goes up in flames, and I know, in my heart of hearts, that House Montu's involvement must have been somewhere in that regime. I have made myself immortal enemies this day, eternal enemies who will hunt me down through the ages for as long as Nefretkheperi is my *Ren*. House Adamastor is finished.

This prompts me to scramble to my feet, my legs unwilling to obey my command. Damn, where the hell is Ashton? I need to find Marlise, if she's still alive, and get both of us out of this place before we're caught.

Who knows what retribution we face? If the girl

child's powers were anything to go by, what could a mature member of House Montu do? Ending Jonathan Binneman was mere fluke, a temporary victory. He'll be back.

I turn and rush out of this chamber of horror.

"Marlise!" My voice echoes in the empty passage, and I try each door I encounter until I enter a bedroom to find her curled in a foetal position on the bed, her back to the door.

She mumbles incoherently and turns, rubbing at her eyes before blinking blearily in my direction. Once again I'm struck by how young she looks, her dark red curls spilling out of the hair band that has loosened during her sleep.

I rush towards her and pull her by her hands into a seated position, kneeling to embrace her hard. Her breath tastes of the bitterness of sleep, but her comforting mint scent offers ease.

"Ash?" she murmurs in my ear.

"I'm here, baby. I'm here. It's going to be okay."

"I've had some terrible dreams…"

I can feel her yawning, the tension in her muscles as she straightens her spine then tightens her grip about my waist. She must register where she is, because she stiffens. "It's so quiet."

"We're okay, but we're going to have to get out of here, like as in yesterday." I can only hope the car I left down the road is still there, that it doesn't have a tracking device…but that would be easy to deactivate.

She lets me help her to her feet, and she sways groggily. We make a cursory sweep of the other rooms where I find her cell phone and wallet on a bedside table, and hand these to her. There's a picture of Cynthia and Paul on horseback in a forest. I turn the picture over.

"I need to call my parents." Marlise snatches the phone from me and switches it on.

I'd like to tell her it's not a good idea, but she scrolls down the menu and presses the call button, her expression one of concern while she waits for someone to answer. All the while I hold her gaze steadily, giving a small shake of my head when I hear the line crackle and someone answer on the other end.

Her pupils dilate and she pulls the phone from her face, killing the call.

"What?"

"It was my mother."

"She's fine?"

Marlise nods.

"Why did you end the call then?"

"I can't go back, can I?"

I offer the slightest shake of my head. The phone starts ringing shrilly, and Marlise ends the call. We both stare at the device in her hand. We should switch it off.

"Put on your shoes." I incline my head and motion at her feet.

"Oh." She hands me the cell phone, which immediately buzzes into life again. Marlise's expression turns to one of wild hope.

The caller ID displays an unknown number, and I answer, just for the hell of it, a small clench of suspicion in my belly.

"Hello?"

A man speaks. "I need to speak to Lucy! Immediately. I've been trying to get hold of her the last two days. Who are you?" He sounds pissed.

A faint glimmer of suspicion rises, and I recall the querulous old granny who's been pestering Marlise with the wrong number for the past week or two. I don't know what it is that makes me say what I do. "You can't speak to Lucy right now. She's in the shower."

I kill the connection then switch off the phone, glancing up to see Marlise's slight grin.

"What did you do that for?"

I can't keep a straight face. Everything that's happened during the past forty-eight hours has me howling with laughter. Ashton would have pulled a stunt like this, and it feels good to laugh until my stomach aches.

Marlise follows suit, realisation dawning. "That sounded like a guy on the other end of the line." She wipes at her eyes. "Her boyfriend?"

"Who knows? Who cares?" I straighten and draw a deep breath. "Okay, let's get out of here."

Hand in hand we sweep through the house, looking for anything that may be useful. Out of spite I trash the computer in the study, stomping the hard drive and other bits and bobs on the inside until they're nothing more than a clinking pile of fragments. We find a wad of cash in a wallet in the master bedroom. It's not much, but hell, two grand is better than nothing at all. It should buy us bus tickets, or something.

I lead Marlise out the front. I'd prefer her not seeing the mess at the back. Her mood is light, her essence giddy. She doesn't ask about what happened, but I see the question in her expression when we go downstairs. I've kept her away from the room where Catherine's *Kha* is cooling.

I stop by a walk-in closet by the front door, intending to rifle through it, and this is where Marlise notices that I'm bleeding.

"Ash! You can't go out like this."

The pain is hardly an issue when my entire being is thudding with exhaustion, but I stop to look numbly at the blood still dripping from my sleeve. I need time to hole up, heal myself, which is time we don't have. Not now. I glance up at her. "We must go."

She grips my jacket and shakes me. "Are you stupid? Besides you bleeding to death, do you think we can go about out there with you leaving a blood trail?"

Marlise has a point, and I allow her to lead me to a ground floor bathroom where, as luck would have it, we find a small first aid kit stowed in cupboard in which the sink is set. House Montu doesn't mess around.

I can't look at the wound. My daimonic senses suggest the bullet has gone all the way through, and I have to bite the inside of my cheek when Marlise dabs spirits on the wound before wadding it with sterile dressing and what seems like an entire roll of bandage. All the while my gut sense warns that we need to leave, we need to get out of here. Someone must be onto the disruption by now, perhaps a security company with dogs and men armed with big guns.

I still can't draw much power to me, and Ashton remains obstinately silent, though I send my thoughts out, nebulously, in a vain hope of making contact. Has he completely blown his souls to smithereens? That he may no longer be in existence upsets me on a deeper level. I may not admit it to him but I've grown fond of my angry ghost.

"Are you done yet, woman?" I ask.

"Patience!" She tugs a few times, sending sharp shooting pains through my nervous system.

The sense of urgency has me on my feet before she can fuss any longer. I grab her upper arm and rush her down the front stairs. We stop long enough for me to get a jacket from the closet—a bulky thing made from dark blue synthetic fabric. A random Blessed memory I encountered a lifetime ago suggests this is a good colour for night-time when stealth is required.

We dash down the front steps not a moment too soon. A helicopter is thudding closer, and a random flash of a search light illuminates the garden at the back of the house. Miraculously the gate is half open. The electronics must have shorted or perhaps the fleeing guards forced it open when they made their escape.

It doesn't matter now. We pelt along the street, our soles slapping on the tarmac. The screech of tyres around a corner has me jerk Marlise into a hedge as a convoy of sleek dark cars screeches past us. I press her face against my chest and allow my hair to spill over my features, praying the headlights don't pick out our shapes. The momentary discomfort offered by twigs pressing goodness knows where is nothing, considering what could happen should we get captured.

The roads are going to be hell, and no doubt they'll have other methods for tracking us. We need to get the hell out of here, and fast.

Desperately I rack Blessed memories, seeking some sort of knowledge to aid our escape. It comes to me in bursts, a child's remembrance of hunting tadpoles in the streams criss-crossing the green belts threading this neighbourhood. It's not ideal, but it's an improvement on taking the obvious routes and risking detection. No doubt they'll trawl the green belts, too, but there's far more cover.

Where the hell is Ashton? I could use him round about now. We crash into a riverbed choked with low brush that slaps into our faces. As fate would have it, the helicopter rattles off to the south. For now. It's quite possible they'll double back. This entire area is veined with tangled greenery. Marlise stumbles, and it's all I can do to stop myself from going down, jerking her onto her feet. Let there not be hidden obstacles. A little to the right our feet find a narrow track that snakes beneath willows.

The rain-swollen stream gurgles and gushes in its bed, but it's so dark I can't see my hands in front of my face. A beam of light slashes through the darkness, and I turn to look into Marlise's grinning face.

"You found a torch?"

"Men won't think of these things. It was in the cupboard next to the first aid kit."

I pause long enough to squeeze her to me, then we run. Sirens blaze though the stillness, in the rough direction from whence we came, lending urgency to our steps. Please let them not have dogs.

For how long we run I don't know. We have to stop often so I can catch my breath, bright sparks wiggling in my field of vision. Marlise asks me if I'm okay for the *nth* time, but I don't want to let on that I'm about to keel over.

We pause again just before an embankment and I look back the way we came, to where torch beams flash.

"They're on to us, aren't they?" Marlise says.

We've switched off our light, and I rise from the rotted log I've been half-leaning against. My legs buckle, my lungs burning from the effort of going.

When I try to snatch at the aethers, desperate for some flicker of daimonic energy, the skeins are mere tatters.

Disappointment burns at the back of my throat. We've made it this far. How can we lose out now?

A car engine rumbles in the distance, and wild hope soars. We've reached Constantia Main Road. Before I can react, Marlise has my hand in hers, and she tugs me upslope. The headlights of the passing vehicle blind us as it roars past, but the level surface of the gravelly verge is a blessing after our mad chase through the bush.

Our pursuers and a chorus of clicking frogs behind us, we stagger along, Marlise dragging me across the flat expanse of tar to the other side of the road.

"What now?" I gasp out the words.

"We're going to hitch-hike."

"Who's going to stop for us? It's dark."

"We won't know until we try."

"What if it's House Montu's people?"

"We don't have any other options. We have to try." She presses a flat object into my hand.

My fingers run over the surface: a leather sheath belonging to a knife. Wordlessly I grip this and shove it into the jacket pocket. I don't want to add anything about taking a knife into a gun fight. Not now.

First one car passes, then another. Marlise turns to face the oncoming traffic, an inane grin plastered to her features as she sticks out her thumb. But who in their right mind will stop to collect a woman who has me as her companion—some six-foot stranger with a mess of long black hair that doesn't look like it has seen a brush in years?

I'm about to point out the foolishness of this and suggest that we use her phone to call a taxi, when against all hope the next car does slow down and pull over to the side of the road. It's a battered Isuzu pick-up truck with a double cab and we pretty much fall into the back passenger seats.

A wiry black fellow turns to grin at us as he switches on the cabin light. His teeth shine white, his hair in dreads falling down his back. "You guys look like you could use a ride."

Marlise flashes him such a sweet smile I'd kiss her right there. "Thank you, mister."

He laughs and turns to face the road. Before he switches off the interior lamp I glimpse the miniature figurine dangling from the rear-view mirror: a small anthropomorphic shape with the head of a jackal.

That's when I allow myself to smile.

EPILOGUE

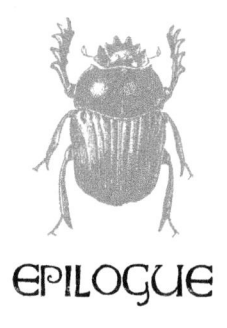

CICADAS SHRIEK IN the ragged gum tree that offers scant shade to Camdeboo Kitchen, a small hole-in-the wall Karoo pub. I lean against the pillar leading down to the chalky dirt road that cuts through the heart of Nieu Bethesda. Even now, six months later and mid-summer since our ordeal, I still find it difficult to sometimes register that we've made it this far.

We've *run* this far—exactly in the middle of nowhere, a House of two, a House that no longer has a name.

Sonja waves at me from the bar, her wild mop of white-blond hair gleaming in the low light as she sets down a crate of beers so she can pack in the fridges for the passing tourist trade. It's unbelievable that I've secured a future here, in this small Karoo hamlet with a population of less than a thousand, and that

I could convince the Wareings to take a ragged pair of strangers in when they themselves are hunted for what they are.

Granted, I'm still looking over my shoulder, still sending out my awareness with each visitor this small hamlet draws. Maybe House Montu thinks we've headed out of the country. That would be the sensible thing to do. That's what I would have done had I had the resources. But we didn't, and we still don't.

We could have gone missing in one of the other cities, but it's not like I can hide this *Kha*, can I? Unless I hide in plain sight in a place where just about every resident is eccentric and has a story to tell. I'm not the only freak with tattoos and piercings here.

Freaks like the Wareings. Who could miss them? A clan with their signature complexions, so pale they look like ghosts themselves. Psychics, seers... Witches, the lot of them.

They took one look at me and Marlise, and just about jumped us with a banishing ritual when we pulled in road-worn and weary. It's an uneasy alliance, but then I've a thing or two I can teach them in exchange for shelter, safety. I've sure as hell not told them about the stele. *The Book of Ammit* has a new hiding place, and I've gone there every other week to lay yet another compulsion on it. When we have to run, I'm leaving it here. And we will have to run. Not today. Perhaps not even tomorrow, but the time will come. House Montu is relentless. Of that I have no doubt.

But it is to Marlise that I go now, and as if by unspoken agreement, she meets me halfway from the door of the cottage we rent. It is situated off a quiet side road, shaded by cypresses, which release their resinous scent when the sun reaches its zenith. Water gurgles in the furrows, bringing life in this land where the summer sun bakes down without mercy in this remote river valley.

Marlise is six months into her pregnancy. I still can't wrap my grey matter around it when we kiss at the gate. I could kick myself for bringing an innocent into the world, but this tenuous peace has been balm to both our souls. I constantly find myself touching her belly, hardly daring to believe this miracle of new life.

"Ash?"

I realise with a start I'm holding her tightly to me, still outside the property. "Hey."

"I don't want to be funny about it, but I need to talk to you about something inside. Where the neighbours can't hear." She casts a meaningful glance to either side. Judging by the frown pulling at her features, something's up, and a cold slice of worry cuts through my veins.

I allow her to lead me inside, my eyes taking a moment or two to adjust to the dim interior of our home. Sinking into the couch, I draw her down with me. "What is it?"

She snuggles into my embrace, her hair tickling my arm. Marlise tilts her head so she can look up at me. "Something weird happened. It's about Ashton."

"I..." I honestly don't know what to say. Since our escape I thought it prudent not to mention my angry ghost, because he has not made contact with me.

Marlise frowns at me, tightening her grip around my waist. "I saw him. I was in the bathroom. I looked up after washing my face, and he was superimposed over me and I felt something...*here*." She moves my hand and presses it to her belly.

A shiver passes down my spine and I summon a smile I don't quite feel. "It's probably the heat, my dear. I told you not to spend so much time in the sun this morning. You probably need to take a nap or something." I press a kiss on her forehead.

Ashton Kennedy, you bastard.

For some reason I can't help but smile, just slightly. Rat bastard.

ABOUT THE AUTHOR

Nerine Dorman is a South African author and editor of science fiction and fantasy currently living in Cape Town. Her novel *Sing down the Stars* won Gold for the Sanlam Prize for Youth Literature in 2019, and her YA fantasy novel *Dragon Forged* was a finalist in 2017. Her short story "On the Other Side of the Sea" (Omenana, 2017) was shortlisted for a 2018 Nommo award, and her novella *The Firebird* won a Nommo for "Best Novella" during 2019. She is the curator of the South African Horrorfest Bloody Parchment event and short story competition and is a founding member of the SFF authors' co-operative Skolion, that has assisted authors such as Masha du Toit, Suzanne van Rooyen, Cristy Zinn and Cat Hellisen, among others, in their publishing endeavours.

Do follow Nerine on Twitter at nerinedorman

OTHER BOOKS BY NERINE DORMAN

Khepera Rising (#1)
Khepera Redeemed (#2)

Those Who Return
Inkarna (#1)
Thanatos (#2) – to follow

Camdeboo Nights

The Gatekeeper Cycle
The Guardian's Wyrd (#1)

Dawn's Bright Talons

The Blackfeather Chronicles
Raven Kin (#1)

In Southern Darkness (2 novellas)

The Firebird (novella)

The Company of Birds

Sing down the Stars